THE
UNDERACHIEVER'S
GUIDE TO LOVE
AND
SAVING THE WORLD

THE UNDERACHIEVER'S GUIDE TO LOVE AND SAVING THE WORLD

A NOVEL

SLOANE BROOKS

ATRIA PAPERBACK

NEW YORK   AMSTERDAM/ANTWERP   LONDON   TORONTO   SYDNEY/MELBOURNE   NEW DELHI

ATRIA
PAPERBACK

An Imprint of Simon & Schuster, LLC
1230 Avenue of the Americas
New York, NY 10020

For more than 100 years, Simon & Schuster has championed authors and the stories they create. By respecting the copyright of an author's intellectual property, you enable Simon & Schuster and the author to continue publishing exceptional books for years to come. We thank you for supporting the author's copyright by purchasing an authorized edition of this book.

No amount of this book may be reproduced or stored in any format, nor may it be uploaded to any website, database, language-learning model, or other repository, retrieval, or artificial intelligence system without express permission. All rights reserved. Inquiries may be directed to Simon & Schuster, 1230 Avenue of the Americas, New York, NY 10020 or permissions@simonandschuster.com.

This book is a work of fiction. Any references to historical events, real people, or real places are used fictitiously. Other names, characters, places, and events are products of the author's imagination, and any resemblance to actual events or places or persons, living or dead, is entirely coincidental.

Copyright © 2025 by SMB Books LLC

All rights reserved, including the right to reproduce this book or portions thereof in any form whatsoever. For information, address Atria Books Subsidiary Rights Department, 1230 Avenue of the Americas, New York, NY 10020.

First Atria Paperback edition September 2025

ATRIA PAPERBACK and colophon are trademarks of Simon & Schuster, LLC

Simon & Schuster strongly believes in freedom of expression and stands against censorship in all its forms. For more information, visit BooksBelong.com.

For information about special discounts for bulk purchases, please contact Simon & Schuster Special Sales at 1-866-506-1949 or business@simonandschuster.com.

The Simon & Schuster Speakers Bureau can bring authors to your live event. For more information or to book an event, contact the Simon & Schuster Speakers Bureau at 1-866-248-3049 or visit our website at www.simonspeakers.com.

Interior design by Davina Mock-Maniscalco

Manufactured in the United States of America

1 3 5 7 9 10 8 6 4 2

Library of Congress Cataloging-in-Publication Data

ISBN 978-1-6680-8126-6
ISBN 978-1-6680-8127-3 (ebook)

For Shawn, who will always be my Chosen One.

And for anyone who's ever felt the magic
of a Home Depot lighting department.

The Underachiever's Guide to Love and Saving the World

PROLOGUE

COURTNEY

There's a reason stories begin with *Once Upon a Time* and not *The End*.

After *The End*, you're left cleaning up carnage and wondering how you're going to afford therapy. You don't feel victorious; you feel tired, hungry, and grumpy.

No one talks about how unpleasant the aftermath of an epic adventure is. No one warns you that you'll return home, after gallivanting around a magical universe, to find your car's been towed. No one mentions the fact that you'll probably look over at the person you're supposed to be having your Happily Ever After with and wonder if a week-long adventure is long enough to truly get to know someone.

That's the predicament Bryce and I currently find ourselves in. It's the middle of the night, and we're in our driveway, staring at our duplex as though it's the strangest thing we've ever seen, even though an undead skeleton stands behind us, clutching an iPhone.

Christmas lights strobe over my half of the building while Bryce's half remains in shadow. It feels like so long ago since the morning when I hung them—the morning everything changed. I'm not sure if I'm supposed to bid Bryce good night and go home to my side, or if I should waltz through his front door and move in.

That's the thing with adventures. If Bryce and I hadn't gone on one, we'd still be nothing more than the petty, bickering neighbors we were a week ago. One measly little romp through a magical portal, and suddenly we've shared our deepest secrets, but not our middle names. We've watched each other cry before we've so much as watched a movie together. We've fought side by side, but his number isn't even in my phone.

Bryce clears his throat. "So."

"Yup," I say.

After facing the undead and a dragon, you'd think a piddly little thing like *talking about my feelings* would be easy. Somehow it's harder outside of life-or-death stakes. Honestly, I'd welcome a monster breathing down my neck. It might make the words come easier. But what words would they be? When the credits roll, the music plays, and the couple rides off into the sunset, what do they say to each other?

Recent evidence suggests emotionally gripping proclamations like "So" and "Yup."

"Now what?" I ask.

Part of me wants to tell Bryce that, obviously, we're going to be together forever and ever. A smaller part reminds me that, a week ago, I was the type of person who rolled her eyes at everyone who believed in true love.

"We'll figure it out," Bryce murmurs as he dips his head and brushes his lips to mine, and for one blissful minute, everything feels like it will be okay.

But then blurry swirls of blue and orange light shine against my eyelids. I squint, looking through my lashes. For a moment, I think the Christmas lights are malfunctioning, but no. It's magic. Wisps of light swirl off our skin—the power left over from the other world slipping from our bodies. The vapor-like energy coils over the lawn like a river. Slowly, the tendrils rise, forming a wide arch.

My eyes snap wide, and I step back.

"What..." Bryce begins.

A pterodactyl-like screech splits the night air. The inside of the arch ripples, right before a bristly black blur bursts through, magic swirling off its wings.

Bryce and I duck as an all-too-familiar dragon swoops over our heads, letting out another earsplitting scream. Our necks arch as we follow the dragon's flight. Its wings snap wide as it dives for the duplex.

Kelly, the skeleton, taps me on my shoulder and shows me her phone screen, where she's typed: THIS IS UNFORTUNATE.

"It's fine," I squeak. "The dragon isn't inherently evil, right?"

"It's also not inherently good," Bryce whispers as the dragon's mouth gapes wide.

Flames roil within.

"If anyone asks, we had nothing to do with this," Bryce is saying. "We're fine. This is fine. I'll leave an anonymous tip for animal control."

Right as the words leave his mouth, flames erupt from the dragon and engulf the house, setting the entire structure ablaze in seconds. Kelly whips out a pair of sunglasses from her long floral dress and slips them over her eye sockets. Smoke singes my nostrils and stings my eyes. I don't think I knew what the word *surreal* truly meant until now, as I watch a dragon burn down a duplex in twenty-first-century America.

I imagine the scene as though it's one of those freeze-frame moments in a movie. You know the one. The one where chaos is erupting, and then everything freezes, and a voice-over goes, *Yep, that's me. You're probably wondering how I got here.*

There's the dragon, its shadowy silhouette suspended before the inferno, wings flared, neck reared back as it drenches the house in flames that shoot into the night sky. There are the exploding Christmas lights, shards of bulbs frozen in the air, zapping blue electricity merging with orange flames. There's Kelly the skeleton in a cowboy hat, lifting her iPhone to take a photo, fire reflecting off the dark lenses of her sunglasses. There's Bryce and me, viewing the scene, not in shock, but with weary dismay, our expressions reading: *Not this again.*

So, how *did* we get here?

It started, as these types of stories often do, with an insufferable, universally disliked child who secretly thinks they're hot shit.

Chapter 1

In Which a Chosen One Suffers from Occupational Burnout

COURTNEY

When I was little, I was 20 percent sure I could use the Force, 30 percent sure I was a long-lost princess, and 40 percent sure I could talk to animals because I was 90 percent sure I was special.

It turned out the 10 percent variable was out to screw me.

I was never shipped off to a magic school without parental consent to lead a troop of grown-ass adults and assorted woodland creatures into battle. I never got to vanquish an evil overlord, subsequently earning the undying adoration of every peasant in the land. I was never anything more than just me.

And eventually, that 10 percent variable convinced me until I was 100 percent certain I was not, in fact, special. I was a raindrop, not a snowflake. Snowflakes were unique, but each drop of rain was the same as the one before it and the one after.

So I decided to make myself into a lab-made snowflake and turn my life into the fairy tale I never had. I'd become something great—a real-life heroine. If I wanted to earn a Happily Ever After, I had to be perfect.

I wasn't totally sure what a real-world Happily Ever After

even looked like, but everyone else seemed to agree that it had something to do with having a dream job, house, and spouse, so I shaped my life accordingly.

The rules of the real world were clear. Regarding relationships: I must be sweet and agreeable in order to be lovable. Regarding my profession: I must be the best in order to earn—well, if not the most, then the begrudging respect of my coworkers and a salary that was 18.4 percent lower than a man's, but which I would receive with a grateful smile because I couldn't become my world's version of a villain: an unlikable woman.

Although I secretly thought Earth's world-building left something to be desired, I complied with the guidelines and set out on my quest.

Initially, I thought I'd be a doctor, but I couldn't figure out all those Latin words. My grades weren't good enough for me to become a scientist. My gag reflex was too sensitive for the everyday heroism of plumbing. During all the time I spent trying and failing to do meaningful things, I began to worry the rest of my Happily Ever After would fall apart too. (Sure, maybe princes in Disney movies had soft spots for reclusive unemployed bookworms, but this was real life.)

Luckily, I ended up with a respectable degree in marketing and then a respectable *job* in marketing. Was it perfect? Maybe not, but it was good enough to get me into the real-world version of a magical ball—the business mixer where I met my boyfriend, Will. With a square jaw, strong nose, and wavy blond hair, Will had the sort of all-American good looks that made him seem approachable and like he was probably good at golf. A modern-day prince.

I'd almost done it. Almost conned my way into a quintessential Happily Ever After . . .

"Courtney?" my mother asked, snapping me into reality. Around me, seated at the long cherry dining room table, my family chatted and ate, no one else noticing my distress. "I asked if there's something wrong with your turkey. You've barely eaten a thing."

I realized my fingers were clenched too tightly around the delicate stem of my wineglass, threatening to snap it. I loosened my grip, fighting the urge to hold on to *something*, even though my idealized future was slipping through my fingers.

"Turkey is excellent." I popped a bite into my mouth and choked it down before I could admit that I had no idea why people convinced themselves that turkey was a special holiday treat and not an atrocity.

The lie seemed to do its job, because Mom smiled, pleased, and returned to her conversation with my uncle. Probably, in her mind, if the turkey was fine, everything was fine; she'd never dream her perfect daughter wasn't.

The house was overstimulating—too bright, too hot, too loud. Silverware clinked and conversation hummed, peppered with the occasional polite chuckle. Heavy Thanksgiving scents assaulted my nose—nutmeg, stuffing, and the sweet tinge of yams. The marble countertops and vaulted white walls were a monochromatic blur. I hated marble countertops. They stained too easily to be practical, yet they were a staple in every Westra home because everyone knew your life had to *look* grand for your life to *be* grand.

I reached up and touched my mouth. My fingers hit teeth.

I was smiling.

I was somewhat of an expert at smiling convincingly through clenched teeth. I'd mastered the art of becoming what people expected of me. I could be everyone's hero. It was just a matter of switching capes to look the part. I was currently wearing the daughter cape, the one that would make me look smart and successful in the eyes of my family.

If it weren't for what happened yesterday, today might have been the beginning of my epilogue—that wonderful conclusion where everything I'd worked for would come together to create my Happily Ever After.

Maybe I wouldn't return to a hobbit hole as a lauded hero

where I'd feast for weeks, but Thanksgiving dinner at my parents' house was a decent compromise.

I wouldn't chop the head off an ogre and bellow in triumph before an army of adoring soldiers, but I would tell my family about my promotion.

There wouldn't be a prince whisking me away to a castle, but there was Will. He even had a ring. I saw it in his sock drawer. We'd discussed it, so it wasn't a surprise. I'd say yes when he asked. Of course I would. That was what you did in an epilogue.

I dug my nails into the edge of the table. My stomach hurt. My stomach always hurt. I couldn't remember a time when it didn't. I'd thought having those ulcers treated in college would fix the issue, but it didn't.

Having ulcers was a rite of passage in the Westra family. It displayed your grit, your drive. You didn't truly want success unless you had the stress-induced medical problems to prove it.

"Ooh, quinoa!" Will exclaimed beside me, reaching for the dish my dad passed his way. It was, perhaps, the most excited anyone had ever been about quinoa in the history of the world.

"Great for the heart," I said. It took all my effort to pretend like I cared about the health benefits of quinoa, but I slipped on a different cape—the girlfriend cape—a perfect blend of cute and sexy. I winked and leaned in. "Which is good news. Taking care of your heart is a priority of mine."

Will smiled and squeezed my hand, which still had a death grip on the edge of the table. He was a good guy who didn't deserve my messes. I still hadn't told him what happened yesterday. Couldn't. Not after I'd been assuring him for weeks I'd be getting that promotion.

I fought the urge to vomit.

For years, I'd been cramming myself into perfect glass slippers, but now the magic had worn off. Once everyone knew of my failure, they'd realize I wasn't the success I'd been pretending to be.

Maybe a girl who squeezed into Cinderella's shoes and fooled a prince didn't even deserve a Happily Ever After.

Will moved from an animated discussion about the country club to one of his other favorite topics: our future. "Courtney's up for this great new promotion at work," he was saying. "Senior marketing director."

He went on to talk about things like Roth IRAs and early retirement, and I tried not to dwell on why talking about our life made me feel so life*less*. At twenty-five, I was definitely old enough that I should enjoy participating in boring adult conversations, yet the topic of retirement made me feel like a clueless little kid and like I was ninety years old all at once.

As everyone started going around the table, sharing what they were thankful for—yachts, vacation homes, expensive handbags—I scrutinized their smiling faces. Sometimes, most times, I felt distanced from everyone, as though my body were just a sim in a game that I was controlling from very far away. My life didn't feel like my own, but someone's idea of what a life should be. I wondered if anyone else felt as lost as I did.

It was like I blinked, and someone thrust this whole life on me that I'd somehow committed to seeing through, even though I never remembered choosing it. I picked a path, thinking I could figure out specifics later, only later was now, and I'd already gone too far to turn back.

I looked at my aunts, cousins, and parents, all at different points on the same sort of road I'd been pushing myself down. The younger ones were full of fire and hope. The older ones leaned back in their chairs with pride, like they'd really accomplished something, when I knew for a fact Uncle Lenny had three stress-related heart attacks in two years, my cousin Dina had a drinking problem, and my grandfather never took a vacation because he planned on enjoying life once he was retired, but he'd been spending his entire retirement in that urn on the mantel.

Everyone was comparing achievements, and they were asking me about mine, and everything became too loud.

But then Will stirred beside me. Before I could ask what he was doing, he stood. Time slowed as he reached into his pocket and pulled out a little black box.

He dropped to his knee.

My ears rang, muffling the delighted exclamations from everyone else in the room.

Once again, my future was here, and once again, I was too far in to turn back.

My vision went dark around the edges. I'd read an article once that said Olympic athletes convinced themselves the feeling they got in the pit of their stomachs before an event was simply excitement, not nerves, seeing as the two emotions felt so similar.

That twisting knot in the bottom of my belly was *excitement*.

In the corners of my eyes, my family's smiles seemed to close in, twisting grotesquely as though distorted by fun house mirrors. I couldn't breathe. Except it wasn't the breathlessness of a blushing bride-to-be. It was the breathlessness of someone dying. This was the life I'd always wanted, and yet the thought of accepting it made me feel as though my life was slipping away.

I sprang to my feet. "I got fired yesterday!" I yelled.

A collective gasp rose from the dining table.

"I'll talk to your supervisor," Will said after a pause, jumping into fix-it mode. "With my connections, I'm sure we can work something out. And if not, we'll polish up your résumé and get you back out there. Everything will be fine."

With a jolt, I realized my employment status was to Will what the turkey was to my mother. Neither saw *me*. *I* was the thing that wasn't fine.

The thought of beginning another job search made me want to hide under a quilt and sleep for the next thousand years. But would they even still love me if I wasn't turkey-loving, perfectly fine girlboss Courtney?

"What if I don't want to get back out there?" I whispered, staring at that black box looming between us.

Dead silence.

Worst of all, slowly, *slowly*, Will shut the lid on that little black box.

I guessed I had my answer.

Fairy tales weren't real. Unicorns were a myth, evil didn't always lose, and trolls only existed on the Internet, but true love...

Well. I'd always assumed it existed.

But if that was true, why did Will shut that box after finding out his princess was a pauper?

He's just saving the proposal for later, some rational part of my brain tried to assure me. *You're the one who ruined the moment.* After we had time to talk it out, he'd propose again, surely. It wasn't like closing that box meant he was kicking me out of his metaphorical castle.

Probably.

I couldn't take the silence anymore.

So I ran away. Out the front door. Into the yard.

And then I felt as though, for the first time, I could finally stop. I had spent my whole life running toward something. Now I walked nowhere. Slowly. Like I'd never walked before.

Outside it was quiet, and I could finally breathe. The cold air was sharp in my burning lungs. I'd only made it to the middle of the lawn, but it was far enough to feel like I'd escaped. I turned to look at the house, the large dining room window like a movie screen displaying the scene of my family within—everyone clustered around Will, comforting him, even while their eyes gleamed with the thrill of witnessing Family Drama.

Thanks to the light inside the house and the darkness out here, I could see them, but they couldn't see me. It didn't feel so different from how I'd felt my whole life. Apart. Distant.

It stung that no one bothered to check on me, but it wasn't unexpected. Why would they comfort me? I was the one who had lost her job and ruined a proposal. Will represented everything they valued. Success ran thicker than blood, I supposed.

I turned my back on them, accepting my place. Every family had a screwup.

I wasn't special. I wasn't a hero. I was some random nameless peasant with delusions of grandeur, wearing underwear outside my pants and a bath towel as a cape. A peasant who picked up the Chosen One's sword and waved it about was only ever a fool.

I looked up at the stars, realizing I'd sort of forgotten they were up there. Earth was still turning, despite the fact some random girl named Courtney lost her job and had a bad day.

It all suddenly felt so stupid. My career had been utterly meaningless yet had felt like the most important thing in the world.

Budget cuts. That was what my boss had told me when she called me into her office. I'd tried to do everything right. I'd worn my Professional Courtney cape. I'd gotten *ulcers* for that job, and yet I'd still fallen short.

Really, though, I'd only been chasing after success because I had no goals of my own other than to do something that people valued, that would make people value *me*. My life had felt like a lie because it was. I'd donned capes to be loved, and so the capes were the only things that were loved. No one knew the real me, not even me. I'd tried so hard to be everything for everyone that I'd become no one.

I turned in the yard, crossing my bare arms against the chill. An abandoned tricycle one of my nieces had been playing with earlier sat in the driveway, lit by a house sconce. I couldn't remember the last time I'd ridden a bike for fun, cardio be damned. I couldn't remember the last time I'd done *anything* for fun.

The average adult spent one-third of their life at work and one-third of their life sleeping. That left you with only one-third of your life left. I'd been spending that third eating quinoa and being stressed and having ulcers treated.

In a burst of resolve, I walked over and got on the tricycle, my knees nearly touching my chest. The wheels squeaked as I pushed my foot against the pedal.

What was the point of trying to meet the conditions of everyone's "unconditional" love when the result was superficial affection?

I could give up. I *would* give up. This would be the last time I'd ever have to feel this way. If I stopped trying, I'd stop failing. Instead of living a miserable lie, I'd find small happiness in a quiet life where I belonged.

I went a little breathless, thinking of the possibilities. If I reclaimed that third of my life I'd spent feeling miserable, I could start caring about the tiny things that used to make me happy that I'd started taking for granted. I could do all the things I told myself I would do "one day" and then never got around to. I could dye my hair a weird color or get a piercing. I could bartend or bungee jump.

I yanked the handlebars toward the street and pumped my legs. Cold air lifted my hair off my neck as I peeled out of the driveway, going up on two wheels for a second before slamming back down as I straightened out. Legs burning, I pedaled, squeaking my way down the street. I didn't know where I was going, and I didn't care. Without a conventional, stifling Happily Ever After looming in front of me, my future was suddenly bright and endless.

Life was too serious to take seriously. I wanted to care deeply about insignificant things, like ice cream flavors and favorite colors and whether I'd rather fight a horse-sized duck or one hundred duck-sized horses. Surely, Will would understand.

CHAPTER 2

IN WHICH I RETIRE FROM THE CHILD HERO RESERVE

COURTNEY

Will did not understand. Will did not understand at all.

The next few months of my life looked like a Disney movie played in reverse. I lost my prince (Will), I left the castle (Will's swanky apartment), and got an un-makeover—which consisted of me transforming into a Boomer's nightmare, to make myself look as un-hirable as possible, in case I ever got tempted to go back to the corporate world.

Sporting freshly box-dyed blue hair and a slightly infected lip ring, I moved to a cheap duplex in a no-name town in Ohio and picked up a dead-end job at a home improvement store, vowing to live my new, insignificant life with one simple goal: have no goals.

Being good enough would never make me *be* enough, so I lowered the bar for my whole life. No more dreams or aspirations, and especially no more relationships. People always wanted those they cared about to succeed, and I'd only let down anyone I dated the way I did Will.

My only personal fulfillment came from volunteering at an animal shelter on weekends. Dogs, I decided, were the only creatures in existence who knew what unconditional love was.

"Who the hell pays fifty dollars for a doorknob?" I muttered to myself, placing the item on the shelf I was stocking. Over the intercom, "Santa Baby" played for the seventh time today.

It was only my first week here, and while I was still happy with my decision overall, I hadn't accounted for just how lonely I'd be.

I was content merely existing, which, for some reason, made a lot of people discontent. Everyone, even my family, disassociated from me, as though mediocrity were contagious. Apparently, phrases like *it's the little things* were reserved to be displayed on plaques in million-dollar homes like trophies, as though contentment itself were something you had to earn. Because if you truly were happy with *little things*, you were unambitious, and if you weren't ambitious, then you must be lazy. Worthless.

"You're deliberately making your life worse. How can I support you through that?" Will had said when I told him I was done chasing material success. "All I want is for you to succeed."

To everyone else, Will's concern sounded valid. My family praised him for worrying over my "obvious cry for help." But I knew Will better than any of them, knew how much he clung to that future we'd imagined together, the one with country clubs and RVs. Unless I continued to max out my retirement account and kept pretending to like tennis, I'd never fit into his "wife" box, and he'd never let me live outside of it. He didn't care that I was happy for the first time. He only cared about what was best for *him*.

I missed Will, though not in the ways I'd expected. I didn't miss things that were uniquely Will. It was the absence of *anyone* in my life that hit me the hardest.

"Where's Courtney?" one of my managers asked from the next aisle over, drawing me from my thoughts.

My coworkers' responses chimed in. "Courtney's working today?" and "Hopefully fired" and "Who cares?"

I checked my phone and realized it was time for my scheduled break. While old-me would have gone running to see what my manager needed, the new me forced herself to ignore the tug that urged me to comply. He'd convince me to help him with something for "just a second," and then two hours would go by, and I'd miss my break entirely without being compensated for it.

Instead, I made my way across the store to the vending machines, which were by the gardening section. The best thing about my new job was, as long as you showed up and pretended to be busy for at least a few hours, no one would actually fire you.

After buying a few candy bars, I made myself comfortable on the floor, leaning against the vending machine for support. Usually, I liked hiding in a coatrack near the lighting department on my breaks, but I'd seen Dave from appliances lurking around there earlier, and I didn't want him to spot me. I loved the lighting department—there was something whimsical about all those twinkling chandeliers—but Dave was just the kind of guy who'd rat you out if you stretched your break a few minutes long, which I was certainly planning on doing. So I settled for the less-aesthetic vending machine alcove.

I'd just taken my first bite out of a KitKat when I experienced the unmistakable sensation of being watched.

I looked up, and there he was—some pale redheaded guy looking lost in the garden department. It took me a minute, but I recognized him as my neighbor—a guy I'd seen coming and going a few times from the other side of the duplex. My landlord had mentioned his name was Bryce. Bryce Flannery.

Bryce turned and looked at me—focused, sharp, intense—in a way that no one had looked at me before. A little thrill went through me because he looked at me as though he *saw* me, the real me, unlike Will, who saw the pretty cape I wore. To be fair, judging by Bryce's frown, he clearly wasn't *liking* what he was seeing, but I didn't mind.

I knew what I looked like: a lazy degenerate slacking off at work. But he wasn't leaving. He was *associating* with me, if only in a small, negative way. He seemed to view me as something worth hating rather than something not worth the effort.

"What do you want?" I asked when he continued to stare.

"Your mom's phone number," he fired back, before looking slightly surprised, like he couldn't believe he had actually just used my mother to insult me.

Something stirred inside me, that competitive spirit that used to get super horny for math tests and tight deadlines. "She doesn't date men who look like a child's crayon drawing of a leprechaun."

"I find it hard to believe her standards are high, considering you came out looking like you belong under a bridge, demanding answers to riddles." He was on a roll now, but I wasn't backing down either.

A few weeks ago, I would have suffocated my snide comebacks under an agreeable cape. Now, I let them fly because there was nothing to lose. I didn't care if this guy liked me or not. "Riddle me this: After listening to your own voice all these years, why do you still think it's a good idea to talk?"

Despite my insult, I hoped he would continue thinking it was a good idea to talk, because Bryce Flannery was my new favorite jerk. His feelings for me, though negative, were based on who I was, not on the things I did. He'd never ask me to be more, *do* more; he'd just hate me for who I was.

This one thirty-second interaction was the only honest relationship I'd ever had.

CHAPTER 3

In Which a Garden-Variety Rake Makes a Fool of Himself

BRYCE

From the moment I met Courtney, I knew.

I'd seen her last week when she moved into the other side of the duplex. At a distance, she'd just been my sad, pathetic neighbor. Now, actually meeting her, I learned who she was on the inside, where it mattered most.

I'd come to the big-box store to buy a towel holder after my old one broke. One hundred and four people died of mold *every day*. Proper towel management was crucial.

That was when I noticed Courtney, sitting wedged between a vending machine and a trash can. Her green uniform vest was the only clue she was an employee; she certainly wasn't *working*.

She was undeniably attractive, and I watched, transfixed, as she sliced open a red KitKat wrapper with a long, equally red fingernail. Warm sunlight danced off her pale skin. Her indigo-blue hair gleamed as she tossed her head back and raised the chocolate to her mouth. As her full lips closed around it, she moaned softly. And I knew. As she *bit into the whole damn KitKat bar without breaking it apart first*, I knew. Courtney was the fucking worst.

And, okay. Maybe it wasn't the act of eating a KitKat incorrectly that made me want to keep my distance. She was an enigma. She viewed the world like it was one big joke, and I wanted in on it. That scared the shit out of me.

I was too curious about her. Curiosity famously killed cats and, less famously, killed my crush-prone heart. I was pretty sure I was reaching my emotional ninth life, so I was done with risks.

My exes always accused me of self-sabotaging—that I was always looking for something to go wrong in relationships. If that was true and my heartache was my own fault, I'd just sabotage my self-sabotaging ways and simply never allow a relationship to form in the first place. Heartbreak: cured.

I needed this woman far, far away from me, so I did what anyone in my position would do. I insulted her mom.

Instead of never talking to me again, she fought back. And now she was—

Oh god. She had her hand out, *introducing herself*, while I stood here, internally monologuing like some kind of Joe Goldberg weirdo.

"Courtney," she said. "Terrible meeting you."

I shied away from her hand. Why we, as a society, still participated in such an archaic tradition was beyond me. Studies had shown it was more sanitary to greet each other with a kiss than—

Great. Now I was looking at her mouth. She was going to get the wrong idea.

The only solution was to continue acting like an egotistical douche nozzle. I was familiar with egotistical douche nozzles from my years of being bullied on playgrounds. All I had to do was channel some of that energy.

Unsolicited advice should do the trick. Hooding my eyes in a look of arrogance, I said, in a patronizing sort of way, "Those things will kill you, you know." I tilted my chin in her direction.

"Candy?" Courtney looked at me like I was a toddler and not a Very Intimidating Man.

"Vending machines," I said, in a dark tone that I hoped conveyed I was the type of good-for-nothing rogue who carried danger with him wherever he went. I was also familiar with good-for-nothing rogues, thanks to having found my grandmother's secret stash of explicit historical romance novels when I was thirteen.

Courtney regarded me with the detached manner of someone examining sidewalk gum—mild distaste, but mostly indifference.

"Anyway, you'd best stay away from me," I said, practically swooping a black cape in front of my face as I began slinking backward into the—well, not shadows exactly, since the store was brightly lit with fluorescents, but metaphorical shadows. "I'm trouble. A maker of trouble, if you would."

"A troublemaker?" she supplied.

"And a rake," I said, because I'd always wanted to be a rake.

"The rakes are over there." She pointed across the garden section.

I drew up short, dropping my mysterious act. "No, *I'm* the rake. A rake is like . . . a bad boy."

"I've never heard of a bad boy who's scared of vending machines."

"I am a bad boy. The baddest of boys."

"Please, I invite you to call yourself a boy again."

Flustered, I raised my voice. "Roughly thirteen people a year die from vending machines, making them statistically more dangerous than spiders, sharks, and even mountain lions, which is why I'm a bad man that you should definitely avoid."

"You're a bad man because you've warned me about the dangers of vending machines?"

This was going poorly. She was a tough nut to crack. I'd been distant and aloof. I'd hinted at danger. I'd even insulted her mother. What was left?

I lifted my chin at a regal angle and gave her a parting, disdainful look, and then I whisked away scornfully.

Which is to say: I ran away like a total baby. *But babies can't run*, one might say. And one would be correct. I ran exactly like a baby who wasn't very good at running.

After returning home, I sat in my living room, typing away on my laptop. Working from home as an accountant was as delightfully boring as it sounded. Boring equaled safe. Boring also meant my mind was free to think about things it shouldn't. Like fatality statistics. Or what kind of illness I might have that I just didn't know about yet. Or how I'd stumbled over my own shoelaces running away earlier. Or how my new neighbor had been desecrating a KitKat like she was laughing in the face of the universe.

She had no right to sit there chomping away at a candy bar like she was happy with a life in retail. She had no right to make me feel like, if I got to know her better, maybe I could be happy with my miserable existence, too, by association. That was unacceptable. Because if I was happy with my miserable existence, it left room for my existence to get more miserable.

Happiness was just the calm before the storm. It made you think that maybe the world wasn't so bad, right before it ripped the rug out from under you. Like when you let yourself get excited about a new relationship, right before you wound up getting dumped out of nowhere and accused of "emotional unavailability." Again.

Or it was like when you were a kid, and your mom gave you ice cream for breakfast and took you to your grandparents' house. Life couldn't get any better, especially since there were a bunch of slugs on your grandparents' driveway, and nothing made little boys happier than looking at slugs. Everything was great. Until your grandparents brought you out of your ice-cream-and-slug-induced trance to tell you your mother had left you, and she wasn't coming back.

But those were hypothetical examples and definitely not real events.

The point was happiness made me sadder than being sad, so I'd decided to just be sad. I couldn't be friendly to Courtney because then she might get the wrong idea. She'd become one of those neighbors who'd say things like *Good morning* and *Nice weather we're having lately, isn't it?* Those types of interactions ventured too close to pleasant for my liking. Luckily, going full theater kid on her had probably weirded her out enough that she'd want nothing more to do with me.

I was pretty sure I'd seen the last of her.

Someone knocked on my front door.

Assuming it was the mail carrier or something, I snapped my laptop closed, went to the foyer, and looked through the peephole. Catching a glimpse of blue hair, I cursed under my breath.

Half-heartedly tugging on a flannel shirt, I answered the door.

"Hi," Courtney said, her voice as dry and monotone as it had been at the store.

I crookedly buttoned my flannel and leaned against the doorframe. "Hi?"

"I shouldn't have been honest about the fact you look like the mascot for Lucky Charms." This was again said in that same emotionless but somehow snarky voice that made her sound like a zombie Valley girl.

"Is this you apologizing?" I asked.

"Yes. I should have been less vocal about your shortcomings. That was wrong of me."

"Unbelievable." I went to shut my door, mostly to hide the inexplicable laugh rising in my chest, but her combat boot stopped it.

"I'm sorry." Now, at last, something cracked in her expression, and the vulnerability shining through made me pause. "I understand if you never want to talk to me again, but maybe—"

"You're right. I don't." I couldn't cave. Couldn't indulge in exploring the intrigue she inspired in me.

Her face hardened once more, and she tossed her head. "Fine. No talking. We don't need to be friends to be neighbors."

"Sounds good to me." With that final dickish sentiment, I shut the door, feeling both pleased and strangely disappointed with myself for having gotten rid of her for good.

I didn't love the type of person I'd had to become in the name of self-preservation. I never wanted to be someone's asshole neighbor, at least not until I was eighty-five and being grumpy was endearing. When I was a child, people described me as kind and sensitive. Now, only half that description applied. I never knew if being sensitive was good or bad. Grandma said it meant I loved too hard. Grandpa said it was a nice way of saying I was weak.

It didn't matter. I would never have to be strong because I didn't plan on loving at all.

Courtney's revenge was swift and sadistic.

Once she left my house, I heard her enter her side of the duplex and turn on the TV. She cranked it up to full volume, but I didn't let it bother me. I'd been a jerk; let the girl blow off some steam.

Seven hours later, *Riverdale* season one was still going strong. I couldn't believe this woman watched *Riverdale* on purpose. Still, I figured she'd fall asleep eventually, and her streaming service would time-out.

She apparently turned off the prompt feature of her streaming service, because her TV blared all night long.

The next morning, I shot awake from my fitful sleep, utter panic striking me deep when I heard Courtney's keys jingle in her front door as she left for work, her TV still booming.

I tumbled out of bed, found a pair of sweats, and staggered out my front door, throwing a hoodie on and blinking back moisture as sunlight assaulted my weary eyes. "Courtney!" I called as she opened her car door. I scampered across the driveway, the concrete freezing my bare toes. "Courtney," I gasped again, rounding her car. "You left your TV on."

She didn't respond. Didn't even acknowledge the fact I was half draped over her driver's-side door. She simply slammed it, nearly taking off my fingers in the process. Seeing her put the car in reverse, I darted back, narrowly avoiding getting my toes run over as she whipped out onto the street.

I knew when I was being subjected to a silent treatment, even if it was the loudest silent treatment to have ever been performed. Even if I hadn't worked it out myself, she'd left me a subtle clue she was pissed in the form of her charming new Wi-Fi network name: Bryceisabuttface.

"No talking," she'd said. "We don't have to be friends to be neighbors." Apparently, the alternative she had in mind was *We'll be mortal enemies instead!* while I'd been assuming she meant we'd be cordial acquaintances.

I would not let her win this petty game. Even *Riverdale* had an end. All I had to do was wait it out. A quick Google search revealed that there were 137 hours of the show, which meant my torture would be over in less than a week, if Courtney didn't get sick of her own warfare by then, which she probably would.

Spoiler: she did not.

By day three, my ears were sore from the earplugs I'd taken to wearing. By day four, I knew more *Riverdale* lore than any human should. By day five, I was reluctantly intrigued. By day six, I was even blinking back a tear as I heard the season finale come to an end, though that might have been because I was so happy it was finally over.

Then at last. At *last*. Sweet, sweet silence.

I removed my earplugs, letting out a little whimper of relief.

Three seconds later, the opening music for *Riverdale* once more thundered through the building, the first lines of season one episode one striking pure terror into my heart.

That was it. I snapped. I shoved away from my desk and burst out the front door. I crossed to Courtney's side of the porch and repeatedly jabbed her doorbell. When there was no answer, I looked over my shoulder and discovered her car was gone. She must be at work and had somehow set up her TV to autoplay *Riverdale* on a loop. Forever.

I'd just have to take matters into my own hands.

Feeling like a criminal, I circled the duplex, checking all her windows in hopes one was unlocked. Desperate times called for desperate measures.

No luck. All her windows were secure. I peered through the last one, trying to see if I could spot the TV. What I saw instead was her bedroom. She didn't even own a bed frame, just slept with her mattress directly on the floor like a college frat guy. I thought she couldn't get more despicable, but then I spied the mug on her nightstand that read: "You're the Ross to my Rachel!" Irritation panged through me. Who gave her that mug? And more importantly, why did she keep it? Did the ridiculous woman think Ross Geller was a good romantic partner?

Really steaming now, I returned to the front of the house, debating what to do. My eyes settled on her mailbox.

No. That was too far. I wasn't a felon.

I developed a rapid and alarming disregard for federal law.

The next thing I knew, I had her mailbox open, and I was riffling through her letters. It was mostly junk mail, but I did learn her last name.

After going back inside, I googled "Courtney Westra," because I was a stalker now too apparently. I got a hit for an inactive LinkedIn account that still had her email on it. I was briefly surprised to find she'd worked in marketing at one point but shrugged it off. Obviously, her abysmal work ethic had landed her where she was today.

I was seconds away from creating a fake ad with her name and email and listing her TV for free, but I hesitated. As hilarious as it would be for Courtney to receive unwanted emails all day, I also didn't feel great about handing out her information to strangers, even if it was easy to find. Not because I was worried about Courtney. I was worried about subjecting innocent strangers to Courtney.

So instead, I created a bunch of new email addresses under fake names and messaged Courtney myself, posing as interested buyers. She'd never have to know I never made an actual ad. I only hoped she had her email notifications turned on her phone, for maximum annoyance.

I needn't have worried. A couple hours later, around the fiftieth variation I sent her of: Hi, Courtney, is the TV still available? I know your listing said your schedule is tight, but I can make your 3 a.m. time slot work, her fist pounded on my front door.

"Wherever you posted that ad, you need to take it down," she demanded as soon as I answered. She'd apparently decided chewing me out was more important than her silent treatment.

"Sorry, I can't hear you," I yelled over the noise of her TV, pointedly bending my ear.

She stalked off, and a few seconds later, *Riverdale* went silent. She did not return.

When I went back inside, I couldn't resist changing my Wi-Fi network name to: Bryceisawinner.

Much later in the evening, when she presumably noticed the change, she released a gratifying shriek of outrage from the other side of the wall that made me grin.

The victory was short-lived, of course, because the very next day she superglued my mailbox shut and changed her Wi-Fi name to: UwillRueTheDay. My mind was already spinning, plotting my next move. This would not be a war easily won. I had a feeling I'd be seeing a lot more of Courtney. But god help me, I didn't hate that as much as I should have.

I told myself it was okay. It wasn't like we were friends. I avoided relationships, but *negative* ones wouldn't do something unwelcome like make me happy right before crushing my soul to oblivion.

Considering all the animosity between us after one week, it wasn't like we'd ever do something as preposterous as *like* each other.

CHAPTER 4

IN WHICH I EXPERIENCE AN UN-MAGICAL AWAKENING

BRYCE

Six months passed. Things were great until I realized how great things were.

Courtney and I were uncomplicated. When we saw each other, we didn't wave; we flipped each other off. Every morning, I'd wait out on the porch to greet her with a preplanned insult as she left for work. Every evening, she'd get her revenge by being the worst neighbor she could—playing music too loud, blocking my half of the driveway with her car, leaving dog turds in my yard . . . which was an impressive feat, considering she didn't own a dog. On special occasions, she'd pop up with some ~~hilarious~~ *heinous* prank.

Unearthing the weaknesses of my enemy required me to get to know her to some extent, which sometimes felt disturbingly like dating, except it was more honest. For instance, my enemy didn't try to hide how much she spent online shopping, nor was she particularly shy about revealing all her gross habits. She once cheerfully informed me she forgot to wash her feet in the shower nine out of ten times, simply because she knew that knowledge would keep me up at night, thinking about gritty sheets and fungus.

All thoughts of dating soon vanished because everything I learned only fueled the special contempt I reserved in my heart for her particular brand of awful. Once, we ran into each other at our mailboxes, and for a dangerous moment, my heart almost softened as I watched her pull a birthday card out of a shopping bag. I couldn't believe I was actually witnessing her do something kind for someone. That feeling lasted right up until she crammed the card into its envelope without even bothering to sign it or write a message inside before she addressed it and shoved it in the box. It was the birthday equivalent of tipping someone a dollar. A way to say, *I acknowledge your existence, but only with my middle finger.*

Of course, *all* of her character traits weren't completely cold and uncaring. Some were just annoying. Last month, by listening through the wall, I learned the correct pronunciation of the word *croissant* made her irrationally furious after she spent twenty minutes trying to order a bakery delivery, stubbornly interrupting every two seconds to correct the cashier's presumably already correct pronunciation of the word.

That evening, I sat outside in my car, waiting for her to come home from work so I could hop out and pretend like I, too, had just returned from an errand, just so I'd have a reason to meet her on our porch. "I think I'm going to have chicken salad on a croissant for dinner," I remarked as we both unlocked our doors, really slathering the French accent on thick around the word *croissant*. "What do you think?"

Courtney responded that she thought I was a fucking asshole, and as soon as she was gone, I burst into laughter. After that, I dedicated my life to using the word *croissant* as much as possible.

But then, slowly, a few weeks ago, I began to sense trouble brewing. Courtney had this way of saying all the rude things

I thought but kept quiet, which had a disconcerting way of making me feel like no one had ever understood me more. Like the other day, she acknowledged how weird all the messages were that Larry down the street kept leaving on the community bulletin board (he kept leaving free lemons for people to take, then getting pissed when people took too many lemons). I'd had a pathetic urge to jump up and shout *I thought the same thing!* like a total dork who needed to impress her by proving how much we had in common. She made me feel a morbid companionship that only came from finding someone to hate things with, something lodged firmly between happiness and misery.

It all came to a head on my birthday. I'd been celebrating in my traditional way—by reading old birthday cards from my mother and expecting her to call, even though she never called.

Then my doorbell rang.

My heart skipped, and it took me approximately two seconds to convince myself my mother had come back to reunite with me. I rushed to the door, opened it, and found nothing.

What a day for Courtney to play Ding Dong Ditch.

When I went to slam my door, my eyes landed on a package sitting on my porch. It was the worst-wrapped present I'd ever seen, parts of a brown box peeking through a clumsy mess of tape and what looked like wrinkled, pre-used wrapping paper. Taking it inside, I set it on my kitchen table before tearing the paper off and sliding the flaps of the box open. On top lay a card. The picture on the front was of a serene landscape with the words *My Condolences* printed across it. Opening it, I found some generic sympathy message printed inside, but beneath it, spelled out with magazine cuttings like a message from a kidnapper, were the words *Happy Birthday*.

Inside the box was a tub of cookie dough ice cream. Pulse thundering in my ears, I pulled it out and opened the lid. The seal was already broken. The ice cream inside was a gloppy mess, like someone had sorted through it and picked out all the cookie dough, which I assumed was exactly what had happened.

Courtney.

She must have figured out I hated ice cream, either by the way I closed my blinds every time the ice cream truck drove by like I was warding off evil, or because she noticed all the ice cream coupons I viciously crumpled and threw away. Using that knowledge, she'd given me the worst gift she could possibly think of.

But she'd somehow known it was my birthday.

And she'd given me a gift. A personalized one.

I scrambled to my computer, and sure enough, there it was: the final nail in my heart's coffin, her new Wi-Fi name and a mostly accurate acknowledgment of my birthday: BryceEST.5/18/1945.

It was the most thoughtful thing anyone had ever done for me. Maybe not thoughtful in the normal way—her thoughts weren't busy considering other people's feelings; her thoughts were full of schemes and malicious intentions. Still, it was a *type* of thoughtfulness.

A sudden desperation to see her took hold of me. I wanted to run to her door and knock until she answered and then . . . and then what? Yell at her? Hug her for the next hundred years or so?

And that was when I recognized the feeling that had secretly crept into my heart over the past few months. Happiness. Courtney had made me feel happy. Then she'd given me ice cream.

I knew what came next.

I could practically feel sticky ice cream melting down my child-sized fingers while hot tears rolled down my baby-fat cheeks. Could practically hear the words *She's not coming back*. Could practically feel the happiness bleeding out of my heart.

I'd done everything I could to ensure we would not form a happy relationship, and yet we had. Kinda. I didn't know what to call her. Friend? Enemy? Frenemy? It made no sense, and it was infuriating.

I smacked the lid back on the ice cream, swiped it off the table, and took it to the trash can. Maybe I could move away, but the likelihood of finding a rental as cheap as this one was slim. No, she had to go. Soon. Before she had the audacity to make me feel full-fledged joy. This girl would wreck me if given the chance, and I needed to put a stop to it.

CHAPTER 5

IN WHICH I DISCOVER A SHITTIER VERSION OF NARNIA

COURTNEY

I smiled to myself as I gazed across my dew-soaked front lawn. A new day stretched before me, full of opportunities that I intended to ignore. The phrase *same shit, different day* was my motto. My days were endlessly unremarkable, and mediocrity was bliss.

I couldn't believe I'd actually apologized to Bryce when I first met him. I guessed some old part of me that still yearned to behave properly felt guilty about all the animosity. Thankfully, he rejected my apology, because I'd rather have an enemy than a friend.

I didn't know for sure why he decided he didn't like me, but it didn't matter. You had to care about something, even a little, to be able to hate it. If you didn't care, you'd simply be indifferent, which had been everyone else's attitude toward me, ever since they gave up hope I'd eventually soften back into the mold they kept for me. I desired Bryce's undesirable feelings, because without them, no one would feel anything for me at all.

So I decided to hate him back fiercely and with all my heart. Some people said love was forever. I said never underestimate the power and longevity of pure, unadulterated spite. Maybe true love didn't exist, but true hate sure did.

Suddenly, I'd gone from one life goal to two.

1. Have No Goals
2. Hate Bryce

The amount of care and attention he and I dedicated toward trying to destroy each other almost made our relationship feel intimate, if you disregarded the fact we both wished the other would fall down a manhole.

My smile broadened as I tore open a new pack of Christmas lights. I had to finish decorating my half of the duplex before Bryce woke up. This was phase two of his special birthday surprise. Hanging lights in May was untraditional, but Bryce was a grinch who hated all things Christmas. He'd demonstrated as much by convincing me he had epilepsy for the entire month of December to guilt me into keeping my lights turned off. Suspicious, I'd kept an eye on his mail until I eventually found a medical bill for a checkup a few months later that revealed the name of his primary physician. A phone call, some sweet-talking, and a borderline HIPAA violation later, I'd learned his supposed ailment was all a lie. A lie he would soon regret.

I hummed while I worked, chewing my gum to the beat of my tune. Though we were well into a balmy spring, the mornings were still crisp. Birds chirped, lawn mowers droned, and the invigorating scent of new life laced the air, fueling the pep in my step as I decorated.

The house and lawn looked like they'd been crop dusted by a fairy. Countless twinkling bulbs zigzagged up the exterior walls. A single strand of lights divided the roof precisely in two, and my side shone like a disco ball, haphazard clusters twisting across the shingles. Wires draped in clumps over the hedges, weighing down the branches until they drooped. I even wound a strand around the left porch railing in messy knots (unfortunately, the right rail wasn't in my jurisdiction). I'd connected the lights to a blinker thingy and fully planned on leaving them on all year, electric bill be damned.

I couldn't wait to see Bryce's expression. Anticipation sent adrenaline coursing through my veins. I didn't think feuds were supposed to be fun, but each interaction with Bryce filled me with an addicting rush of supreme indignation and uncontrollable mirth.

Humming louder, I tossed the roll of lights into the middle of the yard before dragging the end over to a lit strand and plugging it in. Everything blinked for two glorious seconds before a loud zap split the tranquil morning, and my lights went dead.

Confused, I followed my extension cord around to the back of the house where the outlet was. When I rounded the corner, I drew up short, mid–gum chomp, mid-hum.

Bryce held the end of the cord. The plug drooped over his knuckles.

I grinned. "Used to things hanging limply in your fist when you try to use them?"

"Hilarious." His thick morning voice curled around the word in disgust.

Bryce wasn't wearing a shirt because Bryce never wore a shirt. He was one of those people who likely spent a long time making it look like they spent *no* time on their appearance.

My feelings for him had grown so intense, he'd turned into a Bitch Eating Crackers—meaning everything he did got to me, even something as innocent as eating crackers.

His stupid clothes were always the perfect level of worn and rumpled. His scruffy five-o'-clock shadow was a permanent fixture on his stupid face. The ginger hair on top of his stupid head looked three months overdue for a haircut at all times, and it always had a messy *I just had wild sex* look, which had to be manufactured, because who would have sex with Bryce? As a final injustice, he didn't look like he worked out, but he was still sinfully hot in the same way that pale, willowy Victorian men with poor immune systems are hot.

Realizing I'd spent too long staring, I peeled my eyes away from the dusting of orange hair leading from his belly button to the low-slung waistband of his jeans. On anyone else, I'd call it a happy trail, but I had no desire to skip down Bryce's. It was more like a dismal path to the underworld you only went down if you were dying, and the grim reaper dragged you, kicking and screaming.

"You're trespassing." I pointed at Bryce's toe, which crossed the line of Christmas lights separating my half of the yard from his. "Like a good neighbor, stay over there."

"Spare me," said Bryce.

The spark his eyes usually held when we argued was absent today. That was weird. Maybe I'd finally overstepped, even though this didn't seem nearly as devious as the time he signed me up for the alumni magazine of the Ivy League college that rejected me.

"You need to take these lights down," said Bryce. "They're a safety hazard. You're going to turn the house into a fun new Christmas-in-May fire statistic."

God, he was wound tight. "Well," I said cheerfully, "I'll be at work. So as long as you don't get out in time, that's all that matters."

He let out a disbelieving bark of laughter. "Did you just wish me dead?"

Our dance of witlessness stuttered to a halt. Yes, we'd both clearly decided to hate each other for all eternity, but our insults usually remained in the realm of harmless playground clapbacks. It kept the fact that we would not be friends established without getting law enforcement involved. Times had changed. You couldn't go around holding knives to the throats of your arch nemeses anymore.

I crossed my arms defensively. "It wasn't like I said, *I hope you die.*" I lifted my nose. "It was a subtle implication. I'm a lady. I have couth."

"Courtney, Courtney, Courtney." He tsked. "I'm afraid you're so unlovable, even Mr. Rogers wouldn't want to be your neighbor."

A *feeling* took hold of my gut and twisted, sending a sharp sting through my body. Even the unluckiest squirrel found a nut sometimes, but if I kicked the nut away before he realized his success, he'd remain in despair, starved of victory.

I kicked all the nuts, hard and far, before plastering a smile on my face that I prayed was convincing enough to hide the fact I'd just kicked my own emotional nuts. "Geez, Bryce. Who crapped in your cornflakes this morning?"

"More like who de-cookie-doughed my birthday ice cream." He gave me a pointed look.

"Is it your birthday?" I asked absently, as though I hadn't been badgering our landlord for months to tell me Bryce's birthday so I could make it particularly terrible.

"My eightieth, apparently." He let out a long sigh and averted his eyes. "Look, I think we need to talk." The edge of snark Bryce's voice usually held was all rounded over so that it became something ordinary. "We can't keep doing this forever."

Suddenly, *I* felt ordinary, like any old neighbor he might have a polite conversation with. The razor-sharp words he usually reserved for me set me apart . . . made me feel special. With one sentence, he'd lumped me in with the rest of the world.

Bryce held up his phone with the screen pointed in my direction. "I saw this and thought of you."

I leaned in, expecting to see a picture of Gollum or some other grotesque creature. What was there was worse. "A job posting?" The light of his screen blurred in my vision, the words distorting until I could barely read the ad. "You think I should house-sit for someone in California? That's on the other side of the country."

"*Sitting* is literally in the job description. You will excel."

"Ha ha," I said, because this must just be another game. An elaborate insult.

"I'm serious," Bryce said, in that same cordial voice that made me feel like a nobody.

"You want me to leave?" It was as close as I'd ever gotten to asking him how he felt about me. I'd thought he was like me, and some part of him craved this rivalry we started.

"I think you should."

"What the hell, Bryce?" My eyes stung. It felt like rejection, like suddenly I wasn't good enough all over again. Not even good enough to be someone's enemy.

"You can't keep pretending you're happy with all this." He gestured around him vaguely. "Move on. Get out of this damn town. There's nothing holding you back, but you'd rather float through life because anything else is too hard."

My throat tightened. Bryce had never expected anything from me before, except that I would continue trying to make his life worse the same way he did for me. He was the one person who I'd thought wouldn't ask me to be something I wasn't, and here he was telling me I should change. I liked this life. What was wrong with choosing the easy road?

"I *am* happy," I said firmly.

"Oh, really?" He crossed his arms. "You genuinely enjoy pushing everything and everyone away?"

Oof. That one stung. I might be content with most aspects of my new life, but deep down, part of me still wanted to be loved and appreciated.

Maybe I had been pretending a little. I'd told myself I was displaying the real me, but what if what I showed Bryce was just another mask—one that hadn't fooled him for a second?

Despite my thinking I'd shredded all my capes, maybe I was still hugging one around me—an ugly, unsightly thing nobody could like. Because it was easier to be despised by making myself despicable than it was to be despised because, underneath all the layers, I truly was as unlovable as I'd feared.

But maybe I needed this cape. It ensured that, if anyone did manage to care for me like this, at my worst, their love was surely true.

"This could be a fresh start," Bryce was saying, his tone a nauseating, pitying thing that sounded like the faux empathy from my family, right before they realized I wasn't just going through a postbreakup phase. "Find a new neighbor you actually like and let them like you back. Don't let the fear of failure hold you back from wanting more."

I bristled. Bryce, scared-of-everything Bryce, was accusing *me* of being afraid? I didn't want more for my life; I wanted less. That was the whole point that *no* one, not even him apparently, could understand. He was just like Will.

A strand of Christmas lights took the tense moment as the prime opportunity to slide off the roof. One end looped round and round at our feet, while the rest of the strand trailed behind, bulbs skittering merrily over the shingles. When the tail end finally popped over the gutter and plopped on top of the pile of wires, I looked up at Bryce.

"Maybe I do float through life," I said dully, turning to go. "But maybe everyone could afford to float a little instead of sprinting toward death. What about you, Bryce? If I should stop being happy with nothing, maybe you should start being happy with *something*."

I left then, ducking into the house to grab my puke-green work vest and car keys. My shift started in approximately thirty seconds, but I always arrived ten minutes late to maintain my reputation and stop myself from falling into my old overachiever habits— habits that might tempt me into taking Bryce's advice and skipping across the country in search of *more* when I had everything I needed right here.

By the time I went back outside, Bryce was gone. Out of spite, I plugged the Christmas lights back in before hopping in my car. If I pretended today was just another day, maybe I could pretend the only unconditional relationship I'd ever had wasn't crumbling.

When I got to work, I did a little grocery shopping on the clock. The home improvement retail store also sold home goods, which was great because I could get everything I needed—home improvement supplies, groceries, and clothing—all at once and get paid doing it.

Slipping from aisle to aisle, I filled my grocery bags. With my vest on, to an outsider, it looked like I was hard at work. To management, it absolutely looked like I was slacking off, but they hadn't said anything yet. Probably because management Did Not Care almost as much as I Did Not Care.

I picked up some bread, jelly, peanut butter, pizza rolls, and a giant box of condoms, because I had a feeling I'd be looking for a distraction on Tinder later to avoid my feelings.

After I paid for my groceries, it had been a whole hour, and I deserved a rest. And, okay, I knew I wasn't going to be winning any employee-of-the-month awards for neglecting my job so spectacularly, but frankly I was even less in the mood to care than usual. I took a pit stop at the break room to nuke my pizza rolls, then I went to my favorite hiding place in the store. Maybe even the world.

The lighting department.

Hundreds of lights shone overhead and all around, from glittering chandeliers to lantern-shaped outdoor lights. Warm, glowing, magical. It made me feel surreal, like a sliver of magic existed in the real world.

My grown-up daydreams about magic were different from the ones I'd had as a child. All I wanted was a tiny alternate reality where I could simply *be*, somewhere I didn't have to repopulate, run, or save the world to have value. A place like that truly would be magical.

Is Bryce really just like Will? a little voice in the back of my head asked. Will had pressured me to return to the life he liked me in, with his love as the reward for my compliance. All Bryce had encouraged me to do was find happiness and consider letting someone in.

And move to California for some reason, a second, more spiteful voice in my head reminded me. Probably because he figured I'd need to change my whole life to become acceptable enough for someone to even *want* to be let into my heart. Just. Like. Will.

After that fun mental pit stop to refuel my wrath, I made my way to the center of the aisle, where *the* clothing rack stood proudly. It was one of those circular clothing racks, the ones kids hide in the center of when their moms take too long shopping. No matter how many times other employees dragged it back to its own department, I always dragged it back here.

I parted the heavy coats and ducked inside. The coats hung to the floor, creating a sort of tent with an open roof. Overhead, the lights sparkled like stars. Settling in, I rested my back against the metal post in the center, ate a few pizza rolls, and let my eyes shut.

Screw Bryce. He didn't know me at all. How dare he assume I'd never tried to make something out of myself?

It wasn't my fault I wasn't destined to be a hero.

◆ ◆ ◆

As I floated awake, I became aware that the lighting department, usually hot and stuffy, was cool and crisp. I squinted my eyes open. The lights overhead were as pretty as ever.

Prettier, even.

But I could tell that something was *off* in the way the whole world felt different after you learned Santa wasn't real. Like, you'd always suspected the world wasn't the way people told you it was, but you were disappointed all the same.

I squinted, trying to process what I was seeing, but my mind was fuzzy with that post-nap daze where you had no idea how long you'd slept or where you were.

Suddenly, it clicked and my eyes flew wide. Those weren't lights overhead.

An evening sky stretched above me, periwinkle and dusty rose, sprinkled with glittering stars. Stringy clouds webbed across them like strands of spun sugar. And instead of coats creating a circle above me, there were *faces*.

Some old dude hovered over my head, his long white beard tickling my nose. Then, one by one, more people came into focus, framing the sky: a guy wearing a full suit of armor, a guy with pointy ears, and a short guy with a beard.

A middle-aged man joined them, squeezing in next to the ancient dude. The new man looked like he could be someone's dad whose one spark of joy came from his wife letting him play golf every other month—except a giant golden crown rested on his depressed-dad brow.

Maybe I should've been freaking out or in denial, but enough of the little girl who clung to magic was still alive inside me that I *believed*.

I'd been transported to another world.

My first thought was: How? I'd hung out in the coatrack before and had never been shipped off to a different universe. Maybe it was the combination of things I'd brought with me. Between the groceries, a splash of wistfulness, and a side of rage, maybe I'd unwittingly created some kind of portal.

Or, if I didn't create the portal, then for what purpose could I have been brought here?

That last question, at least, was quickly answered as the old dude leaned in closer to study me. He wrung his hands, his beard swaying in front of my eyes. "The Chosen One," he rasped, unwinding his hands and extending one long, shaking finger until it stopped inches above my forehead.

I went cross-eyed, scrutinizing his crusty finger. So, maybe this guy had summoned me?

While part of me screamed that this was exactly what I was leaving behind from my old life—trying to be everyone's hero—the little girl I'd bid farewell to a long time ago flipped with excitement and joy. *It finally happened! I knew I was destined for more!*

I glanced around to find everyone looking at me like I was their savior. Like I *mattered*. After months of dismissal, I couldn't deny the warmth those looks inspired. The people-pleasing little girl inside of me basked in it.

This was my childhood dream—the grand adventure I always thought would come—

Ten years too late.

I reminded myself this wasn't the magical world I'd had in mind as I'd sat dreaming in my coatrack. I didn't *want* to be anyone's hero anymore.

Pushing aside Old Guy's finger, I sat up and saw my groceries laying scattered around me on the slimy cobblestone road. Then I noticed a large horde of what I knew from years watching movies and reading fairy tales could only be described as *peasants* surrounding me. In the background, some guy with his head and wrists stuck through a board was being brutally tortured via tomatoes. Flickering streetlamps reflected in the wet cobblestone road, mirroring the starlight above. White-and-brown timber-framed houses circled the courtyard. Light glowed from thick, milky windows, making the dingy scene look charming, like a Thomas Kinkade painting.

This must be a mistake. I was no Chosen One, no matter what the old dude—who was clearly supposed to be a wise wizard type—claimed.

No one wanted a burned-out twentysomething to save their world. I almost felt bad, smothering the hope-filled little girl I used to be with jaded cynicism, but I felt ridiculous, like some kind of overgrown Percy Jackson poser.

These people were too late if they wanted me to be their champion against whatever evil surely plagued them. Maybe once, when I didn't know better, but not *now*. I'd fail them on whatever quest they were about to send me on. I wasn't hero material—and not in the way farm boys with hearts of gold told themselves they "weren't hero material" right before they saved the world and become the poster child for "hero material."

I was an incompetent deadbeat who paid my rent late. How could I protect anyone when my weakness for deal-hunting on sketchy websites made me a frequent victim of identity theft? I couldn't save the world when I couldn't even manage to save leftovers properly. I avoided commitment to the point I refused to start a Hulu miniseries; no way was I taking on this kind of responsibility. Being special was overrated. Trying to be more only ended in pain and disappointment.

Right as I decided that whatever world I had just been transported to would be better off without me, the crowd started murmuring and pointing. I turned around, and there, standing on the other end of the courtyard, was Bryce.

It finally made sense.

This wasn't about me. It was Bryce's birthday, Bryce's magical awakening, Bryce's world. I must have accidentally been dragged along for the ride.

And that was when unexpected fury began boiling in my veins. How dare he tell me to find a dream to chase, then show up here mere hours later to steal the dream I'd spent most of my life chasing? I'd tried and tried, and when I had finally given up, here he was, taking the thing I'd desperately wanted for so long as though it were easy. Fate wasn't fair, the way it chose some and not others.

For the first time in a long time, ambition coursed through me, awakening my every nerve. Bryce was wrong. I wasn't scared. Screw destiny and screw the universe and screw Bryce. I was taking back my dream.

I imagined all the cheering peasants hoisting me on their shoulders after I saved the day, imagined being knighted and revered and *adored* while Bryce sulked in the shadows.

Maybe I was just a scrappy peasant, and not a Chosen One, but that meant I had grit. Bryce wasn't that impressive. I could be a better hero than an (inconveniently pretty) accountant with a vending machine phobia. That would put him in his place if I, the giant loser that he thought was such a failure, could be a better Chosen One than him.

I'd save the freaking world out of spite.

CHAPTER 6

IN WHICH WE CHOOSE OURSELVES AS CHOSEN ONES

BRYCE

I should have known going to apologize to Courtney would lead to disaster.

After I'd left her outside with her Christmas lights, I tried to lose myself in work, but the memory of her hurt expression haunted me. I'd crossed some sort of line, and I had to make it up to her. I wasn't a monster. I only wanted her safely out of my life forever and ever and ever. Besides, the angrier she was with me, the less open she'd be to accepting my suggestion of moving.

I'd taken the bus to the big-box store because buses were fifty times safer than driving by car. As I rode, I Google searched how many house fires were caused by Christmas lights. The answer was frightening. I hated the holidays. Fire hazards and increased motor vehicle accidents aside, the Christmas commercials filled with happy, smiling families never failed to make me feel more alone than ever.

When I got to the store, it didn't take me long to find her. Courtney wasn't a train wreck, but rather, the avalanche that caused train wrecks. All I had to do was follow the trail of foil condoms, jars of peanut butter, and pizza rolls. I felt like Hansel from the fairy tale. Except, instead of breadcrumbs and a witch's gingerbread house, there was garbage and . . . well, still a witch.

The trail of junk led me to a coatrack in the middle of the lighting department. It looked odd there and strangely ominous, lit in beams of shimmering golden light. A circle of trash surrounded the coats like they'd scattered out from the center as a result of a small explosion.

A half-squished pizza roll by my toe suggested Courtney had eaten her lunch in a coatrack. I didn't like how that made me feel.

"Courtney?" I asked, gently sliding aside a few coats.

And that was when it happened.

I'd waved my hand into empty space.

One second, there'd been hundreds of sweltering lights, Courtney's trash, and a coatrack. The next second, there were stars—real twinkling stars—flecked across a dimming pink and purple sky. I was in some kind of central courtyard, standing on the outskirts of a gathered crowd. Around me were slatted cottages, swinging shop signs, and gross ditches that would send an OSHA inspector into hysterics.

I blinked. *Hard.* Then I compulsively blinked twice more because three blinks felt more complete than one.

This was a dream. It was the only explanation. I must have fallen asleep on my couch while I was trying to work and dreamed about going to the big-box store.

And then I saw her, and my stomach dropped.

There, standing in the middle of the crowd, was Courtney. Her gaze locked on to me, and for a second, she looked downright murderous. Then her expression cleared, and she *winked* before climbing onto the back of a nearby wagon like it was a stage. She smiled benevolently down at the crowd and began doing an honest-to-god cupped-hand rotating princess wave.

A guy wearing a crown and an old man with sickly white skin that looked like wrinkled tissue paper climbed up next to her. The old man addressed the crowd, talking on and on at a barely audible volume. I caught the word *prophecy* a few times, and every time he said it, he got more and more worked up with excitement.

I decided I would not freak out. There was no reason to; I was dreaming and had clearly conjured up a world from one of my video games—one with kings, ancient wise men, and villagers aplenty. My breathing remained regular, my pulse steady. Dreams were preferable to reality. Safer. In dreams, I could be Bold Bryce. Daring Bryce. Irresistible Bryce.

I lifted my hands. They looked normal. My vision was sharp and clear. I'd heard about dreams where you were self-aware and free to make your own choices—lucid dreaming. Well, if I was in a lucid dream with Courtney, there was only one thing left to do—

No. Not *that*, perv.

Granted, she'd wormed her way into my dreams before in rated-R ways that left me extremely hor—horrified. Her being in my dreams was yet another sign that she was getting too close. At least this time, I was in control, and I was going to kick her out of my head. It would be a nice consolation since I couldn't get the real Courtney out of my actual life.

"Courtney?" I called.

A few villagers closest to me at the edge of the crowd turned. Their eyes widened as they took me in, gazes lingering on my *Walking Dead* T-shirt. I took a few steps forward.

The nearest villager gave me a wide smile. "I am sorry to tell you that I'm certain the Chosen One cannot hear you, as she is positioned many meters away, and you stand here . . . many meters away."

"The *Chosen One*," I repeated. "You're joking." This must be because I watched *The Lord of the Rings* the other night.

The villager shook his head. "Verily, I do not jest. The lady simply appeared out of thin air whilst we were gathered here witnessing the public shaming of Winston."

Somewhere in the distance, someone, presumably Winston, let out a scream of agony.

The villager's eyes narrowed. "Now that I reflect on the matter, she appeared much as you have, out of nowhere and clothed in strange garments I have never beheld the likes of before."

"Wordy bastard, aren't you?" I muttered under my breath.

By then, my conversation with Villager #1 caught the attention of a few more villagers. Still, the old man talked on, and Courtney gazed at him with glazed, unblinking eyes, nodding occasionally.

It was my dream, not hers. Time to channel Bold Bryce and take control.

Pushing past a cluster of villagers, I strode for a barrel outside of a blacksmith's awning. The blacksmith worked in the shadows, poking a fire, totally oblivious that the devil incarnate was portraying herself as some kind of Chosen One outside. He was like an NPC, doing his villager duty to create a medieval backdrop while everyone else lived their lives.

I clambered onto the barrel, drawing a lungful of air.

Clang, clang, clang.

The blacksmith's work ethic was admirable but inconvenient.

Clang, clang, clang.

I crouched on the barrel to peer under the awning into the darkness. "Excuse—" *Clang.* "Excu—" *Clang.* "Excuse me?"

The blacksmith looked up, eyes stark against his soot-smeared face.

"Sorry, but I'm having a big moment here," I said. "Do you mind?"

The blacksmith blinked. "'Ello, sir. Might I interest you in a blade, then? If you don't have coin, mayhap we can arrange a trade. You look like a strong warrior. My daughter . . ." He wiped a dramatic hand across his brow. "She was taken by a band of giants not far from here, and—"

Years of video games and a brief D&D obsession in high school had prepared me for this moment. I hopped off the barrel and walked under the awning. "Listen, this isn't personal, but I'm kinda focused on the main storyline right now. Your world needs a Chosen One, which means there's probably a huge war brewing and some sort of dark lord or evil king on his way here as we speak. Maybe I'll circle back to collect your side quest's XP later, cool?" I held my fist out for a bump.

The blacksmith's mouth gaped. "A . . . war?"

"Oh. *Oh*, you didn't know." I cringed. "Okay, well . . ." I inched forward to lightly fist-bump his massive bicep. "Sorry about the bad news." I offered a strained smile. "But I super appreciate you keeping it down."

I scooted out of the shop as quickly as I could. Spying a hammer on my way out, I snatched it up and gave it a few quick bangs against a shield hanging from a post outside.

"Courtney!" I yelled. This could actually be kind of fun. There were no risks in a dream. No consequences. I pounded the hammer harder. *"Courtney!"*

Courtney's gaze zeroed in on me. "Bryce." Her flat voice cut the distance between us. "Go away."

The endless drone of the old man mercifully stopped. He ran a hand over his beard, leaning forward to squint at me. "By the gods," he wheezed.

A few assorted villagers shuffled, muttering, "What did he say?" and "I don't know" and "I barely heard him."

I waved my hammer at the villagers. "Guys. *Please?* Give us a minute."

They averted their eyes.

"He said, 'By the gods,'" one villager whispered to his friends.

I drilled him with a look. He shrank back into the crowd, mouthing, *Sorry.*

"The gods have blessed us," the old man warbled, "with two possible saviors."

Several villagers talked over him, again asking one another if they could hear what he'd said.

"Could you speak up?" a tinny voice called from the back of the crowd.

"The gods have blessed us," the old man amiably warbled again at the exact same volume, "with two possible saviors."

Courtney whirled on the old man. "There can't be two Chosen Ones. There's no such thing as a Chosen Two. Chosen *One*. It's in the name."

I concurred. I didn't super love sharing a planet with Courtney; I didn't want to share a title with her too. Maybe if I convinced everyone she didn't belong here, she'd vanish from the dream.

I walked forward, the crowd parting to let me through. A few villagers bowed as I passed. Now I *was* having fun, doing things I'd never dare to in real life.

"You're right." I smiled, spreading my arms as I walked. "There is only one. And I am"—I paused for dramatic effect, then did a single head bang like I was a rock star and the beat dropped—"the Chosen One."

The villagers gasped, playing their part of background noise/setting/ambiance/etc. beautifully.

"To be sure, whenever we have faced strife and needed saving in days past, there has only ever been one hero," the old man said. "And yet, even though we only have one ancient sword with a great deal of meaning attached to it that we're prepared to bestow on the first person who comes by claiming to be the Chosen One, one great bedchamber and fattened calf, limited sword trainers on standby, and only one World's Greatest Stallion, perhaps we could make accommodations."

Courtney turned on him and smiled that dangerous smile of hers that made me wish I carried bear spray. "I don't want your medieval participation trophies."

The old man chuckled even though he couldn't have a clue what a participation trophy was. Mid-laugh, he had a moist coughing fit and came alarmingly close to asphyxiating before finally recovering. "Relax, child. All is well. It seems the gods have given us two to save us. One to lead, and one to assist."

"You mean whichever one of us isn't the Chosen One is the *sidekick*?" Courtney's eyes bulged.

That simply wouldn't do. Turning, I addressed the crowd like a president about to make a lot of promises I didn't intend to keep. "In addition to her obvious anger issues, Courtney is, in general, a menace to society. She's lazy, legitimately doesn't believe in birds, and regularly uses the word *jelly* in place of *jealous*. I don't know about you, but I think a Chosen One should be able to express her emotions without turning a sugary breakfast spread into an adjective. In conclusion, if Courtney is the Chosen One, she's the poorly Chosen One."

Murmurs spread through the crowd. There was a lot of nodding and arm-crossing.

"You need to leave," Courtney snapped, jumping off the cart, nearly stomping my toes. "I don't know how you followed me, but you're not needed here. This was always *my* dream."

Cute she thought I was in *her* dream. "This is my dream, actually," I said because I would not allow her to assert her dominance in *my* head.

She smirked. Come to think of it, her lips spent most of their time smirking at me, and it was annoying. "Stop pretending you want to be the Chosen One," she said. "We both know you don't. You use safety scissors. There's no way you want to arm yourself with sharp objects and go to war."

It was true. But if I pretended I wanted this, it might make Courtney angry enough that she'd march out of my head. "This is my destiny," I said. "Need I remind you it's my birthday? When have you ever heard of a main character getting swept into an adventure on *someone else's* birthday?"

"I've never heard of a Chosen One having a magical awakening at *thirty*."

"I'm not thirty."

By this time, the prophecy-obsessed old man had slowly worked his way off the cart. Three villagers had to assist him. His joints practically creaked as he clambered to the ground, but he managed. I wasn't sure what his role in the kingdom was—mentor or mage perhaps—but I didn't want to ask because Courtney seemed to know. I couldn't let her know she knew more than I did, even for a second. Especially because it was *my* dream.

"We've . . ." The old man paused for a good thirty seconds to catch his breath.

Crickets chirped. Someone in the crowd coughed. Winston let out a bloodcurdling scream from where he was being tortured on the other side of the courtyard, and a few villagers craned their necks to watch.

The old man straightened at last. "Your claims that Bryce secretly does not wish to be the Chosen One do not alarm me, Lady Courtney. We've had marvelous luck with reluctant heroes in days past."

I beamed. Resident Old Man was an absolute unit of a wingman. "Exactly." I gave him a hearty slap on the back, then winced when I felt something crack. "More evidence that proves I'm the Chosen One, and you're . . ." I gave Courtney a look. "A damsel in distress? Or, at best, the wimpy sidekick who dies."

"Says the guy who's scared of paper cuts," she snarled. "Real hero material."

I only smiled, cooking up my next verbal volley. The game was on, but this was one round she would not win.

CHAPTER 7

IN WHICH INFORMATION IS DUMPED, AND WE DON'T CARE

COURTNEY

When Bryce showed up, I'd whipped out a princess wave and a smile and pretended I had it all together. It reminded me of my old life. Wearing a cape. Faking it. I hated that. But I hated the idea of him getting to live out my childhood dream more.

We argued in the street until twilight melted into night, Bryce's rebuttals growing increasingly pathetic. Though I was clearly decimating him at the Chosen One thing, I was somewhat impressed; Bryce Flannery adapted to a new world quickly for a man who'd once delivered a ten-minute speech on the dangers of flip-flops. (I'd found out that unreliable footwear was a continuous source of annoyance in Bryce's life when he caught me barefoot in our backyard once and decided the way he was going to torture me that day was by listing all the safety hazards of open-toed shoes.)

At last, the man wearing the crown—who I had decided must be the king—got hungry and suggested we head back to the castle. We piled into some stuffy carriages the king seemed deeply proud of, but my kidneys deeply hated, each bump and jolt rattling them around inside my body.

Bryce and I sat on one side of the carriage with the super-old dude wedged between us. The king lounged on the other side, trying to look luxurious and noble but failing because every time we hit a pothole, his crown slipped over his eyebrows, and he had to adjust it.

The farther into the city we traveled, the grander the houses became. The city was layered, each street higher than the next, leading to a castle on the edge of a cliff—the tallest point in the city. With the whimsical, impractical architecture of some of the buildings, the glowing mushrooms recessed in the shadows, and the way everyone we passed gave us a bright smile and a cheerful greeting, I felt more like I was on a movie set than in an alternate reality.

Meanwhile, Gramps had launched into another prophecy spiel that nobody had asked for. I wasn't sure why he was so fixated on the prophecy. Everyone knew prophecies were always more misleading than they were helpful, but I guessed that was the benefit of growing up with books, movies, and video games to reference, rather than living in an actual world with magic.

The old guy said the prophecy was written in an ancient language no one could understand, but he was certain he'd finally cracked the code. Apparently, one of us was destined to overthrow either an evil wizard or a dragon or maybe a hedgehog. (Naturally, the translation grew a bit fuzzy when it came to pinpointing the Evil One's actual identity.) The prophecy stated the wizard/dragon/hedgehog would launch a campaign to destroy the peace the old guy had worked so hard to create. As far as I could gather, the wizard/dragon/hedgehog hadn't actually done anything evil yet, but still, the old dude was convinced they were "on the rise" despite having little to no evidence that was the case.

The only thing "on the rise" was my outrage. Whatever divine power ruled this land could get bent. Clearly, they made a mistake. Either that or they sucked at being a divine power, because who would send for *Bryce* when their world needed saving? Thinking Bryce could save the world was like thinking you could grab on to a spider's web to keep yourself from plummeting off the side of a cliff.

"To clarify," I said, "we've been brought here to save the world, but you're not sure who the bad guy even is?"

"The Evil One's identity will become clear in time," the old guy trilled. "There will be signs. Terrible evils will occur throughout the land. All you must do is follow those evils to the source, and there the Evil One will be."

"Makes sense," I said confidently, even while my inner voice asked me what I thought I was doing. "When the sky blackens, monsters crawl from the earth, and mattress tags are removed by those who do not have the authority to do so, then we'll know that he or she is near."

"Indeed," the old guy said gravely.

Despite all my joking around, a touch of worry began to creep up on me. Maybe I was too quick to accept this job. If there actually was danger lurking, I doubted I would be able to help. What if people got hurt because of me?

"Now, this is very important." The old guy leaned in. "There is a reason Chosen Ones in the past have always been outsiders. Just like your predecessors, you were not raised here; therefore no one has influenced your perception of our world, and your views remain unbiased. It is important you focus on your task at hand. You must not get involved with the politics of this world, nor should you interact with the people, lest they cloud your head with conspiracies, or you make friends who could be exploited and used against you."

That was weird. Most stories featured a little band of heroes that overcame a master sorcerer's thousand-year-old plan for world domination with the power of friendship. Then again, now that my adrenaline was beginning to wear off, I was starting to get the sense that, as much as this place felt like a cartoon, it was a real world in real need of saving, and maybe I didn't know as much about the rules here as I thought.

"We can't talk to any of the actual citizens here?" I asked, to clarify. That felt like believing a CEO's word that he ran a caring, upstanding family-oriented company without actually being allowed to talk to any of the overworked, underpaid employees.

Bryce cocked a brow, seeming to catch on to my skepticism. "How can you say we'll remain unbiased when your opinion is the only one we're allowed to hear?"

The old guy spluttered. "Why, because the king and I are looking out for what's best for the kingdom, of course."

"Of course." I rolled my eyes, pushing aside my worries. Maybe this was a typical cliché fairy-tale land after all, where there were good guys and bad guys, no shades of gray.

"All you must do is defeat evil when it appears, and then you'll be on your way." He reached into his purple robes and pulled out a small flask. "A toast," he said, "to the good we will accomplish together." After pressing the flask to his lips, he passed it to me.

There was nothing I wanted less than to drink some old man's backwash, but I was trying to win him over so he'd believe I was the Chosen One. I pretended to take a drink, wiping my mouth immediately after, when he wasn't looking.

I went to pass the flask to Bryce, but he physically recoiled.

The old man looked at him expectantly. The thought of Bryce actually drinking out of the nasty, warm robe flask was revolting, so I took pity on him.

"Wow, look at that!" Excitedly, I pointed out the window.

When the old guy turned to look, I dumped the flask out before handing it to Bryce.

"I've never seen so many cows," I explained when the old guy gave me a weird look.

But when Bryce handed him his empty flask, he looked pleased.

✧ ✧ ✧

At last, we made it to the castle, which loomed at the edge of the city. Its walls were pale in the moonlight, towers tall and pointy. Behind it, a cliff dropped off, and sounds of whooshing ocean waves rose from the darkness.

As soon as we arrived, servants escorted us to our rooms. On our way, Bryce and I held a long debate over who would take the actual Chosen One's bedroom and who would get the sloppy seconds—until a fed-up servant shoved Bryce into one room and me into another, across the hall, without telling us which was which.

Warm air wafted over my skin as I stumbled inside. A fire flickered behind a grate. With the room's elaborate woodwork and tapestries, it was the definition of *look how rich I am* decor. Heavy furniture sprawled everywhere—a dresser, two chairs next to the fire, a four-poster bed, and a low couch that looked like something an actress would have a melodramatic sobbing fit on in a black-and-white movie.

I smiled. I for sure had the Chosen One's room.

My door opened, and servants entered with new clothes. They helped me undress, exchanging looks over the modern apparel as they peeled away my oversized T-shirt, ratty black shorts, and fishnets, leaving me in my matching set of pale pink underwear, the ones with the little bows in front. Under the black sheep's clothing, there was just a girl, not a wolf. I wondered if Bryce would be surprised by that. Not that Bryce would ever strip back enough of my layers, literally or metaphorically, to find out.

After dressing me in a regal burgundy dress, the maids twisted my hair up, admiring its color. When they were satisfied, they led me into the hall. Bryce's door opened at the same time, and his servants stepped out. Behind them, Bryce fiddled with his sleeve cuffs. As he looked up, his gaze snagged on me, and he paused in the doorway.

I took in his ruffled shirt, embroidered jacket, tight pants, and tall boots.

"Lord Farquaad called. He wants his outfit back," I said, even as my eyes trailed over him again.

If "medieval rogue" were a look, the prick pulled it off. Somehow my meek, gloomy neighbor was *thriving* in this world. With his hair slicked back and curling in damp ringlets at the nape of his neck and his perpetual *I forgot to shave* face, he actually looked like he might have been within five hundred miles of a battlefield at some point in his life. Maybe. Or like he at least watched a gruesome battle scene in a movie one time.

"Look at you, wearing color," he said. "Guess it was a phase after all, huh?"

I made a face at him behind the servants' backs as they led us back through the castle. As we walked, I tried to remember the way, but after a while, one torch-lit hall started to look like every other torch-lit hall.

I smelled the food as we approached the dining room. My primary concern about coming to a fantasy world was not getting killed, it was the *logistics*. Water. Bed quality. Where to pee. What would happen if I got my period? But most importantly, *how would the food be*?

The decadent smells swirling around my nostrils set my worries at ease. We stepped through a wide set of double doors into the dining room. The walls were painted dark. Heavy frames with portraits of dead ancestors I doubted anyone remembered hung on the walls. The long mahogany table gleamed, rich and glossy. Candelabras and chandeliers sparkled in the corners and overhead.

The table was occupied, surrounded by straight-backed chairs filled with floofy people in floofier dresses. At the head sat the king, and on his right sat the old guy from before (I needed to figure out his job description but was afraid to ask since Bryce seemed to understand the dynamic, and I couldn't let him know I'd fallen behind).

"Please, sit," the king said like our butts needed his permission or something.

I hesitated, cringing at the two empty seats placed side by side. When my stomach growled, I sat, positioning myself on the edge of the chair as far from Bryce as possible. I didn't love the idea of bumping elbows with my opponent.

Servants arrived, dishing out course after course of red meat piled on top of more red meat. The king started making a bunch of introductions I quickly lost track of. A few representatives from neighboring kingdoms were visiting to witness the shaming of Winston, which made sense because nothing brought people together like shaming others. Apparently, Winston was being punished for walking around killing chickens all across the land for no reason.

After that, the king introduced a viscount, a few dukes, some favorite serfs, and a visiting princess who was wise . . . within her years—an appropriate amount of wise.

I waited impatiently for the old guy's introduction because he seemed like he might be relevant later. Sort of a mentor type. Like maybe he'd drop a few obscure but vital pieces of knowledge before he tragically died, and I'd reflect back and remember what he'd said to save the day.

Before the king could introduce him, the old man stood shakily. "And I," he said, voice cracking like a pubescent teenaged boy's, "am Amygronkphopoulozeetrop."

Bryce looked up, his spoon scraping loudly against his bowl. "Amyflaflalal?"

"'Gronkphopoulozeetrop," insisted Old Guy.

"Amyphosphorustop," I said confidently, meeting Bryce's sidelong look of confusion.

Old Guy sighed. "Amygronkphopoulozeetrop!"

"How do you spell it?" I asked.

"*A-M-Y-G-R-O-N-K—*"

"*K*?" I asked skeptically. "Are you sure?" I wondered if his parents couldn't decide which letters they liked, so they went with all of them. And in an order that made the least amount of sense.

"The *K* is silent," Old Guy said. "Amygronkphopoulozeetrop. My dearest friends call me Amy for short. *Amy* is a strong name, don't you think?"

"Really rolls off the tongue," I said.

"Very noble," Bryce agreed.

Amywhoeverthefuck looked flattered. "Unique, too, don't you think?"

"I knew a Subaru-driving sorority girl named Amy in college," I said.

Amy lit up. "Subaru? Is that some sort of monstrous beast that only the most powerful warrior can tame?"

"Yep!" I smiled.

Bryce didn't look up but couldn't hide the twitch of his mouth.

"What is *sorority*?" Amy asked.

Bryce sat back. "Only the most elite magic in existence."

My smile widened in surprise, and Bryce shot me a weary look that said, *I can't believe I'm playing along with your ridiculous game.*

"I'm flattered you would compare me to such a sorceress." Amy wore a conceited look that said he absolutely could believe it, and perhaps even expected to be compared to amazing people every day of his life. "Amy, master of sororities, he who causes Subarus to bow under his might."

"This is the best day of my life," I said.

Amy took our apparent interest as an invitation to launch into a whole soliloquy about the origin of his name—how his great-great-grandfather had made it up by mashing four words together, and how it'd been passed down for generations—and Bryce and I continued eating and generally not giving a shit until, finally, the king interrupted Amy. "We must discuss the matter of the Chosen One." He carefully looked at the space between Bryce and me, as though sensing one of us would use his eye contact as proof we were who he referred to when he said *Chosen One*.

"After some consideration," the king said, "I agree there can only be one. It is important to determine who the gods sent to lead us so we know which of these complete strangers we should follow without question to our possible deaths."

There wasn't one ounce of irony in his voice, and the dinner guests expressed their agreement in hushed, earnest tones. It was a bit strange. Like everyone was a caricature of what fantasy people should be like. But who was I to question fantasy worlds? It wasn't as though I frequented them. If I was happy to believe that I had truly been transported to a magical world through a portal, I guessed I could also accept that maybe the fantasy people in my books were more accurate than I'd ever given them credit for.

"What do you propose?" Amy asked, jowls wobbling.

"We will train them each as though they are both the Chosen Ones," said the king. "They will train for three days, after which we will hold a tournament where they will compete for the title, then save us from whatever great evil is approaching."

That got my attention. *"Three days?"*

The king nodded, oblivious to my tone. "We'll test your skills in three categories to ensure you can keep our people safe—magical aptitude, hand-to-hand combat, and jousting."

The visiting princess—who I had forgotten was there in the first place—bounced in her chair as soon as the king stopped talking. "Might we have a ball?"

"I don't see why not," the king said. "We'll make a day of it."

Light gasps and low murmurs filled the room as the nobles expressed their delight.

"You guys don't have much going on here for entertainment, do you?" I asked.

Bryce choked beside me.

"Quite the contrary." Amy blinked his watery blue eyes owlishly. "There was the shaming today and the great famine in the east; that's been going on for quite some time. Not to mention the Chosen One and the Evil One—whoever they may be—and—"

Everyone began to talk about history and languages and kingdoms. Names were dropped, wars referenced, family trees traced back to the dawn of time. Seemingly every random tidbit about the world was described for no reason. At one point, a duke started spouting myths about gods. When he went on to mention oregano had been banished from the land because of its usage in the dark arts, I checked corners for hidden cameras. There were none, which was unfortunate because I'd never been so bored. It reminded me of corporate meetings. God, I didn't miss those.

Something bumped my leg.

I glanced down. A cell phone, of all things, shone up at me. Bryce nudged me with his phone again, so I slid it onto my lap, shielding the glow under the table. There was no service, but his Notes app was open, and he'd written:

This dinner party blows almost as hard as your mom.

I was so relieved to see him return to his normal variety of insults that a surprised laugh threatened to gurgle free. Though I was still annoyed with him for what he'd said in our yard, I felt myself softening. He didn't ask to be dragged here on his birthday. It wasn't his fault fate had blessed him and not me, although I was determined to prove fate wrong.

I hid my mirth behind a smirk as I wrote back:

This whole conversation is about as relevant as you are.

I passed the message as Bryce pushed back from the table, jaw flexing as he finished chewing red meat course number twenty-seven. His hand grazed mine as he took his phone. A little zing shot through my stomach, the sort of thrill that only came from passing notes and sharing secrets and . . . flirting.

We weren't flirting. We were neighbors who hated each other, and rightfully so. The dinner party was boring; that was all.

Nobody used *your mama* jokes to flirt. Besides, Bryce was too timid to intentionally flirt. He probably didn't even know *how* to make a move without being an awkward mess about it.

One time, I'd gone to my window because I'd heard him at his door accepting a pizza delivery. The driver was trying to flirt by starting up the old pineapple-on-pizza conversation, and he'd just looked at her cluelessly and told her the pineapple-on-pizza debate was a tired argument that nobody really cared about anymore.

The statement made me realize Bryce was more of a stick-in-the-mud than I'd ever realized, so I ordered him a pineapple pizza every night for a week afterward, hoping he'd realize he *should* have a stance on the matter (and that stance should be decidedly pro-pineapple). The fact I'd bought the pizza from a different company than the one the flirtatious delivery driver worked for was only because the other brand carried a superior pineapple pizza that would be sure to convince Bryce to care deeply about fruit-on-pizza rights.

I jumped as Bryce bumped my knee with his knuckle, handing the phone back. He raised a brow, sapphire eyes flickering in the candlelight. He had devastatingly pretty eyes that he in no way deserved. Yet another way the universe had favored him and not me. They were wasted on him. Seclusive cave-dwelling creatures were supposed to be pasty, hideous, and blob-like. They were not supposed to look this good in a cravat.

Flustered for no good reason, I took the phone. It was warm from his body heat. I wasn't sure why I noticed that, or why holding his phone felt weirdly intimate.

His text read:

Considering your allergy to work, the healthiest option for you is to go home now. I've never ridden a horse, but when it comes to wielding a large shaft of wood, my skill is unmatched.

My skin flushed, my heart quickening. Okay. So maybe I was

wrong. Maybe Bryce was just particular about who he flirted *with*. But why me? Why now?

It had to be an intimidation tactic. Saving face, I rolled my eyes and texted back:

Nice try. You're going down.

He let out a breath through his nose, resting an arm on the back of my chair so he could lean in and whisper, "Not on you."

CHAPTER 8

IN WHICH I SUSPECT THE PRINCESS IN THE DUNGEON WITH THE CANDLESTICK

COURTNEY

When the final course came out, I sat up in my chair with newfound interest. Dessert was some kind of melty chocolaty affair without an ounce of red meat in sight. Despite my full stomach, my mouth watered in anticipation. A servant had just scraped a generous helping of the stuff onto my plate when the dining room door opened with a bang.

"Your Majesty!" A page boy stumbled inside. "I come bearing somber news indeed."

Everyone fell silent, immediately sobering and forgetting all about the heavenly food before them. I inched my fork toward the mound of chocolate on my plate. Byrce noticed and smacked my hand, gentle enough not to hurt, but firmly enough that my fork clattered to my plate. A few people glanced our way, so I tucked my fingers under my leg and smiled innocently.

"Speak, my boy," said the king.

"Winston, he's . . ." The boy panted. "He's missing!"

Gasps filled the dining room.

I looked around in confusion. "Did you guys really expect the chicken guy to stick around after you canceled him?"

"He did not leave of his own accord, Lady Courtney," the boy said. "Once his punishment was over, guards were keeping him contained until one of his family members could fetch him from the dungeon. A guard heard Winston scream, and when they went to check on him, he was gone."

"So he broke out?" Bryce asked.

The page boy shook his head. "Why would he, Sir Bryce? He was about to be released. We think . . . we believe he was kidnapped. It could very well be the work of the Evil One."

A kidnapping? I hadn't known people were going to be *kidnapped*. This was more than I'd signed up for.

Surely, everyone was just catastrophizing, and Winston had simply broken out, like Bryce said. Constantly going on and on about the Evil One had everybody paranoid. There was no need to panic.

Shakily, Amy got to his feet. "This is troubling indeed. Come. We must go to the prison and investigate."

It took me several long seconds to realize Amy was talking to Bryce and me, so unaccustomed was I to being the responsible adult in the room. With one last longing look at dessert, I sighed and stood before Bryce had a chance to take charge.

This wouldn't be so bad. I'd prove to everyone this kidnapping business was just some Scooby-Doo nonsense, and there was no real threat.

"I will get to the bottom of this." I turned to Bryce and added generously, "Along with the help of my sidekick, Bryce, who is generally useless but occasionally attempts to provide comedic relief."

The look Bryce gave me promised he wouldn't let that snub go without repercussion, but he let it go for now. The heat in his gaze sent an odd shiver through me, but I shrugged it off.

The entire dinner party accompanied us down to the dungeons as though Winston's disappearance were a fun murder mystery party. I wasn't really surprised by their morbid curiosity, though, since these people considered a famine to be prime entertainment.

Grand halls narrowed to dark, musty staircases as we descended. Torches lit our path. The flickering flames cast eerie light over the group's faces, giving them the look of slumber partygoers with flashlights under their chins, telling ghost stories. Despite myself, I shuddered. I still wasn't convinced a kidnapping had taken place, but one time, I fell down an Internet rabbit hole about medieval torture devices, and I didn't really want to witness those horrors in person.

I glanced at Bryce to see if he was displaying similar reluctance as we descended into the bowels of the castle, only to discover him holding a piece of dessert in a napkin and digging in with a fork he'd apparently brought from the dining room. I slowed my pace, falling to the back of the line beside him.

"What are you doing?" I whispered.

"Stress eating," he said honestly.

Well, at least I wasn't the only one with the creeps. "I can't believe you preemptively grabbed your dessert in case you needed comfort food."

"I didn't. I preemptively grabbed *your* dessert."

Ah. Here it was. The payback for my comedic relief comment. He'd seen how badly I wanted my dessert, so he'd taken it. "Sometimes you're a real penis, you know that?"

He laughed, his teeth flashing in the dim light. "Asshole tax," he said, referencing our term for when we stole a bit of the other's DoorDash order whenever it was delivered to the wrong door.

I swiped my cake from his hands, and he relinquished it with surprisingly little resistance. I studied the cake for a second, deciding how best to eat the crumbling mess, but then Bryce wordlessly handed me his fork. My suspicion over the tiny kindness was not enough to keep me from tucking in, nor was the knowledge that his fork had recently been in his jerkish mouth.

The cake was soaked in warm syrup that tasted like smoky toffee. As it melted in my mouth, I let out an involuntary moan.

"What?" I asked, noticing Bryce side-eyeing me.

"You're making sex noises in a dungeon," he said frankly. "Time and place, Courtney. Show some decency."

I was suddenly grateful for the dim passage, as it hopefully hid my burning cheeks. "Please. You couldn't recognize a sex sound unless it was a deeply disappointed sigh accompanied by someone asking, *That's it?*"

"I can recognize *your* sex noises," he said coolly. "The walls in our duplex are very thin. I heard the buzzing, you know."

Oh. My. God. We both knew what instance he was referring to, even if he had the decency not to remind me that The Buzzing occurred shortly after he shipped me a sex toy in very conspicuous, embarrassing packaging as a prank. The catchphrase *Elite thrusting for discerning tastes* still haunted me—well, maybe *haunted* was the wrong word, as the memories weren't entirely unpleasant.

In my defense, what was I supposed to do? Throw it out and contribute to a global plastic pollution crisis? No one could claim Courtney Westra was wasteful.

I delicately cleared my throat, trying to hide the fact I was panicking. "What you heard was my electric toothbrush. I'm very conscious of my oral hygiene."

"Ah, of course. Discerning tastes require elite . . . toothbrushes. Multiple times an hour, apparently."

My stomach twisted and turned like my body was being hurled up and down a roller coaster I'd been peer-pressured to ride. First the suggestive texts, now this. When did Bryce become so bold and goading? It was knocking me off-kilter, and it was all I could do not to let him throw me off our verbal sparring mat.

"I did not pleasure myself with a sex toy *you* bought me. That would be . . ." Well, for some reason, at the time, it had been incredibly hot. It had probably just been a heat-of-the-moment thing; using my enemy's diabolical schemes for personal pleasure had been an exciting and taboo secret comeback. A cumback, as it were.

Looking back now, it was mortifying.

"It was my *toothbrush*," I said again, firmly.

"No one moans while they're brushing their teeth."

"Plaque removal is very satisfying."

"Sure. Plaque removal. Weird turn-on, Courtney."

"Thank the Maker you're here!" A new voice blessedly rescued me from the conversation as we rounded a corner and stepped into an antechamber.

The voice belonged to the distraught guard standing in the small stone room, wringing his hands. The chamber appeared to be a sort of dungeon lobby, if such a thing existed. Behind the guard was a small staircase that led down through an arched opening, presumably to the cells. The room was entirely too small for the dinner party, but they all squeezed in anyway, mushing Bryce and me together near the back.

"We came as soon as we heard your summons," Amy said, stepping forward. "Can you tell us exactly when the kidnapping occurred?" A real Nancy Drew, this one.

"About two hours ago," said the guard.

"Why didn't you alert us sooner?" asked the king.

"We spent a good deal of time trying to track Winston down," explained the guard. "There was no time to send a messenger until after we realized we couldn't catch the perpetrator."

The visiting princess turned to Bryce and me and muttered, "Between you and me, something has always struck me as not quite right about this kingdom."

Amy overheard and shot her a sharp look.

Before things could grow heated, I pushed and wedged my

way through the crowd until I emerged next to Amy. "How did Winston escape? Did he dig out? Squeeze through the bars?"

"Whoever captured him stole a key and unlocked his cell, my lady," said the guard sheepishly. "Come, I'll show you where we keep the keys."

Like an excited group of tourists, the dinner party shuffled after the guard through a side corridor I hadn't seen before. We went down a short hall and stopped before a wooden door.

"The strangest thing is that the key room door was still closed and locked after the key inside had been stolen," said the guard, and the group gasped with horrified delight. "The only thing we can figure is the thief crawled under the door." He pointed at the gap, which was a little over half a foot tall. "Though they would have to be very small in stature."

"Ah, a short king," I murmured thoughtfully.

"The Chosen One utters treason, declaring the criminal our sovereign!" someone whispered, outraged.

Scandalized murmurs rose between the dinner guests.

"*Short king* is just a phrase from my land," I said quickly, before they could get any ideas about trying out any of those torture devices on me. "Let's put aside the fact that you guys really mailed it in when it came to the fitment of a fairly important door for a second. Why would someone even want to take Winston?"

"To use for evil, of course." This groundbreaking revelation was delivered very proudly by the king himself. "Perhaps the Evil One took a hostage as a threat to the rest of us, or perhaps they're carrying out diabolical horrors on the poor soul, testing their vile spells and torture techniques. Poor Winston was already shackled and vulnerable. He would have been an easy target."

The hair rose on the back of my neck. I was out of my depth here.

"Please," a wobbly voice said from the crowd, which parted to let its speaker through. "You must help my son." An older woman emerged, clutching a damp handkerchief. "For all his crimes against chickens, Winston is a good boy. I fear what will become of him in the Evil One's lair."

This must be Winston's mom. I swallowed hard. I'd never had the type of mother who would insist her child was a perfect angel even when everyone else suspected the kid was possessed by a demon. Somehow part of me was a little jealous of Winston. My mother was acutely aware of all my faults. She wouldn't stand up for me like this if I so much as shoplifted. The love of Winston's mom felt realer than any "love" I'd experienced back home in the "real" world, and suddenly the whole saving-the-world thing felt a little too grave.

It had been easy not to take it seriously before, when the looming evil felt like hearsay. But no matter how silly some of the citizens acted, they were real people with dreams and fears and families, and their lives were in danger. Who knew what the Evil One would do next or if they would kidnap someone else's loved one.

Amy seemed so certain Bryce or I were the Chosen One, but I wasn't sure how that was possible. I had no idea how to help these people, and the pressure of responsibility made it hard to breathe. Part of me wanted to run away and find the portal home, but I wasn't ready to admit defeat in front of Bryce. Plus, it wasn't like there were any other heroes stepping up to take the job. Well, except for Bryce, which was unacceptable because, no matter how clueless I was, Mr. Flip-Flops-Cause-Plantar-Fasciitis leading an attack against an evil force was ludicrous. All I could do was keep pretending I knew what I was doing.

"Keep the guards searching for more clues," said Amy. "If we can find Winston's whereabouts, perhaps we can arrange a rescue mission. There is nothing more we can do tonight. The Chosen One must complete their training and grow stronger. Only after then will it be time for them to launch their defense against the Evil One."

The dinner party was somber now. I looked from one face to the next. The guard said Winston's kidnapping had happened two hours ago. That would have been after we arrived at the castle, but before we all gathered for dinner. Anyone here might have been involved. Of course, the suspect could have been an outsider, but the castle inhabitants would have easier access to the dungeons and might not be questioned sneaking around the passages.

There was only one person among the dinner party small enough to fit under the truly half-assed specimen of carpentry that was the door to the key room: the visiting princess.

CHAPTER 9

IN WHICH WE HAVE TWO FUNCTIONING BEDS BUT SHARE ONE ANYWAY

BRYCE

It was the longest, most detailed, most vibrant dream I'd ever had.

After our visit to the dungeons, servants had escorted us back to our beds, instructing us to try to get some sleep so we would be fit for training in the morning.

Now, I shifted in my huge bed, which had to be the Chosen One's bed and not the sidekick bed. The room was large and empty. And silent. So silent.

I couldn't hear Courtney.

Most nights I heard her through the thin duplex walls. She'd sing loudly and off-key in the shower. She'd rehearse excuses for why she couldn't come into work—no two the same, never getting her wires crossed. And yes, sometimes, she'd make sex noises after I'd shipped her adult toys. I hadn't been able to decide that day if I'd made the biggest mistake or the best choice of my life. I'd eventually decided never to speak of it, no matter how often I thought of it.

Reminding Dream Courtney of that day was fair game, though, as was sending her suggestive texts at dinner. I wouldn't have dared to do those things with real-life Courtney, but they were exactly the thing I needed to throw Dream Courtney off her game. And there had been something somewhat . . . exciting about it.

Shadows crept across the wall, reminding me of the creepy turn my dream had taken with the kidnapping thing, and my skin prickled and crawled.

I *obviously* wasn't scared of the dark. But Courtney probably was.

Then again, Dream Courtney across the hall wasn't making a peep.

Usually, I didn't notice being alone. It was the in-between times when it sneaked up on me. When I'd finished work, but it wasn't bedtime yet, and I didn't know what to do with myself. When my growling stomach reminded me to eat, and I cooked alone in a cold, dim kitchen. When I lay in empty sheets at night, repressed memories the only thing keeping me company.

During those times, having a warm body shuffling on the other side of the wall gave me something to fall asleep to. I'd close my eyes and pretend I was back at my grandparents' house, and they were down the hall, watching TV.

I rolled onto my side, the bed suddenly feeling absurdly large for one person.

Furrowing my brow, I thought hard, willing a book to materialize on the nightstand—my usual method of keeping my mind from drifting. I apparently sucked at lucid dreaming, because the nightstand remained bare.

Everything was too dark. The flickering fire cast ghoulish shadows across the wall.

I decided Courtney was for sure scared of the dark. She was probably lying there in terror, expecting a cold hand to close around her ankle and pull her under the bed.

Then I realized I was thinking about Courtney in bed, and something about that felt dirty. Not in a sexy way. Definitely not in the way that made my heartbeat quicken and my thoughts stray to the way that dress hugged Courtney's curves. Dirty in the way that made me feel like I'd contracted a mental plague just from thinking about her.

Briefly, I considered the mechanics of medieval dress laces. I'd never been great with shoelaces, but perhaps dresses could be slipped on and off without fiddling with all those strings, like a pair of old sneakers. There wasn't cell service in my dream, so it wasn't as though I could google it the way you'd google "how to remove a bra with one hand." Not that I'd ever done that.

Just like I'd never done something as absurd as sneak a slice of chocolate cake into a dungeon because some girl looked like she really wanted it.

Okay, maybe I had done that, but she'd had my back earlier, sparing me from Amy's disgusting flask, and I had to repay her before I vanquished her from my dream. I was a gentleman.

She's a plague, I reminded myself. I had to sanitize my thoughts before she ravaged my brain for good.

That viscount, or whatever he was, could have all of Courtney's mind plague germs to himself, thanks. I noticed him staring at her at dinner while a duke prattled on about oregano (I blamed that conversation on last night's dinner). I was disgusted with my own mind for creating him. It probably came from reading my grandma's romance novels, which often featured some slimy viscount lurking in the shadows, being evil and mysterious, kidnapping heroines, and, in general, bringing down the quality of life of all those around them. What a dick.

You couldn't trust viscounts. It was the silent *s* that did it for me, hiding like a snake in tall grass.

A log popped in the fireplace, and I jumped. Sparks crackled and hissed. The fire burned lower, and darkness closed in.

I sat up, sheets falling to my waist. I scratched my bare chest.

By now Courtney was undoubtedly growing frightened, all alone in her room, wondering what was lurking in the dark corners and trying not to think about how well her sheets had been washed.

Since I'd established I was a gentleman, it was only right for me to check on her. I had to get out of here . . . to make sure *she* was safe.

I pried myself out of bed and slid on my jeans from earlier. The floor was frigid under my bare feet as I crossed the room. My walk turned into a run as the feeling of something creeping in the darkness washed across my back. I needed to check on her. *Now.*

I flung open my bedroom door. One, two, three, four steps later I'd crossed the hall. My shoulder hit her door as my hand twisted the knob, and I half fell inside.

Courtney shot up, clutching blankets to her chest. Even in the orange light from the fire, the familiar look twisting her face was unmistakable. Only Courtney could simultaneously look delighted and enraged. "What do you want?" she asked, practically sharpening her fangs, which was a weird way to swoon and say, *My hero.*

"I wanted to confirm I got the Chosen One's room," I said. "I did, by the way. This room sucks." To be totally honest, the rooms were identical. Except her fire did seem brighter. Warmer. Cozier. Damn her.

"You mean you're scared of the dark." She smirked her annoying smirky smirk. "You can't just barge in here. Fuck off."

I should have fucked off. After all, I'd checked on her and confirmed she was perfectly fine—well, *fine* was a kind word for what Courtney was. *Vile* was more fitting.

But as I considered returning to my cold, dark, ominous, foreboding, probably haunted room, I decided that, since I was the hero, staying was the only noble choice. To ensure *Courtney's* safety.

I strode across the room and hopped onto the bed, shouldering her aside and taking her covers. She punched me in the arm, and I laughed as obnoxiously as I could. It felt nice to forget about the kidnapping part of my dream for a second and get back to our usual verbal sparring.

"Why are you here?" she asked, half to herself, like she was baffled as to why she was letting me this close to her.

"We both know you're the damsel in distress who can't be left on her own for more than two minutes without getting kidnapped. I'm here to protect you from yourself."

Her dark eyes narrowed to slits. "If you're such a gentleman, then you'd offer to take the floor."

Ignoring her, I pulled the blankets over my shoulders and hunkered down. Her pillow smelled like her shampoo—jasmine and honey.

I especially hated Dream Courtney. Dreams seduced me with their harmlessness until I loosened my control, and Dream Courtney was always there, eager for me to slip up. Not that Dream Me minded. Which was troubling.

"Bryce?"

My eyes flew upward. Arms crossed, Courtney glowered down at me like I was something unpleasant pulled from a shower drain.

"Huh?"

"Take the floor."

I scrambled upright, sheets sliding to my hips. Her eyes tracked the movement, and I tried not to notice her noticing me, even if it did make me feel warm and nice inside.

"It doesn't matter if I take the floor." I yawned. "I'll wind up here in the end. Haven't you ever read those books where there's only one bed, and the couple has to share? It doesn't matter if I start on the floor because you'll beg me to join you for some half-baked reason we both know is an excuse for you to have your wicked way with me."

By the time I'd finished, her brows were buried so deeply in her hairline, it would have taken an archaeological dig to find them again. "Into romance novels, are you, Bryce?"

My skin felt sticky. I pushed the blankets off my legs. "An ex left one at my house, and I may have perused the pages," I said, because that sounded cooler than *I learned everything I know about sex from sneaking my grandmother's romance novels.*

"*Huh.*" Her eyes sparkled.

I scooped the wad of covers off the end of the bed and dumped them on her head. "Women sleep with guys who read romance."

She shoved the blankets off, hair mussed in an irritating way that gave me a weird urge to lick my hand and smooth it back mom-style.

Why was I thinking about licking Courtney?

Holy hell, that was a thin, thin nightgown.

My throat tightened. This was it. Even in my dream state, I was allergic to Courtney, and I was about to die. It was the only acceptable explanation for why sitting close to her had this effect on my body.

"You're no hero," she said, snapping me out of it. "More like some kind of beta-bro, b-plot villain. You certainly fit the bodice-ripping-womanizer bill."

I tried *very* hard not to look at her *very* see-through bodice. "And you fit the personality-of-a-damp-shoelace sidekick bill."

Her nose wrinkled up. "I do not. I'm full of wit."

I threw a pillow at her nose so I wouldn't notice it again. "Then you're clearly the sidekick. Sidekicks are the witty ones."

She shoved the pillow back at me. "You said sidekicks have the personality of shoelaces."

I tossed the pillow. "Mind your prejudice. Shoelaces are witty."

"That was pretty witty for a supposed Chosen One."

The almost-compliment threw me off. I hated when she did that. Switched sides when we argued until I couldn't tell if she was insulting me anymore. I finally settled on "Thank you." It seemed safe.

Her lips bunched as she sulked. "Knock it off. You came here trying to get in my head. Sleep every night in my bed, for all I care. It won't work. The only reason you want to be the Chosen One is because I do."

I rolled my eyes. Hard. "The only reason you're still here is because I want it. If it weren't for me, you would've dipped as soon as the king said the word *training*."

Her mouth opened and closed a few times, making her look like the fish out of water she was.

Then suddenly a pillow smacked me in the face. Before Courtney could pull it back, I caught it and yanked. She fell forward, tumbling into my lap.

Courtney panted, wide, darkly lined eyes inches from mine. Her fingers wrapped around my thigh, her other hand braced against my chest, the pillow wedged between us like a Bible at a middle school dance.

"I wanted this a long time ago," she said, a bit too theatrically to be convincing.

My brain heard what she meant. My body heard, *I want this*, felt her warm fingers on my leg, and totally lost its shit. Thank god for the pillow between us.

"Huh?" I asked intelligently.

"As a little girl, I always dreamed of being special."

Deep breaths. "Oh, you've wanted to be a hero since you were a kid?" *Buy time, buy time, buy time.* I tilted my head to the side, letting my features grow tender. I touched her chin with a fond finger. "In that case . . . cry me a river, build me a bridge, and get over it." I allowed myself two seconds to recover and relish her livid expression before giving the pillow a shove.

Courtney hooked a leg around my waist as she fell back, pulling me along. I landed with an *oof* over the top of her, bracing my forearms against the mattress on either side of her head, caging her in. "I'm afraid you're just not hero material," I managed.

She wrapped her legs around my hips, tugging me closer. *Fucking hell.* "An appreciation for rest and relaxation doesn't make me an unfit heroine," she snapped inches from my face. "What about hobbits? Those dudes laze around all day, and people think they're great heroes. God forbid I, too, appreciate multiple breakfasts and long naps."

And then the universe blessed me. Because I noticed her cheeks were *pink*. Not their usual angry red, but *pink*. Courtney was blushing.

She'd started a game I didn't think she could finish.

A heady rush washed through me. This was maybe the best dream I'd ever had. I was bold, irresistible Bryce, and this round was mine.

Raising my brows, I shifted my weight, settling against her. Courtney's breath hitched, but she met my unspoken challenge, face set. Her thighs flexed, holding me closer instead of shoving me off. Nerves pinballed around my rib cage. Pulse beating hard, I rolled my hips ever so slightly against hers. Her expression cracked, lips parting as she inhaled softly.

"You can't get everything you want," I said.

Her whole expression read: *Oh, really?* The fire flashing in her eyes seemed to come from inside of her rather than a reflection of the flames lighting the room. Her feet slid lower around my hips as she fit herself snugly against me, expression now reading, *Checkmate*. And fuck my life. She felt good. Warm and soft and—

"I always get what I want," she practically purred.

My stupid fucking mouth was about half a second from saying a stupid fucking thing like *Take what you want as long as it's me*. Instead, what popped out was "Yeah, well, I always wanted to be a slug when I was a kid, and look at me now." Which was also a pretty stupid fucking thing to say. I tried to save it. "A pillar of masculinity."

Courtney's legs loosened, then slid completely off me. The air felt empty and cold. "Keep your pillar away from me." Her entire face tightened in a strange way I'd never seen before. She was likely overcome by the unfamiliar touch of a man, or voluntary human touch in general, and—

Oh. She was laughing. Full-on squirming with uncontrollable mirth, *laughing*. "You wanted to be a *slug*?" Her peals of laughter redoubled. "Oh my *god*. What kid sees a slug and thinks, *Goals*?" She snorted so loudly, she was probably encouraging the villagers' pigs in the city below to begin mating.

I'd never seen Courtney smile like this before—cheeks all crinkled up, umber eyes glittering slits. It caused a heated tug in my gut that must've been anger because it couldn't be anything else. My hands found their way to her sides, presumably to still her, to *shut her up*. But. Once my fingers curved around her ribs, they rested there helplessly, feeling the vibrations as she unknowingly laughed at my childhood trauma. She was such an asshole without even trying, and I couldn't stop her because it was a relief after years of pitying looks and sticky silences.

And screw it, it was a dream anyway. I wasn't breaking my don't-get-close-to-Courtney rules. None of it would matter when I woke. I'd spend a day avoiding her like I did every time this happened. Then after I slept again, my skin wouldn't heat when I was around her anymore.

Her ribs expanded against my palms as she drew in a deep, gulping breath, finally getting ahold of herself.

"Bryce," she said, in a tone I could only describe as *gentle*.

I licked my dry lips. "Yeah."

"You'll *always* look like a slug to me, okay?"

As she fell back into yet another fit of laughter, I rolled off her, flopping down onto the other side of the bed. I shut my eyes. "Sad how a slug is still a better Chosen One than you."

"Wow. What a comeback." Sheets rustled as she wriggled underneath them, shaking the bed.

Silence fell.

"Courtney?" I said into the darkness. "There's something I need to tell you."

"We're not doing the romance-book thing where we stay up all night talking about our feelings and braiding each other's hair."

"I want you to know"—I drew in a fake, shuddering breath—"tomorrow, when I wake up with the most majestic raging boner you've ever beheld, it is in no way your fault."

"If I suffocate you in your sleep, you won't wake up at all," she responded sweetly.

CHAPTER 10

IN WHICH A ~~PLOT DEVICE~~ TALKING ANIMAL ENTERS THE STORY

COURTNEY

The morning after Bryce's surprise voyage into my room, I woke to sunshine streaming through the thick-paned window. Bryce was gone.

While he was always game to hurl insults, he generally avoided touching me, shrinking away from any accidental brush of fingers like a schoolboy scared of cooties. Last night was different. It was as if, in this world, real-life rules no longer applied, and anything was possible.

For a moment, I remembered the weight of his body pressing against mine, the vibrancy of his eyes in the firelight, and the way he kept touching me. The way his fingers—those fingers that had spent so much time shooting rude gestures at me—curved gently around my ribs. The way, for a moment, I wondered what would happen if we kept on touching and touching and *touching*.

Also, why did the man never wear a shirt?

Oh my god. His plan was working. He was already in my head. I'd be an idiot to think he'd come to my room for any other reason.

Time to refocus.

Amy said training should be our priority, and we should wait until after then to organize a proper counterattack against the Evil One, but I wanted to dig into the investigation more. The memory of Winston's worried mom urged me to get to the bottom of the kidnapping, and that started with interrogating the visiting princess. It couldn't be a coincidence that the day she came to the kingdom, someone went missing. Maybe she had a personal vendetta against Winston. Maybe he'd stolen her pet chicken or something. Once I solved the case, everyone could rest easy. Well, everyone but Bryce, who I hoped would rest terribly, kept up by the knowledge that I'd bested him at being a Chosen One.

I was drawn from my thoughts by a barely audible knock against my door. I slid out of bed, crossing my arms over my embarrassingly thin nightgown before answering.

Nobody was there.

Someone cleared their throat, a tiny, high-pitched throat-clear. There, next to my foot, was a mouse standing on its hind legs. "Are you the one they call Lady Courtney?" he asked.

A scream tore out of my throat. Instinctively, I ducked behind the door, using it as a shield as I gaped at the *tiny talking mouse*.

Unfazed, the tiny talking mouse extended a hand. "Greetings. I'm—"

"Nope." I slammed the door.

Was it a bit mean to slam the door on a small woodland creature? Perhaps, but I wasn't keen on the thought of enduring the annoying antics of a no doubt snarky, no doubt cringey, no doubt ridiculously over-the-top animal companion. God forbid he broke into song.

Plus, I didn't want the bubonic plague.

Before I could do anything else, another knock came at the door. This time, it was a servant telling me I was expected at the training grounds. I'd have to wait a little longer to interview the princess. In the meantime, I could only hope the city guards found Winston soon.

After dressing in puffy brown pants, a loose cotton shirt, and a hobbit vest, I ate a quick breakfast in the kitchen before the servant led me down to a central courtyard.

Bryce and another guy stood waiting. Bryce looked like a low-budget Jareth the Goblin King wannabe in a thin white shirt and leather breeches, and the other guy looked like an overeager camp counselor. He was youngish and blondish and shortish.

"Greetings!" The camp counselor smiled a pearly white smile, which was impressive considering dental hygiene couldn't be great here. He was practically vibrating with a level of joy I considered obscene, given the early hour. "I have been instructed to help you refine your swordsmanship skills in preparation for the tournament! Which of you noble warriors wish to start us off?"

Bryce stared at the guy like he was trying to figure out if this was real life.

A few townspeople grew curious and walked over. Their expectant eyes reminded me of Thanksgiving. That moment after all the cousins flaunted their successes, and it was my turn to impress, proud familial eyes glowing brighter with each of my achievements even as my exhaustion grew heavier.

I remembered how dim the eyes of my family were when they didn't look at me through the rose-colored lens of my accomplishments. Who did I think I was, volunteering to save the world when I couldn't even keep a meaningless marketing job?

"Well?" Castle Camp Counselor asked, bouncing on his toes. "I am sure you're both naturally adept warriors, seeing as all Chosen Ones effortlessly slay legions of monsters with little to no training." His smile widened as his excitement grew. "Nevertheless, I daresay there are always ways to improve!"

"Before we begin, I'm going to need you to take it down about ninety-eight percent," I said.

"Pardon me?" Castle Camp Counselor asked.

I sighed. "You're up here." I raised a hand above my head. "And I'm going to need you about here." I bent until my palm grazed the dirt.

"Ah! Indeed!" Castle Camp Counselor ambled over and lay on the ground at my feet.

It took me half a beat to recover. "Look at that, Bryce. Most men know to bow before me."

"Have you ever had a dream where you go to bed, and then you wake up still in the dream?" Bryce asked, swaying a bit, a dazed haze in his eyes. "That's impossible, right?"

Did Bryce think we were in a dream? Suddenly, his unexplained confidence made sense, as did the comfort he displayed last night when he . . . Oh my god. Why was Bryce *comfortable* with crawling into my bed in his dreams? And why was I okay with him crawling into my bed when I knew it wasn't a dream?

"You're definitely in a dream, Bryce," I said, and his shoulders sagged with relief. I'd considered telling him the truth, but I was too curious to see more of this Bryce, the Bryce that was only free to be his true self in the deepest, safest corners of his mind.

"When one's whole life is a dream," Castle Camp Counselor was saying from where he still lay on the ground, "you live in paradise whether sleeping or awake."

This dude loved his job way too much.

"Do people usually worship me in your dreams, Bryce?" I nodded down at the counselor.

"Please. The poor bastard is under the illusion you could be the Chosen One." Bryce walked over and held out a hand for Castle Camp Counselor. "Arise, good citizen." His voice took on a booming cheesy quality. "For a good leader will raise you up, not put you down. It is I, your Chosen One. You can tell it is me by my flowing red hair."

Castle Camp Counselor rose, a look of reverence on his face as he grasped Bryce's hand.

"Red hair proves nothing," I said.

"Sure it does," said Bryce. "All Chosen Ones have flaming auburn hair and piercing eyes."

"It is known," Castle Camp Counselor said, gazing at Bryce with adoration.

Bryce had a point for maybe the first time in his life, but I had to keep my cool if I wanted to convince everyone I was the Chosen One. I narrowed my eyes in a challenge. "Fine. Where did you grow up?"

Bryce placed a hand over his heart. "You're taking an interest in my childhood? I'm touched. Truly, truly touched."

Still grasping Bryce's other hand, Castle Camp Counselor reached for me, his overly happy smile still plastered to his face. "It warms my heart to see such comradery between—"

"Shut up," Bryce and I said in unison.

"Where did you grow up?" I tried again. "Because I grew up only ten miles from a farm, which means I'm basically a farm child and therefore the Chosen One."

Bryce's Adam's apple bobbed, but he recovered quickly. "I have a weird birthmark. I'm sure Amy could relate that back to the prophecy somehow."

My heart clenched. I couldn't compete with weird birthmarks.

"Shall we begin?" Castle Camp Counselor started demonstrating fencing positions, movements exaggerated as he transitioned from pose to pose.

"What about parents?" I asked, while Castle Camp Counselor waved his sword around next to us. "Is one or both of your parents dead or dying?"

Bryce averted his eyes. "I'm sure they're fine."

Disappointment overcame me. "Mine too." I kicked at the ground angrily. "Even still married." Probably because they hadn't found time to draft their own divorce papers yet. I wished they could see where I was right now. They'd take back all those years of telling me to get my nose out of fantasy books and start focusing on real life.

That was when I remembered. "I have a talking animal sidekick."

"Sure you do. Where?" Bryce glanced at the space around my feet. "I was under the impression sidekicks were supposed to be . . . by your side."

I shouldn't have slammed the door in the mouse's face. He'd never come back, and I'd never be able to prove he was real unless Bryce saw him.

The only way to claim the Chosen One title was to beat Bryce at the tournament. To do that, I needed to train . . . which would be a challenge, considering I couldn't walk up a flight of stairs without getting winded.

✧ ✧ ✧

We were given phenomenally unimpressive wooden swords and subpar instructions, thanks to Castle Camp Counselor, whose name was actually Cuthbert.

Everyone watched as Cuthbert casually crushed us. They shared how disappointed they were with our performance with grumbled insults like, "*These* are the Chosen Ones?"

We "trained," which was a loose term for "Cuthbert cheerfully kicking our asses," for hours. The grime and physical abuse wore me down, but I sought solace in the fact I was marginally better with a sword than Bryce, which I attributed to all those tennis matches I'd pretended to enjoy playing with Will.

Now, I took a break while Bryce and Cuthbert dueled. I stood outside the dirt ring with a few assorted castle employees who should've been working but were instead watching Bryce lose on company time. I felt a companionship with them on a spiritual level.

"And thrust, and thrust, and thrust," Cuthbert said, as I whispered, "That's what she said," between each "and thrust."

Cuthbert unleashed a flurry of attacks that Bryce tried and failed to block. Bryce fell to the dirt. Dust swirled around Cuthbert's boots as he approached. Bryce dove for Cuthbert, but he dodged, rapping his stick smartly over Bryce's back and sending him sprawling.

Groaning, Bryce rolled onto his back, limbs spread-eagle, face covered in sweat and dirt. Cuthbert tossed his hair as he sheathed his sword, his blond locks gleaming like he belonged in a Pantene commercial. He went to help Bryce up, but Bryce threw his wooden sword to the side, rocked into a sitting position, and clutched his head. "*I'm* the Chosen One, and this is *my* dream, damn it. I don't understand why I'm not immediately good at this."

My own frustration flared in sympathy, aggravated all the more by hunger and pain. Various bruises all over my body throbbed in time to my heart.

Bryce lifted his head. Clean tracks trailed from his eyes, cutting through dust and blood. He quickly swiped his sleeve over his face, smudging mud across his cheek.

I couldn't look away from the shimmering wetness brimming over his red-rimmed eyes. Guilt seeped into my veins. Maybe I shouldn't have lied to him about the dream. Then again, if he knew this was real, he'd freak out even more.

"Ancestors above," a maid said at my elbow. "Is the Chosen One crying?"

Mutters spread through the gathering of castle extras. "We're doomed!" someone wailed like they were going for their Oscar.

"The gods have sent us a squealing infant," a gruff guy said, crossing his meaty arms.

I turned in a circle, taking in all the dissatisfied, angry faces. I was the only one allowed to mock Bryce. It was an art form, and other people didn't do it properly.

These people had done nothing but provide unhelpful commentary all morning. It was our first day, there was no caffeine here, and a cheerful man had given us a hearty beatdown. Anyone would shed a few discouraged tears, but these people looked at Bryce like one drop of water from his eyeball discredited his abilities completely. It was *wrong*. Tears didn't make Bryce pathetic. His personality did.

Grabbing Gruff Guy by his collar, I yanked him down to eye level. I lowered my voice so Bryce wouldn't hear me defending him and get the wrong impression. "I swear, if you or your pathetic peasant pals say one more negative thing about Bryce, I'll request the king have you hung—hanged? Hung." I deliberated a second more, then whispered, "Hanged?"

Gruff Guy swallowed hard. "Apologies, miss, I didn't mean nuffin' by it."

"Sure." Releasing him, I stepped back and raised my voice. "Everyone, back to work." The words, which had often been yelled *at* me, felt odd coming *out* of me. "Or at least go slack somewhere else," I called after their retreating backs so I could sleep at night without hating myself.

Meanwhile, Bryce staggered to his feet, wincing as he rolled his shoulder. "What did you say to that guy?" He pointed at the dissipating crowd.

"Nothing. I think watching you repeatedly fail got monotonous."

He gave me a weird look. "You must've said something to get them to leave me alone. They clearly hate me."

I smiled gently. "I don't think your issue is that you wield a sword like a toddler playing T-ball, or that your leather pants make it super clear you've skipped leg day one too many times, or even that you bear an uncanny resemblance to a garden gnome."

"Gee, thanks." Bryce tried to pull away, but I hooked an arm around him and pulled him back. His skin burned through the thin linen of his shirt.

"It's the tears. Fantasy heroes aren't allowed to cry. Like, sure, unicorns are real, and magic is a thing, but a place without toxic masculinity? Inconceivable."

"I wasn't *crying*. It's my allergies. The real evil lurking here is this world's astronomical pollen count. I can practically see it in the air. How am I supposed to fight anything without my Claritin? God, and hand sanitizer. I miss hand sanitizer."

Bryce looked about one second away from losing it, so I didn't push the issue. Though I had noticed he had no problem braving pollen every time he helped Doris, our elderly next door neighbor, mow her lawn.

"Whatever the reason for your watering eyes," I said instead, "it's not okay for men to show emotion—not even in a fantasy world—the one exception being if their entire army has been massacred by the evil foe, and they're alone on their knees in the middle of a foggy battlefield. Then, and only then, are they allowed one singular tear. And only if their face is super battered and dirty, and their loyal companion has been captured, and also their girlfriend has dumped them for some obscure reason."

Bryce looked down at me, his blue-fire eyes bright in the midday sun, orange hair a messy halo around his head. He let out a soft puff of air through his nose, almost a laugh, though his face remained set, and I knew he caught my sarcasm. The settling dust lit golden around us made me feel like we *were* in the middle of a foggy battlefield. That was the only explanation for why the air felt charged with significance.

"I don't have one, you know," he said. "A girlfriend."

"I know you don't" popped out of my mouth. "I mean, not because I care. I just noticed you stay in on weekends, so I figured."

"And you?" Bryce asked, averting his eyes. "Do you have someone special you keep locked up in your basement?"

"Believe it or not, I'm more of a serial dater rather than a serial killer."

"Oh." He sounded disappointed.

Some weird urge to explain made words build up in the back of my throat until they burst free. They tumbled over one another, each one faster than the last. "It's easier that way, you know? Besides, it's not like anyone is lining up to date me long-term. There's a list of questions everyone asks when they're looking for a relationship." I ticked them off with my fingers. "Kids, job, aspirations, and with each box you fail to check off, their interest goes down. My life is enough for me, but it's not enough for anyone else. Even you told me I should change."

Bryce frowned for a second, then his eyes widened as though he'd had an epiphany. "That's not what I—"

"I thought I might find you here," a decrepit, crackly voice interrupted. The old guy—or Amy, as we'd been calling him, since he had a keyboard smash of a name—wobbled across the courtyard, his purple robes billowing underfoot. "The servants have prepared a luncheon for you. After that, it's time for magic practice."

◇ ◇ ◇

The luncheon had been set up in the castle gardens and appeared to be attended by everyone who was at the dinner last night. This was good news, as I hoped to get a chance to interrogate the princess a little.

The gardens looked like a surrealist painting, with twisting topiary spiraling from sparkling rock gardens and strange trellises supporting flowering vines that coiled and arched over cobblestone pathways. Vibrant purple, green, and blue foliage spilled over garden beds, and pillowy trees with blooms the size of my head cast pleasant shade over the center of the garden, where a long table had been erected. A fountain gurgled to the side. The bizarre statue in the middle was of a woman with cropped hair wearing a fringed flapper dress, of all things, while she rode a rearing horse and wielded a broadsword. A Chosen One from days past, maybe.

Beside me, Bryce dissolved into a sneezing fit, the fragrant pollen in the air apparently rendering him helpless. I abandoned him in his time of need, spotting the princess seated toward the far end of the table.

The meal appeared to be a free-for-all—people coming and going, some eating at the table while others milled about with their plates of finger food.

I slid into a chair opposite the princess and began piling my delicate porcelain plate with a heap of bite-sized sandwiches, some kind of fruit that looked like purple watermelon, and a delightful array of poofy pastries. As I shoved an herby sandwich layered with something that resembled a cucumber into my mouth, I let my eyes roll back into my head. After a morning of exertion, I was famished.

"So," I said to the princess, after I'd swallowed. "I feel like we didn't get a chance to talk the other night. Tell me about yourself."

The princess looked pleased to have been addressed by a potential Chosen One. "My name is Clementine. Princess Clementine of the Seven Isles."

"Ah, we come from similar backgrounds. I looked after sixty-eight aisles in my land," I said, thinking of the store where I worked. "Do you ever have intrusive thoughts, Clementine?"

"Ever heard of small talk?" Bryce asked, pulling out a chair beside me.

I ignored him and kept my focus pinned on Princess Clementine. "You ever think about kidnapping someone? Not that you'd ever do that, of course, but have you ever considered it? Just for the funsies."

Clementine blinked in shock. "Why, of course not. I'm a princess. I would never think of such things."

"Of course not. How silly of me." I took a bite of the melon, which tasted like a banana had had sexual relations with a hayfield, and nearly gagged. "What kind of things do you like to do for fun, Clem? Specifically, yesterday right before dinner?"

"Subtle," Bryce said under his breath.

"I was in my chambers, doing everything a princess ought to do," Clementine said slowly, deliberately. The way she looked at me was a little intense, like she was trying to tell me something without actually saying it—probably that she didn't appreciate the cross-examination. "You can ask the king, if you'd like. When I left my chambers, I ran into him coming from the direction of the dungeons."

Bryce and I exchanged a sharp look. "Are you implying something?" I asked, leaning in.

"I could never imply that I saw your dear king sneaking suspiciously around the castle," Clementine said with a shrug, taking a dainty sip of her bubbly purple drink.

I risked a peek at the king where he stood by a hedge maze talking with Amy. There was no way he could fit under the door, but he was the king. He probably had a master key and could have broken Winston out without needing to go into the key room at all.

I shifted uncomfortably. I'd have to be more subtle with my investigation when it came to the king. I couldn't have people muttering *treason* again. Tonight, I would follow him and see what he was up to.

CHAPTER 11

IN WHICH WE ARE TRAINED IN EVERYTHING EXCEPT HORSEBACK RIDING, WHICH FEELS LIKE A MASSIVE OVERSIGHT, CONSIDERING THE IMPORTANCE OF HORSEBACK RIDING IN FANTASY

BRYCE

After lunch, Amy led us back across the courtyard. I hoped magic training would be less violent than this morning's lesson, but I doubted it. Very few things were pleasant in this hell *not* on Earth.

Because, yes, after the incredible pain inflicted on me during sword training by Cuthbert, aka the happiest man I'd ever met, I'd concluded I was not in a dream. And yes, maybe I did shed a tear or two upon discovering reality, as I knew it, was a lie. But who could blame me? I was stuck here with *Courtney*. That would make anyone cry. Nothing was familiar here, except for her, as infamous as that notorious tickle you get in the back of your throat right before you come down with the common cold.

I didn't understand how this happened. In all my googling, I'd never seen any warnings that coatracks in lighting departments could create accidental portals to dangerous new worlds.

(Oh god. Did I remember to lock my front door when I left the house yesterday?)

And the kidnapping. That wasn't just a dream either. A real man might be in the clutches of an Evil One, and *we* were supposed to fix it? Courtney with her terrible interrogation techniques, and *me* with my . . . with my what? Ability to make spreadsheets? I was an *accountant*. If destiny had grand plans for my humble life, I would prefer to avoid them the way I dodged weekend outings: by telling everyone something had come up, when that "something" was just my reluctance to be social.

The fact none of this was a dream also meant last night was not the off-the-record indulgence I'd thought it was. I'd slid Real Courtney suggestive Notes app messages under a table and mentioned The Infamous Buzzing *That Must Never Be Mentioned*.

Worse, I'd had Real Courtney on her back. Under me. In bed. Never. Again.

My skin grew clammy. Familiar panicky fingers clenched around my heart, trying to suffocate it quietly before it could be stabbed to death. No more slipups. No more touching.

Inching closer to Courtney, I tapped her arm. This touch was okay. It was a normal touch. A necessary one.

Courtney fell back as Amy continued ahead, still talking about who knew what.

"Do you think it's strange how weird everyone acts?" I asked. "Like, the blacksmith's sole purpose in life is hammering stuff. Amy's whole existence revolves around a prophecy. The princess's daily activities literally involve *doing princess things*."

"Why is it strange?" Courtney asked.

"This isn't a dream," I said.

She gave me a look. "Obviously."

She knew it wasn't a dream. The whole time last night, she'd known.

My mind replayed the evening over and over. I could practically feel her thighs tightening around my hips. Drawing me closer. *Not* pushing me away. And then today. The way she criticized the whole world for its intolerance instead of criticizing me for my weakness.

I stopped touching her arm. She terrified me—a flashing red button I couldn't keep my hands off of.

"You could always give up, find the portal we came through, and go home," Courtney said, a challenge in her smile.

The thought was tempting, but though I'd had the best teacher, I'd never been good at leaving. "If you thought getting back home was that easy, you would have quit already."

"Nope." Courtney began walking again. "I have to make something of my life, don't you remember?"

I let out a growl of frustration. I'd shown her an easy minimum-wage job I thought she'd love and suggested she stop wasting her time torturing me so she could find some real friends, and all she heard was *change everything about yourself*. I hadn't meant to imply I thought her life wasn't good enough. In truth, I didn't give a shit about her life; I'd just wanted her out of mine.

I opened my mouth to tell her she'd misunderstood, that the whole reason I'd followed her to the store was to apologize, but then I shut it. Maybe it was better she was angry. I needed to maintain whatever distance remained between us, especially after I'd already gone and told her I didn't have a girlfriend, like I was offering myself on a silver platter. *Stupid, stupid, stupid.*

The situation was growing dire. I was a bug thrashing in a web, getting myself increasingly tangled up in *Courtney*. I had to escape before she sank her teeth into me.

My mind took the opportunity to present me with a detailed image of tangled sheets and Courtney beneath me, biting her teeth into my shoulder around a muffled whimper.

I pushed aside the image.

Pulled it back. Considered it. Just for science.

Pushed it away again.

Feelings weren't constant. That's why I liked numbers. One plus one always equaled two, whereas feelings came and went for no reason whatsoever. Best to avoid the variable and keep them out of my life. Zero feelings equaled zero risks, which equaled zero damages.

I carried a past, the weight of which wasn't heavy but light. Empty, thanks to all the people who walked out. I hadn't exercised the muscles needed to hold someone in my life. If I tried, it would break me. Even if I grew strong enough, she'd leave anyway, and the empty memories left behind would feel lighter—and more crushing—than ever.

Courtney said she'd wanted to be a Chosen One since she was little. I'd never seen her care about anything. This might be my only opportunity to beat her at something she actually valued. She was such a sore loser; she'd never speak to me again. We'd go home, and she'd get out of my life. That would be that.

"Look." Courtney pointed.

I followed her finger. A woman knelt by a fountain on the other side of the courtyard, comforting a little girl with skinned knees. Over the sounds of steel clashing from training soldiers, the hum from servants' conversations, the clip-clopping of hooves on stone, I could still catch a few words as the mother kissed her daughter's tears away, murmuring comforting nonsense: "Are you all right?" "Brave girl," and "Mommy's here."

The little girl smiled. Love shined from both their eyes. Strange ribbons of light swirled around them, orchid purples and sunshine yellows.

"Is that magic?" I asked.

The colors reflected off Courtney's dark eyes. "It must be. I wonder how it feels."

I was silent a moment before saying quietly, "Me too."

Amy called for us to catch up, drawing us out of our reverie, and we hurried after him. When we got to the stables, Amy climbed onto a donkey while grooms gave Courtney and me horses and no instructions on how to operate them. I looked up at the tall beasts and swallowed hard.

"Come on, Bryce," Courtney said, already on her horse. "Horses are basically grass-powered motorcycles."

Was that supposed to help me feel better?

"See?" Courtney was saying, making gear-shifting motions with her foot, which the horse ignored. "Motorcycles."

I steeled myself before grabbing the saddle and hauling myself awkwardly onto the horse. Before I could adjust to my tall, unstable perch, a groom gave my horse a firm slap on the haunch, and I had no choice but to hold on for dear life. Meanwhile, Courtney did Absolutely Nothing—her signature move—simply letting her horse follow ours.

Amy took us out of the city, along the bluff overlooking the glittering ocean, and across a series of rolling picturesque hills, like he was a producer trying to show off his movie's budget by creating a series of cool, wide-angled scenic clips.

Before long, we left the open air behind and plunged into the woods. Amy was droning on about a library or something, but I was too distracted by the landscape to pay much attention.

I'm touching grass.

That was what Courtney had said one day when I'd stepped outside to find her sitting, crisscross, in our front yard, her hands in the grass, her eyes closed. It wasn't until she'd said that, *touch grass*, like a real action and not a sarcastic response found on the Internet, that I realized how long it had been since I'd actually touched grass too.

Later, when she went back inside, I put aside my fear of dirt and germs, kicked off my shoes, and stepped onto the lawn. With the cool blades between my toes and the soft dirt staining my heels, everything felt less scary. Inconsequential. Small.

I tried to find that peace now. A breeze whispered through leaves, cool against my skin, made cooler by the canopy of branches overhead. Massive trees, their trunks larger than any found in our world, towered around us. Strange foliage nestled around their mossy roots. Red and white mushrooms. Yellow flowers the size of basketballs. Plants that grew orbs of luminescent purple fruit, glowing in the shadows. The mulchy scent of the wet forest floor floated through the air. Birds bickered overhead, and cicadas whined underfoot.

We rode until we came to a gurgling brook. A waterfall seeped through moss and stones, trickling into a larger pool at the bottom. Amy dismounted, saying, "Now we can talk."

"I wonder if there's a reason we had to traipse into the woods to learn magic," Courtney said as she halted her horse beside me. "Traveling all this way for the aesthetic seems wildly impractical." She remained in her saddle, probably because she couldn't be bothered to *not sit* for the two seconds it would take to climb off.

I peered over the edge of my horse. It was a long way down. My stomach flipped. I'd just have to live here now, on top of this horse, forever.

"Aren't you going to dismount?" Courtney asked, tilting her head toward where Amy squatted, preparing some kind of medieval charcuterie board next to a fallen log. "Amy went all out to make this a special day for us, and now you're not going to enjoy the nice picnic he prepared?"

I fiddled with my reins. "I don't want to get off until you do." I caught what I said and knotted my jaw, feeling my ears heat.

"Such a gentleman."

"I'm scared of horses, okay?" I said, with about as much aggression as one might use to say, *I'm going to force you to drink bleach.*

A delighted smile spread across her face. "A Chosen One who's scared of horses," she crowed.

"It's not so bad once I get going. I can close my eyes and pretend it's fun."

"I don't wanna hear about your sex life."

I would do anything to get her to stop thinking about me and sex in the same brain wave because it made me think about her thinking about it. "Could you maybe help me down?"

A smug smile crawled across her face. "If I leave you there, you'll be stuck forever, and I'll win by default."

"All Chosen Ones need help from their sidekicks every once in a while."

"I'll manage."

"No." I huffed. "I mean *I'm* the Chosen One, and if you leave me, you'll be failing to do your sidekick duties."

"You said *doodies*."

"Real mature, Courtney."

Releasing a long sigh, she watched Amy putter with his picnic basket. "My butt fell asleep," she admitted. "I'll probably fall if I try to dismount, so couldn't help you even if I wanted to."

"Well, well, well." How the tables had turned.

A pale green moth the size of a kite dive-bombed Amy, and he spun around, swatting at thin air as it fluttered off.

My horse grew skittish from all the excitement. I gripped my reins hard. Remaining on the horse was suddenly scarier than getting off it. Before I quite knew what was happening, I'd swung a leg over my saddle.

What do you think you're doing? my mind screamed at me. But my body dismounted, even though my heart pounded in my throat. My feet hit the dirt, and I rested a hand on my horse until my footing steadied.

Still shaking, I shoved my horse out of the way and walked to Courtney's side. Her eyes went round as she looked down at me. She still wore the makeup from our world she'd had on the morning of my birthday, but it was dark and smudged, making her look like some kind of feral forest creature—an unimpressive one who devoured pizza rolls and Starbucks. "What are you—"

"Don't make this a thing," I said, lifting my hands. "Get off the horse."

She did, a little quicker than I'd anticipated, slinging her leg over the saddle and half falling over the side. She slid between me and the horse. Her boots hit the spongy forest floor, her legs wobbled, and she fell against me, winding her fingers in my shirt. I barely caught her. The horse snorted in protest. Or maybe that was me.

My jaw ached. I willed myself to unclench my teeth, but warning bells blared through my head with the trumpeting intensity of a wailing Death Star alarm.

The no-touching rule had been shat on.

My breaths shallowed with each passing second.

Her vest had laces crisscrossing up the front. I started to visually trace the paths of the strings through the eyelets, then stopped, realizing my brain was calculating how best I might go about loosening those strings if she let me. My hands, fixed to Courtney's waist, grew clammy. I trained my eyes on a spot above her head.

Unknotting my jaw, I rasped, "You have terrible blood pressure if you still can't stand."

"It's been three seconds."

"They make medication for that, I think. Cheerios. Running. I don't know."

"That would lower my blood pressure, which would be the opposite of helpful in this situation."

Fuck me, fuck me, *fuck me*. If I avoided eye contact, I'd be fi—

She adjusted her hands, sliding them over my chest, wrapping her cool fingers around my biceps. My muscles tensed. I tried to remind myself she'd only touched me to keep from falling. I shouldn't analyze.

Courtney blinked up at me. *"Bryce?"* She said my name all breathy in a way that sent my brain straight to the gutter.

"Courtney," I said. Because all I could do was say her name back. My gaze fell to her mouth. The thin gold hoop dividing her bottom lip in two suddenly felt like it was placed there for the singular purpose of tempting me.

Her breath warmed my neck, so different from the cool spring air. It was odd how such warmth could come from a woman with a heart of ice.

"The sausage is ready," Amy said.

I released Courtney and eyed the charcuterie board Amy had laid out. I needed to get a grip. A firm one. On anything but Courtney.

We joined Amy on the log, where I focused harder on cheese than I ever had in my life. While Courtney dived in, Amy stared into the distance and prattled on about gods and the foundation of the world. He briefly mentioned the unknown Evil One we were supposed to vanquish, before talking about a maple leaf for a good half hour. It might have been a metaphor for something deep and important, but the main point got lost along the way.

I kept stealing glances at Courtney over my sausage. Now I knew I wasn't in a dream, things had become . . . different. I couldn't shake the memory of Dream Courtney because Dream Courtney was Real Courtney. I'd slept in Real Courtney's bed and woken up with an arm slung over Real Courtney's hip and was imagining Real Courtney saying my name *in that same bed* and in that *same pleasantly concerned voice she used earlier*.

Shit.

I couldn't sleep this one off. I was stuck with horny brain, which wasn't good. Horny brain made me fixate. It made me see a random thing, like, say, Courtney's nose, and suddenly it was the most beautiful thing I'd ever seen. It made me momentarily forget all her unappealing qualities like her selfishness and arrogance and how nice her fingers felt wrapped around my arms—

Damn it. At least she was making me horny now instead of happy. Horny was just another form of misery, and misery was safe.

"And so," Amy was saying, his trembling lips smacking around a wedge of cheese, "how do you two plan to use your magic to defeat the Evil One?"

My thoughts scattered. "Magic?"

"Of course. I assume your powers manifested, leading you from your ordinary lives to ones of adventure, calling you to overthrow darkness?"

"Not . . . exactly." Courtney looked at me like we shared a secret—dirty gossip whispered in church with horrified delight—and I felt myself unraveling at my very tight seams.

The whole thing pissed me off. Basic things like her looking at me or saying my name should not affect me. I willed my heart to calm. After my *oh my god, this is not a dream* moment this morning, I was on edge. That was all.

"What if our powers haven't . . . manifested?" Courtney asked. "What if we aren't capable of using magic?"

"Of course you're capable," Amy said. "Just because magic doesn't exist in your land doesn't mean you're incapable of wielding it in a place where it does."

That sort of made sense. It was like if you grew up having never seen a spoon, then you were handed one as an adult: You could use it even though you'd never seen it before, if only you learned how.

"But how do we get magic?" I asked.

"You must chase the sensation of others' positive perceptions of you to find the power inside," Amy said unhelpfully.

"Huh?" I asked. "What does that mean?"

"Exactly what I said." Amy swayed on the log. "Charisma is the source of magic. Once you feel it inside you, you can use it to your advantage."

"Charisma," Courtney deadpanned.

My day turned around in an instant. "You mean we need to be charming to have powers? Courtney, you're going to be so great at this." My smile hurt, it stretched so wide. I leaned against the log and crossed my ankles.

"Charm is all well and good, to be sure." Amy stood, closing his eyes as he placed a solemn hand on an oak tree for no damn reason. "But there are other things that can help others see you in a positive light—good deeds, wit, and general kindness can all influence people's perceptions of you."

"General kindness." Courtney paled. Her eyes searched me out, giving me an *oh hell no* look.

"You'll do great," I said, trying not to notice the freckle under her left eye. "I'm sure people will like you. Just be yourse—actually, in your case, don't be yourself."

To my surprise, Courtney flinched, the sparkle snuffing from her eyes, and I immediately felt like the world's biggest jerk. Usually, no insult, no matter how heinous, made her flinch like that. Something about this conversation had her on edge.

Amy stepped away from his tree bestie and looked from me to Courtney. "I must say, I've never heard of Chosen Ones completely unable to feel their Charisma. Most of them are universally liked."

"Why, though?" Courtney asked.

He blinked. "Well, I . . . I don't know."

"How can we get people to like us when you told us not to make friends while we were here?" Courtney asked shrewdly. "It's hard to build connections when you're not allowed to talk to anyone."

Amy chuckled. "Oh no, no, no. You mustn't do something so ridiculous as *talk* to the people. For their safety, it's best if you keep your distance. You will be admired from afar, loved by society—an icon, a legend." Amy clasped his hands. "I propose we try an exercise."

"I hate exercise." Courtney whimpered. I focused on not focusing on her whimper.

"Close your eyes," Amy said.

"Oh, this is more my speed." She shut her eyes.

Amy crossed to Courtney and placed what was probably supposed to be a comforting hand on her shoulder, but it came across creepy. "Think about your interactions with people, how their approval felt, then chase that feeling deep inside of you. There, you will find your power."

"This seems like a toxic magic system," Courtney said. "Do your children have a lot of self-worth issues if they aren't immediately liked by others?"

"Oh, extreme issues," Amy said gravely. "Power is strongest and easiest to wield during the initial rush of admiration a person feels for you, following whatever specific event sparked their adoration. Once that fades, so does your power. Though, if you have strong, constant appreciation surrounding you to draw from, you can be trained to pull upon it and awaken your magic at will. However, it is hard to access and takes much practice. See if you can feel any of that power now. I'm sure you have already amassed many admirers throughout the kingdom."

"Like chasing likes on the Internet." Courtney shook her head ruefully, eyes still shut.

I pretended to join her, knowing I'd find nothing. I knew no one here liked me. But if I dedicated myself to trying to tap into my magic, maybe it'd keep my mind off tapping anything else.

CHAPTER 12

IN WHICH OUR MENTOR IS A MISOGYNIST

COURTNEY

I closed my eyes and tried to do Amy's assignment, even though I knew I'd find nothing. To keep up appearances, every once in a while, I furrowed my brow or made a low humming noise, so it looked like I was going through some heavy character transformations. I'd have to figure out a solution to my magic problem quickly. I'd never read about an unlikable Chosen One, and if I didn't gain Charisma soon, everyone would see me for the fraud I was.

Squinting one eye open, I peered at Bryce. I'd seen how his hands shook when he helped me off the horse. I'd also felt it, his fingers hot at my waist, trembling against my skin. He wasn't joking about being scared, and yet he'd pushed past it. For me.

My mind went back to a day a few months ago. It was after I'd gotten into an argument with someone on the Internet who tried to convince me cilantro tasted like soap. He'd told me to touch grass, and that actually seemed like a good idea, so I went out and sat in the front lawn, my palms pressed to the earth beside me. It was one of the first warm days of the year, and a green, earthy smell filled my nostrils.

"What are you doing?"

I'd looked up to find Bryce leaning over the porch railing, a bemused expression on his face.

"Touching grass because some idiot thinks cilantro tastes like soap."

"Cilantro does taste like soap, so you should stand up. You're going to get grass cuts."

"Is that really how you see the world? You go through life seeing everything that can hurt you?"

"No," he said, "I see people who can be hurt by everything."

That was the difference between him and me. He still tried, still fought for people. Didn't he know they wouldn't fight for him back?

Hours passed. From time to time, Amy murmured particularly useless encouragements like "Reflect on where your own positive perceptions of others stem from," and "Feel the validation of others flow through you."

At last, Amy figured out neither of us was going to shoot fireballs out of our butts, so we headed back to the castle, the setting sun behind us.

"How can I convince people I'm worthy?" I asked. My shoulders hunched as my mind flashed back to exhausting years of working to earn love.

"How do I convince anyone to pledge their devotion to me?" Bryce asked, sounding equally weary.

I glanced his way. Perhaps he had his own insecurities.

"You must inspire the kingdom," Amy said, voice shaking along with the hoofbeats of his ass. "The people expect a sort of silent strength from you."

I perked up. "I can do stoic. I'll be a freaking inspiration."

"Oh no, I mean Bryce. *You* must be a kind, genteel woman." Amy tapped the side of his nose, a grandfatherly twinkle in his eye that I suddenly wanted to punch out.

I pulled on the reins, dragging my horse to a halt. We stood on the bluff, a steep drop to the ocean on one side and rolling hills on the other. "Excuse me? Bryce can be all sulky and mysterious, and people will find him charming, but I have to be *nice*?" I hissed the word.

It was the Mr. Darcy conundrum. Men could be antisocial assholes and people thought they were hot and wanted to understand them. If I was an antisocial asshole, people told me to smile more.

Bryce turned his horse to face me, knuckles white around the reins. Amy sat trapped in the middle on his dumpy ass, eyes wide. Probably, since he'd given us one singular magic lesson, he knew he'd served his purpose and his time drew nigh. Typically, after mentors in stories found a Chosen One and told them enough information to keep them alive but withheld enough for no other reason than to make the journey difficult, they were expendable.

"The people expect a certain feminine grace," Amy explained. "They need to see your empathy, your womanly, healing touch—"

"A healthy choice for you would be to stop talking," I said.

Bryce looked between us. Salty air lifted the hair off his neck, and his horse pranced, impatient to get going. I waited for him to gloat or mock. He probably agreed with Amy, seeing as just yesterday, he'd urged me to change too.

Amy opened his mouth.

"No," Bryce said. "She has as much right to be a dick as I do."

I sputtered as everything inside me recoiled. There he went again, *helping* me. This was *disastrous*. Helping led to caring, which led to expectations.

This not-hate only started after we came here, after I appeared to be making an effort to save the world. He'd expect it now: effort. His hate was simpler than his *bothering*. While him liking me would help me get magic, it wasn't worth losing our dynamic— a dynamic I was beginning to realize I valued more than I'd thought.

Collecting myself, I lifted my chin. "On second thought, I'll pass on the problematic inner magic. I'll defeat the Evil One without it." I nudged my horse into a walk.

Amy kicked his ass, hurrying after me. "Without Charisma, why will anyone follow you into battle? Who will care? What bards will sing your glory if no one is moved by your story?"

My stomach began to hurt.

I was losing myself and my only honest relationship. Tempted by glory and adoration, I'd been morphing myself back into something society deemed acceptable. I'd dug myself deep, surrounding myself with more and more lies to convince people I was worthy. But I wasn't, and I'd never get magic because no one ever liked me genuinely, not the real me; they only liked my pretty facade. If I didn't claw my way out soon, I'd lose myself again for nothing.

If I backed out now, maybe there was still time for Bryce to face his fears and figure out how to become the Chosen One he was. I was wrong before. I couldn't be a better Chosen One than him. I couldn't do this at all.

I didn't know these people, didn't even know they existed until a magical portal brought me to their world, but their lives were real, and they deserved a chance to live, even if they were foolishly putting their hopes on someone who didn't deserve their confidence. In the end, maybe Bryce was right to challenge the validity of my devil-may-care attitude, because I *did* care. I cared too much about these innocent people to stay.

I'd quit this, just like I quit my old life, and flee back to the safety of perpetual failure, where I couldn't let anyone down.

"Defeat the Evil One yourself," I choked out. "I'm going back to the portal, and I'm going home."

"Thank god," Bryce said on a sigh of relief. "I'm out too."

"You can't be," said Amy.

"I don't even want to be a Chosen One!" I said. "I only said it to piss Bryce off. Can I please, please just go home?"

Bryce's face softened. He opened his mouth, but Amy cut him off.

"I'm sorry. You cannot. It's impossible." To his credit, Amy's eyes held pity. "In the past, when a Chosen One was summoned, the portal for them to return home didn't open again until they left the world better off than when they came."

Darkness flirted with the edges of my vision. My stomach twisted in on itself. We were *stuck* here? I guessed I sort of assumed Bryce and I could dip if things got too hairy.

"I thought *you* summoned us," I said through gritted teeth. "Undo it."

"Though I did summon our last Chosen One, it was not I who cast the spell this time," said Amy. "According to our history books, we often never discover who summons Chosen Ones. Sometimes it's fates. A skilled mage. A farmer who happens upon the spell. Sometimes the universe itself summons warriors forth, as though the gods themselves have sent them to us. Indeed, since the dawn of time—"

Amy's droning voice faded as rage swelled in my ears. I loathed this world. It was a sick parody of everything I used to think I wanted. I'd bet anything the universe dragged me here after I'd finally broken free to say, *You're not allowed to give up. Now run along and save the world.*

There were milestones everyone was expected to reach in life. Gatekeepers stood at each of those milestones, guarding the path to happiness. When you were a kid, you were allowed to be content. You weren't allowed to do that once you'd reached a section of your life that said you had to go to college or get married or have a child before you could continue to achieve joy.

When I wouldn't perform, I got shoved into this place as punishment, where I would be stuck until I broke.

I urged my horse into a run, leaving Amy in the dust. My fists balled around the reins, my pulse loud and hot in my ears.

By the time Bryce caught up to me, I was already back at the stables, handing my reins off to a groom. Bryce's horse slid to a stop, puffs of dust swirling from its hooves.

"Thank you so much," I said to the groom, lifting my voice to a high falsetto. "However can I show my appreciation?"

"Cut it out." Bryce dismounted, shoving his reins at the same flustered stable boy. "That Yoda guy is an out-of-touch fossil. We're going to find a way out of this. You don't have to smile to save the world."

Claustrophobia pressed in. The stable roof felt lower, the shadows darker. Who did I think I was, playing hero again? I was as naive and stupid as I was when I was ten, trying to use the Force to levitate my stuffed animals. The mental strain felt the same—exhausting, desperate, futile.

"This isn't me," I said. "It's all an act. I'm not a hero. I can't get anyone to like me, and I can't get us home."

"You *can* do it," he said. "I can tell you're trying."

While I was pretending to be someone else, the compliment felt like he was saying, *Thank you for not being you.* I'd slipped on a cape to play the part of a hero, and Bryce had fallen for it. Instead of me showing him that even losers could save the world, he simply thought I wasn't a loser anymore.

I couldn't even set him straight because, in order to get home, I'd have to keep wearing the cape. I missed what we used to have. He'd made me feel seen, even if he only saw me as a nuisance. Now, it was like he didn't see me at all.

Distance. We just needed distance again. Straw crunched under my boots as I marched for the stable doors. My nose filled with the musty scent of manure and hay.

Bryce's footsteps pounded closer. "Wait." He caught up, slowing to walk beside me. The light streaming through the cracks in the stable boards flickered over his face with each step, highlighting the stubble along his jaw, the angle of his cheekbone, his eyes. His lips. The light swept across them, and my finger itched to do the same—to trace the ridges of his cupid's bow, to see if his breath would catch.

Something under my ribs jumped and tingled at the thought.

Touching Bryce should inspire existential dread, not tingling. I shouldn't want his breath to catch unless it would catch and stop altogether.

His brows furrowed as he looked me up and down. "Damn it, Court, say something. I'm sorry, okay? I'm sorry it's unfair."

I stopped, and he plowed into me, nearly knocking me off my feet. Turning, I shoved him off. "Why did you do that?"

He pressed a hand over his chest where I'd touched him. "Do what?"

"Court," I breathed. "You called me *Court*." My voice grew louder. "Then you *sympathized* with me?" My heart pounded in my ears. Last night. His lingering looks and half smiles . . . they all added up to something. Something bad. "Why'd you call me Court?"

"I don't know? I couldn't be bothered to say the whole thing? Would you rather I go with the second half of your name and call you Ney?"

I shook my head, already backing away. Everything felt too fast, like I could suddenly feel the whole world spinning and slinging around the sun at sixty-seven thousand miles an hour.

Real-world, part-time job, paid-the-rent-late Courtney never caught his eye. Only fantasy-world, aspiring-Chosen-One, planning, scheming Courtney. Whatever positive feelings he felt for me were built on a lie. Just like Will's had been.

"I don't want a friend, Bryce," I exclaimed. "Friends want what's best for each other. I don't want what's best for me. I want what everyone believes is worst for me, and no friend can understand that!"

I always knew, if someone started to care for me, they'd try to help me. If I cared for that someone back, I might just let them, and then I'd be living a lie again. I'd change to try to keep them, to convince them I was worthy of their affection. The next thing I knew, I'd be serving Thanksgiving dinner ten years from now with ten million goals involving PTA, HOA, and every other type of stifling, mind-numbing acronym. And then, one day, all the lies would come to light, and I'd be left alone again.

I turned and ran.

✧ ✧ ✧

I burst into my room back at the castle, buried my face into my pillow, and screamed.

Someone tapped my arm.

I lifted my head and screamed again. There, standing on the bed, was the mouse.

"I found your dragon," the mouse announced, which didn't make me want to scream any less.

I shot upright. "Why'd you come back? I slammed a door in your face."

"All is forgiven, my lady. 'Tis an occupational hazard." The mouse plopped onto the bed and sat like a human beside me.

I shrank away because I was still pretty concerned about the bubonic plague.

"The prophecy states—" he began timidly.

"Not you, too, with the vague prophecy nonsense." But he looked so earnest that I wearily waved for him to continue.

"The prophecy states that on the eve of the second day of the Chosen One's arrival, they will venture north-northeast into the woods for two miles, whereupon they will come across an abandoned barn, inside of which they will discover a dragon."

"Oh. Well, that's actually—highly specific."

"According to ancient lore, the wrath of a dragon can be tamed by a Chosen One," the mouse said. "If you should accomplish the task, having such a mighty force on your side will aid you in the fight to come."

Slowly, I nodded. This was more doable than Amy's popularity magic. I wasn't sure why the mouse still had my back after I'd slammed the door in his face, or why he believed I was the Chosen One when his only interaction with me was the aforementioned door slamming, but he wasn't such a bad sidekick after all.

This was the quick solution to getting us out of here. Once I figured out who kidnapped Winston, I could swoop in on a dragon and rescue him before incinerating the Evil One's fortress—wherever it was. I was pretty sure Bryce was the Chosen One, not me, but I couldn't ask Bryce, scared-of-grass-cuts Bryce, to try to tame a dragon. How hard could it be?

I was sort of in the mood to burn something down anyway.

CHAPTER 13

IN WHICH A WHITE KNIGHT GETS SCARED

BRYCE

Courtney didn't come to dinner.

"I don't want a friend," she'd screamed at me back at the stables. Words that should have stung made my heart ache with how familiar the sentiment was. Her dysfunction fit with my dysfunction. Maybe the fact both of us were avoiding relationships was what had made our weird not-relationship work so well.

"Where is Lady Courtney?" someone at the table asked.

Maybe she found a way home, the catastrophizing voice in my head whispered. She'd seemed pretty upset. Maybe she'd done a small, good deed—like helped an old lady cross the street—and it had bettered the world enough to open the portal for her, and she'd abandoned me.

Sure, I wanted her out of my life, but not like this. Not before we were both safely home.

"I saw her head into the woods." The faint voice of a maid in the shadows snapped me from my thoughts, and my self-pity morphed into a new kind of dread.

I was well-acquainted with fear. I thought I knew it inside and out until that moment. Until I stopped feeling scared for myself and started feeling scared for someone else. It was brand-new and a thousand times more terrifying.

"The woods?" I repeated, words sharp, mind filling with horror stories of murdered joggers and bear attacks. "Where? *Alone?*"

Ten minutes later I'd mounted a living death machine and was galloping into the forest. As the shadows closed around me, my mood darkened further. The sun was fading fast. Fog hovered above the ground, opaque wisps weaving among the foliage. It split around the horse in coiling ripples as we galloped through. As the trees grew thinner, the horse's hooves scrambled for purchase over stone. I slid from its back and rushed forward on foot. The stones took shape as the ruins of a house, its chimney the only thing still erect—like a skeletal arm bursting from the ground, reaching for the sky.

I crashed into a clearing, boots sliding over slick bricks as I fought off rosebush thorns and spiderwebs. Light from the orange-sherbet sunset poured through the opening in the tree canopy above. Below, a stone barn stood forlornly in a circle of brown, matted grass.

A cloying burnt smell stung the back of my throat. Fog rose off the ground, turning the dying sunlight into something hazy and dreamlike. Spindly forms twisted from the hovering fog here and there, maybe the blackened remains of farm equipment . . . no, they were trees—what was left of them, burnt and twisted. A foreboding chill swept up my spine.

Through the sound of crickets and tree frogs, a metallic clinking met my ears. My head snapped toward the sound. Courtney stood before the barn doors, fiddling with a chain that was looped through their handles. She let the chain go, the padlock securing the ends together, smacking against the heavy steel doors.

I took a step, boot snapping a charred twig, and I noticed the grass underfoot was blackened too.

Courtney whirled. "Bryce? Why are you here?"

It was strange seeing her like this. Usually, she went around so *unfazed* by everything. "Are you okay?" I asked, momentarily ignoring my creeping suspicion that the clearing was created by an unnatural and deadly fire.

Giving me the cold shoulder, she turned back to fiddling with the padlock. "Why do you keep *bothering*? You're like that guy. That character in a TV show who dies, but their body is never shown, so you know they're going to come back."

I crossed the eerie clearing, wishing I didn't recognize her defense mechanism—lashing out when vulnerable. Wishing I didn't care.

"The first time the character returns, it's this whole cute, clever thing." She grew more agitated with each word, rattling the chain every few seconds for emphasis. "But then they keep dying and popping up over and over, and soon everyone just wants them to meet their graphic end on-screen so we can be done with it."

I drew up short behind her. "You think I'm cute and clever?"

Ignoring me, Courtney slammed the chain against the side of the barn. "Why is any of this our problem, anyway? We don't even live here. Isn't it unrealistic for these fantasy worlds to expect one person to save them?"

"I . . . guess?" She was upset and rambling, and I was having a difficult time keeping up.

"Back home, our own world is falling apart, but no one is expecting a single random pedestrian to save us." Courtney grew more impassioned with every word. "But go to a fantasy world and suddenly everyone looks to the least qualified person in existence for salvation. If they say no, suddenly they're the selfish bad guy."

"What's with the barn?" My fists clenched. "What are you up to? Are you all right? You shouldn't be out here alone."

"No, I'm not all right. I'm *angry*." Courtney wiped roughly at her brow. "Don't you see what I've been driven to? It's disgusting. An all-time low. I've set aside my personal beliefs and betrayed everything I've ever stood for." She shuddered. "I'm out here, sweating my butt off, *working*. Because—stupid Amy and stupid Charisma and stupid *you*. You're ruining everything."

"How am I ruining everything?"

"With your *bothering*," she said, like that explained everything. Shaking her head, she dropped her voice to a condemning tone. "You feel something for me."

What? What gave her *that* idea?

Perhaps internally I'd been experiencing some weaknesses toward her, but she couldn't know that. I needed to shut this down now so she wouldn't make the same mistake again.

"Sure, yeah, you do make me feel things." I shook my head ruefully—a man bested. "You make me feel the same kind of intense irritation I experience when I step in water while wearing socks."

She rolled her eyes, but her shoulders eased slightly.

Stepping around her, I took the lock from her hands. "Here. Let me try."

"Don't tell me you conveniently know how to pick a lock."

"I don't conveniently know how to pick a lock." Stretching, I plucked the key off the top of the doorframe. "But I am taller than you and saw the key." I twisted the key in the lock and gave the chain a sharp tug. "What's in here, anyway?"

Courtney pushed me aside, using all her body weight to pull open one of the doors. It creaked. A slit of sunlight slashed across the dusty barn floor. Something stirred in the shadows.

"Courtney," I asked, trepidation tightening my muscles, "what's in there?" For the first time, I noticed the bag at her feet—some kind of white material stained with red. A red that resembled blood.

She hoisted the Disturbing Sack (possible band name?) and pushed the door open farther. A low clicking issued from the depths of the barn. Something glinted and shifted in the far corner.

Courtney strode inside. I tiptoed after her, blinking as my eyes adjusted. The barn smelled of decaying straw and musty grain. Heavy cobwebs coated every surface like sheets over furniture in a mansion.

"The prophecy says—" Courtney began.

"You were paying attention to the prophecy?" I failed to keep the impressed tone out of my voice.

Her back stiffened. "*Actually*," she said, as though she were a stranger in a social media comments section about to say something deeply untrue with a great amount of confidence, "yes. But don't get used to it. The prophecy states the dragon will help the Chosen One."

I choked and almost tripped over my own feet. "Dragon?"

Her teeth flashed in the gloom. "Scared?"

Snick tick tick tick.

The sound slithered forward, sending the hairs on the back of my neck on end.

Something peeled itself off the far wall of the barn. I staggered back, cursing under my breath, heart hammering the inside of my chest. "Courtney," I whispered.

Ignoring me, she opened the Disturbing Sack, withdrawing a slab of raw meat. "Even if I'm not the Chosen One, I've always been pretty good at taming strays." She extended her bleeding offering, inching farther into the barn.

The clicking picked up excitedly. Shadows took shape as the dragon emerged from the darkness, its four wings reared back and twitching. It had eight spindly legs ending in dual hairy tarsal claws. They jabbed the barn floor one after the other in halting, inhuman movements as the creature came closer, closer, closer. Its pinchers clicked together in front of its wide, fanged mouth. Its eight eyes blinked independently, never letting Courtney and me out of its sight.

Adrenaline whooshed through my veins, setting my muscles

alight. I did not sign up for winged, fire-breathing spiders. The spider dragon took another step forward, long talons crunching bones littering the ground.

"Uh, Court, maybe this was a bad idea."

All eight of the dragon's eyes clicked in succession, swiveling toward me.

Courtney flapped the raw steak around. "Here, dragon, dragon, dragon."

Eight eyes snapped to her.

The dragon struck at a speed I couldn't track. *Zip, zip.* Courtney's jaw dropped as she stared at the quivering, bleeding scrap of meat left in her hand.

The dragon pulverized the steak like an infomercial juicer, pulp flying. My stomach churned. "Run." The word came out a raspy nightmare whisper.

The dragon snapped its wings wide, stirring up a tornado of dust within the barn. It arched back its head, toothy maw gaping wide. Fire roiled to life in the back of its throat, sending a heat wave blasting over us.

I stumbled away, but Courtney stood frozen, that bag of scraps dangling uselessly at her side.

"Run!" I yelled, but she didn't move, silhouetted in the blinding light filling the barn as flames churned and licked around the dragon's razor teeth.

I darted forward, grabbed Courtney's hand, and yanked her away as the dragon unleashed a stream of flames. I dragged her out the door, fire literally hot on my heels. I risked a peek back. The dragon burst from the barn, its side banging into one of the steel doors and crumpling it like a tin can. It shrieked at the sky, unleashing another stream of blinding flames.

My legs pumped faster, my hand clammy in Courtney's. "Run," I said again. "Run, run, run."

We burst into the tree line, the subwoofer thumps of the dragon's wings pounding against my eardrums. The trees bent as the beast lunged into the sky. Waves of air battered against us, forcing us to our knees. Spotting an alcove tucked between massive, gnarled tree trunks, I pointed, urging Courtney forward. We crawled into the space and hunkered low, willing the dragon to move on.

I couldn't see it through the trees and darkened sky, only heard its pounding wings. They went on and on for what felt like hours but must've only been a few minutes. At last, with one final scream, the sound of its wings faded.

The air grew still. I panted, slumping against a tree root.

Courtney slipped her hand from mine, letting out a shaky breath. Then she hopped to her feet, tossing the Disturbing Sack aside. "The mouse must've translated the prophecy wrong. Even though I'm not the Chosen One, you were there, too, and it still tried to eat us both. But you should have been able to tame it. The mouse said the Chosen One could tame the dragon."

"Why are you listening to prophecies from random mice?" I was too busy undergoing acute chest pains to pay much attention to what she was saying.

"It wasn't a random mouse. It was my sidekick."

"Right," I wheezed, "the famous sidekick nobody but you has seen. And look where it landed us."

"There are worse things."

"Are there? Are there really? Because I can't think of much that's worse than an oversized, flying, *fire-breathing spider*."

"We weren't in any real danger," she said.

"We weren't?" Slowly, the vise of fear loosened around my heart.

"Nah. Now, if it had been a flying vending machine, we might've been in trouble."

"You ass." I scrambled to my feet, my temper flaring, numbing the fear away. Her words weren't soothing, but, in a way, they did manage to chase off my panic. It was the emotional equivalent of telling someone you had a headache, and them offering to smash your finger to make your head feel better—drowning out a smaller feeling with a bigger, new one.

"What happens when the dragon starts ravaging the countryside?" I asked. "It won't take much to figure out who's to blame."

Her reaction caught me off guard. It was the same look she had when I told her to start over with her life, the same look she had when Amy said she had to change if she ever hoped to save the world. There was a familiarity to the crack in her expression, like a mug with a handle that had been glued back together in the same spot time and time again. She wasn't surprised by the fact she'd royally messed up. I guessed that made sense.

Everyone told her she was a screwup; I'd heard the phone conversations with her parents through the thin duplex walls. Her family, Amy, even I had tried to push her to do something different with her life. I hadn't considered the fact that the constant berating actually got to her, that maybe she *did* try, and it always led to disasters like this one.

"Maybe it will fly away," she said weakly, and now I caught the edge of panic in her seemingly unconcerned voice. "Maybe it's happy, free and chilling in the wild. Maybe it'll never hurt anyone, and no one will ever have to know."

I held my tongue before I could remind her there was a lock on that barn, implying the dragon had been caged for a reason. She knew that as well as I did, and she felt bad enough as it was.

"Listen," I said gently, "we need people to like us if we want to gain Charisma. If the dragon comes back and starts causing destruction, we're going to have to blame the Evil One for its release, otherwise the people will never forgive us."

"We can't just let it eat people, Bryce."

"Of course not. When it returns, we'll recapture it before it can hurt anyone, and no one will ever find out we're to blame." My tone was soothing, even though the thought of facing the beast again made me wish for an asteroid.

But if we wanted to get home, to get the portal open, we had to make the world a better place than when we came to get the portal open. Which meant, if the dragon started hurting people, we had to put a stop to it. Yet another thing to pencil in to the Chosen One to-do list between *find Winston* and *defeat the Evil One*.

Courtney thought about my suggestion for a moment. "Okay. It can be our secret."

Normally, phrases like *it can be our secret* were used for fun, harmless things. Like grandmothers sneaking you cookie dough. Not—oopsie daisy—accidentally releasing a fire-breathing spider.

"If you don't tell, I won't," she said.

We were accomplices, whether we liked it or not, and if one went down, we both did.

CHAPTER 14

IN WHICH I WORK THE (MAGIC) SYSTEM

COURTNEY

The two-mile walk back to the castle was a tense one. I'd almost been roasted and slurped like a cappuccino by a giant spider, and yet all I could think about was Bryce. I accused him of having feelings, and somehow, he said exactly what I needed him to. *You're like a damp sock.*

Nothing had ever been more comforting.

It was also disconcerting because no matter what he said, he still came to make sure I was okay. I didn't understand why he kept *bothering*.

I needed to focus. I could only pretend to be a hero for so long before I actually had to do something heroic. I *had* to stop failing, and this time, I couldn't do that by quitting. I was going to need magic to fix this, which meant I was going to have to play the part of the perfect savior. I would suffocate under the layers of capes I'd have to wear.

A stray, hot tear rolled over my nose. Rage crying was inconvenient. It was hard to be convincing with tears streaming down my face. I stood in the middle of the darkening woods, sniffing miserably.

Up ahead, Bryce looked over his shoulder, noticing me several yards back. The next thing I knew, he stood before me. His eyes were still frantic and darting, movements jerky. "What's wrong?" he asked sharply. "You hurt?"

I shook my head.

He reached for me, hesitated, then placed his fingers under my jaw as he scanned my face. He tilted my chin and brushed the tear from my nose with his thumb.

My chest lurched. My head filled with dangerous *what if*s. I wanted to hold on to this Bryce forever, this strange in-between Bryce who was my friend enough to not be my enemy, but still my enemy enough that he was safe.

"You saved me," I whispered.

"I guess I'd die for you now." Bryce sighed heavily. "Hate that for me." His usual bite was absent from his voice, like he truly did hate that for himself. "We really need to work on your fight-or-flight response."

He looked like a fairy-tale prince standing here, surrounded by golden twilight, fog swirling around his body, red hair curling in the humidity and falling over his bright eyes.

"Why are you crying?" He released my jaw, tucking his hands under his armpits. "And don't say it's the dragon, because I already know it's not. I don't think you've ever known what fear is. I bet you were one of those horrible, adventurous children who thought everything was better in the dark. Hide-and-seek in the dark. Tag in the dark. Blanket forts in the dark."

I blinked through my tears. "Games *are* better in the dark. Where's the fun in the expected?"

"You need the light so you can see what's coming. So you know when to run." Shaking his head, he took a few steps away. "Fuck, Courtney. A dragon? A spider dragon? How was that a good idea? We could have died. Actually died. Fuck!"

I realized then how hard he'd been fighting to keep his cool, to soften his words. He'd shown me considerable kindness, considering my massive screwup, but finally his fear had broken through. The fear that was my fault. He was right. We could have died. At once, the world felt very large, and I felt very small.

I closed the distance between us, wrapping my arms around Bryce's waist and resting my cheek against his shoulder. "I'm sorry."

He went rigid in my arms, his heart thumping against my ear. I squeezed him tighter, willing his pulse to calm. I was suddenly aware of every inch of his body pressed against mine, the firm contour of his chest, the slope of his stomach, the dip of his spine under my palm.

As nice as it felt, he and I could never work. I was a quitter. The only reason I hadn't quit being a hero by now was because I couldn't. Once Bryce saw my true colors again, he'd stop his *bothering*. This in-between moment was all we could ever have.

I placed my palms on his chest to push away but hesitated.

His hands shot to mine, peeling them away from him. "Let's get out of here," he said. "Your hands are cold. They're making my nipples pebbly."

I arched my brows, shoulders easing because I'd been handed A Gift, and I mustn't squander it. There was a lot to dissect. A lot to ridicule. I settled on "Pebbly?" as I held back a laugh and tried not to look at our entwined fingers.

"Yeah," he mumbled, voice soft now. His eyelids fluttered as he glanced at our hands. "Pebbly. Like, all prickly and hard. Like I'm a heaving-bosomed countess being seduced by a wealthy rake or something. It's a well-known word. Stop acting like I'm the weird one for knowing a normal word."

"So, wait, I'm the rake in this scenario, and you and your nips are helpless to my charms?" I couldn't fight it anymore. I snorted, helpless laughter gurgling forth.

He detached his fingers from mine. "Is everything a joke to you?"

"Yes," I said, wiping a new kind of tear from my eye. "It's my working theory that, if life isn't a joke, then it's a tragedy."

He shook his head, and the tension between us eased. We started walking again. It was odd how he seemed to grow more scared when I tried to comfort him. He only relaxed once I started teasing him again, distracting him from danger.

"When I think *pebbles*, I think fish tanks and gravel roads," I mused, following him through the woods. "I can see how it's an erotic word. Nothing gets me going like a gravel road."

He kept his back to me as he ducked under a limb. "I'm so happy you took nothing our wise mentor said about kindness to heart today."

"That's some awfully pebbly dirt you're standing on. Don't get too excited."

I kept stealing glances at his profile, at the way dying sunlight danced over the exquisite angles of his face. And a plan began to emerge.

Screw the universe. I'd save the world my way, quick and dirty, and get Bryce home safely, whatever it took. Maybe I wasn't a hero, but that meant I didn't have to worry about things like honor or morals. I'd fight dirty. I'd use all the tricks in the book. My methods wouldn't be pretty, but I'd get the job done.

I scooped a rock off the ground and sidled up to Bryce. "In case you ever get lonely," I practically purred, pressing the stone into his palm.

Maybe I couldn't be a hero, but I could be a hell of an anti-hero.

◆ ◆ ◆

When we made it back to the castle, Amy updated us on the search for Winston. There were no new clues, which only made the urgency in my gut build. I had to get a handle on this Chosen One thing, and quickly.

I'd meant to lightly stalk the king, but he didn't come to dinner.

It seemed suspicious to me, but all his staff insisted he was in bed and would not leave his chambers until morning, so I supposed I'd have to continue my investigation tomorrow.

We met in Bryce's room after dinner without addressing the fact we were about to sleep together for a second time. We were like the sheepdog and the wolf in that old cartoon, shaking hands after clocking out from a long day of fighting. I had my reasons, but I wasn't sure what his were.

My plan was simple. If Amy wanted me to be nice, I'd be nice. Very nice.

Forget pushing Bryce away when he repeatedly kept *bothering*. Instead, latch on to it. Encourage it. Maybe I wasn't allowed to make friends with the other people in this world, but if Bryce found me fascinating, hilarious, and irresistible, my Charisma tank would fill up. I wouldn't let it go too far, of course. Nothing physical would happen. But if he grew attracted to me, I'd use the magic to defeat the dragon, find Winston and overthrow the Evil One, and deal with the fallout later. A tiny crush never hurt anyone. I could almost smell sweet, sweet victory.

Oh. That was the smell of Bryce. I'd never noticed it until then, until I slid my legs between the sheets of his bed. It was some generic *guy* smell, like mint-leaf-chewing-bear-fighting-octopus-near-pine-forest or something, but it smelled good, clean, comforting—

"Courtney?" Bryce asked. "Hello? I made a hilarious joke, and you're not appreciating it."

"I'm sorry I'm missing all your greatest moments," I said, rolling my eyes.

"I'll have to start calling you dad."

I paused. "Oh my god, Bryce."

"Don't 'oh my god' me. Tell me you're my daddy or something. Come on, I thought going too far was our thing."

"You'd like to go too far with me," I said, but my mind drifted elsewhere, remembering how Bryce said, "They're fine," when I asked about his parents. Remembering the way Bryce didn't get any Christmas cards or packages in the mail. The way I ate microwave spaghetti sitting against the shared wall of our duplex on December 25 because I heard him shuffling around over there. Maybe he just didn't celebrate Christmas, but I'd pretended he was as lonely as I was because then at least we could be alone together.

Guilt over what I was about to do trickled into my heart.

It was for Bryce's own good, I reasoned. I'd confess after we were safely home that I'd used his emotions for power. He'd be irate and would probably hate me for real. If that meant we were done being frenemies when we got home, that was a consequence I could live with, so long as we were both alive.

Maybe it was for the best. Bryce threatened the lifestyle I worked so hard for (or rather, did *not* work hard for), because suddenly I had all kinds of bothersome new goals like: protect Bryce at all costs.

What came next was simple. I pretended to have a sex dream. A loud one.

CHAPTER 15

IN WHICH WE ROLL FOR SEDUCTION

BRYCE

I didn't know how long I'd been asleep, but when Courtney moaned my name beside me in bed, I'd never been more awake.

I was almost certain she was screwing with me. Not in her supposed dream, but in real life. Courtney did not simply press her body up to people and hug them. It was a 180-degree shift, and something was definitely up.

And yet a large, majestic, throbbing part of me did not care.

For the hundredth time that day, my brain replayed the hug. Earlier, I hadn't thought about it in a sexual way. For one, my brain was busy thinking things like *Oh my god, a giant spider*. For two, it didn't feel like *that* kind of hug. It was the sort of hug that made you realize how long it had been since you'd been hugged at all. The kind of hug that set off quivering, tight feelings in your throat and chest.

Now, though, my body remembered her warm curves. With one touch, each of my muscles committed the feel of her to memory, as though us touching was a skill long practiced—so deeply ingrained, it would always feel right and natural when returned to again. Like riding a bike. Only I wanted to be the thing being ridden.

"Mmm, Bryce," Courtney groaned in her sleep, and something tugged at my gut.

Fuck. Sheets shifted as she tossed and turned. Itchy sweat broke out in hot waves across my skin. Images of my own dreams flickered behind my eyelids. Everything below the belt tightened. Aching pressure creeped in, threatening to destroy my common sense. I slid to the far side of the bed because I feared, if her skin brushed mine, I'd simply die.

"Bryce, you idiot." She sighed thickly, seemingly still asleep.

Damn it, why was that hot? I clenched my fists in the sheets.

Her eyelids twitched back and forth, thick lashes fluttering, barely visible in the dying firelight. "Just like that," she murmured. "Perfect, oh, *oh*. You sex master. There has never been one so proficient in the art of pleasuring a woman, nor will there ever be one after."

Okay. That was highly specific, and there was no way Courtney was capable of such flattery, even in sleep. She was messing with me and making no effort to pretend she wasn't.

I wouldn't give her the satisfaction of telling her to knock it off because then she'd know it affected me. Instead, I lay there and listened as the phrases she uttered "in her sleep" became so specific and filthy that every cell in my body nearly shattered. It was torture, and I hoped she'd never stop.

As I lay there listening to her panting breaths and shallow moans, the way forward became clear. It was all I could think about. I just had to channel a bit of brave Dream Bryce.

✧ ✧ ✧

"I have a plan," I said the next morning.

Two could play her game. If I had to see her in this new, horny light, she had to suffer the same fate until the sight of me gave her hell, exactly like the sight of her did to me. It was a sexy game of chicken, and I was sure she'd back down.

Courtney squinted her eyes open, morning sunlight turning the dark irises mahogany. She'd finally washed the last of her makeup off, and she looked—still pretty unapproachable, if I was being honest.

"A plan?" she mumbled.

I sat up. Her little sex-dream stunt was going to get her more than she bargained for. I would call her bluff—if it was a bluff.

It had to be a bluff.

"Yes. A plan," I said. "A plan to get magic."

She perked up. "I'm all ears."

I bit my lip, anticipation pulling at the corners of my mouth. "All we have to do is like *each other*."

She shot up, her blue hair haloing around her head like cotton candy. "*What?!*" she exclaimed, like she hadn't had the same idea herself.

I ran my thumb over my bottom lip, trying to get my thoughts in order. Noticing her watching the movement, I paused. Channeling irresistible Dream Bryce, and feeling a bit like a douchebag, I gave her a slow wink. Her eyes darted away. A thrill of exhilaration went through me. I couldn't help the smile curving my mouth. Her cheeks were flushed, which was fascinating and surprising—and could this actually be working?

Innocently, I raised my brows. "As long as we find, say, two qualities we don't totally despise, then we'll have some Charisma."

"Like, one single Charisma. I'm pretty sure you need more than one person to like you to be powerful enough to overthrow the Evil One whenever they arrive."

I leaned in and let my voice go husky. "We'll like our two qualities, really, *really* hard."

She gave me a sideways look. "Why do I get the feeling I'm going to loathe whatever you're about to say?"

I held back a smile. "I think we should have sex."

She made aggressive gagging noises, shoving the blankets away.

"Hear me out."

"Nope." She hurried for the door.

"Would it help if I told you that day you were super into brushing your teeth, it made me really want to brush my teeth, too?"

That made her pause. "You're lying."

I actually wasn't, but I'd let her believe that. She'd sounded unbearably hot that day I'd shipped her a sex toy, and imagining what she was doing to herself on the other side of the wall had nearly driven me to . . . well, needing to brush my teeth. But brushing my teeth at the same time she was brushing hers felt slightly icky when she didn't know I could hear her, and so I resisted.

For a day.

When I finally caved and brushed my teeth, it was frantic and depraved, and I definitely did not make it the recommended two minutes.

"Look," I said, "I'm just saying there's no point in denying that we don't find each other totally repulsive."

Courtney started for the door again.

"I'm not saying we have to like each other's minds," I called after her. "That would be ridiculous. We can work the system. All we have to do is like each other's bodies. I think you'd like my spectacular *pulsating* manhood, and I'd like your—"

The door slammed.

I burst out laughing, falling back onto the pillows and slinging a hand behind my head. Idly, I picked up the pebble she'd given me off the bedside table and turned it over in my fingers. Hopefully, my planting that little idea meant she'd spend the day tormented with the same thoughts plaguing me. She'd be so angry I used her own game to get under her skin, she'd never try it again. Which was a shame, because it was her most intriguing game yet. It filled me with the same exhilarated curiosity I felt as a child when I contemplated sticking my finger in a light socket just to see what would happen.

In both situations, my fingers were best kept to myself.

CHAPTER 16

IN WHICH ONE CANNOT SIMPLY GIRLBOSS THEIR WAY THROUGH BEING A CHOSEN ONE

COURTNEY

My entire body ached for him.

Bryce had somehow turned the tables. I'd wanted him to have a tiny, harmless crush. Instead, he'd suggested sex, and now all I could think about was him. It was all because of the wink he shot me when he propositioned me. Winks were evil. They had the power of making anyone hot.

No. It was before then. In those moments when his brow was pinched in worry or fear, but I'd make a wisecrack, and his expression would smooth when he turned my way. When I found myself looking at his mouth. When his shoulder brushed mine, and shivers raced over my skin.

Or maybe it was last night, listening to his agonized sighs as he buried his face in a pillow and cursed my name. Or what he'd confessed this morning about The Infamous Buzzing. Whether it was true or not, the unbidden mental images that arose from it had me ready to combust: Bryce desperate and unwound as he listened to me getting myself off—

Well, suffice it to say, my scheme had backfired. I hated my body for reacting this way to the human equivalent of a dial tone.

I had to come up with a plan B. Who knew how much time I had before the dragon showed back up, or something happened to Winston, or worse, the Evil One made an appearance.

Screw Amy and his irrational rules. I couldn't get people to like me from a distance. I needed to interact with them. I'd win them over the old-fashioned way: face-to-face bribery.

After a much-needed morning bath, and checking with the servants that the king was still asleep in his chambers, I got to work.

Grunting, I dragged a giant golden chair down a narrow stone staircase. The legs clunked loudly, bouncing from one step to the next. Sweat poured down my back, and my labored breaths echoed off the stone walls.

Maybe bribery wasn't the most morally pure way to win affection, but it was the quick way, especially because it wasn't like my personality alone would win me any points.

I called my plan Operation Dave. Everyone has one coworker that they can't stand, but everyone else loves. For me, that coworker was Dave from appliances. It was obvious to me that Dave from appliances was a major kiss-ass, but everyone else was under his spell. That was my plan. Being genuine would get me nowhere because I was a genuine, grade-A disappointment. So, since I wasn't terribly good at being good, I'd just have to be good at faking it. Amy would never have to know.

After what felt like an eternity, I finally reached the bottom, emerging outside the castle in a small, abandoned courtyard. With a final heave, I hoisted the chair into the back of a wagon, which was full of all the other chairs I'd already stolen from the council room. Amazingly, no one at the stable had questioned me when I showed up, still in my nightgown, asking for a horse and buggy.

After tossing a few blankets over the chairs, I clambered into the driver's seat and flicked the reins. As I emerged from the courtyard into the busier castle grounds, I smiled and waved as though it were totally normal to be out and about in the early morning in a coat and a nightgown, hauling a conspicuous heap of covered cargo.

Everyone smiled and waved back without a second thought. It was like Bryce had said. Everyone acted more like video game characters than real people. Strange. But convenient, given that normal people would have definitely realized Bryce and I sucked at being Chosen Ones by now.

I exited the castle walls and headed into the city. As I neared the market, the crisp morning air filled with the incredible smells of street food—the homey scent of warm dough, the savory aroma of spiced meat and caramelized onions, the sweet whiff of pastries.

Turning a corner revealed the busy main street. Women bustled from shop to shop. Children scampered underfoot. Traders' carts and stands packed the street, displaying their wares—from colorful scarves to food to baubles and trinkets. Their shouts rang over the laughter and conversation.

It was slow going, but at last I found a spot to park my wagon between a flower stand and a meat pie vendor. I hopped off the wagon, unveiled my stolen wares with a flourish, and propped up a sign on one of the chairs that read: *Free. Limit: One per customer.*

Grinning, I pulled down one of the chairs for myself. "And now we wait," I said to myself as I settled onto the plush purple upholstery adorning the gold frame.

Ten minutes passed.

Then another ten.

People would glance at the heap of blindingly reflective furniture, then scuttle away as though afraid. Growing impatient, I stood on top of my chair and began shouting along with the other hawkers, putting my marketing degree to good use. "WHY DO NONE OF YOU WANT A FREE, SUPER-VALUABLE CHAIR?"

Okay. So, it wasn't my best work. But it didn't make sense. One chair could turn someone's whole life around.

I began to grow antsy, worried about what the king might get up to once he woke and left his chambers. I needed to be around to spy on him, in case he was involved with Winston's kidnapping.

Catching sight of a cluster of young girls at the flower shop next to me, I turned. There were five of them working the stand, all appearing to be sisters, ranging in age from toddler to teen. They all had the same giant green eyes, snub noses, and dark hair.

They giggled and whispered to one another as they cut stems, arranged bouquets, and greeted customers. Aside from Winston's mom, it had been difficult to see the humanity in everyone else I'd met here. Wizards, kings, people like Cuthbert who were genuinely happy with their jobs—they didn't exist in my world and therefore didn't quite feel real.

But these were normal girls. Put them in jeans and T-shirts, give them cell phones instead of flowers, and they'd be just like the kids back home.

My mission felt even more personal now. *Real, actual* children were counting on me. Yes, I had to fix my mistakes and overthrow an Evil One for my own good to get back home, but I also had to do it for these girls and everyone else just like them. Familiar pressure to succeed pressed against my lungs, but I would endure it. I had to.

Back in my coatrack, I'd dreamed of a magical land, a place where I wasn't held responsible for other people's comfort and happiness. Ironic how, now that I'd actually gotten my magical land, I was responsible for the fate of the world.

With new resolve, I scooted my chair over to the flower shop girls, the gold screeching over the cobblestones. Straightening, I planted my hands on my hips. "This is for you."

Five sets of eyes blinked back at me. "We can't accept this, my lady," the oldest one said at last, with an airy laugh.

"Don't be ridiculous. This isn't the time for pride. I insist."

"No. We cannot," said a girl who appeared to be the second oldest—maybe eleven or twelve. She stuck her hands in her worn apron. "It is not the way of things."

I inched the chair a little closer, wagging my eyebrows enticingly. "If you sold this, you could be rich."

"We cannot be rich," said the oldest with a little shrug. "We are peasants."

Sighing, I rested my forearms on the back of the chair. "That's what I'm saying. You won't have to be peasants anymore."

"We can never not be peasants," she said with a cheerful smile.

I was about to give up and turn away, but my eye caught on her placid expression. Before, I hadn't paid much attention to any of this world's cardboard cutout characters, writing them off as storybook clichés, but now I took a closer look. The girl continued staring at me, a serene smile on her lips, but I almost thought I could see a hard glint of something deep in her eyes.

Then she blinked, and it was gone. "Would you like to buy a flower?" She held a daisy under my nose.

An idea struck me. "If you can't accept the chair for free, would you take it as payment? You could even have it melted down before you sell it, if you're worried about people realizing where it's from."

All the girls exchanged looks. "We don't have enough flowers," the littlest said.

I squatted to her level and grinned. "Tell you what. I'll buy them all, and if you help me with a little project, we'll call it even."

◇ ◇ ◇

Phase one of my little project was a shopping spree. With the girls staggering behind me carrying chairs, I went from booth to booth, purchasing clothing, junk food, and useless trinkets, and paying for everything with the furniture until it was gone.

Unfortunately, even overpaying everyone with life-changing

amounts of wealth wasn't enough to awaken my magic. I thought I could buy the people's approval, but Charisma was not so easily fooled. They loved me for what I could give them, not for who I was. I probably should have known better.

Still, the morning was not altogether unpleasant. The flower girls (who were all named after plants, of course) took one look at my nightgown and coat and insisted on dress shopping. I bought them all dresses, too, and even if their awe for me was only inspired by gold, it still felt nice. It still spoke to that part of me that craved adoration. Still teased me with the idea that maybe, just maybe, I could be the amazing person they thought I was.

After the shopping spree, the girls piled the contents of their flower stand into the back of my now-empty wagon. Some of them squeezed onto the seat beside me and the others wedged in the back, then we were off.

The conversation back to the castle was joyous. They showed off the day's spoils and passed around the food we'd bought so everyone could try everything. Their questions were incessant. *How is it being a Chosen One? When did you first know you were different? What's the worst monster you've ever faced?*

They *ooh*ed and *aah*ed over my answers (terrifying, I still don't believe it, and late-stage capitalism) as though they were impressive.

"In the stories of old," said Lavender, the eldest, who was seated beside me, "Chosen Ones always found time to visit the less fortunate and listen to our opinions. Our last Chosen One, Edna Johnson, was said to have joined us in our festivals, visited our orphans, and made friends with members of our community. Quite a fan of mulberry ale, that one. Legends say she insisted on sharing her brew with everyone in the kingdom."

Edna Johnson? I wondered if that was the flapper girl immortalized by the fountain in the gardens where we'd had lunch. I guessed being free of Prohibition for a while must've been exciting for her, which would explain her hipster-ish obsession with craft beer. But damn, if Amy had summoned her as he claimed, that meant Amy was even older than I thought.

"I must admit," Lavender went on, "when you showed no interest in venturing outside the castle walls, we began to worry for the future of our kingdom. But I see now how lovely you are. You must have been quite busy with important matters, then, if it took you so long to come into the city?"

My stomach shifted uncomfortably. We'd been under instructions from Amy not to get involved. But even if we hadn't been... would I have bothered to learn more about the kingdom? "We were told not to." The excuse sounded weak even to me. "For safety. For *your* safety. They told us if the bad guys knew we were friends, they may hurt you to get to me. Which is why you can't tell anyone you met me. If anyone asks where you got the chair, say a traveler traded it to you."

Her features softened, which made me feel even worse. "Of course."

If what Lavender said was true, and other Chosen Ones, like Edna, were allowed to make friends with the people, what had changed in the last hundred years that made Amy so convinced it was safer for Chosen Ones to keep their distance? Had something happened with Edna herself?

Rose, one of the middle girls, piped up from the back, disrupting my thoughts. "What's the other Chosen One like?"

My thoughts fluttered away. "Oh, Bryce?" I asked flippantly. "He's okay, I guess."

A brief silence ensued, followed by shrieks of delight and teasingly dramatic proclamations of Bryce's name. Ahead, our horse's ears twitched in annoyance, and I concurred.

"I didn't say his name like that," I called over them.

"Like what?" said the tiniest girl, Poppy. "*Ooh, Bryyyyyce?*" She spun on her heel in a swoon and collapsed onto a heap of flowers, a pudgy hand thrown over her ruddy brow.

"Is he handsome?" the quiet girl, Sage, who sat on the other side of me asked, stars in her eyes.

"No."

The prickliest girl, aptly named Thistle, gave me a withering look.

"Fine, yes." I sighed. "Unfortunately, he is." They begged for details, so I stammered through a brief explanation of the Sickly Victorian Man phenomenon. "He's not, like, muscly or conventionally attractive. He's the kind of gorgeous that sneaks up on you."

That was enough to convince them we were soulmates.

Their enthusiasm was contagious, and I found myself smiling as I described Bryce's quirks. The way I sometimes noticed him secretly grinning after I found a particularly clever way to annoy him. The way he stuck by me, no matter what, even when it involved battling a dragon. The way he cared so much about everything, even if it was starting to make me feel bad for caring about nothing.

I lapsed into silence for the rest of the trip as the girls planned our wedding. As we neared the castle, a strange sort of lightness fluttered behind my ribs—anticipation and excitement wrapped in fuzzy warmth. Inexplicably, I *missed* Bryce, and I couldn't wait to see him again.

Something dreadful was happening, something I hadn't felt since grade school, when I'd draw gel-pen hearts around my initials coupled with some pubescent boy's.

I was developing a freaking *crush* on my asshole next-door neighbor.

CHAPTER 17

IN WHICH WE GET PHYSICAL

BRYCE

Courtney was late. I'd been waiting with Cuthbert for hours, listening to him excitedly talk about the hand-to-hand combat we'd be practicing today. We were inside this time, in a training room—a large, rectangular space with stone walls and dark wooden arches. High windows let in streams of pale, early-morning light. We weren't the only ones practicing, and the clanging of clashing steel echoed around us.

Thankfully, I hadn't heard anyone talking about a dragon on the loose yet. Either Courtney and I had gotten incredibly lucky, and the dragon was breaking stereotypes and truly wasn't interested in terrorizing villages, or it was only a matter of time.

Sighing, I sank onto one of the benches placed around the perimeter of the room while Cuthbert exaggeratedly showed me a takedown move. Today, he had a little handkerchief tied around his forehead like a sweatband, and every time he moved, his hair sticking out of the top flopped this way and that.

At least I'd gotten a bath this morning. Even though I still yearned for Germ-X with the intensity of a thousand suns, I felt almost clean for the first time since coming here.

I sighed again and leaned against the wall. Still no Courtney. I could only assume her absence was due to the fact I'd seduced her senseless, and she was unfit for warfare.

"Good morning," a benevolent female voice cooed.

Everything halted as everyone looked up to find the source of that impossibly sweet voice.

Courtney swept through the doorway in a fluttery pink gown, every inch of which was covered in ribbons and lace. Now the only noise was her heels clicking across the polished floors. Her eyes landed on me, and she smiled. Generally, her smiles were stuffed full of sarcasm and schemes. This one was not. It made me feel weird and like I was definitely losing.

A handful of young village girls bustled in behind her, clutching bouquets of wildflowers. They all wore bright dresses like hers, fluttering with yards and yards of ribbons. Their excited voices overlapped, turning into an unintelligible babble punctuated with giggles and squeals. The girls flocked around Courtney like she was their leader, and she amiably doled out attention and approval until she good-naturedly shooed them off.

They began placing bouquets around the room, planting daisies in the visors of the empty suits of armor and tucking bouquets behind crossed decorative weapons hanging on the walls. The flowers immediately wreaked havoc on my allergies. Upon closer inspection, the bouquets included sprigs of ragweed and baby's breath. This was chemical warfare. Unbelievable. First moaning my name in her sleep, now this. Even after we'd formed a shaky alliance, she was still finding ways to mess with me.

"It was far too gloomy in here!" Courtney proclaimed, clapping her hands together. "This is much better."

Those who had been training before Courtney came in now paused to smile fondly at her. A few pressed fingers to their hearts, clearly taken by their seemingly kindhearted and agreeable new hero.

I ground my molars as she simpered at the nearest guard and

sweetly asked him to check to see if the king was awake yet—probably so she could kiss his ass too.

Then Courtney made her way to Cuthbert and me, her dress fanning out and twirling with each step like the wind itself was on her side. Apparently, she hadn't considered my proposition at all and was on a mission to make the entire world like her instead. I wasn't sure I could stand a whole day of watching Courtney flouncing around, being *kind* and *smiling* and doing upsetting, heartwarming things like *resting her hand on Cuthbert's shoulder* and planting a *kiss* in the air next to his cheek. "Good morning, Cuthbert." She narrowed her eyes at me. "Bryce."

Standing, I mimicked her narrowed eyes, hoping to show her how ridiculous she was. "Courtney." Unfortunately, my eyes were still watering profusely from the flowers.

"Look how touched he is by your kindness, Lady Courtney," Cuthbert bubbled.

"What was that you were saying about choke holds?" I asked pleasantly.

✧ ✧ ✧

As Cuthbert talked us through exercises on footing and balance, I tried to focus, but my gaze kept sliding back to Courtney. She practiced several feet away, and her entourage of flower stand girls surrounded her, playfully taking part in the exercises with her. She smiled at them like I'd never seen her smile at anyone, and they gazed up at her with wide, adoring eyes. What had she done to win them over? And, if she was so good at winning people over, why did she spend her life being completely awful?

She poked the smallest flower girl in the stomach while they were practicing a balancing move that required them to stand on one foot, and the little girl toppled over, sending squeals and giggles rippling through the cluster. Pain tugged at my heart. I felt like a sad zoo animal, trapped behind a glass wall, watching people live while I merely survived. I wanted to be a part of it, and I'd never wanted to be a part of *life* before because life was so intertwined with pain.

I sidled up beside her. "Where were you this morning? What's with the fan club? Why are people acting like they *like* you?"

"Because they do," she said breezily, swiveling her arms as she moved from position to position as Cuthbert instructed.

Oh hell. Her flouncy pink dress had laces up the back. Why were *laces* suddenly my kryptonite? They both baffled and fascinated me. A scene glowed behind my eyes—firelight, my fingers hooking into the ribbons at the small of Courtney's back. Her skin warm against my knuckles through the dress. Her, smiling over her shoulder at me.

I let out a choked cough, refocusing. "What did you do to kiss up to everyone?"

She grinned. "I Robin Hooded the castle. I stole a bunch of gold-plated chairs last night and gave them to the villagers. No one from the castle even noticed, and now everyone loves me. Look at me now. Petty theft to Chosen One. It's an inspiring character arc."

"It inspires people to gaze into the sun, so they won't ever have to read stories about you." Her unwavering smile made me feel bad for being surly, so I asked, more pleasantly, "Isn't stealing against the rules if you're the Chosen One? Besides, Amy told us to mind our own business."

She picked at her nails. "Rules are like glow sticks."

"A feeble but steady light to help you navigate your way along the dark and dangerous road of life?"

"Made to be snapped in half."

"So your stunt won you magic?"

Her face fell. "Well, not exactly. Strictly speaking, I think everyone likes gold-plated furniture, not me. But it's a start."

Courtney, the girl who was prickly with everyone, would rather be nice to the entire universe than even consider my plan. I should be relieved by that. Not insulted. Not disappointed that I'd never get the chance to figure out those perplexing laces.

"Now that we're warmed up," Cuthbert said, interrupting our conversation, "we'll practice a few takedowns. We will start with a move called the Rear Naked Choke."

"The what?" My question came out as an inaudible whisper. Was this hand-to-hand combat, or the Kama Sutra? I refused to be on the receiving end of a Rear Naked Choke.

"One of you can practice the move on the other," Cuthbert said. "We will start in the rear mount position—"

"No way am I letting Courtney subject me to something called a *Rear Mount Position*."

"You might like it," she crooned.

"Oh, definitely not." Cuthbert beamed. "It can be quite painful."

"Nothing like a little light choking to start the morning, right, Bryce?" Courtney asked sweetly.

CHAPTER 18

In Which I Suffer a Crush-ing Defeat

COURTNEY

"Sex with me is sounding pretty good right now, isn't it?" Bryce hissed, his forearm around my neck, his thighs caging my hips. "All this training, all this being nice to everyone, it must be killing you." His arm held me almost protectively against his chest. It was perhaps the softest and least impressive attempt at a choke hold ever.

Him throttling me should not make me need to throttle my feelings, yet it did. His touch spread awareness through my nerves, sparking a needy desperation between my thighs.

"I would rather volunteer at a hospital, help raise a neighbor's barn, and give a compliment to a stranger than have sex with you," I whispered viciously, trying not to notice the pale hair dusting his freckled forearm.

"That's the meanest thing you've ever said to me."

After approximately two minutes of watching Bryce and me half-heartedly flailing around as we tried to grapple without actually touching each other, Cuthbert realized we were a lost cause and hollered for us to move on to sword training.

Bryce detached from me and stood. Fixing a pleasant expression on his face so no one would know we were arguing, he held out a hand for me.

Taking his hand and hoisting myself up, I followed his lead and arranged my face into a frozen mask of friendliness. "Sex with you would only make me like certain parts of you less," I said under my breath.

"I think you'd like it," he said brightly, talking through his smiling teeth. "I'd whisper dirty things about plaque in your ear. I know how that gets you going."

I released his hand and made a show of wiping mine on my dress. "Why are you obsessed with me? Am I, like, the light of your life?"

"If that light is a burning trash fire, then sure."

Being called a trash fire should not make me feel giddy and special. Except that I bet Bryce wasn't calling other girls his trash fire, and that fact made me want to go around bragging to everyone that, sure, maybe I was a trash fire, but I was *Bryce's* trash fire.

Eager fire licked between my ribs. Bryce's insults felt like pulled pigtails on a playground; I knew it was messed up, but they made me feel like the most special girl in the world.

I was like a crush-prone hormonal teenager, blinded by glitter-gel-pen hearts. The whole world had turned into the magical white-and-blue landscape of a homework margin. I could practically see purple and pink doodles surrounding everything Bryce did. At his every movement, the word *hot* danced before my eyes, underlined three times. Swoopy arrows pointed at all his best features, like his veiny hands, his intelligent eyes, and the lines bracketing his mouth that appeared when he was holding back a smug smile.

Oh my god. This was truly sad. Even watching Cuthbert beat the snot out of Bryce during sword practice couldn't dampen my crush. Every time Cuthbert's sword connected with Bryce's body, little imaginary hearts and butterflies sprang out. I rested my chin in my hand while my mind had a field day with a fantasy of nursing Bryce back to health that would, of course, involve me gently removing his clothes in the firelight, and him wincing and gasping, our eye contact the only thing keeping him tethered to the mortal plane. I'd give him alcohol to numb the pain, and he'd grimace, his Adam's apple lurching and sweat rolling down his chest. He'd probably grow delirious and confess that he'd been in love with me since, like, the dawn of time.

As the training session went on, Bryce's posture began to slump, the life in his eyes chipping away, exposing something hollow and empty inside. A feeling nagged within me, intensifying with each passing minute. Nervous energy built up until I thought I might explode.

Worry. That's the only thing it could be.

I had to occupy my hands before they did something unsavory. Like try to fulfill my fantasy of nursing him back to health.

All I wanted to do was march across the room, smack the sword out of Cuthbert's hands, and tell him, *Enough*. Bryce was never going to be that kind of fighter—the type that was bold and flashy and violent. His strength was the type that went unnoticed. He persevered. He stayed. He *felt*. It was admirable, the way he worried on behalf of the whole universe, fighting, in his own way, for people like me who had given up fighting for themselves.

The unsettled feeling within me grew more unsettling. Something was compelling me to try to make Bryce's life *less* miserable instead of *more* miserable. I . . . was *bothering*. The very thing Bryce did that pissed me off.

What did Bryce *do* to me? Quitting things had become easy, but I couldn't quit him.

It didn't help that my village groupies were encouraging the situation. They sat clustered around me, whispering and giggling, prodding me and smiling knowingly.

An agonized moan snapped me out of my fantasy.

"Rally, soldier!" Cuthbert barked like an excited Chihuahua, prodding Bryce's prone form with the tip of his wooden sword.

Bryce lay flat on his back, eyes squeezed shut, his sword a few feet away.

Before I could stop myself, I passed off the daisy chain I'd been making to Sage and sprang up. I swept to Bryce's side like he'd collapsed on a battlefield. My crush had apparently crushed my kneecaps, because they buckled, and I half fell beside him. "Bryce?" With one finger, I pried his eyelid open.

Bryce's blue eye snapped to look at me. Letting out a weak cough, he whispered, "I downloaded the Bible app on my phone a month ago in the event that, if we both died, I might make it to Heaven and avoid this reunion."

"We're not in Hell, silly." I laughed the laugh of a pick-me girl who's just squealed the phrase *You're sooooo funny!*

Bryce opened his other eye. "It feels like it."

I tugged on his arm, more as an excuse to sink my claws into him than anything else. He begrudgingly stood. Awkwardly, I tried to do that thing where you loop someone's arm over your shoulder to support them, but his arm was too heavy, and he gave me a *What the fuck are you doing?* look, so I stopped.

"Sorry. Just trying to help," I mumbled.

"Thanks, Court," he said, brushing off his shirt, and the damn nickname made my damn heart soften.

"Don't expect it ever again." I tried to add my usual bite to the words but couldn't quite manage it.

"Trust me." He snorted softly. "I never expect anything from you."

I rolled my eyes. On the inside, I treasured his words—*I never expect anything from you*—like a love letter. The thing I ran the risk of losing every time we touched, every time one of us *bothered*. If we grew too close, he'd stop saying rude, beautiful things like *I never expect anything from you*. Love expected everything, and I had nothing to offer.

"I don't want to do this anymore," Bryce said, barely audible. "I can't fight anything."

Back when being a Chosen One felt like a competition, a game, I would have been gloating, but not now, after meeting the village girls and realizing how vital our success was. Bryce couldn't quit. He was the Chosen One, the reliable one. The gravity that kept me tethered to the earth. My moral compass. Without him, I couldn't navigate what it meant to be a hero. I would lose my way and fail like always.

"Nonsense. You're fit for war." I fetched Bryce's sword and tucked it into his limp hand. He immediately dropped it. "Whoops. Looks like someone has a bad case of the dropsies."

Cuthbert's eyes grew wide. "Dropsy? Lord Bryce has come down with dropsy?"

"No," I said. "No, no. I only mean he dropped his sword."

But more people started gathering around murmuring, "Dropsy? The Chosen One has fallen ill with dropsy?"

"It's a phrase!" I yelled over the chaos. "'Having the dropsies' means you're prone to dropping stuff."

"His limbs are already failing him!" a soldier wailed and fell to his knees, his own limbs apparently failing him.

"We must boil water," Rose yelled frantically.

"How do you think water will help?" I asked, pulling at my hair. "What do you plan on doing with it?"

"We will boil it, my lady," said Rose.

I let out a frustrated growl. "I know he looks like a sickly, fragile Victorian man who's constantly on the verge of death, but he's *fine*."

"He's on the verge of death?" a third person sobbed.

Bryce's eyes focused, flitting from one concerned face to another. "Yes," he said quietly. Then, louder, "Yes!" He dramatically clutched a hand to his chest. "How I suffer so! How misfortune has struck the land! How the mighty have fallen!"

The castle folk nodded and clapped one another on the back, fighting off tears.

"Behold, my appendages already retain fluid. See how I have been rendered useless!" Bryce raised his arms, which were the opposite of swollen. "I fear I will no longer be able to serve as your leader. My henchwoman will take my place until I feel better." With that, he collapsed onto the ground.

CHAPTER 19

IN WHICH COURTNEY TRIES TO SUCK ME DRY

BRYCE

Faking a dangerous ailment to get out of training wasn't my proudest moment, but the opportunity dropped into my lap, and I couldn't let it pass me by.

I lay in my bed, staring at the ceiling, trying not to feel guilty. I was exhausted and bruised, and my mind had started trying to convince me that maybe I had a fatal illness after all. Back home, I would have been googling my body's normal functions like they were symptoms, self-diagnosing with four different diseases and deciding that I had mere hours left to live—my go-to hobby.

Touch grass, I told myself.

An image of Courtney smiling as she placed a daisy chain on a little village girl's head floated into my mind's eye. It destroyed me when she was nice, wrecked all of my carefully crafted convictions that she was The Worst. Slipping a hand into my pocket, I found the pebble she gave me and pressed it hard into my palm.

My bedroom door flew open, and Courtney marched in. She stood over my bed and crossed her arms, eyes half-lidded. I'd changed out of my clothes into fresh pants, but she still wore the pink dress from earlier, now dirtied and torn. "You are being so dramatic. I've faked plenty of illnesses to get out of work in my day, but convincing everyone you have *edema* takes the cake."

"I'm dying," I rasped, letting out a feeble cough. "Show some compassion."

"So this is it, then. You're giving up." She pressed her lips together, giving me a weird look. All morning she'd been looking at me like that, eyes boring into me like she wanted to eat me alive. Likely, she was actually planning to eat me, maybe chopped up in a stew or something.

"No." I moaned, throwing an arm over my eyes. "I'm sick. There's a difference. I'm unfit for fighting dragons and overthrowing darkness and competing to be a Chosen One and whatever the hell else we're supposed to be doing."

Unexpectedly, her voice softened. "You put up a good fight, soldier."

"Yeah?" I lowered my elbow and peeked over my arm.

"Oh *yeah*," she said in an extremely patronizing way.

"I don't love your tone."

A smile tugged at her mouth. God, she was acting weirder than normal. I side-eyed her, my paranoia kicking into overdrive. I wanted to demand she tell me what she wanted from me—why she could never let me go.

Courtney walked over to the washbasin and wet the rag hanging there. Returning, she sat at my side, bending over me to dab at a cut above my eyebrow. "What tone would you prefer? *Oh yeah*." The way she said those two words was borderline indecent, and now I really didn't love her tone for the way it made a hard thrum of desire pound against the inside of my skin.

I swatted her hand away. "You are the worst caretaker. You're, like, a care *taker*. You take all the caring away."

"Au contraire." Her smile dripped with venom. "I've arranged for the best physician in the land to see to your affliction." She snapped her fingers, and a gaunt-faced man wearing a slouchy red hat and carrying a bowl entered. "Gird your loins, Bryce," she said.

The physician walked closer, closer, closer.

I shrank against the headboard. "Why are my loins in need of girding, Courtney? Are my loins in danger? *Courtney?*"

"It is time for your bloodletting," the physician intoned. He reached into the bowl and plucked out a slimy black leech. With a crazed expression somewhere between reverence and fascination, the physician lowered the leech toward my naked chest.

A strangled sound left my mouth. I leaped out from under my blankets and hid behind Courtney. "You absolute *tonsil stone*," I snarled into her ear.

"Look at that," she said. "He's healed. A Christmas miracle."

Looking disappointed, the physician let the leech plop back into the bowl.

"We won't be needing you anymore." Courtney waved the physician out of the room before turning to face me. "This was the saddest cry for help I've ever seen." Scooting closer, she knelt beside me and went back to dabbing at the scrapes that covered my body.

I caught her wrist. She was so close that, when she looked up, I could feel the air move past my mouth as she inhaled. When I told Courtney to have some compassion, I didn't expect she would listen. Yet she'd helped me in her own twisted way by getting me out of bed when I felt bad. I couldn't bear it. Her caring about me made me feel happy, and all my happiest memories were drowned by the hurricane of misery that followed.

"You and I are gonna save the fucking world, Bryce," she said, a grit to her voice I'd never heard before.

I didn't know what had brought about her new determination, but in that moment, I believed anything was possible, so long as it was proceeded by the words *you and I* in that resolute tone of hers.

My bedroom door opened for a third time, and Amy hobbled

in. "Lady Courtney, you are going to miss the council meeting." He looked between us. "Bryce, glad to see you are feeling better. You can join us. I imagine we will talk long into the night!"

Long, boring council meetings were a favorite hobby of the castle's inhabitants. You could make a comment on the weather, and they'd call a council meeting to order to discuss what implications the day's forecast might have for the next seventeen harvest seasons.

"What's the meeting about?" I asked.

"Our general, Theodora Thimblepop, has gone missing," said Amy, and Courtney's spine went rigid. "She was apparently swiped right off the streets last night as she was doing her rounds."

"Another kidnapping?" Courtney asked in alarm. "Shit. Where's the king?"

"Do not fret," Amy said. "He was safe in his chambers. Servants are alerting him to the news now."

"He's been there all morning?" Courtney asked, and I shot her a look. Did she suspect him?

"Yes, the dangers his kingdom faces have put such strain on his constitution, and he needed rest." Amy looked between us as Courtney continued to absentmindedly dab at my brow. "Lady Courtney, why on earth are you tending to Lord Bryce's wounds? We have an infirmary for such things."

"No reason." Courtney's face flushed bright red. "Amy, someone told me today that heroes used to be very hands-on when it came to hearing the people's concerns. Is it true Chosen Ones like Edna Johnson were allowed to make friends?"

Amy waved a hand. "Who told you such nonsense?"

She bit her lip. "No one. I just heard it . . . in passing."

"Utter hogwash," said Amy. "When I summoned Edna Johnson, she mingled with the citizens, but only because it was necessary to keep them calm while she and I worked to deliver the people from calamity. Now the Evil One is trying to destroy the utopia we created."

"What calamity?" I asked. "Did this Edna person face the same Evil One we're going to have to face?"

"No, of course not," said Amy. "Now come." He teetered closer. "You must share your plan for stopping the kidnappings and vanquishing evil with the council."

"What if we don't have any plans?" I asked.

Wringing his hands, Amy perched himself between us on the bed. "Of course you have a plan. Why, if you search your memories, I'm sure you'll find the solution to all our problems has been with you for months. Chosen Ones always hear voices or see visions or have dreams that they forget about until the precise moment when they feel all is lost. Then they remember their premonition, and everything becomes clear." His watery blue eyes gazed up at me.

"Courtney's had some really interesting dreams lately." I couldn't resist throwing her under the bus after the leech incident.

"Not true," she said quickly, flashing a demure smile.

Amy turned to me. "What about you, Bryce?"

I hesitated. While my dreams lately hadn't exactly contained illustrated step-by-step IKEA-style instructions on how to destroy evil, they had been . . . intense. If there was any chance revealing them could help us get to the bottom of the kidnappings, wasn't I obligated to reveal them in hopes Amy could translate their meaning?

"I've had a few dreams," I confessed, feeling my hands grow clammy. "Maybe Courtney shouldn't hear them, though. They aren't fit for the ears of a . . . lady."

The smile melted from Courtney's face as she gave me a long, calculating look. "You've had dreams?"

"I prefer to call them nightmares."

Amy nodded wisely between us. "Ah yes. Oftentimes such visions can be disturbing."

"Especially when Courtney's in them." My face heated.

"What was I doing in your *dreams*, Bryce?" Courtney hissed.

"Praising my name, mostly," I said dickishly to hide how desperately I wanted to melt into the floor.

She snorted. "Then your dreams are the most fantastical thing to happen to you."

I leaned back, propping my arms behind me on the bed. "We literally stepped through a portal and wound up in a world straight out of a dungeon master's fever dream."

"My statement stands."

"If Lady Courtney was praising your name, perhaps it is a prediction that you are the Chosen One, and she is indeed your henchwoman," Amy mused, but neither of us was listening.

Courtney narrowed her eyes. "Tell me about one of these dreams." The challenge in her voice told me she thought I was lying.

Figuring I might as well get this over with, I leaned forward so I could see her past Amy. "In my dreams, we're at the big-box store where you work."

"Hot."

Amy gasped. "You were hot in your dreams? That could be a sign of a drought to come." He started mumbling about stockpiling food and alerting the council while I continued.

"We're arguing," I said, "really going at it, me yelling, you just . . . talking like you always do, one zinger after another without batting an eye. That shit makes me angry and *inspired*, like . . . you make me want to be a better asshole."

"Wooow." She drew out the word, brows high. "I'm so damp right now."

"Don't use *damp* in that context. I'm begging you. Anyway, we're arguing, and I yell something, and you deadpan something back, and it takes me a second to register that you said, 'Are we going to fu—'"

Amy stopped muttering and looked up with interest.

I dropped my voice. "You said, 'Are we going to *do this* or not?'"

Courtney peered around Amy. I wished I could see into her brain, because her expression was unreadable. But if eyes were the windows to the soul, Courtney's opened into an empty void.

"And then?" she asked.

"And then I say, 'Well, yeah, I guess so.' And you yank me forward and kiss me right there among a bunch of sink displays."

"And then?" Amy whispered, literally on the edge of his seat, suddenly overly invested in our lives.

I cringed away from him. "That was it."

Amy stood. "This is very troubling indeed. Why, I cannot make heads nor tails of it. What does it mean? Kissing and arguing? Should we be wary of those closest to us, for they are our enemies? Or perhaps our enemies are actually our friends."

As usual, Amy's input was exceedingly unhelpful. I'd apparently shared this mortifying tidbit for nothing.

Before I could rise, though, Courtney caught my hand. "And then?" she whispered.

Her piqued interest was more gratifying than I wanted to admit, and my embarrassment morphed into profound smugness. Maybe she'd run away this morning not out of disgust, but because she'd actually been tempted.

I leaned in. "You pull me to the break room, and you yell at me to take off my clothes, and I yell at you to take off your clothes, and then we both yell at each other to shut up."

She swallowed hard. "And then?"

"And then we shut up." I stood, her hand falling off me. "If you want to know more, you'll have to find out for yourself." I added that last part because I knew she would never, ever take me up on the challenge. I only hoped to tease her apparently desperate libido enough that, by the time we got home, she'd happily move away as quickly as possible, lest she succumb to my apparent charms.

"Come." Amy waved a hand over his shoulder. "We must tell the council about this."

There was no way I would be discussing my sex dream with *the council* for the next six hours.

CHAPTER 20

In Which the Council Talks about Bryce's Sex Dream for Six Hours

COURTNEY

No matter how many times I repositioned, my hard wooden stool found a new angle to make my tailbone ache.

When we got to the council room, everyone noticed the fact that all the cushy gold-plated chairs that had surrounded the long stone table were missing. Servants had to rummage up a hodgepodge of assorted stools, wooden folding chairs, a couch, and a giant velvet pouf, which the king immediately called dibs on, even though he now sat so low, his nose was barely higher than the top of the table.

I'd blamed the missing stuff on the Evil One. The presence of an Evil One had upsides. They were a convenient scapegoat to take the blame for all my screwups and nefarious activities. Everyone bought the lie, which succeeded in taking the spotlight off me but added to the length of the council meeting because everyone had to speculate what kinds of ghastly things the Evil One was planning on doing with the chairs. People started throwing out ideas, ranging from using the chairs as weapons, using the chairs as torture devices, and then, finally, using the chairs as chairs. This last suggestion was the one they settled on, deciding (with great thoughtfulness) that the Evil One probably needed somewhere to sit.

The whole time, I kept a shrewd eye on the king, watching him for signs of guilt. It couldn't be a coincidence that the night he was absent, supposedly sequestered in his rooms, another person went missing.

After the chair debate, the meeting moved on to Bryce's sex dream, and Bryce's face discovered eighty-seven interesting new shades of red.

The phenomenal waste of time made me antsy. Right now, General Thimblepop and Winston were enduring who knew what kinds of terrors, and I wanted to *do* something about it. Training was all well and good, but I didn't feel like we were making progress.

And then, of course, there was still the looming tournament where we'd have to compete for the title of Chosen One—something that now felt like yet another meaningless waste of time. I was 99 percent sure Bryce was the Chosen One, but when I tried to secretly tell Amy that (because I didn't want Bryce to hear me forfeiting), Amy insisted the tournament was the only way to truly know who they should trust with the fate of the world. We were nearing the end of our second day of training, which meant we only had one more full day before we had to compete.

"We can't rule out that the kiss might be a metaphor for a kiss of death—something which will lead to our downfall," wheezed one of the six decrepit old men seated around us.

I rubbed my dry, gritty eyes, stifling a groan. A kiss from Bryce likely *would* lead to my downfall. I shouldn't have lied to him by faking the stupid sex dream. This was karma. The beauty of our relationship was its honesty. I was a scumbag, worse than a breaker of pinkie promises. Encouraging Bryce to *bother* only got me bothered in all the wrong ways. It was a reckless idea, and I needed to undo it. If I told him it was all an act, he'd be furious, which would effectively un-seduce him, and, as a result, un-seduce me.

I pulled out my phone. I'd turned it off to save the battery, but I figured powering it on for a few minutes wouldn't hurt. Bringing up my Notes app, I tapped out a message. I owed Bryce the truth. He'd been honest and had to endure six hours of embarrassment for it.

I faked my sex dream.

Before I could chicken out, I slid the phone onto Bryce's thigh.

I fiddled with the edge of the cold stone table as he glanced down and read the message.

Only a moment later, he gave the phone back.

Say it isn't so.

I mean it. I faked the dream.

His knuckles brushed my hand as he passed the phone.

I know you did.

What, how?

He paused. Then typed for a long time. Paused. Typed. Paused. Typed. When he finally passed the phone back, six words stared up at me.

Why else would you hug me?

Hug? Did he mean after the dragon got loose? Bryce thought there was no scenario in which I'd genuinely want to hug him? Not even after he came to rescue me from a *dragon*?

My insides began to soften like Jell-O left out too long.

Shoving my traitorous Jell-O innards back into the metaphorical fridge, I typed:

For the record, the hug was real, but I can see where the confusion came from. You're probably so used to people faking things around you that you've grown to anticipate it.

When he read that, he chuckled so low I didn't think anyone else heard.

Have I ever made you feel like you had to fake anything?

My stomach twisted. No. He never had. And I lied anyway.

Well. I just thought you should know. I didn't want to take advantage of you, if you thought the dream was real.

I showed Bryce the message before tucking my phone away as the discussion around us shifted to General Thimblepop's disappearance. I didn't dare note his expression; I didn't want to see if he was disappointed, or worse, relieved.

I focused instead on listening intently to the debrief on the kidnapping situation. Once again, there were no clues to lead us to the victim's whereabouts. General Thimblepop had gone out to patrol the outer edges of the city and never returned. Before the meeting adjourned, I suggested a buddy system, so that no guards would go out on their rounds alone anymore. The temporary solution was a feeble Band-Aid slapped over a hemorrhaging artery, but it was all I could think of to do.

At last, the meeting came to an end, and everyone started standing up and saying their farewells. They all trickled out, giving us nods and telling Bryce to let them know if he had any more visions. Then they were gone, and it was just Bryce and me seated at a long, empty table.

A weighty moment humming with tension passed between us. I glanced at his lips. He noticed, eyes hooding, jaw ticking.

I had other things I should be thinking about, like discovering exactly what the king had been up to last night. I stood, banging my knee on the bottom of the table.

Before I could beeline for the door, Bryce hooked a hand around my elbow, spinning me back. Though it was still afternoon, the council room didn't have windows. The only light came from flickering sconces recessed into the walls. The dim fire and the aristocratic angle of Bryce's cheekbones slashed seductive shadows across his face, but his eyes were soft and unsure, flitting as they struggled to maintain contact with mine. He was just awkward enough that I didn't think he knew how damn pretty he was. "For the record, you can take advantage of me. That is, if you want to."

A heavy wave of heat coursed through my veins. Maybe I should be concerned about how much I liked this gorgeous, fragile man telling me I could take advantage of him. I cleared my throat, trying to get ahold of myself. "No, I'd never—"

"Take advantage of me," he said softly, taking a step closer. I couldn't tell if he was begging or daring.

Gently, I pressed my fingertips against his stomach. He paused, stomach flexing tight under my palm as he sucked in a sharp breath. "You don't want—" *me*, I thought, but didn't say. "You don't want that. I'm the worst, remember?" I whispered, because he *must* have forgotten. "I . . . I don't RSVP to weddings."

"I don't either, so what are you scared of?" It was amazing how *not yelling* softened his voice.

"I'm not scared. You're scared."

"I'm not," he said, in the steadiest voice I'd ever heard him use, even though vulnerability stabbed through his expression.

My pulse drummed like impatient fingers on a tabletop. *Kiss me, kiss me, kiss me,* my stupid crush-filled heart said. But kissing made things complicated. If we kissed, I'd catch feelings for him the way you caught any other fatal illness—by licking something you have no business licking. Kissing led to me losing myself as I searched desperately for True Love, only to find out, yet again, that it didn't exist.

I took a step back. "I watch TikTok videos at full volume in public spaces. I unironically chew on toothpicks sometimes. I'm a *toothpick* guy, Bryce. No one likes a toothpick guy."

The corners of his mouth lifted. "That's what I thought," he said, backing out of reach. "Don't start games if you can't finish them."

So that's what this was. Him teaching me a lesson. Calling my bluff. Ensuring I'd never do it again. It had to be. That was why he was so confident; he knew I wouldn't say yes.

I desperately wanted to say yes.

✧ ✧ ✧

My secret love for stalker romance books had given me a surprisingly useful skill set when it came to tracking down the Evil One. Like now, for instance: I was tailing the king like I was in love with him.

The king had a cushy schedule for someone who was supposed to be leading a country. As far as I could tell, it was Amy who made most of the actual decisions, and the king was more of a mascot. I followed him around as he drifted aimlessly through the castle for a while. Then we spent an hour in the parlor for tea, during which a bunch of other nobles sat around talking shit about everyone who wasn't there. It reminded me of work; the parlor was a break room, and tea was basically the water cooler.

The king looked a little shifty when he finally got up and left the parlor. I crouched around the corner in the hall as he stepped out and murmured something low to his attendants. I couldn't hear what he said, but I heard the servant's reply.

"We'll tell everyone you retired early. You won't be disturbed."

It was still light out, far too early for bed. No doubt his real plans involved more kidnapping. *The king is a traitorous sneak, leading the downfall of his own country.* Though I wanted to leap out of the shadows and shout *gotcha!* I refrained. I needed further proof.

So, after I heard the servant's shoes clicking down the hall, I scuttled from my hiding place and resumed my pursuit.

The king displayed more excitement than I'd ever seen from him as he moved swiftly through the castle. Probably, the sick bastard enjoyed whatever evilness he'd been up to.

We stopped at his chambers, where he collected a large black pack—probably his murder tools. After that, we traveled all the way out of the castle, across the courtyard, and into the garden. I nearly lost him when he entered the hedge maze but managed to find him again by cheating the maze and burrowing through the hedges.

I tripped and nearly crashed out of a bush in full view of the king but managed to catch myself on a limb. In the center of the maze, the king sat on a bench drenched in late afternoon sunlight. I peered through leaves, trying to figure out what he was doing as he reached into his pack and drew out—

A lyre.

He fiddled with the strings, tuning the instrument before he launched into a catchy little tune about a frog and a unicorn.

The king wasn't the culprit. He just had a secret, harmless hobby. I doubted kings were allowed to perform, so he probably did it at night in disguise, and that was why he'd been absent yesterday evening and slept in this morning.

While part of me was relieved I didn't have to accuse the kingdom's monarch of being evil incarnate, now I was back to square one.

CHAPTER 21

IN WHICH WE FIND A FAMILY

BRYCE

By early evening, Courtney had been missing for hours. A maid said she spotted her heading into the city. Having a suspicion that her whereabouts had something to do with the village girls she'd befriended, I asked a villager where the flower shop girls lived.

I found Courtney sitting on a curb, eyes fixed on a tiny, leaning house on the other side of the twilit street. She had a sword strapped to her hip, and every so often, she looked up and scanned the dimming sky.

"What are you doing out here?" I settled beside her.

She tossed a few flakes of cobblestone into the street, watching them skitter and bounce. "You know what Amy said . . . about how we'd only endanger people we grow close to. Plus, with the dragon on the loose and the kidnappings . . . I wanted to make sure they were safe." She tilted her chin toward the house. "I don't think I could handle it if one of them went missing next."

I could hear the faint ring of laughter from inside. Shapes moved within, silhouetted against the sheer curtains hanging in the windows.

Someone inside pushed the curtain away, revealing the scene of a very full kitchen. It looked like they were all working together to bake something, with flour-dusted cheeks, rolled-up sleeves, and doughy hands. "It looks like a Christmas commercial," I said, and I knew I sounded a bit too wistful for someone who hated Christmas.

"Or Thanksgiving, if your family was functional and actually liked one another," she said, her voice heavy, maybe with the weight of her own memories. Even though she'd mentioned having a mother and a father, I wondered if she felt like I did sometimes. Alone. Apart. Maybe they were distant in a different way than my family had been distant. Distant while present.

"When you asked Amy about where the king was earlier . . . You don't think he's the Evil One, do you?" I asked.

She shook her head. "No. Well, I did think he might be, but I don't think so anymore."

"You don't have to do this alone, you know," I said, though I didn't know what help I'd be.

Truthfully, she seemed to have a better grasp on how to be the Chosen One than me. I'd been so busy just trying to survive that I'd been happy to leave the investigation up to the guards, while she was apparently Sherlock Holmes–ing all over the castle.

She snorted softly. "Oh, good. I feel much better about the chances of two people being able to save the entire world than I did about one." But her sarcasm was gentle enough it held no real bite.

The door to the house banged open, spilling lamplight onto the cobblestones. "Are you going to come in and help or not?" An older woman, who must have been the girls' mother, stood in the doorway, her hands on her hips. "Lavender saw you out here. She says you're the traveler who gave her the chair."

A few pudgy faces peeked around her waist. "Mama!" one of the girls said. "You can't ask them to help. They're the Chosen . . ."

She fell silent. To keep them safe, Courtney must have instructed her not to reveal our titles.

Courtney stood. "Of course we can help."

Together, we followed the woman through the doorway and into a delightfully disheveled home. Clutter covered every rickety piece of furniture in a haphazard but somehow organized way that indicated every item had its place, as chaotic as it might look. The kitchen and dining space were all in one room, while the sitting room was separated by a door. In the corner, a staircase wound up to what I assumed were the bedrooms.

Gathered around the worn table in the middle of the room were the rest of the family: an older man, who must be the father, and a plethora of daughters—even more than the ones who had been with Courtney earlier. One of them bounced a baby on her knee while the others were preoccupied with the bag of coins spilling out onto the table.

"This is from selling the chair you gave us," one said, sounding almost guilty, as though she needed to explain, as though she wasn't allowed to have it.

The mother introduced herself only as "Mama" and the father was simply "Pop." The girls' introductions were a jumbled mess of laughter and squeals, but I found if I uttered a random name of a plant, I had a good chance of one of them responding.

"We're baking tarts to sell at the market tomorrow," Mama said, indicating the pastry mess covering the counter by the hearth. "Maybe we cannot give our money to others in need, but if a few coins happen to slip into the batter, and if a few good people happen to find those coins in their tarts, well they might as well keep them."

"Wait," I said. "I'm confused. Why can't you just give people the money?"

"It is not the way of things," she said simply.

Courtney stepped forward. "Is that why your daughters didn't want to accept the chair at first? They had to view it as payment before they would take it."

Mama shrugged. "Things must be done a certain way. We are peasants. We must work to earn our keep. The soldiers must fight. The servant must serve. It is not our place to accept wealth."

Maybe this was why Amy wanted us to stay away from the villagers. The social infrastructure of this world seemed deeply rooted in tradition, with rules about what you could and couldn't do, depending on what class you belonged in. If the world ran smoothly this way, maybe Amy didn't want us shattering the walls of decorum and tradition by telling people things could be different. Maybe Edna Johnson, the last Chosen One, had tried to do that, and that was why it was now forbidden.

Still, it was strange these rules were just accepted, especially because people like Mama were actively trying to find ways around them. But this was a different *world*. If someone from this world came into mine, they'd probably find our cultural norms senseless too. Like the way everyone universally agrees to say *big stretch* when their cat stretches, or the unspoken one-urinal-buffer-zone rule, or how, if anyone says, *this one time*, you're legally obligated to throw in, *at band camp*.

"Do you wish to help, or not?" Mama asked. "Idle hands have no place here."

A few of the girls who knew we were the Chosen Ones cringed and offered apologetic looks, but Courtney brushed them off. "Let's get to work."

CHAPTER 22

IN WHICH CHEKHOV'S CONDOMS FOIL OUR PLANS

COURTNEY

This family was so different from mine—their smiles real, their interest genuine. One of the oldest girls had recently had a baby, who was now happily bouncing on Bryce's lap. Bryce himself looked shell-shocked to have found himself holding a miniature human. He handled the child as though he thought it might break apart. Meanwhile, the baby thrashed around unconcernedly, cooing and dribbling drool over Bryce's fingers.

Instead of asking the new mother what milestones the baby had reached like it was a competition to see which infant in the family would achieve things faster, her family asked questions like *How are you?* and *What's it like being a mother?* and *You'll let us know if you ever need help, right?*

The kitchen was nothing like my parents' either. Not a trace of marble in sight. It was all warm woods, cream plaster, and cast iron. Thanks to Mama's brisk instructions, I soon had a decent idea what I was doing. We formed an assembly line—some making dough, some rolling, some forming the tarts. It was efficient, but there were also plenty of shenanigans, which Mama loosely refereed, and Pop blatantly encouraged.

The girls had some sort of ongoing game they called *shleekshelock*, which, from what I understood, roughly translated to Kill the Guy with the Ball. The rules of the game were what you would expect. They had a small wooden ball, and if someone spotted you with it, they were allowed to obtain it from you by whatever means necessary. Physical violence was encouraged, though there was also a certain amount of strategy involved. The trick was to sneakily pickpocket the ball and hide it before anyone knew you had it.

They'd already roped Bryce into the game, though I declined after learning "Once you agree to play *shleekshelock*, you're a player for life."

Every so often, I looked up from my work, seeking Bryce, *needing* to see what he was doing. Each stolen glimpse was a reward, sending endorphins straight to my heart, whether a ten-year-old was commanding him to toss berries into her awaiting mouth, or he was being dogpiled by every child in the house as they wrestled him for a ball.

Sometimes I caught him looking at me, just grinning, with a thoughtful look in his eyes.

I sprinkled flour onto the smooth wooden counter before plopping a new ball of dough onto the surface and pressing my rolling pin on top of it. I didn't notice when the voices around me faded, so focused was I on making this batch less lopsided than the last.

"Flatter," a low voice said behind me, hot breath tickling the tiny hairs on the back of my neck. Bryce's arms circled me from behind, his hands coming to rest overtop my flour-covered ones gripping the rolling pin. "Like this."

Slowly, he guided my movements, his chest pressing into my back. As if by magic, the stubborn dough I'd been struggling to roll evenly transformed into a perfectly smooth circle.

I glanced to the side, noticing we were suddenly alone. Everyone else had gone to the sitting room to watch the baby gurgle and laugh over a silly face one of the girls had been making. The sounds of joy from the other room combined with the closeness of Bryce and the taste of sugar on my tongue sent bliss curling through my heart. Maybe this was what family was supposed to feel like. Maybe this was what *belonging* felt like.

"How do you know how to make a tart?" I asked, my voice hushed.

"My grandma taught me. I lived with her and Grandpa for a while."

He reached around me, picking up one of the tart molds and placing it in my hands. I held it as he expertly pressed dough inside with his thumbs, his fingers cradling my hands. Maybe he couldn't sword fight. Maybe he was scared of horses. But the man could competently make a tart.

"This is nice," he said into my ear. "Just like a Christmas commercial."

The more I pieced together of Bryce, the more I realized the universe had not blessed him as I'd once supposed. He was as lost as I. From the clues I'd gathered, it sounded like he had less of a family than I did. At least mine were around, even if they didn't like me.

I turned in his arms, and he didn't step back, so my back pressed into the counter. "You weren't alone last Christmas, you know. I was there too."

A soft smile touched his lips. "Yeah, I know. I sat against our shared wall so I could listen when you started playing a song called 'It's Beginning to Look a Lot Like Fuck This' on repeat."

"I turned it on for you," I confessed. "I thought you might appreciate the sentiment."

Flour floated lazily in front of the windowpanes. The smell of cooking tarts rose warmly from the stove. Distant baby belly laughs sounded from the other room, followed by delight and praise. The perfectness swelled, the warm, solid, *right* feeling too much to bear. I was too happy. I wanted to laugh. I wanted to cry. I wanted to—

"I want to hug you again," Bryce said simply.

All I could do was nod.

One step, and he was holding me. His arms were sure when they banded around me. I'd never felt so snug and secure, so used to the obligatory featherlight side hugs from my old friends and family. He smelled like warm sugar and soap. I pressed my face into his chest, overwhelmed by everything I was feeling, positive emotions on top of positive emotions. He cradled my head, stroking my hair, tucking his face against my neck. God, he was a good hugger.

"I need to tell you something," he whispered into my hair.

I nodded against his chest, braced for whatever he might have to say.

"I've had the ball for like half an hour, and I think they're beginning to suspect."

I peeked over his shoulder to find giggling faces stacked in the half-open door to the sitting room.

"I knew it!" one screamed.

They attacked like wolves, ripping Bryce away from me. When he begged me to save him from their clutches, I only laughed and blew him a kiss.

✦ ✦ ✦

Too tired after the evening of baking to walk all the way to the castle, we checked into an inn Mama recommended down the street.

"We need a room," Bryce said to the innkeeper. "I'm sure, what with the tournament in a couple of days, you only have one available, right?"

The innkeeper smiled. "It's your lucky day! We just had a cancellation. We have two empty rooms."

"What a shame. Only one room." Bryce tsked and shook his head.

The innkeeper's smile faded. "You must have misheard, sir. I said—"

"And, let me guess," Bryce cut in coolly. "That room doesn't have two beds."

I smiled, catching on to what he was doing. Bless Bryce and his fondness for romance novels.

"Of course we have multiple beds available upon request." The innkeeper puffed up. "We are a reputable establishment, good sir. To only have one bed available?" He scoffed. "Unacceptable."

I sighed. "Whatever are we going to do. Only one room with only one bed."

The innkeeper protested. "Have you not heard a word I have said to you?"

Giving up, Bryce leaned over the counter and held out a hand. "I'd like one room, please. With one bed."

✧ ✧ ✧

The room was small but cozy, with a simple, small bed, and a fireplace that coated the wooden beams and cream plaster in hues of warmth.

I wasn't sure if Bryce had requested one bed because we'd come to an unspoken agreement not to sleep alone in this strange world, or because . . . because our perfect afternoon had affected him like it had affected me.

But he didn't make a move as we readied ourselves for bed, and soon, we were bidding each other good night as we pulled the sheets over our shoulders.

I closed my eyes. The fire burned low, the air chilled, and still, sleep didn't come.

Sleep didn't come, but I wanted to. I tried to remember all the reasons we'd agreed to never grow close. I couldn't recollect a single one.

Slowly, I scooted my way toward the center of the bed. The unused sheets were freezing, but Bryce's body radiated heat inches away.

Bryce made a soft noise, rolling onto his side, his hand flopping across my stomach. I looked from his face to his hand and back again. He breathed evenly, eyes closed. Asleep.

Inch by inch, so as not to wake Bryce, I scooched closer until I pressed against his side. His hand slid to my lower belly, then over my hip. The contact burned through my thin underdress. I almost forgot the reason I'd come over here was because I was cold. *Cold* was a distant memory.

I jumped when Bryce spoke. "What are you doing?" His voice was deeper than normal—slower, too, thick and sluggish from drowsiness. It slid over me like a heavy blanket, providing the same false sense of security a blanket did—because, let's face it, the thought of Bryce protecting anything was hilarious.

I found my voice. "I was watching you sleep. In the creepy way, not the cute way. You look so peaceful with your mouth shut. If a person didn't know you, they'd never guess what a massive doorknob you are."

He grinned wickedly and cracked an eye. "You think my knob is massive—confirmed."

"Shut up, Bryce."

He closed his eyes again. "If you wanted to cuddle, you could've asked."

"I don't want to *cuddle*. I'm cold."

"What am I supposed to do about that if you don't want to cuddle?"

"We should huddle for warmth."

"So, cuddling."

"Huddling."

Bryce grunted. "Fine, but I'm little spoon." But he didn't move, thumb trailing a slow circle around my hip.

His touch was painfully affectionate. The unfamiliarity of it washed waves of raw vulnerability over me. I clenched bedsheets in my fists but couldn't hold back a shiver.

"Are you actually cold?" Bryce sighed, and I nodded, teeth chattering from things that had nothing to do with the temperature. The strange, nervous lightness to my stomach sent trembles through my limbs and made it hard to think.

Bryce seemed to debate for a long, *long* moment.

"C'mere," he mumbled, fingers tightening around my hip as he pulled me back into him, tucking me against his chest. His heart thudded between my shoulder blades, his breath tickling my neck. His arm around my waist tightened, and he sighed against my hair.

I twined my feet with his, and he grumbled a protest at my chilled toes, but let me stuff them between his calves anyway.

"Bad night," I wished him with a fake yawn, nestling myself against him comfortably.

Bryce caught on immediately, murmuring back a soft "Sleep loose."

"Sour dreams."

"Shithead." The word sounded like an endearment, our usual bickering turning into something new and sweet.

He pulled me tighter, fitting our hips together. I pretended to stretch my legs, moving against him, slow and languid.

Bryce's breath caught. "God, I hate you." His lips moved against my neck.

"I know you worship me, but 'Courtney' is perfectly fine." I let the nonsense leave my mouth, unsure if it made sense because all I could focus on was the feel of his body against mine.

He caught my waist, stilling me. "I don't worship the devil." His teeth grazed my ear, and desire pooled low in my belly. "But you sounded pretty worshipful yourself when you moaned my name last night."

"I'm incapable of feeling pleasure when you're around." Every one of my nerves buzzed and tingled in—you guessed it—pleasure.

"I feel the same." Slowly, he shifted his hips, pressing against me so I could feel him, hard and unmistakable.

And, oh my god. He really did feel the same as me, though not in the way we both claimed. That knowledge loosened my restraint. My pulse drummed white-hot between my thighs.

"You feel the same?" I managed.

"You know I do." His words were rough and low in my ear. I never would have suspected the anxious accountant next door had a feral sex voice that could melt me. "Every minute spent with you feels like an hour, but not in a good way."

It was as though we both believed that, so long as we continued to verbally insist that we despised each other, anything we did to the contrary wouldn't count.

"For perspective," Bryce went on, "given the choice between sex with you and sitting through a distant relative's graduation ceremony, I'd take the graduation."

I clenched my jaw so I wouldn't turn into a whimpering, begging mess. "If that random french fry everyone has lodged under their car seat were a person, it would be you."

"A delightful and unexpected snack?"

All I wore was the shift I'd been wearing under my dress, and it slipped up, skimming my upper thighs. Bryce's hand trailed to my hip, and he sucked in a breath when he discovered me naked underneath.

"Unwanted, forgotten, soggy, gross, flaccid," I spat through my teeth.

"Uh-huh," Bryce murmured, slow and soothing. He slipped his hand to my inner thigh, and I arched against him.

"Given the choice between sex with you and helping a friend move, I'd—"

His fingers tightened. "Don't. That's too far."

"I'd help the friend move," I gasped.

"You're awful." His teeth found the back of my neck, and he nipped lightly, sending my every hair on end.

"Maybe you had a point this morning." The words tumbled

from my mouth in a breathy rush. "I mean, I tried being kind to others for twelve whole hours, and I'm still not beloved by all, so—"

Bryce moved so quickly I barely had time to register it, flipping me onto my back and rolling on top of me. Firelight glinted off his bare chest. His eyes were dark, glazed with lust. "For the sake of the world, yeah?"

"Yeah, yes," I said. "To awaken our magic. To save the world. Just a physical thing, no strings attached."

"Yes. Good."

"Good." Tugging him closer, I ground against him.

"Good," he choked out, breath hot against my jaw. His nose skimmed over my cheek. He dipped his head, lips angled for my mouth.

My hand shot between our faces. I stared at his beautiful, soft, tantalizing lips in horror. "No kissing."

"No kissing?" Bryce repeated against my hand. He pulled back. "What am I supposed to do with my mouth?"

"A moment of silence for your past lovers."

He gave me a withering look. "You know what I mean. It's weird not to."

"This is no strings attached. Kissing is stringy."

"You're doing something wrong if kissing is *stringy*. On second thought, maybe I'll pass."

I wavered, then compromised. Because I was generous. Not because I wanted his lips on me. Now. "You can kiss me, just not on the mouth."

Bryce shook his head. "Fine. Okay."

He dipped his head, hair tickling my ear as he pressed his warm mouth to my neck. I sighed and immediately wondered why I'd said no kissing. Skimming my fingers over his back, I nipped lightly at his shoulder, tongue grazing his skin. He shivered.

"Don't fake a damn thing," he said roughly, lips against my ear.

"Stop being annoying," I whispered. "Touch me."

Eyes darkening, he slipped a hand between my legs, making a helpless sound low in his throat when he felt how badly I wanted him. Reaching down, I adjusted his hand, and he groaned against my shoulder, somewhere between agony and want. I rocked into his touch, needing more, more, more.

"Wait," I gasped. "Before we get further. Condoms?"

His eyes tightened.

I grimaced.

Bryce let out a long sigh. "Yeah, right, I'll just ask *Amy* for some *condoms*." Pulling away, he closed his eyes. "Where exactly do you think I have condoms?"

"I don't know, in your wallet? Aren't you an accountant? Accountants are supposed to *account* for things."

His eyes opened, lust-hazed irises flashing. "What do you think I am, some sort of sexual vending machine, ready to dispense protected portable sex at any time?"

"You're not nearly as menacing."

"You think you're funny, but you're not."

"Condoms aren't an unusual thing to keep with you, Bryce."

"Shopping cart handles give me anxiety. You think I'm out there braving the casual sex scene?"

"Shit."

"Shit," he agreed, pushing off me and flopping onto the mattress.

I scrubbed my hands over my face. There had to be a solution. If only I could stop thinking about Bryce's fingers between my legs long enough to focus.

"Listen," he said, sitting up, his hair a ruffled disaster, "my grandparents tried to raise me to be a good Catholic. I know every way there is to have sex without having sex. This is fine. We'll adapt. Overcome."

"Wait, I've got it." I shot up. "We have to go to the courtyard where we first appeared. I had a bunch of groceries, and some made their way through the portal with me. It was mostly food, but I also had condoms."

While obviously I knew there was plenty we could do together that wouldn't require condoms, if I was only going to get Bryce for a night, I wanted to do *everything* with him.

CHAPTER 23

IN WHICH WE CHICKEN OUT

BRYCE

I was happy my indignant dick was distracting me from how terrifying medieval cities were at night.

As it was, all I could think of was the objective: Condoms. Sex. Once.

Twice, if necessary.

Whatever it took to get back to the normal *the world is a little bit worse because she's in it* feelings instead of these new *I need to remove her clothes with my teeth* feelings.

I'd miscalculated Courtney. No matter how much I tried to push her away, she kept popping back up, the herpes of my heart, ready to ruin my life.

The concept of no-strings-attached sex was foreign to me, but it was the only solution that made sense. Touch a lot so we could never touch again. Perfect. Never mind how that hug had ripped my heart from my chest. Never mind how, for the first time, during one afternoon with Courtney by my side and genuine, familial love surrounding me, I'd felt wanted.

◆ ◆ ◆

Unfortunately, in the dark, we couldn't find our way back to the courtyard where we'd first appeared. Tired and frustrated, we decided to wash our sorrows away at a pub.

When we walked in, no one seated at the candlelit rows of tables along the walls looked up. They kept talking and drinking, silverware clanking and laughter booming. The man behind the bar at the end of the room gave us the stink eye.

We found a seat toward the back, recessed in the shadows. Courtney slammed an open hand on the table, and I jumped. "Bar wench," she said to no one in particular. "Your finest ale, if you please."

Those seated closest to us turned to give us dirty looks. Many a large burly man occupied the tables. "If you start a bar fight," I said solemnly, "I want you to know I don't have your back."

I shifted as I thought about that very back pressed against my chest, her swiveling hips, and the filthy sounds she made when I--

A shadow dropped over us. Craning my neck, I looked up. The barman was bigger close-up, and he didn't look *the most* happy with being called a bar wench.

"'Ere." He slammed two mugs on the sticky wooden table and waited expectantly, holding out a hand for payment.

"Oh, I'm the Chosen One," Courtney said with an inspiring amount of unearned confidence that would likely get us killed. She flashed the royal crest embroidered on her jacket like she was whipping out a VIP fast pass at Disney World.

The barman grunted. I imagined it was close to the same sort of grunt a rhino made right before it impaled you.

"I've got this," I tried, digging around in my pocket, which was extraordinarily empty.

Luckily, our situation was interrupted as the front door of the bar opened with a mighty crash, and Winston of all people tumbled through. Everyone stopped what they were doing, murmuring his name in shocked voices as he stood there panting in the doorway. My heart pounded in my chest. Maybe this was when he'd confess he'd just run away for a few days, and there wasn't actually an Evil One on the loose. Of course, that wouldn't explain General Thimblepop's disappearance, but maybe there was a normal explanation for that too. Maybe things weren't as dire as they felt.

"Winston!" the barman bellowed. "Where have you been?"

Winston slid into the nearest chair, which happened to be at the end of our table. The patrons of the bar quickly crowded around until we found ourselves in the midst of a large group.

If Winston thought about the fact that several of the people in the crowd had likely thrown tomatoes at him a few days ago, he didn't seem to mind. Instead, his eyes fairly glowed as he basked in all the attention directed his way.

"There I was in prison." He launched into his tale with relish. "I'd never felt lower in my life, and I thought to myself, *Winston, things need to be different after this*. It doesn't matter how tempting it might be when chickens step into your path, just asking to be snatched or eaten, they don't belong to you, and you must cease this life of crime."

"That's what you promise every time after a shaming," someone in the crowd called out.

"Aye," Winston agreed, leaning in. "But this time, things went differently. I was waiting for me mum to fetch me from prison when everything went dark, like I'd nodded off to sleep. I found out later, I must have been poisoned or spelled, for when I woke up and found myself out on the streets, someone told me I'd been missing for days. I still had rope about my wrists when I came to my senses. I must have found a way to escape whoever took me, despite my delirium."

"You have no memory of who took you or where they kept you?" Courtney asked, and a few people turned our way, as if they'd forgotten we were here.

"Ah, Chosen Ones!" Winston took off his dusty hat and tucked it under his arms. "Apologies. I didn't see you there."

"Please continue." I slid him my untouched drink, hoping to encourage him to keep talking.

Winston took a whiff of the beverage. "Oh, good. I was afraid it was mulberry ale. Stories say the last Chosen One, Edna, all but forced that rubbish down our gizzards." He blushed, looking a little surprised at himself for bad-mouthing a former hero. "Pardon me saying so. I don't quite know what came over me. I seem to have lost my manners."

"You were saying you have no memory of who took you?" Courtney prompted, seeming to share my thoughts that the last Chosen One's questionable propensity for fruit beers was the least of our problems.

"No, indeed," said Winston. "But something must have happened, because after I woke up, several chickens clucked their way right up to me boots, and I didn't feel the slightest inclination to harm a single one."

"I guess your experience was the scare you needed to start making better choices," I said.

"Or . . ." Winston leaned across the table even farther and dropped his voice. "Whoever captured me did something to me that changed me very nature."

The crowd gasped, and I resisted the urge to sigh as Winston proceeded to ham it up, his theories about what had been done to him growing more and more preposterous, fueled by the way everyone held on to his every word.

Still, it was an overwhelming relief that Winston was okay. I only hoped General Thimblepop would find a way out soon too. And hopefully she'd remember something more useful.

Courtney touched my hand and tilted her chin in the direction of the door. No one noticed us slip out, too occupied by Winston's storytelling.

"Do you think he actually escaped, or did the Evil One let him go?" she asked, once we were out.

"I can't imagine they would have just released him."

"Unless they were tired of his tall tales," Courtney pointed out.

"None of it makes any sense." I scuffed my boot along the cobblestones, sending a few tiny rocks skittering along the road.

In a way, I was grateful we had this distraction, so we didn't have to talk about what had nearly happened in the inn. With space away from the evening's earlier activities, my stomach filled with that shrively, cowardly *run away* feeling so familiar to me anytime I felt a connection forming.

"It's weird no one notices anything suspicious before people go missing," Courtney said. "That's why I thought it was an inside job, maybe the princess or the king, but both of those were dead ends."

"The people being stolen have nothing in common either," I said. "There's no pattern. Capturing a general makes sense strategically, but why *Winston*?"

Courtney shook her head. "I don't know."

"Maybe he was just in the wrong place at the wrong time and was an easy target," I said. "He didn't look like he'd been tortured or mistreated, though, so I wonder what the Evil One took him for."

"We'll get to the bottom of it," Courtney said with confidence I didn't feel. "Working together will double our chance of solving this . . ." She seemed to realize what she'd said, because she paused, then added, "If you want to work together, that is."

I wasn't sure when we'd started becoming a *we*, but we had. Instead of fighting against each other, we'd already started working toward the same goal, and we'd have to continue doing so if we hoped to solve this.

"Of course we can work together," I said, even while I suppressed a shudder.

Teamwork meant communicating, helping each other, spending time with each other. All of my plans to remain distanced were crumbling. It was getting harder and harder to believe my heart would escape this adventure unscathed, even if my body did.

It wasn't supposed to be us against the world. It was supposed to be us against each other.

CHAPTER 24

IN WHICH AMY'S STORIES DRAG-ON

COURTNEY

By the time we returned to the inn, whatever mood the night had started with was officially killed, and things were weird. We didn't touch, and Bryce seemed preoccupied. His guard was back up and stronger than ever. What we'd had before coming to this world was uncomplicated, wild, and weirdly perfect. I worried what we'd done had ruined it, and nothing would ever be the same.

A mile of empty sheets separated us as we lay in bed, completely silent—the kind of absolute silence that made it clear neither of us was sleeping.

Maybe it was all too much too soon, between our heated moment earlier, finding Winston, and my suggestion to work together.

Teamwork was a strange notion, but I figured having the Chosen One around might be like a good-luck charm that encouraged the pieces of the mystery to fall effortlessly into place.

Besides, we'd worked well together once before, even if neither of us talked about it. It was a few months ago, and I'd noticed Bryce doing some yard work for Doris, the sweet old lady across the street. He'd mowed her grass and trimmed her hedges, and naturally, that evening, I'd changed the name of my Wi-Fi network to mercilessly tease him about it: Bryce<3sBushes.

I'd gone to close my laptop, but my breath caught when I saw his own Wi-Fi name switch before my eyes. We frequently changed our Wi-Fi names as a way to get the last word in, but the switches happened days apart, where they didn't feel like an actual conversation. Not like this.

Pulse pounding, I watched as IknowU8myDoorDash disappeared to be replaced with: DorisBrokeHerHip.

I hadn't known Doris was down with a hip injury. Hell, I barely knew my neighbors at all. But Bryce did.

At once, I'd wanted to try. Just a little bit. Not because anyone expected me to, but because a small part of me admired the way that, for all his doom and gloom, Bryce quietly did his best to make the world a little less shitty.

I'd changed my Wi-Fi name again: IllDoHerTrashOnTue. A pause, then his name changed again: IveGotHerMail. And I changed mine once more: IllMakeSureSheHasFood.

And that was that. All the chores were silently taken care of until Doris recovered.

Saving the world was a larger task than helping out a neighbor, but it gave me hope we could work well together.

Bryce stirred. I heard the sound of skin sliding over sheets, then his hand brushed against mine. I held my breath. A moment's hesitation. His ring and pinkie fingers slid gently over my knuckles, his skin warm. He wove his fingers with mine. Two of his entwined with two of mine. Not holding hands, but not *not* holding hands. In between. Just like everything with us lately.

My heart thumped, and I was sure he could hear it as silence again enveloped the room. Feelings in my stomach popped and fizzed like a freshly opened can of Pepsi. It felt nice, and I was too tired to remind Bryce that holding hands had nothing to do with saving the world.

When we returned to the castle the next day, instead of our morning beatdown, Amy led us to a secluded conservatory for breakfast, saying he had an important matter to discuss.

"I gathered you here in secret because I do not want this matter to spread alarm," Amy said in the loudest whisper I'd ever heard as we settled around a small table, which was filled with plates of pastries, breakfast meats, and fluffy eggs.

I poured myself a cup of tea, the herbal steam clearing my sinuses. Leafy plants covered every available surface. Ficus trees and palms grew from planters set into the cobblestone, making the room feel less like a room and more like a tropical jungle. Morning light filtered through vining plants hanging in the windows of the octagon-shaped space.

"Has the Evil One made an appearance?" I asked. After our evening with the village girls, I was even more eager to end the Evil One's reign of terror.

"Not quite." Amy buttered a scone. "I fear it is as the prophecy states. The rise of the Evil One brought with it other great evils. There have been stirrings—dangerous signs that the end draws near. There has been news of a dragon not far from here."

My blood went cold. I'd known it was only a matter of time before news of the dragon came out, but part of me had foolishly hoped it had simply flown away into the wilderness somewhere, never to be seen again. I took a sip of tea, trying to clear the tightness in my throat.

"One of our knights had ensnared the beast several days ago," Amy went on, "but when he returned to the place where he caged the monster, it was gone—freed by the Evil One, no doubt."

It seemed like fate, the way the dragon had apparently been captured just in time for the Chosen One to come and fulfill the prophecy by taming it. I decided not to tell Amy I'd probably fucked up destiny by messing with the dragon before Bryce had a chance to properly domesticate it.

"So, we gather the troops and attack at dawn, right?" I asked instead.

Bryce shot me a dubious glance. I didn't blame him. I hadn't been this enthusiastic about anything other than break time in a while. When our eyes met, his expression morphed into one of those awkward, tight-lipped smiles you reserve for when you run into someone from high school at the grocery store, and you pray they keep walking. We hadn't talked about last night, and I got the sinking feeling we were doing the *let's pretend it didn't happen* thing.

Amy stroked his beard. "This needs to be dealt with quietly, lest it disrupt tomorrow's tournament."

I'd almost forgotten about the tournament.

"The beast has been spotted flying around an ancient burial ground half a day's ride east from here," Amy said.

Struggling to breathe, I said, with bravado I didn't feel, "So, let's gather a bunch of soldiers and recapture it."

"Nay," said Amy. "Best to keep this between the three of us. No need to spread panic. Why, Chosen Ones in days gone could take care of a dragon single-handedly in mere minutes. With the two of you working together, I'm sure there will be no issues."

It would take us all day to get there and back. Thanks to my mistake with the dragon, we were losing our third and final day of training, if not our lives. Tomorrow, if we survived, one of us— no doubt Bryce—would win the tournament and be declared the Chosen One. Everyone would expect him to lead the attack against the evil lurking in the city. The thought was preposterous, like expecting someone to perform brain surgery after watching *Grey's Anatomy*. My stomach began to hurt.

"Do you have any . . . tips?" Bryce asked weakly. "For ensnaring a dragon?"

"No doubt victory will come at a great price," Amy began.

Bryce perked up. "That's wonderful news. I love a bargain."

I gave him a withering look, but he looked totally sincere, which was painfully adorable. He was like a bird who'd hit a window. I just wanted to scoop him up and hug him.

I was immediately annoyed with myself for the thought when Bryce was over there so effortlessly Pretending Like It Never Happened.

"How about a step-by-step guide?" I asked, shoving aside my breakfast plate. "Defeating Dragons 101."

"Oh, of course! Why, I forget how new you are to all of this." Amy launched into a cryptic monologue that had more to do with vibes, headspace, and feelings than it did actual strategy. The leaf metaphor even made a reappearance. Whenever Amy tried to make a point, he reminded me of one of those food blogs where you have to scroll through seven pages of someone telling you how green beans are sentimental in their life before they give you the actual recipe. He could never just deliver pertinent information in a timely manner.

He told us about gods, the creation of the world, and an emotionally inspiring phrase that he saw embroidered on a throw pillow one time, before launching into a botany seminar covering the entire history and evolution of a nearby plant.

"And so," Amy said, standing, which hopefully meant he was wrapping up his TED Talk, but we'd already been through several false endings—like when you go to the ballet, and the song seems like it's done, so you start to clap, only for the song to begin again. "And so," Amy said, "I will leave you now. You should make haste, as we will need you back early tomorrow morning for the start of the tournament. When you face the beast, search yourselves. Search each other. But most of all . . ." He looked from Bryce to me. *"Feeeeel."* He whispered the word and backed away, palms spread.

A chill shivered along my spine.

Amy tripped on a flowerpot and went down.

I figured that was *finally* the end for him, but he scrambled to his feet, flapping dust off his purple robes. He glanced over his shoulder to see if we were watching. I gave him a tight-lipped smile and raised a hand.

Nodding awkwardly, he hiked his skirts disgraced-princess-style and scuttled away.

✧ ✧ ✧

Armed to the teeth with weapons we didn't know how to use, and baffled by travel directions we didn't fully understand, we rode out of the castle, heading for the wilderness. It was bold of these people to assume I knew which way east was without Siri.

We were just outside the city when a tiny voice caught my ear. "Wait! Wait, my lady!"

I drew my horse to a stop, looking for the source of the voice. A scuffling sound grew louder until I caught sight of a leather sack, seemingly levitating a few inches off the ground. It bobbed to and fro as it approached. When it reached the ground below me, it rose a few inches, then plopped onto the grass.

Where the bag had been seconds before, doubled over and panting, was the mouse, who I now realized had been carrying the sack. "Some victuals for your journey, my lady," he said. "I'm sure you will be hungry by the time you reach the burial ground. I included flint and steel for a fire. I suggest you thoroughly cook your meal to rid it of any impurities it may have gathered throughout the day."

Dismounting, I threw a smug look over my shoulder at Bryce. "Told you I have an animal sidekick."

"Gregory Percival Von Squeak the Third, at your service," the mouse said, eyes all aglow.

"Excellent, thank you, Greg." I placed a finger on the mouse's tiny shoulder. I'd underestimated how handy having an animal sidekick would be. He was like medieval DoorDash. Maybe I could take him home and coerce him into performing domestic tasks for me, like Cinderella did to her mice.

"I'm sure Greg the *mouse* will come in handy as we attempt to slay a dragon," Bryce said, voice full of innocent sincerity that I knew was sarcasm.

Ignoring him, I addressed Greg again. "Would you like to join us? You wouldn't have to fight a dragon, but you could keep me company." It didn't seem like Bryce would be a very good traveling companion, seeing as he was so fixated on Pretending Like It Never Happened. The idea of swapping lively banter with the mouse while Bryce sulked and felt left out was appealing.

"Nay, madam." Greg shook his head gravely. "I must return to the castle and keep a lookout."

"A lookout for what?" I asked.

"Anything that seems suspicious," he said darkly, which was actually helpful, since we wouldn't be there in case there was another kidnapping.

Before I could ask Greg if he'd happened to notice anything shady around the time of the first two kidnappings, he'd already disappeared.

✧ ✧ ✧

Around the second hour of riding through the forest, my entire body hurt. I swatted at a mosquito buzzing by my ear. Humidity made my shirt stick to my back. Bryce rode a few paces in front of me, and the sight of his stiff back marred the view of every misty waterfall, sunbeam clearing, and multicolored ring of toadstools we came across.

Needing something to take my mind off the discomfort, I broke the silence. "Should we talk about it?"

"How we're going to fight the dragon?" Bryce responded immediately, shoulders growing even more rigid. "Absolutely. We need a plan."

I sighed. If he didn't want to talk about it, fine. The dragon was more important anyway. "Do you think we could provide our own Charisma? You know, one of those self-love situations everyone hates to see. Like, the power we always had within us fixes everything in the end."

His shoulders rose and fell, but despite his sulk fest, he slowed his horse so I could catch up and ride beside him.

"Maybe we have to figure out our personal journey in order to make progress," I went on, refusing to let his sullenness irritate me. "In stories, it's always the people who need to fix their lives or learn something about themselves who get swept into adventures that force them to change. It's only after they experience growth that their adventure comes to an end."

"So, why are we here?" Bryce asked. "Out of everyone, why were we picked to be heroes?"

I frowned bitterly. "Isn't it obvious? On the day you told me to do something with my life, I refused and then got shoved into a world where I'm *being forced to do something with my life.*"

"It's not that," Bryce said quietly.

"Care to elaborate?"

"Not really."

I pointedly scratched my ear with my middle finger. Out of the corner of my eye, I caught him breaking into a reluctant smile—which had been my intention all along. It was always best to combat Bryce's gloom with cheerful harassment.

"If anything, it's my fault." Bryce sighed, smile fading as he plucked a cherry blossom off a passing tree. He twisted its stem between his fingers. "That morning, when you thought I was telling you to do something with your life, I didn't care about your life at all. I was only thinking of mine, and I wanted you out of it. I was trying to push you away because . . . because I was scared. You remembered my birthday, and I freaked out because it felt like you cared. I'm not good at trusting people who care about me."

My blood slowed in my veins. I wanted to ask if his trust issues had to do with his *I'm sure they're fine* parents and the reason he'd been raised by his grandparents, but if kissing was stringy, this was ropy. Still, if the reason we were brought to this weird fantasy realm had to do with our buried backstories, we had to talk about them.

"Oh?" I asked, feeling shitty that I couldn't manage more.

"It can't be a coincidence that, on the day I tried to get you out of my life, I got stuck in a magical world with you. Maybe I'm the one who has to learn a lesson. Like in *Groundhog Day*, Phil Connors only escapes the time loop by changing into a better person . . . and winning Rita's love."

"It's not that," I said quickly, shaking my head, even though a nauseating feeling in my gut told me he might be right. "This has to be about something else."

"How do you know?"

"Because love isn't real! How can it fix anything? It's not some magical, selfless thing. All you have to do is watch a reality dating show to know that. It's all about: What can this person do for *me*? And: How does this person make *me* feel? Love is just taking and giving, taking and giving, swapping tiny pieces of yourselves back and forth until you both end up more broken than when you began."

Ever since I stopped changing myself in order to make other people more comfortable, I started keeping all the pieces of me for myself instead of using them to buy the affection of others, which meant I'd been alone. Whole, but alone. The glue was still drying on the messy pieces of my soul, feebly holding them together. I couldn't fall in love because I would fall apart.

"You don't believe in love?" Bryce asked, as though I'd just revealed I was a flat Earther.

"You do?"

"Yeah. I believe it's terrifying."

"You believe everything is terrifying," I reminded him, not unkindly.

"I believe it's smarter to run from monsters than close your eyes and pretend they don't exist." Bryce leaned over and handed me the cherry blossom. "Unless that monster is only pretending to be a tough guy while she secretly mopes around believing no one cares about her. Then, I can't seem to resist poking her big soft heart with a stick, even if I am pretty sure she'll eat me for it."

Rolling my eyes, I picked at the petals of the blossom, trying not to like how nice his gesture made me feel. How seen he made me feel with his gentle teasing and his stupid kind eyes and his *making me feel desirable and sweet and not like a deplorable burden to society.*

I plucked the last of the petals from the flower. *He hates me. He hates me. He hates me.* And now I was the one who was terrified—too scared to give *He hates me not* a chance.

CHAPTER 25

In Which Courtney Steals a Pizza My Heart

BRYCE

I'd been hurled into a fantasy world, was almost punched by a stocky barman, and knew some Evil One was lurking, but the scariest thing yet was participating in a semi–emotionally deep conversation with Courtney.

She didn't believe in love, and suddenly, I was consumed with the desire to change her mind, even though I knew happy endings and love didn't go hand in hand. Maybe it was the argumentative nature of our relationship; if she said something, I instinctually wanted to prove her wrong, no matter what that thing was.

Or maybe I wanted her to believe for the same reason parents lie to their children and tell them Santa is real; experiencing the magic was worth the letdown.

Except I'd never believed happiness was worth the letdown, so it was troubling that I wanted to convince Courtney it was.

I clenched my fingers around the pebble in my pocket. Something about the rock grounded me. It warmed until I could imagine the heat of Courtney's hand against mine when she'd pressed the stone into my palm.

We reached the burial ground by late afternoon. It was just a big, empty field surrounded by trees and lit by golden-hour sunlight. It looked like the default background on a new laptop, all big blue skies, swaying grass, and wildflowers. The only reason we knew we were in the right place was because there was a stone marker that said: Burial Ground.

I scanned the grass and darkening sky. No dragon, though massive claw prints marred the earth, dirt staining the grass. "So, we just... wait and see if it shows up?" I asked.

"Weren't you listening to Amy's dragon-fighting lecture?" Courtney asked, eyes dancing. "We must search. Not, like, for the dragon, but for *ourselves*, and *each other*."

I chuckled. "And don't forget, we have to feeeeel."

The jovial mood disintegrated at the mention of feelings.

"I'm gonna just"—I jerked a finger over my shoulder—"do stuff... over there."

"Absolutely," she said. "And I'm going to"—she pointed in the opposite direction—"do things over here."

"Good." I smiled in what I hoped was a warm, unconcerned way.

"Fantastic!" She gave me a slightly unhinged thumbs-up before spinning on her heel and practically skipping away, going so far as to whistle as though she hadn't felt the same tension in the air that I had.

◇ ◇ ◇

Hours passed. It was nearing evening now, and if we didn't find the dragon soon, we'd never make it back in time for the tournament in the morning.

We spent the time wandering the field, avoiding each other, and fiddling with our many weapons, hoping to spontaneously develop mind-blowing fighting skills. The only thing I spontaneously developed was mind-blowing shoulder pain after hyperextending my arm trying to throw a dagger.

A little way away, Courtney drew her bow from her back and

notched an arrow. She pulled the string and went to let the arrow fly, but her fingers slipped. The string slapped against her arm, and the arrow fell pitifully to the ground.

Clutching her arm, she let out a unique arrangement of curses—something about *fudgebiscuitsmotherfuckingfuckfuck*, and I tried not to find it adorable.

I walked over. "Let me see."

"I have been filleted," she announced in a raw whisper, baring her arm and averting her eyes as though she feared what she might find.

Her forearm was slightly pink. Considering neither of us was even strong enough to pull the bow back all the way, I doubted it hurt as badly as she claimed. I cleared my throat. "Court."

"What," she whimpered.

"I don't want to alarm you."

"Oh my god."

"Have you ever seen *Cast Away*? Where the guy had to pull his own tooth?"

"Bryce." She said my name like a plea, and I hated how much I liked it. "Where are you going with this?"

"We're going to have to amputate. Here. Right now. I know it's not ideal, but you won't survive otherwise. You've lost too much blood."

She risked a peek at her arm. Her wide, scared eyes narrowed to slits, and she yanked her arm away. "Hey, I have an idea. Why don't you go fuck yourself?"

"And deny you the pleasure?" I fired back before I thought better of it. We'd made it all day without talking about last night, and here I was getting dangerously close to it.

Her stomach growled, snapping me out of it.

"Tell you what," I said. "You recover from your mortal injury, and I'll see what the mouse packed us to eat."

Before she could protest, I swiftly walked back to our horses. We were on the cusp of something. A boulder resting on the edge of a cliff. All it would take was one featherlight touch, and everything would crash down. I'd always known Courtney caused avalanches, just like I'd always known touching her was a bad idea.

Last night would've been a mistake. Who did I think I was? If her shoulder so much as brushed mine, my brain imagined deeper attachment. No way could I detach my idiotic *feelings* from my dick enough to pull off "strictly physical" with *love isn't real* Courtney.

It would be fine. These types of feelings never lasted anyway. I just had to wait it out like you'd wait out a hurricane or a stock market drop or any other undesirable thing.

I unhooked the leather bag from Courtney's horse and flipped open the top. The logo of the store where Courtney worked greeted me, printed on a plastic bag. It was so unexpected, I almost dropped the bag. Then I realized what it meant. Courtney had mentioned she had groceries when she came through the portal. Greg the mouse must've returned them to her. My heart drummed against my ribs.

Courtney walked up behind me, her hip bumping mine. Gritting my teeth, I tried not to sniff her hair like a weirdo. "Well? What's in there?" she asked. Her stomach growled again.

"Nothing." I tried to flip the top back over the bag, but she snatched it away.

She pulled out the grocery bag, fished around inside, then produced a box of pizza rolls.

"No way am I letting pizza rolls that have been left out for three days inside my body." But my stomach growled, and questionable pizza rolls would be better than foraging for probably poisonous mushrooms.

Courtney dove back into the grocery bag. "I had stuff for peanut butter and jelly, but maybe the mouse ate it? Mice like peanut butter, right?"

Then she froze, letting the bag drift down to her side. "We

have condoms." Her tone was unreadable, and it was hard to make out her features with the setting sun behind her.

It was as I'd suspected. Condoms. Delivered from above. I heard angels singing.

I hushed the angels. Things were too rocky. If a feather would send the metaphorical boulder of doom off the metaphorical cliff, then sex would crack the world in half. Which would be inconvenient, considering our mission to save it.

Gently, I removed the bag from her fingers. I almost couldn't resist the tantalizing idea of pushing aside her uncertainty and admitting *I want you so badly I can't breathe.* "Food is more important." I didn't recognize the robotic voice issuing from my mouth.

Courtney looked at me like I'd unironically told a *Why did the chicken cross the road?* joke.

Maybe I did owe her an explanation, but there wasn't a good way to say, *You're not my arch nemesis, and maybe you never were, but you have to be, because if you so much as hug me again, my pathetic ass will offer you my heart as a sacrifice and thank you when you inevitably destroy it.*

No. That was too complicated. So I grunted, "Food," again, my jaw locked to hold back everything else.

CHAPTER 26

IN WHICH WE FUCK... UP

COURTNEY

Half an hour and lots of hangry bickering later, Bryce and I managed to get a small fire going. The wood crackled, cicadas whined, and fireflies flickered among the swaying grass.

"What do you think?" Bryce pulled me from my thoughts, presenting a slab of bark with a pile of pizza rolls on it. He wouldn't meet my eye. He hadn't met my eye properly all day.

"The bark will burn," I said.

"This is how the cavemen did it."

"You have a fully stocked kitchen of bark cutlery and dishware?"

"Ha."

"The instructions said to arrange them in a circle," I said, trying not to notice how nice his skin looked in the light of the flickering campfire because only serial killers had creepy thoughts like that.

Bryce arranged the pizza rolls in a circle, fingers deft and sure.

I crossed my legs a little tighter, trying not to think of the places those fingers had been.

Bryce Flannery was mouthwateringly attractive when he was obliviously excelling at something, like fingerbanging or accounting or cooking. Maybe him heating pizza rolls for me shouldn't have been a turn-on, but it was.

His competence had always stirred something in me—like that time I almost got scammed by a door-to-door vacuum salesperson before Bryce stepped out on the porch to spew a bunch of numbers, outlining how the payment plan was a total predatory rip-off, leaving the salesperson nearly in tears. His brain was like a fleshy calculator. Meanwhile, I didn't even understand why the word *mortgage* had a silent *t* because I'd always been too scared to ask; it seemed like one of those things that adults had silently and collectively agreed to accept and never discuss.

I'd never had anyone stand up for me like that—without prompting and not out of familial obligation. But Bryce had gone out of his way to rescue me from debilitating vacuum debt, and I'd never felt more noticed or cherished. Our whole duplex had felt safer, like as long as he was on watch, protecting us from solicitors, I could breathe a little easier. I didn't need to know why there was a silent *t* in *mortgage*. I didn't *need* to know everything or be perfect. Bryce didn't expect me to fix my shortcomings; he anticipated them, silently stepping in to have my back when he noticed me struggling.

In return for his help, I'd decided to repay the favor. For some reason, spiders liked to build their homes in the corner of his doorframe, and he was always walking through their webs and shuddering with revulsion. So I started checking every morning and rehoming any eight-legged friends I saw. I didn't know if Bryce noticed their absence, but it made me feel good to make his life a little better where it truly mattered, even if I enjoyed making it worse in every area it didn't.

After the vacuum incident, I'd thanked Bryce via my Wi-Fi router name: ThxForMansplaining.

A few hours later, his Wi-Fi name had changed from cwww wwwoissants4lyfe to: SucksUcantSuck.

I'd happened to catch the switch, and approximately thirty seconds passed before he corrected his name to: BecauseUdont HaveTheVacuum.

And again: NotInASexualWay.

And again: ImSureUcouldSuckIfUwanted2.

InASexualWay.

AndAlsoNot.

And finally: AtLeastURpersonalityStillSux.

I'd never mentioned the blip. I told myself it was normal for my enemy to think about how I sucked.

But now here he was making me food. And he'd braved my sharp teeth to poke my supposedly soft heart with a stick. Perhaps my make-Bryce-like-me plan had worked a little too well. Then again, I still wasn't shooting light from my hands, so it couldn't have been that effective.

"There. Pizza roll summoning circle complete." Bryce waved his hands over the bark platter.

"It'd be great if it could summon us some power because Amy's methods are worthless," I grumbled.

"Maybe you have to trust the process. Wax on, wax off, and all that."

Annoyance flared in my empty stomach. "I bet that cantankerous old man could tell us in two seconds how to save the world, but he won't because he wants to teach us a lesson."

Bryce positioned the bark on a forked stick and held it over the flames. Sparks crackled against the underside of the dry wood. Flames rose around the pizza rolls. An odd chill prickled across my skin.

"Have you tried asking him nicely?" Bryce asked.

"Nice. That's the key to everything, isn't it? Just *be nice*." I knew I was being prickly, but my stomach wouldn't stop growling, and we'd spent all day out here for nothing while the Evil One was free to inflict who knew what kinds of horrors at the castle.

"It wouldn't hurt to try occasionally." Bryce sighed. "You walk around with a chip on your shoulder like the world owes you something when you've done nothing but laugh at it your entire life."

I fought to keep my expression unbothered to hide how, in all his poking around, he'd found a few old wounds. I hadn't always laughed at the world. Once, I'd smiled demurely under its shadow. And it had gotten me nothing meaningful in the end either.

"I think the world does owe me," I said with a shrug, "and maybe it does make me entitled—that I don't think I should have to have a career, two-point-five kids, and a 401(k) to earn my value as a human being."

Orange light danced across Bryce's face as he studied me. Leaning over, he tucked a tendril of hair behind my ear, fingertips like butterfly kisses across my brow. "It's never too early to start thinking about retirement, Court," he said, softly, throat bobbing. "Social security is so uncertain. If you don't want a 401(k), you could consider a Roth IRA, or a SEP, or—"

I'd opened myself up to him more than I had to anyone in a long time, and here he was trying to sell me a retirement plan. Trying to get me to *be better*.

Then again, his response probably wasn't intentionally malicious. He simply didn't understand. No one did.

I pulled away, brushing off the hurt. "Between a minimum-wage salary and the money I make off of selling pictures of my feet on the Internet, I do all right."

"Selling your feet on the Internet?" Bryce rubbed his temples.

"There are two types of people in this world. People who sell pictures of their feet on the Internet, and liars."

"That's not even a little bit true."

"Look, I have my future under control." Digging my phone out of my pocket, I powered it on before flipping to the appropriate screen and handing it over to him. "My retirement portfolio."

"This is just an album with over three thousand pictures of your feet."

"Retirement. Portfolio," I corrected him, taking my phone back and powering it off to save battery. "I can keep selling pictures of my feet forever, even when they're old and weird."

"Oh my god." Bryce scrubbed at his eyes.

He was sort of hot when he was peeved. When we got home, I was going to blackmail him into doing my taxes. The prospect of getting to distress him like this for hours on end made my skin tingle. I was an attention whore, if craving the undivided annoyance of one man counted as being an attention whore.

Seeing his expression and knowing he wasn't going to let this go until I gave him a serious response, I gave in. "My employer provides retirement benefits, not that it's any of your business." Needing to defend myself, I went on, "I never wanted to be a burden to anyone. I told that to Will—my ex. I made this whole spreadsheet to show him that I could take care of myself, that my lifestyle wouldn't hold him back. He still said I was being selfish for not wanting to strive for more. *Everyone* says I'm selfish. Maybe they're right. I don't want kids, and my parents certainly have enough money to take care of themselves. It's a selfish choice. It impacts nobody but me, and it's astonishing how many people take that personally."

Bryce's gaze flitted over my face. "I get that you want a life that not many can understand, but you don't even give people a chance. You just say something off-putting or insulting to make them dislike you immediately. Does that truly make you happy?"

"No." The truth came easier with darkness pressed around us. Bryce was scared of the dark, but it made me feel safe, like any secret told in shadows would never come to light. I didn't like pushing people away, but it was easier than letting them down.

"I want nothing," I said after a moment, "but I want to be something to someone."

"Well, you'll always be a delightful pain in my ass, so that's something," Bryce said tenderly. I saw the real truth swirling in his gentle gaze: *So you can stop believing no one cares about you.*

Being his pain in his ass used to be enough, but it was starting to feel like we'd never be able to go back to how things were. All his kindness lately was due to the fact he thought I had a secret soft side that made me redeemable. And maybe I did, but I wondered if anyone could like all the hard, cold, ugly parts of me, too, or if the only affection I could have was a half love. I wanted someone to like me *because* I was an unambitious smart-ass, not despite it.

Forcing a mischievous grin, I lightened my tone, casting away the shadows, secrets, and unspoken confessions. "Fine, we can try things your way. I'll humble myself before the world, apologize for laughing at it, and politely ask for help. *Oh, universe, we offer this pizza roll platter as a sacrifice.*" I lowered my voice to the wavering cadence of a Bible thumper on channel three calling down the wrath of god onto old people sleeping in recliners. "Please send a divine power to deliver us from these trying times in return for our zesty offering."

"Why are you the way you are?" Bryce ran a hand down his face.

"Oh, pizza god, bestow your greasy glory upon us—"

"Gross."

"That we might shine as well."

"This is a supremely impressive display of maturity, Courtney."

The fire popped, sparks exploding. I yelped and fell back. The bark pizza roll platter teetered. Bryce fought to rebalance it. It swayed, almost fell, but then righted itself.

I let out a sigh of relief—

Eeeeeaaaaakkkkk!

A deafening, high-pitched screech split the night, followed by the bone-chilling beat of dragon wings. Wind swept my hair back. A dark blur shadowed the corner of my eye. Then rows of wicked teeth filled my vision.

"Watch out!" I yelled, ducking.

The dragon dove for us, its wings snapping open at the last second. One claw grazed my cheekbone, barely a brush, not even hard enough to scratch. Its wing clipped Bryce, throwing him off balance.

I glanced up, but the dragon was already soaring toward the horizon, its chilling scream fading away.

I looked down in time to see the pizza roll platter tipping in slow motion.

"Nooooo!" I reached a trembling hand.

One square pillow of goodness after another plopped into the white-hot coals. Logs popped, sending embers prickling across my skin. The fire flared high as it consumed our dinner.

Anger fueled by hunger burned in my gut. I pushed myself off the ground and flailed around for my weapons. Finding a knife, I ran a few steps farther into the field, scanning the sky. "Come back here, you overgrown arthropod!"

"We missed our chance, Courtney," Bryce said. "It's gone."

A stress migraine throbbed behind my eyeballs. "So are the pizza rolls." That fact shouldn't have felt critical after the reappearance of the dragon, but I hadn't eaten in hours, and my temper had ignited faster than my dinner had. "We're going to starve."

"I'll get right on that next time." Bryce scrambled to his feet. "Saving pizza rolls from *giant flying spiders* will be my number one priority."

"Well, you certainly weren't busy chasing the dragon."

"At least I bothered to make food in the first place."

I marched up to him. "I haven't asked you to do any of the things you've done for me. I never *wanted* you to *bother*."

"No, your stomach *demanded* it." Bryce waved his hands over his head, his shadow stretching behind him like one of those red dancing men found outside sketchy car dealerships.

"What does that even mean?" I asked, temper and voice rising.

"Oh, you knew what you were doing." His lip curled. "Standing there looking all innocent in the wildflowers while your stomach growled and growled and *growled*." Bryce let out a growl of his own, running a hand through his hair until the wild orange strands springing around his head resembled the still-growing fire.

"You think I can control my *stomach growls*?" I practically screamed.

"God, you're annoying!"

"I didn't do anything!"

"Your voice gets scratchy when you yell, and it's really hot!" he yelled, a vein standing out on his forehead.

A strange mix of desire and white-hot anger shot up my spine. When he yelled, his voice got all throaty and rough, and it. Was. Really. Hot.

"Yeah, well," I said. "You make me so angry with your stupid shirts that you *never wear* and your annoying five-o'clock shadow."

"How is *that* annoying?" he bellowed.

"Because it's impractical! I bet it takes you *more* effort to look like you don't care than if you actually didn't care."

"If I actually didn't care, then I'd look like you, and what a nightmare that would be!"

"Fuck you!"

"Fuck *you*!"

We panted and glared. Fire and heat raged between us.

Oh. No.

Actual fire raged between us.

The flames roared as tall as us, wild and out of control. Somewhere, in another universe, Smokey Bear cried. Argument forgotten, we stared at the pillar of flames as it raged taller.

Strangely, it didn't spread much, only mounted higher and higher, lighting the entire field in flat, white light.

"Either dragon fire is the trick candles of the fantasy world, or pizza rolls are more flammable than I thought," I said.

"Amy is going to be so pissed if we burn down the sacred field," said Bryce.

"There's no *if*," I said, backing away from the flames. "The sacred field is toast."

"I like toast." Bryce's arms dangled pathetically as he looked up at the flames.

"You know," I remarked after a minute of watching the sparks dance overhead, "if you die here tonight, consumed by the pizza roll fire, nobody back home will ever find your body."

Bryce turned on me. "Did *you* know that every time you wish me dead, you look at my mouth?"

"I do not." I looked at his mouth, and an ache tightened between my thighs.

He wet his lips. "You can pretend you're frustrated about the pizza rolls, but we both know—"

"Don't speak of the pizza rolls," I hissed. "It is *too soon*."

"Oh no." His eyes widened. "The condoms."

I gasped. "The condoms."

United once more, we charged into the flames, gathering as many stray condoms as we could. As the heat licked around my skin, all I could think about was each foil wrapper and what it represented. Each one a symbol of what could be. The burning within me transformed as the world burned around me. I met Bryce's eyes, lit by the inferno. I didn't know what the burning transformed *into*, only that it made me want to sacrifice my eyelashes to gather as many condoms as I could. Which meant a lot. Because getting my eyelashes done took up a substantial portion of my minimum-wage budget.

At last, when we could bear it no longer, we tore away from

the fire. We burst into the forest, breathing very hard for two people who had just run very little.

Gasping, I looked from the strands of condoms in my arms to Bryce's face.

Chest heaving, he nodded, dropping everything he held. With a giant, determined *fuck it* written all over his face, he stepped over all the crap littering the ground and strode forward until he stood right before me, toe-to-toe.

"Don't stop shaving to try to look like you haven't shaved," I said, weirdly choked up—maybe from the smoke, maybe not. "You look ridiculous how you are, but you'd look worse any other way."

His eyes were glassy, no doubt stinging from smoke like mine. "I don't shave at all," he said simply with a little shrug, like we were sharing a deeply intimate moment of revelation. "This is legitimately all I can grow."

My breath hitched. *"Oh."*

Holding my gaze, he slipped a strand of condoms from my fingers, tearing one off and tossing the rest behind him. "I want you. Now. Against a tree," he said hoarsely. "Or something."

"Uh-huh," I squeaked out because I couldn't think of anything I wanted more than Bryce pinning me against a tree and spreading my legs. Not even pizza rolls.

Everything tumbled from my arms. The distance between us vanished. Bryce's hands found my waist, pressed, urged. Back, back, back. My heels scrambled over roots. Before I could decide if I was falling, my shoulders crashed into a wide, smooth tree trunk.

He hesitated, palms pressed to the bark on either side of me. I saw the question in his eyes. When he tried to voice it, he only managed a whispered "Please."

I nodded, and he collapsed against me, his mouth finding my neck, all hot breath, gentle teeth, and urgent lips. He didn't ask to kiss my mouth, and I was glad he didn't push it. I clutched my fingers around his arms as he grabbed my hips, sliding his hands low to pull me against him. My blood ran heavy in my limbs. My head spun. I might've been asphyxiating, not entirely because of Bryce's charms, but also due to the fact I'd never caught my breath, and I was very out of shape.

His lips found the space where my ear met my jaw, mouth caressing my skin. While heat from the raging inferno out in the field wafted over my skin, a different sort of heat ravaged my insides. Molten rivers of desire flooded my veins.

His thigh slotted between my legs, and he pressed against me, hard. A muffled sigh escaped my lips. I slipped my hands under his shirt, around his back, drawing him closer, closer, closer. I tried not to moan as he rocked against me. It rubbed me the wrong way, him knowing how much I liked it when he rubbed me the right way. It felt like giving him the upper hand in an unspoken power struggle.

Regaining my footing, I brushed my hand over his hip, found his belt. My fingers fumbled. Reaching down, he helped me, and metal clinked as the buckle unfastened.

A tremor ran through his fingers, and I paused. "Good?" I whispered.

When he nodded, I slipped my hand past his loosened waistband. Eyes shuttering, he moved against my palm. The only evidence of pleasure he displayed was a barely audible groan stifled by tight-pressed lips and a knotted jaw, but it was enough. Enough to validate my own burning want. Resting his forehead against mine, he watched me with glazed eyes, his breaths matching the rhythm of my hand.

He explored the bodice of my dress, thumbs trailing over my nipples and sending a tug of desire down to my core. His lips skimmed across my cheek, breath warm where it ruffled the hair at my temple. I arched against him as he teased me through my bodice, letting a gasp slide free of my lips, and at last, he smiled. Movements growing urgent, his fingers tangled with ties and fabric.

"Fuck these damn laces," Bryce growled, as though laces had been his personal vexation his entire life.

"Do the bodice-ripper thing," I urged in a breathless rush. "Rip it."

For a second, Bryce looked at me with the wonder of a man who'd been handed keys to a Ferrari. Then he gripped the top of my dress with his fists and pulled. And pulled again. "It won't tear."

Scrunching my neck, I looked down. "Have you tried trying harder?"

"Wow, stellar advice." His voice rose.

"I'm sorry!"

"Stop yelling at me, you dick."

"I'm not yelling; I'm encouraging," I yelled, coiling my fingers in his shirt and yanking him against me. "Forget it."

I redirected his hands to more accessible locations, and we became a blur of hands under hems, fingers over skin. There was an intense moment where my heavy skirt threatened to best our frenzied fingers. Bryce dug through yards and yards of fabric, and the sight of his frustration made me suppress a laugh. Then his hands were on me, skin against skin, brushing over my hips, nudging my thighs apart, and my laugh turned into a sigh. He hiked my leg to his hip, hooking my ankle around his waist. An ache, heavy and empty all at once, swelled between my legs.

He slid his hand between us, thumb finding the spot that needed him, fingers filling the emptiness until I clutched his shoulders and arched against the tree. I ground against the heel of his hand as his fingers massaged a place deep inside me that made my vision tunnel. My breaths quickened as pressure built. My limbs trembled, then trembled again, *harder*.

A low rumble filled my ears.

If Bryce turned out to be my most earth-shattering sexual encounter, I'd be shook.

My whole body shook.

CRACK! The sound split the night.

Bryce flinched, dropping my leg. My eyes flew open.

The ground rattled beneath our feet.

"Oh," I said, "that makes more sense. It's just an earthquake, not your sexual skills."

"*Just* an earthquake?"

A second gut-wrenching crack thundered across the field. I stumbled away from the tree, staring out into the clearing. The earth churned as though it had transformed into a raging ocean, sucking grass and wildflowers into its earthy folds.

Bryce began gathering condoms.

I straightened my skirt and helped, scooping up everything I could. Because when the earth splits open, the first thing on everyone's mind is *save the condoms*.

I found my senses somewhere under the subsiding sexual sensations ebbing from my body. "Let's get out of here." The ground rattled, and I stumbled, catching myself on a branch.

The dirt boiled under my foot. I tried to back away, but more earth gave way beneath me. Clods of soil bubbled up, revealing pale flashes of bone, lit by the blazing field.

A skeletal hand burst from the dirt and wrapped around my ankle.

I screamed.

Bryce looped an arm around my waist and pulled, but the cold bones tightened, squeezing sharp pain into my ankle.

The dirt churned, and a smiling skull rose to the surface, soil trickling from its eye sockets like tears. Another scream ripped from my throat. I clutched the condoms to my chest like a security blanket, pulling helplessly at my ensnared foot.

Bryce stepped around me and stomped hard on the skull, driving it back under the dirt. "Back to Hell, asshole." He stomped again, heel connecting with the skeletal wrist, bones crunching under his boot.

The fingers released, and I flew backward.

Bryce steadied me until I found my footing. I looked toward the field and caught one glimpse of a skeletal army clawing its way from the earth, silhouetted in the flames of the unnatural pizza roll fire that should have long ago burned out.

Then Bryce was yelling in my ear, "Run!"

CHAPTER 27

IN WHICH WE OREGA-KNOW THESE ARE GRAVE TIMES

BRYCE

I was uncomfortable with many things in life. If I had to rank the top three things I was most uncomfortable with, it would probably go something like this:

1. That moment when you go to a show, and the guy on the stage screams into the microphone, for the third time, "I said, are y'all having a good time?"
2. Flash mobs.
3. Skeleton flash mobs.

However, at that moment, my mind was not capable of ranking fears. I was really only capable of thinking thoughts such as: *Holyshitholyshitholyshit.*

The undead had spooked our horses, causing them to run off, so we crashed through the forest on foot, vines slapping our faces and thorns scraping our skin. Bioluminescent fungi grew out of tree trunks and rotting logs, like stars had fallen and settled in the forest. I tried to find comfort in the beauty, but my limbs shook.

They felt like they hadn't *stopped* shaking since we came into this world. Trying not to catch feelings for Courtney while simultaneously chasing after Courtney as she repeatedly endangered herself meant I existed in a continuous state of acute panic.

Courtney happened to remember the sun was in her eyes this morning on the way to the field, so we figured out which direction we needed to run to head back to the castle. Thankfully, the skeletons were too preoccupied with rising from the dead to be concerned with chasing us.

We ran for what felt like hours before the fear buzzing in my ears subsided enough for me to think. They were frantic, nonsensical thoughts, but at least I could form words.

"Do you think those pizza rolls had oregano in them?" I gasped for breath.

Courtney limped as she ran. "Are you saying you think *oregano* had something to do with us raising the dead?" Her words came out choppy as we maneuvered over roots and undergrowth.

"Amy said oregano was used in the dark arts, and you called upon some unknown god while we burned a circle of oregano. You do the math." My voice came out sharper than I'd intended, fear tightening my throat. "What are we going to do? We have to fight a dragon *and* the undead now?"

Her pace slowed. "It was an accident. Really, the dragon's fault."

"Right. The dragon *we freed* made me drop the pizza rolls into a fire and raise the dead. I'm sure everyone will be understanding." My chest hurt. I could hardly breathe.

Moonlight caught Courtney's face as she fell against a tree and rubbed her ankle. "We can blame the Evil One again."

"You're hurt." I couldn't breathe. I hurried over and knelt at her feet. "Where? Do you think it's broken? *Can you see bone?*" I couldn't breathe. I couldn't breathe. Oh god, I could not breathe.

Courtney wore a strange expression. If I didn't know better,

I might say she was concerned. Then she smirked. "I told you most men know to bow before me. I knew you'd come around."

My chest was constricted so tightly, I expected a rib to crack. "Would you stop joking around for once? Why can't you take anything seriously? It's like you don't even care about safety."

"I have the ultimate respect for your love of caution, Bryce. I even hope you have a warning label written about you one day. Imagine the honor."

"Gee, thanks." Wrangling my frantic fingers, I managed to wiggle her shoe off her heel. She dug her fingers into my shoulders, drawing in a sharp, pained breath. Purple bruises swelled around her ankle. Visions of her being sucked into the ground, echoes of her screams—they flashed in my memory before settling in my gut to fester. My vision swam, darkening around the edges.

"Relax, Bryce." Her voice sounded distant. "One day the sun will explode and consume the universe, and none of this will have mattered."

The shock factor of her words momentarily distracted me from my fear, and when she slipped her hand into mine, slowly, slowly, my pulse evened out.

I grimaced. "You are the most negative positive person I have ever met." If she were the sunshine, she'd be happy, not because of how brightly she shone, but because she could give people sunburns.

Favoring her unharmed ankle, Courtney slid down the tree to look me in the eye. As she scanned my face, the fight seemed to leave her body. "What are we going to do? People here need help, and all we do is make things worse. It's not as though three-to-five armies are going to rush to our aid at the last minute and save us. We haven't done any of the things heroes are supposed to do. We don't have a band of misfit sidekicks. We haven't slain any beasts or traveled thousands of miles on horseback. All we've done is make everything worse."

I stood unsteadily, hand gravitating to my pocket, where I found the pebble Courtney gave me. I held on to it for dear life. "We need to itemize all the bad shit and tick off our problems one by one," I said, as though I could simply spreadsheet our way through being Chosen Ones. "Step one, figure out who the fuck the Evil One is. As soon as we get back, we find Greg the mouse and ask him if he learned anything while we were away."

"And what about the dragon and the skeletons?"

"I don't know. We'll talk to Amy about increasing guards around the city to buy us time until we figure it out."

◊ ◊ ◊

As morning light touched the horizon, the city finally came into view. We kept looking over our shoulders for signs of the skeletons. My ears prickled as I strained to hear the telltale crashing of bony feet through the forest, and my neck developed a crick from how often I kept searching the sky for the dragon.

Forcing ourselves to act natural, we walked through the gates to discover the streets bustling with activity. I scrutinized everyone around me, looking for signs of fear that would indicate people had seen the dragon or undead, but everything seemed normal. Carriages stretched down the main roads as far as we could see. Banners waved on every house. People were setting up booths. Children laughed. Hawkers' shouts zipped back and forth as they tried to sell their wares. Women gossiped in clusters. Smells of street food filled the air. Somewhere far away, music played. An eerie sense of foreboding settled over me, raising the hairs on the back of my neck. It was the calm before the storm. It was only a matter of time before calamity swept through the city, and it was all our fault.

My eyes caught on a banner praising the return of a Chosen One, and that was when I remembered. "Oh, shit. The Chosen One tournament is today." Frustration tried to claw its way out of my throat. None of this mattered anymore. We had bigger problems to worry about.

"We don't have time for that," Courtney said, echoing my thoughts. "There's a dragon and a zombie army on the loose. We'll come up with a reason to delay it."

Just then, Amy materialized out of nowhere. "Ah, there you are. When your horses returned without you, we grew concerned. I trust you took care of the dragon?" He didn't wait for a response. "Wonderful. We must make haste. The trial is about to start." He beckoned for us to follow.

"I think we should postpone the tournament," I tried, scampering after Amy as he ushered us through the crowd. "I'm . . . not feeling well." Faking an illness had worked well enough before.

But Amy ignored me. "Come quickly. We must get you prepped. Everyone's waiting!"

"What do you think about increasing security?" Courtney asked Amy, struggling to catch her breath as we trailed after him through the city.

"Pish posh," Amy said absently. "Last night was peaceful. The Evil One seems to be lying low for now."

"I just thought, with the increased crowds for the tournament, it might be wise," Courtney pressed.

"Nonsense." Amy waved a hand. "The citizens are well-behaved. There's nothing to worry about from them."

Courtney gave up arguing and fell back to hobble beside me. "I'm going to let you win so we can get this over with quickly and figure out how to stop the skeletons. You're the Chosen One anyway. All that matters is fixing things and getting home."

Hearing her give up the title so easily was no longer the triumph I'd once thought it would be. I had no idea why she thought I was more capable than her of saving the day. The thought of having to organize a defense against the Evil One only increased my panic.

I didn't have much time to think about it, though, because Amy dropped us off at an armory where a guard strapped a bunch of metal to my body. A few minutes later, I was being pushed outside, where I found myself in a dirt arena, surrounded by loud, packed bleachers.

As someone shoved a blunt sword in my hand, I figured out that hand-to-hand combat was the first test of the tournament. In the bleachers, people talked and laughed.

I glanced toward the horizon, waiting to see a zombie horde approaching. Nothing yet.

A trumpet sounded, and I jumped in fright, expecting a dragon to drop from the sky. Instead, a herald, who was predictably named Harold, stepped forward and spoke at an unnecessarily loud volume as he held a giant broadsword aloft, declaring it the award for whoever turned out to be the Chosen One. The sword's name, origin, and significance were discussed at length. Basic human needs, like breathing, didn't seem to apply to Harold the herald. In the bleachers, Amy nodded along, and I half expected him to leap up and shout, *Amen!*

A second later, Harold the herald ran through a points system I didn't understand, the trumpet blasted again, and I jolted once more, armor rattling. A servant shoved me forward, and I stumbled into the arena. Courtney limped into the other side of the ring carrying a shield and sword. Her gaze was heavy, like she was a battle-worn warrior instead of a woman whose exhaustion stemmed from missing a singular meal and enduring one sleepless night.

"I forfeit." Courtney stabbed her sword into the ground, stepped back, and crossed her arms.

The crowd fell silent. Amy wheezed. The king looked perplexed—more than usual.

"You can't quit, Lady Courtney," the herald said under his breath.

"Why, though?"

"There are no records of a Chosen One ever having quit before," the herald said. "They've come close, to be sure, but the power within always rejuvenated their broken spirits, and they persevered."

In the bleachers, Amy stood and drew in a large lungful of air like he was about to deliver a three-part presentation over all the reasons Courtney couldn't quit.

"Fine, fine." Rolling her eyes, Courtney faced me and spread her arms. "Attack me. Let's get this over with."

I took a few steps toward her. Murmurs spread through the crowd. Amy sank back into his seat, momentarily satisfied. I kept expecting to hear screams of fear rise from the city as the skeleton army breached the wall, or for the shadow of the dragon to drop across us.

My eye caught on something as it moved beneath the bleacher nearest to me. It was Courtney's sidekick, the mouse, Greg, hiding behind someone's tankard of beer. He obviously couldn't tell how spooked Courtney and I were, because his whiskers twitched as he caught my eye, and his tiny mouth curled into a smile. If only he knew what happened on our trip, he wouldn't be so happy about seeing us again.

Forcing myself to focus on getting through the task before me, I tried to lift my blade. Unbidden, pictures flashed in my head—Courtney's wide, shining eyes, full of shock and pain. The pure terror twisting my gut when the skeletal hand grabbed her ankle.

"I can't," I said, realizing it was true. My arm refused to lift the sword. I couldn't hurt her. Physically *could not*. I had mental erectile dysfunction. Instead of being unable to use my dick, I was incapable of *being* a dick.

Courtney huffed, yanking her sword from the ground. "Then call it self-defense, if it makes you feel better."

She lunged, and I jumped back, barely managing to parry. She attacked again, her blade a flashing flurry of steel that I barely batted away. Relentless blow after relentless blow rained down upon me.

Our blades locked, and she stepped in close. "What are you waiting for?" she growled, nose inches from mine. "Fight back."

"What if I hurt you?" Courtney gave me a disbelieving look, so I added, "I mean if you're hurt, you'll be a worthless sidekick if I need you to pull a Samwise and carry me up a volcano."

"Unbelievable." She pressed her sword harder against mine. "You've gotten soft."

"*No.*" The muscles in my arm trembled. Not because they were particularly fatigued from holding her off me, but because they *didn't want to hold her off me.*

"What did it? My pebbly, *pebbly* nipples?"

"*Shut up.*" I scoffed, trying to sound dismissive.

She pushed away, our blades separating with a metallic *shink*. Realizing she was right and we needed to end this, I tossed my sword aside and strode purposefully toward her. Lowering my shoulder, I aimed low and charged. At the last second, I eased back my speed, so my shoulder lightly tapped her hip.

She looked down at where I stood, my shoulder stuck to her hip. "Literally, what are you doing?"

"I'm letting you let me beat you," I said into her waist. "Go with it." She shifted, and her chain mail smashed against my mouth. Spluttering, I tried to maintain my grip. "I'm tackling you."

"I'm quaking."

"You're kinda supposed to fall now." I grunted. "So if you could cooperate, that would be great."

"Yes, I'm sure you fondling me is convincing the city of battle-hardened warriors this is a legitimate fight." But she stiffly bent her knees, and we began jointly lowering ourselves to the ground.

It was the slowest tackle in the history of the world. Hardly even a tackle—more like two fragile old people helping each other to bed. Our feet shuffled as we negotiated our landing.

I adjusted my hold halfway down and caught a glimpse of her blank face. "Would it kill you to look scared or angry or *something*?"

"I'm trying not to laugh during my devastating defeat. How's this?" She opened her mouth and widened her very dead eyes.

I staggered as my bent knees threatened to collapse. "Worse. Much, much worse."

In the bleachers, the crowd grew restless, denied their display of graphic violence.

"Watch your sword," I said.

"*My sword?* Watch your knee." She grimaced. "Maybe if you put your hand here, and my foot there. Yes. Like that."

With a mighty creak of armor, we made an awkward landing. Off balance, I half fell over her.

"You okay?"

Courtney gave me a look. "Are you even trying to make this believable?"

She had a point. I straddled her hips, pinning her limp arms over her head. "I have bested you, foul cur," I announced to the crowd.

"What's a cur?" Courtney wanted to know.

"No idea. Could you scooch like a foot to your left so I can reach my sword?"

"Sure thing."

We inched ourselves across the arena. Each scuff of our bodies over the dirt was amplified in the dead silence of the crowd.

"Little more. There." I stretched and grabbed the sword, then returned to my position and held the blade over her.

Her eyes sparkled up at me, full of mirth, despite all the trouble we'd been through and all the impossible tasks still before us.

I wanted to kiss her.

It was the simple truth, and to deny the feeling would be like denying the sky was blue or the ocean was deep. I wanted to feel her annoying smirk against my mouth and figure out her stupid laces once and for all, then let her lock her disgusting feet around my hips and forget everything else for a while.

A trumpet wailed, snapping me out of my fixation. With much confusion, the herald declared me the winner. Shaking myself, I stood and helped Courtney to her feet, brushing dirt off her back, then drawing away when my fingers wanted to linger.

I should have grabbed her right there, told her what I wanted, asked her if she wanted it too. Instead, I let her go, telling myself, *Later*. There would be time for kissing later. But, since there was an undead army on the loose, I had no idea if that was true.

"Psst," a tiny voice whispered.

I turned to find Greg gesturing me closer from his hiding place. Inconspicuously, Courtney and I sidled closer. "What is it?" I asked. "Did something happen last night while we were gone?"

"No," Greg said. "I was curious if your dinner was to your liking? Both of you look so weary, I was worried you did not receive proper nourishment."

Courtney and I exchanged a look. Greg was so eager to please, I didn't want to tell him that the meal he'd so thoughtfully packed had led to a crisis, so I only nodded and said, "Oh yeah, it was great. We really appreciate your help, dude."

"Have you heard anything more about the general?" Courtney asked. "Has she been found?"

Somberly, Greg shook his head.

Amy called for us then, so Courtney gave him a quick "We'll catch up with you later," before turning and muttering to me. "I'll let you win this one as quickly as possible, too, so we won't even have to waste our time with whatever the third challenge is, then we'll figure out a way to talk Amy into increasing security."

We were taken to a large amphitheater down by the beach, the crowd following after us. Crashing waves drowned out the noise from the multitude seating themselves in the circular gallery.

Amy led us into the basin of the theater, where he instructed us to stand facing each other. "Defeat your opponent using magic alone," he said, tucking his hands into his sleeves and backing away.

Well, there went our plan to get through the tournament fast. We'd be here until one of us starved to death. There wasn't anything Courtney could do to let me win this one.

Unless there *was* something she could do.

When I'd called Courtney on her sex dream bluff, I'd told her all we needed was physical attraction to bring our magic to life. Magically speaking, physical attraction had gotten us nowhere. Maybe we needed to allow an emotional connection. I'd felt one forming that night we baked the tarts at Mama's house and in the sacred field, but we were both still resisting. Courtney had always been as adamant about hating me as I was about hating her, but I needed her to sympathize with me for one minute.

"I had a rough childhood," I said, low enough no one could hear it over the waves. "Remember when I told you I wanted to be a slug when I was a kid?"

"Yeah." The ocean breeze lifted her hair off her neck, whipping it around her face.

"I was nine. My mom had me young, and all I heard my whole life was how she had to sacrifice everything for me. And I get it. I do. But what nine-year-old wants to hear how their existence crushed their mother's dreams?"

"I'm sure she didn't mean it like that." Courtney's eyes darted like she was searching for an escape.

"Oh no, she did," I said, hands sinking into my pockets. Finding the pebble. Clenching it. "One day, she took me to my grandparents' house and told me to wait out on the porch. I sat on the step and listened as their voices rose until I heard her yell, 'Raising him is ruining my life, and I can't do it anymore!'

I didn't look up when the back door slammed, not when her car fired up, and not when she pulled away without me. I watched the slugs on the driveway instead, and I wished I were one. All slugs cared about was avoiding salt and eating fungus. A slug wouldn't hurt like I did."

CHAPTER 28

IN WHICH I FALL THRICE—METAPHORICALLY, CLUMSILY, AND WITH THE HELP OF A BATTLE-AX

COURTNEY

I stared at Bryce, and Bryce stared at his feet, shoulders hunched and brows furrowed.

"Oh," I said so softly I wasn't sure he heard. I didn't know what else to say.

Though I tried to hold it back, my heart went out to him like a runaway puppy down a street—recklessly, with no thought for the consequences. My throat clogged, and my eyes prickled. I wanted to run to him and throw my arms around him, but I'd noticed traditional forms of comfort often scared him more than anything else. Now I knew why. The people who felt the closest to him were the ones who hurt him.

So I just stood there, helpless, imagining little Bryce at nine years old, feeling so guilty for something that wasn't his fault, so hurt he wished he were a slug. It made sense why he kept people at a distance, maybe even why the thought of being the Chosen One when no one had ever chosen him might be appealing. I was wrong about him. He didn't fight for people because he thought they'd reciprocate his effort. He fought for people because no one had ever fought for him. My heart constricted slowly, like a neglected old machine whirring to life, dust flying and rusty cogs groaning.

Bryce, the guy who'd fretted about me getting grass cuts, who'd faced a dragon for me, who'd lost the person he loved most, he deserved someone to fight for him too.

Gasps from the crowd rose above the crashing waves. Navy-blue light rolled like smoke off Bryce's shoulders. His head snapped up, and when his eyes met mine, they shone even bluer than normal. Magic.

I'd let him win the Chosen One competition, and while he was at it, he'd also won me. The proof of my feelings shone before my very eyes. Like it or not, I cared about two things: nothing, and him.

Woman down.

I was a goner.

The light billowed, roiling to the ground like a cloak made of storm clouds. Bryce lifted his hands, color curling off his fingertips. He was too beautiful to look at, and even while my heart burst with affection, some darker part of me squirmed with envy. Bryce with his red hair and his tortured backstory and his throbbing magic. And yes, maybe I'd let him win, but destiny was destiny, and yet again events fell in just the right sequence that resulted in me taking my place in the shadows.

He was light, as bright as the glow of a Thanksgiving dining room, and I was the darkness watching from outside the window. He surpassed everyone's expectations, and all I did was let people down. He was a Chosen One, and I'd . . . accidentally unleashed a dragon and raised an undead army.

I was like . . . the anti–Chosen One.

No. It couldn't be.

. . . Could it?

Slowly, a sticky, uncomfortable feeling spread through me. It reminded me of the same sort of feeling I got trying to chase success, then failing. The same sort of feeling I got when Will dumped me. The not-good-enough feeling.

The kind of feeling I tried to ignore when I failed to tick all those boxes on a first date. The feeling that told a truth I couldn't run from: there was still some part of me deep down, a little girl who wanted to be liked. A little girl who thought, if she tried hard enough, maybe someone would think she was special. A frustrated little girl who hid her face in her pillow and cried at night because it seemed so easy for everyone else.

It was quite the villain origin story.

My mind raced, putting together the pieces.

As soon as I got here, people started getting kidnapped. Granted, that wasn't my fault, but Amy said the presence of an Evil One brought with it other great evils, that bad things happening were a sign the Evil One was near. Perhaps my very presence was a catalyst that awoke evil in everyone's hearts and began spreading crime and chaos throughout the city. Maybe the kidnappings were just a manifestation of the darkness I'd brought into the world . . . as the Evil One.

I licked my dry lips and took a tentative step toward Bryce. "Bryce." I swallowed hard. "I need to tell you something."

I'd always been pretty sure I wasn't a hero. It hadn't bothered me too much until now, until learning I was the villain. Now I felt a particular brand of ick, the same sort of feeling you get when a guest steps into your home, and all the things you used to be content with suddenly feel shabbier. Inadequate.

As a child, I believed I was a hero. Even later, when I knew better, I at least thought I was a peasant. I never would have thought I was my worst nightmare: the villain.

I'd inadvertently put on a new cape. The villain cape. I'd done the thing I was so convinced I was avoiding: I'd lost myself. Again. I'd failed. I'd failed like I'd never failed before, and everyone would suffer for it.

"Bryce," I whispered, gazing into the eyes of the man I was predestined to destroy, "I'm the Evil One."

Bryce's lips parted, and his head shook infinitesimally. Of course he was in denial. He was too pure not to think the best of me.

Someone screamed.

And then another scream, and another.

Except they weren't screaming at my proclamation. They hadn't even heard it. Instead, they were leaping to their feet and pointing down the beach.

I pushed past Bryce and ran up the amphitheater steps, stomach plummeting. As Bryce caught up, the magic around him dissipated in the wind.

The shadowy silhouettes of the skeletal army we had accidentally summoned emerged from the fog. They were probably drawn to me somehow, and they'd shown up because they assumed I'd want to start planning world domination.

Fuck. I needed to figure out how to control my own army, and quickly.

"Back to the castle!" the king yelled, hiking his robes and charging away, heels kicking up sand in the faces of the peasants who followed.

I turned to retreat, only to find Amy standing behind us, looking at us with watery, expectant eyes. "It's time," he said, like we were supposed to understand what he was talking about. "You're ready."

"We need to run, Amy," I said. "The king told us to retreat, so not running away from the murderous skeletons would not only be stupid, it'd basically be treason."

Amy shook his head and smiled a toothless smile. "This is the true trial. The Evil One is on the rise. It's up to you."

"Can we count on your sword?" I asked, trying to imitate the inspiring speeches from my books, reaching past Bryce to squeeze Amy's knobby shoulder.

"This isn't my fight," Amy said mysteriously, backing away. "I must leave this place. But remember . . ." He spread his hands in front of his face. "The strength of a maple leaf."

And then he ran away in a flurry of flappy robes and flailing appendages, all frailty apparently healed.

Bryce and I stood alone on the beach as the dry clack of bone on bone grew louder, signaling the army's approach. He lifted his hands, now empty of magic. "I need you to go back to thinking nice thoughts about me, or we are going to die."

I did want to think nice thoughts about him. It was *all* I wanted to do. But I didn't trust myself not to hurt him. I was a *villain*, and he was . . . he was my world. Villains did nothing but destroy worlds. As much as I tried, I couldn't free my feelings.

Bones clattered. Rusty blades glinted. Sightless eye sockets and toothy smiles provided a backdrop to Bryce's face like the most deeply upsetting school picture background ever.

Desperate to reawaken his magic, I drew Bryce's hands out of his pockets to entwine our fingers, but he held something in his hand. Turning his wrist, I opened his fingers. There in his palm was a smooth, oblong pebble. I looked from the stone to his face.

He'd kept a rock I'd given him. Ridiculous man. It made my heart ache.

To awaken his magic again, all I had to do was tell him how much I truly, truly liked him, and how I was so fucking grateful he was not a slug because he was the best man I knew, and I would make sure he never hurt again—but something held me back.

Because I knew I'd inevitably *be* the one to hurt him again.

Someone like me would have to be a complete asshole to entertain the idea of being with someone like him. He had abandonment issues, and my literal one goal in life was to have no commitments. I couldn't let him know I cared for him, only to break his heart one day—not after what he'd told me about his mother.

Before I could decide what to do, one skeleton detached from the mob and jogged toward us, gangly bones swinging and clanking. We were out of time.

"Move. Go, go, go." Frantically, I pushed Bryce, trying to get him to run.

Instead, he tripped and went down. I stumbled over him and fell hard. My foot got caught under his leg. I yanked on it, twisting around to see behind me. The skeleton slowed as it came up to us. Sunlight streamed through its rib cage, half of which was exposed by deteriorating rags that might have once been a magnificent gown. A tarnished tiara rested crookedly on the skeleton's brow. The skeleton queen.

"I'm your leader, remember?" I tried, raising my hands, palms out, in the universal sign for surrender.

The universal sign for surrender must have only been universal in our universe, because the last thing I saw was the blunt end of a battle-ax swinging for my head.

CHAPTER 29

In Which We Dance Around Our Feelings

BRYCE

I squinted an eye open.

Amy's face snapped into focus, inches from my own. Too tired to even flinch away, I simply cursed under my breath and shut my eye again.

"My lord," Amy said, his foul breath washing over my face, "you and Lady Courtney defeated the undead horde!"

Reopening my eyes, I pushed myself upright, forcing Amy to take a step back. "We did what?" All I could remember was Courtney spouting some nonsense about how she was the Evil One and trying and failing to control the army, and then—

"Indeed," Amy said. "When you didn't return, we sent out a search party, which found you and Courtney, injured, but the army was gone!"

"Courtney." Panic squeezed around my heart. I shot out of the bed I was in, turning in circles, searching for her. I must've been in the infirmary; rows of cots separated by white sheets stretched along the walls. I began running from bed to bed, pushing aside curtains as I searched.

The last image seared into my brain was of a skeleton

smashing a battle-ax against Courtney's temple . . . and then I'd passed out. Not because the skeleton came for me next, but just because I passed out. Not that anyone would ever have to know that.

"Lady Courtney woke long before you and is preparing for the ball," Amy called.

I stalked up to him. "Is she okay? Take me to her."

Amy blinked. "She's quite all right. She regaled us with the tale of how the two of you single-handedly destroyed the army by using your magic to banish them back to their graves."

What was going on?

Her voice echoed in my head. *I'm the Evil One.* A little stab of betrayal slipped between my ribs, but I tried to shake off the sensation. We had to trust each other if we had any hope of getting out alive. Courtney was not evil incarnate, despite her twisted love for pineapple pizza.

There was no way she'd been able to command the skeletons back to their graves. I needed to find her and figure out what really happened.

✧ ✧ ✧

When I changed into fresh clothes and made my way downstairs, the ball was in full swing. Apparently, everyone had decided to go ahead with the day's festivities, confident we'd taken care of the skeletons. Bell-shaped skirts swept across floors of glistening cream marble. Candlelight gleamed off white, gold-gilded walls. A string quartet performed on a balcony overhead. Clinking champagne glasses mingled with flirty giggles and buzzing conversation. A feeling of victory and celebration hummed through the entire room.

People patted me on the back or bowed, expressing their thanks. Although their admiration was misplaced, it felt so nice to *not be sucking* at something that I swiped two glasses of champagne off a passing tray—one for me, the other also for me. I downed them both and set the empty glasses aside, just as everyone hushed and turned as one toward the curved grand staircase. I followed their gazes, lifting my eyes as Courtney appeared at the top. The room tilted a bit, the champagne announcing its presence as a soft buzzing in the back of my skull.

Courtney wore an indigo-blue dress that matched her hair, which was piled on top of her head. Tendrils hung down to brush her bare shoulders in a vexing way that made my fingers itch to push them back. The slow speed at which she descended the stairs was also irksome. Lately, everything she did touched a deeper nerve than normal, like she was somehow antagonizing me on a subconscious level.

Courtney looked down at everyone, wearing her signature mask of boredom. I didn't understand why she pretended not to care when she cared so much.

My head swam, thoughts growing fuzzy and pleasant, the alcohol loosening my control. My mind wandered, free to imagine all sorts of dangerous things, like: Who was to say she wasn't pretending to not care about me like she pretended to not care about everything else?

Maybe it was the alcohol that made her so intoxicating. Maybe it was how intoxicating she was that made me feel drunk. I didn't understand her. She wanted nothing and fought for it like it was everything.

Her presence pulled me in. Almost unconsciously, I drifted across the ballroom. We met at the base of the staircase. Courtney extended her black-gloved hand for me to take. A large purple bruise spread across her face, next to her eye. My arms ached to pull her to me, to hold on and never let go. I wanted to find somewhere I could stow her away, safe from harm, the same way I'd been stowing away my heart for years.

I didn't think she'd take kindly to any of that, though. I shouldn't fool myself into thinking Courtney's and my relationship extended past a brief union over a mutual goal, even if the story of my past briefly inspired her sympathy enough to awaken my magic.

I choked down everything I wanted to say and focused on the matter at hand. "What happened with the skeletons?"

Her big brown eyes swept up to meet my gaze. "When I woke up, they were gone, so I lied and told everyone we used our hero powers to order them to go back to the sacred field and return to their graves. Which I *will* do with my *Evil One* powers just as soon as I figure out how to command the undead."

"You're not the Evil One," I said, even though, a few days ago, I would have heartily agreed that she was The Worst.

"I am," she said, a bit too breezily, shrugging like she didn't care one way or another. "It's good news, actually. All we have to do is stop the kidnappings, then I'll go find the army and tell them to go away, and then do the same for the dragon. We'll do a few good deeds around the city so the world is in a better state than when we came, then leave before my presence can inspire anyone else to do evil."

A tray passed by, and I snagged two more flutes of champagne. While I drank one, Courtney plucked the other from my hand and downed it in one swallow.

"If you're the Evil One," I asked, "why did the skeleton whack you over the head with a battle-ax?"

"Maybe she didn't recognize me as her overlord until after she knocked me out, but then she realized her mistake and didn't murder me."

"But I was there, and everyone's decided I'm the Chosen One," I pointed out. The champagne began to hit me hard, and between that and whatever witchcraft Courtney's dress was working on her cleavage, it was becoming hard to focus. "So why didn't she kill me?"

"Maybe she didn't want to step on my toes and ruin a big villain monologue I might have planned for you later by killing you before I got a chance to really drag out the ordeal? I don't know."

Courtney squinted over her empty glass. "People are looking at us weird. We should dance so we don't look suspicious. We're supposed to be celebrating our victory."

"It wasn't a victory," I pointed out.

"You did have magic for two seconds," she said.

A laugh burst from my chest, surprising me as much as her. "I had magic for two seconds!"

"Come on." She tilted her head toward the dance floor. "Or would you rather keep standing there looking like a loser?"

"You're right. I shouldn't be seen with you. I should go."

Rolling her eyes, Courtney took my hand and dragged me to the middle of the room.

I liked that she didn't treat me differently after learning of my past. She didn't let me wallow, didn't coddle me, didn't pity me with fake niceties like so many others.

She'd been battered and bruised. Put down and discouraged. And yet she still found time to mercilessly tease me out of being scared. She'd been doing anything she could think of to get us out of this, even if her methods had landed us in more trouble than where we'd started. All I'd done was give her headaches and half an orgasm. I didn't think she'd go for the other half, but maybe I could give her something else.

She'd told me she'd wanted to be a Chosen One when she was a little girl. I could give her back a small part of her dream. That herald had said something about a special sword . . .

I'd find it later and give it to her. Even if she was the Evil One in everyone else's eyes, she deserved to know at least one person would choose her.

CHAPTER 30

IN WHICH A WIZARD TRIES TO CANCEL US

COURTNEY

I couldn't focus on saving the world, not with Bryce standing before me looking like this. I should tease him about his frilly shirt, tall boots, and gold-stitched black coat and pants—but those pants were tight in all the right places, and if I opened my mouth, I worried I might up and say so.

I blamed the head injury.

The song that had been playing ended as we reached the middle of the dance floor. In the silence, the words hanging unsaid between us roared.

As the music started up again, I shifted forward. My knuckles brushed Bryce's palm, and his fingers closed around mine, quickly, before they could slip away. Before *we* could slip away. His skin burned through the thin fabric of my silk gloves. His eyes dropped to our conjoined hands, and he visibly swallowed.

Other dancers scooted to the edges of the room to accommodate us, smiling for once instead of glaring. I was too preoccupied to be annoyed with their superficial approval. Too preoccupied to even care about my aching ankle and head. Bryce curved one hand over my hip, the other tightening around my fingers.

As he took the first step toward me, my breath caught. For a moment, I was frozen, then my foot fell away from his, barely managing to land on beat. Again and again, he advanced, and I retreated. All it would take was one of us to stop. We would either crash together or fly apart. Instead, we kept up the dance.

Ever since Bryce's story about his past, I understood him. He wasn't uptight. He was careful, and no one had been careful around me in a while—the girl with the lip ring and the bad attitude.

"We should be saving the world, not dancing," I said, letting my steps grow tighter. Our bodies moved with the music, closer with every measure, every spin.

"We can save the world tomorrow," he said. Procrastination looked sexy as hell on him. "It's not like we can go monster hunting in the dark." His hips pressed against mine, his breath hot down the side of my neck as his temple brushed my hair. Even when he spun me, he was never far, hand skimming my waist, shoulders relaxed, anchoring me to him. "Besides, you have a head injury." Bryce brushed a knuckle over the tender skin covering my temple.

"You can't just ask the world to stop ending because I have a headache."

"If you had a paper cut, I would let the world burn until you recovered."

I wanted to tell him to be so for real, that he was just an accountant and couldn't stop the world from burning even if he wanted to. But scorching heat rushed through my veins, pooling in my lower belly. I should *not* be pleased that Bryce was willing to sacrifice an entire world for me, but I wasn't a hero, and my impure soul liked impure things.

I thought I'd gained control of my puppy-dog heart, but a faint blue halo of light glimmered to life over Bryce's skin. Luckily, he didn't seem to notice, his gaze never leaving me. My pulse pounded to the rhythm of the music like my common sense was trying to beat its way out of my skull.

The music faded and my heart crescendoed. Anticipation mixed with apprehension rushed to my fingertips.

As the last note drifted away, Bryce stepped closer. Twined his fingers with mine. Dipped his head until our mouths hovered an inch apart.

Would one little slipup really hurt? What happened in the bonkers-lighting-department-pocket-universe stayed in the bonkers-lighting-department-pocket-universe, as the saying went.

Yes, it would hurt.

"I need a drink," I blurted, and then I ran.

Champagne dulled the pain in my ankle and softened the throbbing in my head, but I still stumbled, my feet feeling bigger and heavier than normal thanks to the alcohol. My thoughts spun, trying to catch up with my body, but mostly drowning in bubbles.

There was only one advisable thing left to do after catching undesirable feelings: self-medicate. I swiped a glass off a passing tray and downed it, teeth clinking against crystal in my haste.

"Hello there." The visiting princess, Clementine, sidled up to me. "Have you made any progress with the kidnappings?"

"The king was a dead end," I said distractedly.

"I heard you went into the city the other day," Clementine went on. "Our last Chosen One loved spending time with the people too. Some might say too much time."

I looked at her sharply. "By 'some,' do you mean Amy?"

"No, I heard he was quite supportive of Edna's fraternization," Clementine said cryptically. "I only mean that, if some of the good citizens *didn't* enjoy Edna's company, they couldn't exactly say such a thing about a Chosen One, could they?"

I focused my full attention on her. "What are you trying to say?"

She sighed wearily. "So many things." Then a plate of hors d'oeuvres caught her eye, and she drifted away.

I couldn't decide if she was trying to tell me there was something suspicious about Edna Johnson, or if Clementine was just tipsy and spreading gossip. Her last lead hadn't exactly been eye-opening either.

Besides, I knew who the Evil One was, and it wasn't a long-dead Chosen One.

Feeling a prickle on my neck, I looked over my shoulder and found Bryce watching me from the other edge of the room. Did he think I couldn't see him there? Eyes half-lidded, head lolled back against the wall.

My heart gave a painful twang. He'd stuck by me this whole time, and now I knew enough about him to know he would *never* be the one to leave. He might have tried to push *me* away, but he couldn't even leave me when I was his enemy.

I needed to let him go. I'd tell him to turn me in, which would effectively rid the world of the Evil One. Maybe without their leader, the dragons and the skeletons would leave, and the kidnappings would stop, and Bryce could go home.

Across the room, Bryce pushed off the wall, giving me one last long, lingering look before disappearing into a doorway. The skin between my shoulder blades prickled. His smoldering look had *come hither* written all over it.

The alcohol was not doing its job. I was not getting over him. It shouldn't have been this hard to *not* fall for Bryce.

Finishing my second drink, I passed my champagne glass off to some dude wearing a crown and strode after Bryce.

I expected Bryce to let me catch up so he could grab my hand and pull me into the nearest room, but I barely kept up with him. The hall was dark. I skimmed a hand along the wall to keep my footing. My vision wavered like I was trying to look through a pool of the very champagne currently making my thoughts spin.

He kept glancing over his shoulder and peeking into rooms like he was looking for something and didn't want to be caught. Suspicion spiked in my gut. I fell back a bit so he wouldn't see me.

At last, he stopped in front of a guarded door. A murmured

word to each of the soldiers had them nodding and leaving their posts—the power of being the Chosen One, I supposed.

When they were gone, Bryce opened a door and, looking pleased, stepped inside the room, pulling the door shut quietly behind him. The suspicion faded. He wasn't up to anything, just finding us a secluded spot.

When I reached the door, I paused and readied myself for what needed to be said. He'd probably protest, but I couldn't back down. It was a sacrifice that had to be made. Setting my face into a mask of solemn serenity, I pushed open the door.

My look of solemn serenity slipped.

My jaw dropped.

"What're you doing?" I slurred.

The room was some kind of treasury—weapons, armor, and jewels locked in glass cases. One of those cases was open, its red velvet insides bare. Before it stood Bryce, and in his hand was a fancy-ass sword.

Bryce looked from the fancy-ass sword to me. "This," he slurred back, "this isn't what it looks like."

My heart pounded, skin hot, alcohol-muddled brain firing on all cylinders. He hadn't led me here for a romantic romp. He'd sneaked here to claim the Chosen One's sword. But why? Had he thought of the same thing I had—that he could embrace his title, betray me, and go home?

"It looks like you're holding the Chosen One's sword." My cheeks felt fiery, whether from the champagne or the confusing mix of hurt and resignation curdling in my gut. It was one thing for me to tell him to turn on me. It was something else for him to have come to the decision on his own.

Shutting the door behind me, I made my way forward, setting my shoulders and hiding my heartache. In the end, I guessed it didn't matter if it was my idea or his. It was time for me to accept my fate.

"I can explain." Bryce backed down an aisle flanked by tall

shelves full of glittering jewels. Massive arched windows took up the end of the aisle behind him, displaying an endless view of stars and city.

"No, you're right." I reached for him. "It's better this way. I won't hold it against you."

His face went ashen. *"What?"*

We neared the end of the aisle now where the shelves butted against the wall, leaving no escape. "I get it. It makes the most sense." I couldn't think straight. Tears blurred my vision. It would be enough to know he would be out of danger, even though nothing with him felt like enough anymore. "Why should we both have to stay when it's my fault we're stuck?"

Bryce gave me a weird look, lifting the sword between us, eyes hazy and unfocused. "I didn't steal this for me." He gave the blade a little shake and took a step forward right as fireworks exploded outside the window behind him. A resonating *boom* rattled the panes as blue sparks erupted into crackling fountains, bathing the room in flickering light.

Bryce staggered. Tripped over his own feet. Grabbed on to the shelf behind him for support. Time slowed for two breathless heartbeats as the shelf wobbled, rocked on edge, teetered—then plunged forward, slamming into Bryce. He crashed into me. My back smacked against the opposite shelf. More fireworks thundered, vibrating in my chest. I squeezed my eyes shut, waiting for the shelf behind me to fall like a domino, squishing Bryce and me between them like marshmallows in a s'more.

It didn't fall, though. It groaned, shuddered, but held steady, pressed hard against my spine. The heavy weight of Bryce and the shelf rested against my ribs.

I cracked an eye open. A steel blade glinted under my chin.

I felt my entire face morph into an expression of shock as every inch of my skin tried and failed to shrink away from the sword millimeters from my neck. I blinked back tears, even though I knew this was for the best.

He, just like Will, had seen the truth about me; all the effort he'd found appealing was a facade. Realizing I was not worth caring about, he'd gotten over his infatuation. He hadn't stuck by my side to be supportive. Since finding out I was the villain, he'd been biding his time, getting close, waiting for the perfect moment to strike.

"There's no need to hold me at knifepoint," I said bitterly, the alcohol in my veins igniting over the way he was treating me after everything we'd been through, as though I really were evil. "I would have given myself over willingly, you know. I would have done *anything* for you, and you—"

"Stop moving." Bryce's wide eyes glinted inches from mine, sparks reflecting off his irises.

"Or what?" I spat.

"You'll get yourself hurt."

Fireworks crackled.

"Is that a threat? You couldn't. You *wouldn't*." My mouth twisted, and I lifted my chin. Orange light bounced around the room. When I next spoke, my voice was grave. "Do it, then."

"Would you *shut up*?" Bryce bellowed.

Startled by his unusual display of assertion, I did, indeed, shut up.

"Look at the damn sword." He jerked his chin down. "It's not even pointed at you."

I carefully looked at the sword. To be fair, it wasn't pointed at me, the sharp edges aimed up and down.

"Now look at the million-pound shelf currently wedging me against you."

And okay, the shelf was hard to miss, tipped over the top of us, Bryce's back the only thing keeping it from crushing me. The elbow of Bryce's sword arm was braced against the shelf by my shoulder, which meant the blade, by default, extended across my neck.

Bryce grunted as he struggled to hold said heavy-looking shelf. "On three, help me push." His expression was hard and unreadable. "One. Two. Three."

Gingerly, I reached around him, avoiding the sword, and pushed the shelf. For a moment, nothing happened, but then I dug in my heels, and Bryce chanted a deranged string of curses under his breath, and it gave, swinging upright, where it almost seemed like it would stay before it decided not to. It plummeted backward, smashing to the floor in a mess of flying jewels, splintered wood, and shattering glass.

When the last pearl rolled across the floor and the last shelf creaked and settled to a new resting place against the marble, Bryce turned to me, jaw set. He threw the sword to the side. It knocked over an important-looking display case holding a very large crown, which promptly joined the rest of the priceless artifacts littering the floor. It was a good thing the fireworks concealed all the clanging and crashing, otherwise, someone might barge in to see what the commotion was about.

"You think I followed you into a weird magical world, almost had sex with you, and SAVED YOU FROM AN UNDEAD SKELETON, only to decide to *kill you*?"

I pressed my lips together and nodded. "When you say it like that, it does sound like there are some logical steps missing."

"*Some* logical steps missing?" he repeated, a vein throbbing at his temple. "If logic were a Fitbit-wearing suburban mom competing with a bunch of other Fitbit-wearing suburban moms to see who could collect the most steps in a day, she would *fucking lose* because she would *have no steps*."

"None? That's a bit harsh. I don't think you should shame logic like that. Exercise can be a very triggering topic—"

Bryce crossed the floor, jewels crunching under his boots. Strobing light from the fireworks show bounced off his body. Reaching me, he grabbed my chin, firm and gentle all at once, blazing eyes boring into mine. "I'd never hurt you. I stole the sword to give to you because being a hero used to be your dream."

I was way too drunk for this. "Okay," I squeaked. "That's... neat."

"I was trying to be nice," Bryce said, gentler.

There he went again, poking at my heart with a stick—or in this case, a sword. "You really should betray me," I said meekly. "It makes sense."

"I will never abandon you, you donut. Also"—his eyes flicked down—"your no-kissing rule is annoying."

He released my chin.

Before I knew what was happening, I followed after his retreating hand. Slotted my feet between his. Wove my fingers in his shirt. In the back of my foggy mind, I wondered what on earth I was doing. At the forefront, I heard only Bryce saying not kissing me was annoying, and that felt like the least annoying thing he'd ever said.

"If you don't like the rule," I said, "then break it."

A challenge, a challenge that scared me far more than when I'd told him to "do it" a few minutes ago when he held a blade to my skin. I lifted my chin, pulse points in my neck pounding.

Without hesitation, he grabbed my waist, cupped my jaw in his hand, and pressed his lips to mine.

My stomach dropped to my toes. His lips caressed mine, once, twice, and all my thoughts fluttered away. The world was topsy-turvy, wibbly-wobbly, completely perfect, and utterly frightening.

I didn't expect him to kiss me like he did, hard and slow all at once, like he could go on just kissing me forever. His hand found the back of my neck, pulling me closer, angling my head and coaxing my lips apart. The ring in my lip clicked lightly against his teeth. Sweet champagne lingered on his mouth, and I pulled his bottom lip between mine, gliding my tongue across to taste it. He shuddered and sighed—a ragged sound of sweet, blissful torture. My heart twisted in anguished relief. All my pain and worries melted away.

This was all that mattered for now. In this moment, I did not care about anything else, and it was wondrous. I did not care, did not care, did not care. There was only the scent of him, the tender glide of his lips, and the gentle press of his tongue.

I never would have suspected my gloomy neighbor kissed like he belonged on the front of a romance novel. I never would have imagined someone so prickly had such impossibly soft lips. I never would have thought a man who hated happiness was adorably sensitive, vulnerable, and sweet in his own broken kind of way. It made my heart ache, knowing all this time, he'd been just as lonely as me.

"There you two are."

Bryce and I peeled apart. I nearly fell, the floor tilting up with my sudden movement, my head still sloshing with champagne. Amy, the biggest cockblock ever, stood in the doorway. Outside there was darkness, the room now eerily quiet.

"What do you want?" I snapped.

"I am saddened to report the undead are not dead as you supposed," Amy said, and my stomach lurched. "That is to say, the re-animated have not been rendered re-un-animated." His frown deepened. "That is to say, you did not kill the dead—oh, heavens. The undead are still alive. You did not defeat them as you thought."

"We didn't?" I repeated, trying to act surprised. "Are you sure they're not dead—re-un-animated—fuck—*defeated*?"

Nodding, Amy stepped farther inside. "I am afraid so. They must have simply run away of their own accord, not because of your magic, and certainly not back to their graves. It seems their attack was not in earnest, but rather a diversion."

"A diversion." I gulped.

"In all the chaos, the king's hand has gone missing," said Amy.

Bryce squinted. "Oh, damn, the skeletons chopped it off? We'd better find it quick if we have any hope of reattaching it."

Amy gave Bryce an odd look. "The hand of the king, Marty."

"Does the king name all his appendages?" Bryce asked with interest.

"The king's right-hand man, Bryce," I hissed with forced patience.

If the skeletons were a diversion for the kidnapping, then that meant the skeletons were working with the kidnapper. How was that possible? We *knew* who had resurrected the army, and it certainly wasn't the kidnapper. Maybe the kidnapper had found the army and somehow coerced them into working for them? My thoughts were too muffled from champagne to make sense.

"This is obviously all the work of the Evil One," said Amy. "They took General Thimblepop, and now the hand. We should gather the council and discuss matters, perhaps over a nice bottle of mulberry ale. It seems the Evil One is targeting those in command."

"Except for Winston." I pointed out the perplexing exception to the kidnapper's pattern.

"Indeed," said Amy, but his voice faded as he finally took in the scene around him. The shattered display cases, splintered wood, dented gold, and scattered jewels.

"It was like this when we got here," Bryce said unconvincingly, nudging a fist-sized diamond under a rug with his toe.

Amy shook his head sadly. "The two of you may very well be the worst heroes in the history of all Chosen Ones."

A touch of guilt nagged at my stomach, the same sort of guilt you get when you refuse to participate in an interactive magic show you never wanted to go to in the first place. Like you're somehow a bad person for letting a total stranger down, and it's your fault a grown man's magic career is crumbling.

"It was his fault." I pointed a finger at Bryce, only to find him already pointing a finger at me.

Amy's eyes narrowed shrewdly as he looked between us. "Perhaps you two aren't even the heroes we supposed you to be," he said slowly.

"Of course we are," I blurted. This was bad. Now that I'd had Bryce's lips on mine, I wasn't exactly ready to turn myself in. I wanted to get home safe *with* him.

Bryce stepped forward, wobbling a little. "Relaaaaax, Amy." He spread his palms, expression mellow, dulled by alcohol. "We're definitely legit. Courtney is my not-evil sidekick, and I'm the Chosen One. I can prove it. For one thing, I won the tournament. For another . . ." Gingerly, he plucked the sword off the ground, letting it dangle between his thumb and pointer finger. "I have the sacred sword . . . sssssSusan?"

Amy shook his head. "Its name is—"

"We call her Susan," Bryce said, sticking to his guns.

"Sue, for short." I linked my hands behind my back, nodding wisely.

Bryce spun on me, stumbling over his own feet. "*Sue?* Come on, Courtney."

"Like *Susan* is better?" I hissed back. "Why is this the hill you chose to die on?"

"Shh, he'll hear us," Bryce said, very loudly.

"*Susan* is a bad name for a sword, and you know it." I rolled my eyes. "Ooh, feel the wrath of Susan. A blade with a name that will strike fear into the hearts of all who hear it. Strike me down with Susan, and together we will rule the galaxy. Even Karen would be a more infamous name, if not fearsome."

Amy's eyes bounced between us like he was watching a Ping-Pong match. He paused, as if waiting to see if we were finished, before continuing, "Ever since you two arrived, the people have been uneasy, and chaos has taken over the land." Amy wagged a finger. "Very suspicious. I will assemble the council and sort this matter out once and for all."

I sobered up real quick. If Amy was onto us and everyone

figured out I was an imposter, they might lock me up and have me hung—hanged—hung? Which was something I definitely hadn't considered when I'd thought turning myself in was a good idea.

"Hold up," Bryce said. "Let's talk this out like adults."

"Yeah, Amy, grow up." I primly brushed invisible lint off my dress.

"We have an animal sidekick, so there's nothing to worry about," Bryce said. "We're definitely the heroes."

Amy looked between us. "A talking animal approached you? In the prophecy . . ." His face went white, and he backed toward the door. "I thought it was a hedgehog, but perhaps I mistranslated. I must discuss this matter with the king. I fear things are not as they seem."

Before his fumbling fingers could turn the knob, a tiny brown blur dashed under the door, darting between Bryce's feet—Greg, the animal sidekick in question.

Greg ran, gait off-kilter, as he lugged a jar of peanut butter on his shoulder. The blood drained from Amy's face as he looked at the rodent by his toes.

"I knew he stole my peanut butter!" I said.

Amy tried to stomp on Greg—a real dick move—gangly limbs flying.

Undeterred, Greg heaved the lid off the peanut butter and shoved his fist inside. "All disputes can be solved over peanut butter," he said confidently. "It's how my kin settle matters."

"I don't think—" I began, but Greg was already scrambling up Amy's robes. Amy flapped his arms, trying to shake him free, but Greg clung to the fabric. He wriggled onto Amy's shoulder.

"Get off me," Amy yelled. "Cursed beast! Evil foe!"

Greg shoved his peanut butter–coated fist into Amy's mouth. Bryce and I both cringed.

Amy sputtered, smacking at the peanut butter. Slowly, the agitation bled from his face.

"See?" Greg hopped to the floor, brushing off his hands and slinging goo everywhere.

Amy coughed several times, working his tongue along the roof of his mouth. He tried to say something, but only a gasp escaped his lips. His face grew red.

"What's going on?" Blood pounded dully in my ears. My vision was too fuzzy, too unsteady. I drilled the mouse with a glare. "What did you do?"

Amy clutched at his throat. Hives broke across his skin. He fell to his knees.

"Oh, shit," Bryce said, which was the understatement of the century.

Our mentor, it seemed, had a peanut allergy.

Greg wrung his soggy paws. "I only wished to help by giving him a tasty morsel as a peace offering, my lady."

Panic seized hold of my limbs. "You call shoving your fist into someone's mouth an *offering*?"

"I was trying to save you," Greg said.

Bryce ran a shaking hand through his hair. "What do we do? We don't have an EpiPen. We can't call nine-one-one. Should we . . . should we boil water?"

"Why would we boil water?" I bellowed.

"I don't know! That's, like, a medieval cure-all, right?" He sank to the floor, scrubbing at his eyes like he could wash away the sight before him.

Amy's breaths grew ragged and loud. Crawling over to him, Bryce propped him up against a display case and began fanning his face.

"What if we can't save him?" Bryce's breaths became as concerning as Amy's, but where Amy couldn't get enough oxygen, Bryce gasped in far too much. "He'll die because of us. And then we'll go to prison. I won't do well in prison, Courtney. I need Germ-X. I've been known to *moisturize*. What if they torture us?

I've read about those medieval stretching machines. I take back ever wishing I was taller."

"I was only trying to save you, my lady." Greg gave me one last pitiful look, his eyes welling with tears, then he scampered into the nearest hole in a wall. This was the problem with animal sidekicks. They caused more problems than they were worth.

I took a deep, shuddering breath. I couldn't reasonably blame a mouse for thinking peanut butter would solve the world's problems. Besides, there were other things to worry about. Exhibit A, Bryce on the verge of an anxiety attack. Exhibit B, Amy on the verge of dying.

Squatting, I placed my hands around Bryce's upper arms and looked him in the eye. "Focus. I know you're the Chosen One, but stop making the mentor's tragic death all about you."

Strangely, that steadied Bryce. He nodded, swiping at his nose with the back of his hand. "We have to make it look like an accident."

"Oh my *god*, Bryce. We have to save him. Stop freaking out." I paced. "We need to find a doctor. Someone discreet."

Amy let out a phlegmy snort.

"Shh, Amy," I said distractedly. "We're trying to think." I snapped my fingers. "I've got it. Remember Leech Dude? I gave him a golden chair the other day. That's how I got him to tend to you. I'm sure he'd help Amy without telling anyone about our involvement."

"Amy will tell everyone about our involvement," Bryce said, practically sobbing.

"No, he won't," I said darkly. "Will you, Amy?"

Amy quickly shook his head *no*.

I jerked my chin at Bryce. "Pack up and follow me." The high-stress environment was familiar. Not wanted, but familiar. And I knew how to function in high-stress situations, even if I hated being stressed.

Bryce threw the gasping Amy over his shoulder and followed as I sneaked into the hallway. The physician lived deep in the city. We'd have to take the back way out of the castle so as not to be stopped. The problem was, I barely knew the front way.

Several wrong turns and near-misses with servants later, we emerged into the courtyard. It was a good thing Amy looked like he weighed as much as a large cat; otherwise Bryce never would've managed.

"We need a horse," I said. "We'll never make it on foot."

"And what," Bryce asked, panting as he readjusted Amy on his shoulder, "we stash Amy in a bush while we ask the groom for horses?"

I could ask Bryce to wait outside with Amy, but I didn't think he was in any condition to help the old man if things got worse. If I asked Bryce to go in alone to get the horses, he'd probably panic-confess our entire accidental murder situation to the first person he saw.

"We'll *Weekend at Bernie's* it," I said with a lot more confidence than a plan that involved the phrase *Weekend at Bernie's* deserved.

"Oh yeah, that'll be much less suspicious. Great thinking, Court. We'll just '*Weekend at Bernie's*' our medieval wizard mentor around the city."

"He's not dead yet," I pointed out. "It's like . . . *Weekday at Bernie's*. Far lower stakes. Here, set him on the ground between us, and we'll prop him up together."

Shaking his head, Bryce did as I asked. I threw Amy's arm over my shoulder and wrapped my hand around his back for support. Bryce did the same on the other side.

Amy's breath rattled moistly in my ear. "Perfect," I said. "This is fine. Everything is fine."

"You being supportive makes me feel like everything is *not* fine."

Together, we crossed the courtyard, Amy's feet dragging between us. He was fading fast. When we entered the stable, a groom stopped sweeping and gave us a strange look.

"We need horses," I said. "Chosen One business."

"Is Amygronkphopoulozeetrop quite all right?" the guy asked, ducking his head to try to see Amy's drooping face.

My hand that was around Amy pressed into Bryce's side. Bryce was shaking, nervous tremors quivering through his muscles every few seconds.

"He's fine," I said firmly, trying to send a telepathic message to Bryce: You're *fine*.

"Are you certain?" asked the groom.

With a nudge of my shoulder, I sent Amy's head swinging and talked in a gravelly old person's voice like a ventriloquist. "Quite all right, youngster. In fact, I could compare my strength to that of an oak leaf, the origin of which can be found ten thousand years ago, when a swamp nymph flew over a field and accidentally dropped an acorn—"

"All right." The groom waved a hand. "I'll fetch horses."

CHAPTER 31

IN WHICH A KISS DOES NOT SAVE THE WORLD

BRYCE

My heart pounded so hard it hurt. I couldn't breathe. Maybe I was dying too.

Dying. Oh god, oh god, oh god.

One minute, I was being kissed like it was my last day on Earth. Now, it actually felt like it might be my last day on Earth.

I'd never been kissed like that in my entire life, with pure, raw *want*. And now this, the instant reminder that no matter how good something was in the moment, it was sure to come crashing down.

Courtney's knuckles jabbed against my side. The warm light of the stables stung my eyes. Then I was pushed onto a horse. The cold darkness of the city streets hugged me, suffocated me. Streetlamps flashed by.

My thoughts were sharp, staccato, firing off to the rhythm of my horse's hoofbeats.

This was why it was better to never chase happiness. It felt so much worse when everything fell apart. Courtney wouldn't leave me, and I couldn't leave her, and she'd made me progressively more and more happy until—until this.

Clomp, clomp, clomp, went the horse's hooves. Amy was still breathing, though shallowly, and I focused on that to avoid spiraling more.

With a jolt, I realized we'd stopped, and Courtney was standing at my knee, looking up with wide eyes. "Help Amy off the horse. Something's wrong."

Together, we helped Amy down. He didn't look good: eyes bulging, skin going blue around the mouth. We hadn't made it far at all. There was no way we'd get to the doctor in time.

Garbled choking noises issued from Amy's throat. He gestured wildly, trying to tell us something.

"I think he's trying to talk," I said.

Supporting Amy, we dragged him to an abandoned alley and propped him against a building.

"Is there something we can do to save you?" Courtney asked, going to her knees in front of him. Her hair was falling free from her updo, and her dress was dirty and wrinkled. Dark smudges rested under her eyes. She looked like the human embodiment of stress.

Amy opened his mouth, but only a croak came out. Croaking in every sense of the word. He pointed at me, then opened and closed his fingers rapidly like he was miming small explosions before pointing at himself.

I started to laugh, a high-pitched, hysterical laugh that was almost a sob. I couldn't help it. The whole situation was too ludicrous. Here we were playing a high-stakes game of charades with our mentor, who we'd had a hand in poisoning.

"How many words?" I heard Courtney ask. "Five. Okay. Ten. Fifteen? Amy, no, I'm not sure you understand the concept of this game. Brevity is key."

I sank to the wall opposite Amy and clutched my hands, still half laughing, half crying. Emotionally and physically, I was spent. Hopeless.

"Person, place, thing, book?" Courtney asked.

I peeked through my fingers.

"Oh my god, Amy," Courtney said. "Just write it in the dirt."

I blinked. "That's not how charades works, Courtney."

Courtney gave me a look of disbelief. Right. We weren't actually playing charades.

Amy bent to the side, gnarled, shaking finger tracing wobbly letters in the dirt.

He wrote:

Magic has healing properties. Bryce has awakened his, and, with focus, he could coax the poison from my body.

"How, though?" I asked hopelessly, feeling as lost as the time someone told a waiter it was my birthday, and everyone stared at me as though I were instinctually supposed to know how to act correctly when faced with ice cream I didn't want and the racket of a public domain birthday song.

Amy started writing in the dirt:

The first man to discover magic was my ancestor Urphomptemtust a million billion years ago . . .

Courtney turned her back on Amy as he proceeded to write his memoir in the dirt. "Come on, Bryce. Heal him. You can figure it out."

Behind her, Amy wobbled, then slid farther down the wall, eyes drifting shut.

I pointed, wheezing, my dismay too extensive for words.

Courtney looked over her shoulder. "Oh my god. He died." Her voice was blank and uncomprehending.

My chest tightened. "No. He can't be gone." I crossed the alley, scrambling to my hands and knees, sweeping Amy's bony wrist into my hands. His pulse fluttered weakly against my fingertips. "He's still alive," I said, latching on to that one hope.

Courtney's hand found mine, her slender fingers weaving into my cold, stiff ones, and my focus steadied. "You can do this. Use your Care Bear love magic and heal him."

I laid my hands on Amy, reaching inside for that tiny glow I felt earlier that day. But I couldn't find a single glimmer. Pressure built in my head as Amy grew weaker. My hands shook. "I don't think I can," I said.

Releasing my hand, Courtney rocked back on her heels, creating space between us. "Are you serious?" Before I could react, Courtney scooped up a handful of pebbles and started lobbing them at my boots. "You. Have. To. Try. Harder." Lob, lob, lob. "They're going to throw us into the streets and stone us for killing Amy. Which, actually, you'd probably like, considering your pebble fetish. Your body won't know if it should die or be aroused."

I deflected the tiny rocks. "Joke's on you; not knowing if I'm dying or aroused has been my body's resting state since coming here!"

"All your body does is rest."

"That's rich coming from you!"

"At least I'm not obsessed with rocks."

"Don't hate on geology!"

Amy made some concerning snuffling noises.

Courtney flung her hands, letting the pebbles fall through her fingers. "Move." She elbowed me out of the way. "Think some nice thoughts about me to turn on my magic, and I'll heal him."

My mind was blank. I'd been so intent on feeling nothing but hate for Courtney for so long, I couldn't manage anything else. The dark, swirling memories clenching my chest wouldn't *allow* me to manage anything else. Me, at nine years old, so happy one second, so devastated the next. Courtney and me kissing, so happy one second . . . so devastated the next.

I stood to shake out my cramped legs. "What if, as soon as I stop hating you, something else bad happens?"

A raindrop splattered across her forehead, and she swiped it off her brow, movements jerky. "You're giving yourself too much credit if you honestly think your *feelings* can alter the course of the universe."

"We are in a fairy-tale world. Who says they can't?"

"If we were in a fairy tale, positive feelings would save the day, not ruin it," she said, voice rising. "If we were in a fairy tale, all we'd have to do is kiss again, and everything would be fine."

Something in my chest constricted, all my fears reaffirmed. "Instead, everything fell apart after we kissed," I whispered. More rain fell, spattering in cold drops across my skin. I struggled to allow myself to feel the things she needed to awaken her magic. With each new piece of evidence suggesting she and I were a doomed idea, new walls formed around my heart.

She licked her lips. "Bryce—"

"Courtney," I sighed wearily. "If you want me to infuse you with some love juice—"

"Don't call it that."

"—you're going to have to give me something new to work with. You used to work in marketing, right? Pitch yourself until I can't help but like you."

CHAPTER 32

IN WHICH A MANIC PIXIE DREAM GIRL WANTS NOTHING

COURTNEY

Try, try, try. The never-ending mantra echoed through my head like a short but petrifying two-second clip of a horror movie commercial. My inner voice shook her fist, saying, *See? One kiss and he already needs more from you.* And not *more* in a fun sexual way. *More* as in more *effort.*

Still, Amy's life was on the line, so I had to let it slide for now.

"I don't have a tragic tale of love and loss," I began. "It's not that deep."

"Then make something up."

I couldn't. Not when he didn't. I had to hope the truth was enough. Had to hope *I* was enough even though I hadn't been enough for anyone in six months.

I rubbed my forehead. The rain fell harder, splattering dirt onto my dress. "When you're a kid, you play house and pretend to be an adult. No one tells you that, when you grow up, we're all still pretending, and we've gotten tired of the game. Last Thanksgiving, I had a career and a boyfriend, who had a ring and plans to pop the question after the pumpkin pie."

I took a deep breath and quickly told Bryce how I used to want to be special, how exhausting it was, how I thought it was the only way for people to admire me. I told him how my fear was proven the day I lost my job, decided I was better off without it, and Will broke up with me. Bryce leaned against the wall on the other side of the alley, full attention on me.

Absently, I pet Amy's arm, partly to urge him to stay alive, partly because I didn't know what to do with my hands. "After I made my choice, no one asked if I was okay or tried to understand. They went into fix-it mode. I was the happiest I'd ever been, and they wanted to fix it because it wasn't good enough for *them*. My boyfriend went from wanting to propose to me one day to dumping me the next. My grandmother practically disowned me. Even strangers write me off." My eyes stung, my throat growing tight and achy. "I'd been wearing masks, pretending to be someone I wasn't so people would love me." I lifted my eyes to Bryce's. "When you showed up, I discovered how much more honest it is to hate people than it is to love them. I never wanted to stop hating you because I couldn't lose you. So that's me. Nobody's hero. Everyone's villain."

One by one, the muscles in Bryce's face softened. In my chest, a tiny, warm something fluttered. It was unfamiliar and nostalgic all at once. A feeling of contentment and quiet joy and acceptance. It felt like that evening, baking in the village, surrounded by love and comfort.

My breath caught with surprise as a faint glow rose from my hand. I pressed my palm to Amy's chest, hoping it would be enough to help him hang on. He was barely breathing now. A few moments went by. His breathing didn't worsen, but it also didn't improve.

"More," said Bryce, crouching on the other side of Amy. "Tell me more."

The rain had picked up and I looked at the water pooling

around my knees where they pressed into the mud. "That's it. There's nothing more to tell."

"You told me about a thing that happened to you," said Bryce. "That's not *you*. I know you." A smile flirted with the corners of his mouth. "You forget to wash your feet nine out of ten times. You don't own a bed frame. For some reason, you think Ross Geller is a good romantic partner."

"Ross was persistent," I said defensively. My face felt strange, strained and tight in unfamiliar places. Keeping one hand on Amy, I reached up and touched my face. I hit teeth. I was smiling. And for once, I was not wearing a cape. Not the cape that made me more, and not the cape that made me less.

"You don't believe in unconditional love," Bryce finished softly, gazing into my soul in a way that said he was not disgusted by what he found there, and for the first time, I began to doubt my doubts about unconditional love.

We sat there, the ground growing into slippery mush from the rain, Amy barely breathing between us. None of us moved, Bryce and I because we were rolling over everything in our heads, and Amy because he was preoccupied with not dying.

"Courtney . . ." Bryce swallowed hard. "Tell me who you are, the pieces I don't know."

The light glimmering off my fingers was feeble at best. "What if who I am isn't lovable?" I asked meekly, because I truly didn't know.

That was the half of me I was too scared to explore. Too scared the truth would crush me the way it did when I learned superheroes didn't exist, or when I decided true love wasn't real. I didn't want to bring those soft, vulnerable parts of myself to light. When the whole world continued to prove itself to be darker than I supposed, why not blend into the darkness so the monsters passed me by?

"*Court.*" Bryce said my name in a voice so tender and broken, it felt like a tragedy. "You remember people's birthdays, even if you only acknowledge them with unsigned cards. If you forget to wash your feet in the shower, it's because you only shower for five minutes to save water." He held up his hand. "I hear your timer through my wall every night, so don't try to deny it. You've been protecting my front door from spiders for months. You hide your kindness, only displaying it when you think no one's watching, but I've been watching. Even if I tried not to."

Unexpected tears pricked at my vision.

"Now, your turn," he said.

I rubbed my eyes. I couldn't do this. Couldn't.

"One tiny thing," Bryce urged.

"I almost stepped on a worm last week," I mumbled, "but I moved him off the sidewalk." Inside me, something flickered, encouraging more words. "I volunteer at an animal shelter on my days off." Sensing Bryce's fond, half smile directed my way, I squirmed. "It's not, like, A Thing. I'm only there to hang out with dogs because our landlord won't let us have pets."

"Sure, sure," he said, that smile not budging.

I sighed. "Okay. I'm the world's best puppy pusher. Everyone at the shelter says they've never seen anyone able to find as many puppies homes as I have." I thought for a second. "When people with hazel eyes claim their eye color changes depending on their mood, I refrain from telling them it's just lighting."

"That's big of you."

"I'm also hilarious. My jokes are way funnier than yours."

"Whoa, whoa." Bryce held up his hands, fully grinning now. "Let's not get cocky."

"I think you're so attractive—ridiculously attractive," I blurted out. It was as though Bryce had rifled through an old chest in my soul where I kept every positive thought, every nice attribute, every compliment, and now that he'd started taking things out, more kept tumbling forth, never to fit back inside correctly again. "You're funny, even if you're not as funny as me, and so damn sweet I want to hide you from everyone else, like you're the best candy in a shitty communal Halloween candy bowl."

His smile widened, but that joy wouldn't last. Bryce had unleashed my nice, and it was going to hurt us both more than our "hate" ever did.

Gathering his hands in mine, I leaned over Amy as though Bryce and I were making eyes at each other over a candlelit dinner instead of a thousand-year-old wizard dude. "You want more, but I want less. I want Nothing, and that's the thing, Bryce, that makes us so difficult." Releasing his hands, I twisted my fingers together, clenching them until they hurt. "I have no future, so neither can we. I'm good for nothing and bad for you. I'm irresponsible, which is why I have to be responsible enough to never tell you if I happen to adore you."

As Bryce's expression broke into one of wonder and confusion, the spark in my chest ignited, flaring into a warm glow of affection. It was schoolyard whispers tickling down necks and crisscross applesauce traced on backs. Cool breeze, tight squeeze, shiverees. It was summer night carnivals, the smell of funnel cakes and mosquito spray. It was the giddy anticipation of counting down the days to your sixth birthday. It was how you imagined touching a cloud must feel like before anyone told you the disappointing water-vapor truth.

More warmth trickled into my chest. Faster until I could hardly stand it, until my heart raced, and I could barely breathe. Until I *couldn't* stand it, and pale orange light exploded from my body so bright it forced me to squint. It streamed from my palms, a wavering mix of transparent and opaque. Without thinking, I laid my hands over Amy's bony chest, pushing all the best-parts-of-living feelings inside of him.

Amy's eyes drifted shut. A heart-wrenching beat passed where I thought he was gone.

Slowly, his breathing smoothed, air flowing unrestrained in

and out of his lungs. The light faded from my hands, and I sat back. Amy's skin was still puffy and blotchy, and his eyes remained closed, but he breathed deep and steady.

"So," said Bryce.

"So," I said. "What do we do now?"

Rain rolled off the end of Bryce's nose. "We'll get him to the doctor. He can look after him and alert us when he wakes up. After that, we'll have to somehow convince him we didn't *mean* to make all the mistakes we did."

That hadn't been what I was talking about, and I had a feeling Bryce knew it. I'd been talking about *us*. What *we* would do now.

Together, we helped Amy back on the horse. After dropping Amy off at the doctor's house, the ride back to the castle was long, wet, and miserable. And silent. So, so silent. Thoughts raced through my head—what Bryce said about being scared to love because everyone he loved left, and my own problems—how I always fell just short of being enough.

When we got back to the castle, instead of our usual ritual where we climbed into bed together, we stood in the hall between our two doors, dripping water onto the woven carpet.

"We had a moment in the rain," I said, feeling him out, needing to know where we stood after I practically threw my feelings in his face.

"Sure did."

My heart was scared to beat. "Isn't this the point in your books where the hero declares his love?"

Bryce looked down at me, a sort of pain in his eyes. His wet hair curled over his devastating sapphire eyes. "Court, darling, sweetheart, beloved, I confess I have frequent urges to prepare you romantic candlelit dinners, using all your dearest, most treasured possessions as the candles."

It was a half-hearted attempt at our old fire, but it fizzled out and died in the cold gray between us. There was no going back, and there was also no going forward.

I realized what he must have too; it was better never discussed. It was like a dream you hold close, knowing telling others would destroy the magic. As you sleep again and again, the memory slips away, growing faint and distant until you can't remember if it actually happened or not.

We turned away from each other, and a moment later, our separate doors clicked shut.

CHAPTER 33

IN WHICH WE THINK WE ARE ABOVE MISCOMMUNICATING

BRYCE

I simply did not have the testicular fortitude needed to make grand declarations.

We *did* have a moment in the rain. I *did* have feelings. This *was* the point where we should be confessing them. I liked Courtney. *Really* liked her. She finally let me in on her joke. While everyone else strove for success, she'd already won. The whole time I was hiding inside, she was living, too brave to conform.

My head was dull and fuzzy, and every beat of my heart hurt. My soul felt fractured, broken on the outside, but with tentative rivulets of hope trickling from the cracks, stinging my wounds. She didn't want me and wanted me at the same time. What was I supposed to do with that?

I could ask her to explain.

Or I could tell her how I felt.

If we would have admitted neither of us cared about being Chosen Ones from the beginning, we might've worked together and been home by now. A misunderstanding. Which led to more misunderstandings. Which led to dragons and skeletons and Amy, oh my.

I paced around the same way I had on The Infamous Day of Buzzing, when I'd listened to Courtney's beautiful moans through the wall in agony, unable to decide what to do with myself. I'd finally sat at my computer and typed and deleted three different names for my Wi-Fi network: ~~YoureKillingMe~~. ~~LetMeComeOver~~. ~~FuckMe~~. That last one had been both a curse and a request.

In the end, indecision had run out, and I'd ended up typing nothing. All the possibilities of what might have happened if I'd knocked on her door stayed locked away in fantasy.

Not this time. I'd take a page out of Courtney's book. She didn't filter herself, and neither would I.

Before I could change my mind, I raced across the hall and barged into Courtney's room. Her bed sat empty.

Cold sweat broke out across my skin. I charged into the hall, where I almost bowled over a maid.

"Don't get yourself worked up." The maid sighed. "*Honestly.* She's only in the library."

She gave me directions, and I was off, careening around corners and sliding through doorways.

I found the library and quietly went inside. Utter darkness consumed the room, save for a faint glow from the far side. The glow—candlelight—flickered through tall bookshelves, barely providing me enough light to navigate the room.

The library had that musty, ancient smell to it, a room locked away from time itself. Books overflowed the wooden shelves, dusty tomes stacked in tall haphazard piles. One of Amy's signature purple robes draped over the back of a chair. He must spend a lot of time here doing various Wizard Tasks.

I weaved among stacks of books and overstuffed chairs until I spied Courtney through a gap in a bookshelf. She sat on a wooden stool at a cluttered desk, one foot pulled under her, a cloak wrapped around her shoulders. Her messy hair stood on end, bright blue, backlit by candlelight. She hunched over a giant book, finger trailing over the page.

I started forward, stubbing my toe against a tower of books. I stifled a curse as it toppled, dust flying and pages scattering over the floor. Courtney whirled.

"Bryce?" She squinted into the darkness. "What are you doing here?"

"I need to tell you something. What are *you* doing in here?" I didn't know why I was whispering, only that it was a library, and it felt like I should.

Courtney avoided eye contact, faking casual a bit too hard, considering our last interaction. "I'm trying to find information on dragon hunting. No luck so far. I did find this weird potion book, though—"

"Who cares about that," I said, even though a dragon terrorizing the countryside was arguably a higher priority than my feelings. I strode across the room. "You know what the leading cause of death and trauma is in books? Hint, it's not what you think."

Pushing back her stool, she looked up at me. "Gee, BuzzFeed, I don't know."

"Miscommunication. It's miscommunication." I hoisted myself onto the desk and scooched her stool with my foot until she faced me. "We need to talk this through, but don't freak out. It's not like we have to act on anything."

Courtney pulled her cloak tighter around her nightgown. "Act on . . . what?"

"From now on, no more hiding things. This is about survival. We need to communicate." When she nodded, I steadied my resolve and blurted, "That starts with me saying I have a moderate-to-severe feeling. For you."

Courtney visibly recoiled. "Oh my god, Bryce. It's not rheumatoid arthritis." She made a face. "Is this supposed to seduce me?"

I caught her knee and leaned forward. "Courtney, would you listen for a second?" My voice rose to a level that was probably making every librarian alive feel a prickle in their neck. "I'm trying to wax poetic, and you're being such a dick about it."

She threw up her hands. "I already know what you're going to say. I know you think you like me, but you don't. You really don't. You only like me because you're impressed with how hard I've been working."

"If I were attracted to people who worked hard, do you think I'd be attracted to *you*?" I scrubbed a hand down my face, regaining control of my soaring emotions. "You know what?" I said, softer. "I'm scared of pretty much everything, but you're the real coward. You're so afraid of people finding you unlovable that you've made yourself unlovable. You won't even try."

"I am unlovable, Bryce. I am what I am, and no one can tolerate it."

"You are what you are, but you act like you're not. Hate to break it to you, but you're still wearing a mask, Courtney, a mask for yourself."

"Wow, very deep. Thanks, Dr. Phil."

"Shut up. You are. You pretend not to care about anything, but you steal chairs for people and make daisy chains for little girls and save dying old guys, and you help me view myself and the whole damn world less seriously, and I can tolerate that, Courtney. I'll tolerate the shit out of you."

Scrambling off her stool, Courtney gripped my shoulders and gave me a little shake. "You want to communicate? Fine. You've built a fantasy of me in your mind, and one day, I'll let you down. A handful of redeeming qualities doesn't make me unique or special. I don't have some deeper insight into the world. I'm just a girl who's *tired*." Her eyes shone, refracting glimpses of something shattered within her. "You know why this can't work? You have abandonment issues, and I have commitment problems. Don't you see? My favorite thing to do is quit things, and I can't make promises to someone who deserves promises of forever."

My heart fluttered in my throat. She cared, and that was the issue. She cared too much.

For the first time in my life, a feeling of wild recklessness seized me. "Maybe we could learn," I whispered. "Maybe we're capable of more than we think. Maybe you're the type of girl who can keep a promise, and maybe I'm the type of guy who can learn to play tag in the dark."

I bent to the side and, with one quick puff of air, extinguished the candle.

"Bryce?" Her voice came softly through the shadows.

Reaching out, I pressed my palm to her cheek. "Tag. You're it." *Your move.*

I hopped off the desk and darted away. It was nearly pitch black, a soft touch of gray on the horizon outside the window providing the only light. Vague outlines of objects kept me from becoming a complete bull in a china shop. Even so, I slammed right into two more stacks of books, sending them thundering to the floor.

Courtney's surprised laughter rang out behind me, free of irony, full of genuine happiness. My pulse raced, a few of my old fears trying to creep back in with every murky shadow I passed. I skimmed my fingers over a shelf, guiding my way. Her footsteps padded behind me, closer, closer, closer. My breath quickened. Every cell in my body strained, screaming to shut this down because whatever happened next was sure to kill me with happiness. I wanted to run.

I came to a stop.

Courtney slammed into my back, flinging her arms around my waist to keep from falling. "Tag." She gasped for breath. "Take off your shirt."

My fear morphed into a rush of exhilaration. Maybe she was right. Activities were more exciting in the dark. "You sure you want to start that game?"

"Take it off." Then she was gone, footsteps receding into the shadows, rows of books muffling their noise.

I started after her, fingers working my shirt buttons loose. I shrugged it off, thin material fluttering to the ground. My other senses expanded in the darkness. "Cooouuurtney?" I drew out her name. "Where are you?"

A flutter of paper to my left. I pivoted, stalking the sound. *THUD.* A book hit the ground to my right. I spun. She played dirty. I'd play dirtier. Feeling around, I found a bookshelf and leaned against it. Closed my eyes. Focused.

I pictured Courtney, waking up early to hang Christmas lights in her yard. Pictured her saying rude things to scare me out of being scared. Pictured her hands in my shirt and her lips against mine.

"Bryce, that's cheating!" came her yell.

"Gotcha." A triumphant smile spread across my face, and I opened my eyes. A blinding orange light shone a few aisles away.

I took my sweet time. There was no point in her running.

She obviously hadn't figured that out, because she still tried, an orange blur streaking among the books. No longer feeling patient, though, I ran after her, cornering her quickly in a dead-end aisle.

She turned, arms crossed, pale orange magic floating around her skin like a beacon.

I strode up to her and poked her in the forehead. "Take off your nightgown."

"That's not how strip games work." Courtney scowled. "You have to work up to it." She yanked the cloak off her shoulders and tossed it at my head. Trying to catch me off guard, she lunged forward, but I jumped back and took off.

About ten seconds later, a telltale tingling warmth trickled down my neck, and I drew up short. It was the intensity of someone's full attention mixed with the soft feeling of drifting off to sleep on the couch in the middle of the day.

Blue light swirled from my skin in wisps. She had me. I glanced over my shoulder. A blur of orange grew brighter.

I was off, Courtney right behind me. Blue and orange flashed among the bookshelves. Laughter and giddy breathlessness wrapped up in anticipation. The sun outside finally burst over the horizon. Sunbeams gleamed through cloudy windows, swirling with lazy dust mites. For a moment, we were cocooned in our own little world of joy and safety.

My lungs ached and my pulse raced by the time she caught me back by the desk, slamming into my chest so hard I nearly fell over. I kicked off my socks and tagged her before she could run.

She wiggled out of her own socks and tagged me right back.

We panted, standing frozen in a sunbeam. Golden light cast long shadows across her face. Her smile faded. So did mine.

"Courtney," I said, voice hushed, "it's been one interruption after another. If we're going to do this, we should do it. Now. Before we get eaten by a dragon or speared by a skeleton or some new horror finds us." I pulled a condom from my pocket. "I didn't want to presume, but, well, after last time, I figured it was better to be prepared—"

A gleam ignited in her eyes, and she crashed into me, smooth palms skimming down my bare torso, my skin quivering at her touch. I stumbled back and would have fallen if I hadn't backed into the desk.

"Fuck," I cursed, reaching back to grip the edge of the wood.

"That's the idea," she whispered, breath hot against my lips.

My hands grasped her hips, yanking her hard against me, and I brought my lips down on hers. Tongues and teeth and lips mingled, overwhelming me in sensation. I splayed my fingers over her jaw and neck, thumb brushing hair from her eyes. Her lips were soft as they ravaged mine, the sweetest oxymoron I could imagine.

She flicked her tongue into my mouth, and I chased after her when she pulled away, cradled her neck, and drew her back. The table dug into the backs of my legs as she ground against me, breaths soft and shallow.

Pushing off the table, I turned us, pinning her against the space I just occupied. Toeing her feet apart, I stepped between her legs, hoisting her onto the desk, her butt crushing many an ancient tome.

Reaching behind her, I shoved everything I could reach off the desk. Books, jars, and other library junk crashed to the floor, plumes of dust swirling into the rays of light surrounding us. Every librarian alive probably just woke up in a cold sweat.

Our lips met again. I slid my hands up her nightgown. Her thighs were so soft, I let out an almost pathetic groan. She shivered, shifting closer, smiling against my mouth. With frantic fingers, we helped each other free of our clothing.

"We could be in one of your books," she whispered. "Library sex seems like a thing people with pebbly nipples do. This must be like a dream come true for you." She pressed her lips tight, eyes dancing.

I grinned. "It would be something like, *His tongue worshiped her heaving bosoms, suckling one pebbled peak after the other. Her silky flesh writhed and undulated against his steely,* incredibly *muscled body in response to his ministrations. He knelt before her sweet love canal—*"

"It's not a fjord, Bryce." Courtney dissolved into giggles.

"Shh, respect my craft." I raised my voice over her snorts. *"You could say the noble, and impressively well-endowed duke, knew a thing or two about fording fjords, and as a result, was skilled in the art of . . . fjordplay."*

Courtney covered her ears. "La, la, la, stop it! I'm not listening!"

I smiled, letting my gaze drift over her. "Good. I'm done talking."

CHAPTER 34

IN WHICH I SPEAK AT LENGTH ABOUT THE UNSPEAKABLE THINGS WE DID IN A LIBRARY

COURTNEY

Holding my gaze, Bryce dropped to his knees before me.

My vision swirled. His hands coaxed my legs apart, mouth trailing kisses up my thighs. When he nipped the side of my knee, I yelped, swatting the back of his head.

He laughed, his hot breath against my inner thighs, tickling sensitive skin. I gasped at his touch, my hand winding in his hair. My world narrowed until all I could focus on was the swirl of his tongue, the feel of his lips, the gentle pressure of his teeth. He gave before I asked, coaxing me higher and higher. My hips rocked, and he let me follow each sensation. When I fell, I didn't think of the fragile pieces of my soul. I thought only of him catching me.

Standing, Bryce pushed his hand lightly against my chest, guiding me to lie flat on the desk. He crawled up after me, pulling my legs around him as he went, kissing me long and slow, his mouth soft and warm from my skin, his eyes feverish. He whispered steamy nonsense into my ear, and goose bumps tickled along my neck. With each murmured assurance about how good

I was, how perfect, how right, I let myself go, losing myself in his fantasy, letting myself believe him.

A pleasant shiver went through each of my nerves, a warm feeling of absolute happiness radiating behind my ribs. Orange light tinged my eyelids, and I opened them to find the magical glow around my skin brighter than ever. Ribbons of it swirled from my body and coiled around Bryce, twining and mingling with his own blue light.

I hooked an ankle around Bryce's hip, pulling him closer. He searched blindly for the condom, hand sweeping across the desk, sending ancient texts fluttering through the air. And then he found it, and he was whispering into my ear, asking me if I was sure, and I was pulling him tighter and nodding because I, the girl who wanted Nothing, also wanted *him*.

Bryce touched his forehead to mine and held my gaze through that first breathless, pleasure-filled moment. He moved slowly at first, and I arched back, relishing the sensations.

"You're so pretty," he whispered, breath ragged against my neck, and I burst out laughing.

"You talk so much shit," I gasped, "and now all you can say is 'You're so pretty'?" It was ridiculous and somehow ridiculously sexy.

He rocked into me. "If you keep laughing and wiggling around like that, this is going to last about five more seconds."

That only made more giggles bubble up. He was the most precious human I'd ever encountered, and it made me . . . furious and confused and blissfully happy. That he, of all people, could make me feel like this. I felt free. Free of all expectations. Free to be myself.

Bryce paused, propping his hands beside my head, drawing back to look down at me, a dry *Really?* expression on his face that made me laugh harder.

Looking at him made it worse, so I closed my eyes and tried to breathe deeply.

Bryce peeled my hands away from my face, pinning them on the desk. He shook his head, mouth cracking into a smile. Then he laughed, and when he laughed, it made me wonder why we spent so much time not laughing. It was stupid, him inside me, and us laughing over nothing, but that only made it funnier.

The tendrils of blue energy swirled off his skin like early-morning fog over still water. It tickled over my skin like butterfly kisses. Our laughter faded as the magic wisps melted into the golden light around us, vaporizing and mingling with streams of sunlight, opaque with dust.

As he began to move again, he smirked at me, but it was a nice smirk. "You *like* me." The words were slow and teasing.

"You like *me*." I sighed back dramatically.

He laughed and swung me up, sliding me to the edge of the desk and hooking my hands around his neck. "You can't take any part of me seriously, can you?"

"Do you have a problem with how I'm taking you?"

"God, no," he managed weakly.

Orange magic shone from my skin, sheer streaks of it cascading to the floor like a waterfall, pooling to hover over the ground. I grasped Bryce's shoulders, meeting his movements, our breaths quickening and smiles fading. Subtle moans, light whimpers, and half words created our own language in our own world where only we existed.

He brushed hair off my sticky neck, winding it tightly around his fist at the base of my skull. My muscles tightened and tingled. He kissed me once, a gentle, barely-there caress, focused eyes never leaving mine as his breaths grew broken. His nose brushed my cheek, hand slipping between us, pressing where I wanted him. When I gasped and clung tighter, the corners of his mouth twitched, his smile ghosting over my lips.

As my legs clenched around him, he whispered my name into my ear like a curse—something widely considered foul that he liked having in his mouth. It sent a shiver down my spine, triggering my release. Wave after wave soared through me, making me feel lighter than air. It was like the adrenaline-filled satisfaction of getting the last word in during an argument or the heady exhilaration of ditching work. He followed shortly after, breath hitching into a soft sound that nearly undid me all over again.

✧ ✧ ✧

After, we lay on the desk, Bryce's arm tossed over my ribs and our legs entwined as we caught our breath. He turned to his side, gaze flitting over my face.

"You're shadows," he said softly, trailing a finger over the slope of my cheek.

"Hmm?" I let my head roll to face Bryce, the hard desk digging into my spine.

"You have to have shadows to have light. That's you."

"Gross," I whispered, smiling. "Is this you trying to say I'm the light of your life again?"

"It's me saying you're the dark hellish abyss that makes the rest of my life look brighter in comparison."

I warmed with pleasure. Being with Bryce made me feel discovered, like I was a crusty old painting yanked down from someone's attic and appraised on *Antiques Roadshow* for eighty-five dollars. Which admittedly wasn't much, but it surpassed all expectations, so he was pleasantly surprised. The painting didn't become something too grand to hang in a home. Instead, it was something to cherish, to hold on to a little tighter because there was more to it than once supposed. I liked being the mediocre keepsake Bryce had a soft spot for. I liked that he looked at me like he thought I was worth far more than any rational person would suspect.

The lazy blue glow around him flared a little brighter. I tucked in closer to him, the overwhelming, comfortable do-not-care feeling I experienced the last time we kissed settling warmly behind my ribs. I'd be happy to stop the world and melt with him.

"What are you thinking about?" he murmured against my hair.

"If a volcano exploded right now and lava engulfed us, when archaeologists come to explore years and years from now and fill our magma body shells like they did in Pompeii, we'd create the cutest little plaster people."

"Fucking hell. What goes on in your mind?"

"Well, I was thinking about melting—"

"Shh." Rolling over me, he pressed his lips to mine, cutting off my words.

Thinking about the end of the world reminded me we had to save it, which reminded me why I'd come to the library in the first place.

Just like that, our magical little space really was engulfed by a metaphorical volcano. The do-not-care feelings trickled away, replaced by doubts and fears and hesitation. Bryce said he'd tolerate me as I was, which was all I'd ever wanted. To be tolerated. The bare minimum.

And yet.

When we were trying to save Amy, Bryce listed all the things he liked about me—and they were all my positive traits: I saved water and sent birthday cards and rescued puppies. But I was still difficult and stubborn and prickly, and I wondered if he accepted my less desirable traits, too, or if he was actually just looking past them—and if he was, how long would he be able to ignore them.

"I found a book," I said around kisses, voice muffled.

He smiled against my mouth. "In a library?" he breathed. "Inconceivable."

I elbowed him lightly in the ribs. He caught my hand, thumb rubbing slow circles around my knuckles.

"A potion book." I furrowed my brow. "I wasn't able to read it thoroughly before you arrived to seduce me, but there's one in there called a hero potion."

"Like a superstrength potion or something?" he said distractedly, trailing kisses down my neck.

"No. Like I think it would turn us into heroes. I think it would change us, make us stop being bad at everything."

He went still. I imagined he was wondering the same things I had. The consequences of a potion like that. What would be left after everything bad was removed—if there would be anything left at all.

In order to get home, I needed to be a hero. Becoming a hero would have the added bonus of removing my less lovable side. With it gone, I'd never have a reason to doubt Bryce's affection because I'd be so genuinely good and perfect inside and out that every piece of me could finally be loved fully.

The temptation of the potion called to me, promising that for once, everything could be easy.

"No," Bryce said quietly.

"What if it's the only way? The only way to get home, the only way to . . ." *To be together*, I thought but didn't say.

Just then, something caught my ear. A faint ringing. I shoved Bryce off me and sat up. "Do you hear . . . bells?" I asked.

He planted a kiss on my open palm. "If you're hearing wedding bells, we have more miscommunications to hash out."

"Hush." Stretching, I plucked my nightgown off a stack of books and slipped it on.

I ran to the nearest window and peered out. Bryce came up behind me, buttoning his pants and squinting against the sun. The city bells clanged their warning louder by the second. A sinking feeling settled in my stomach.

The dragon soared over the city, huge wings creating dull thuds that made my ears throb. Below, villagers scattered away from its shadow. The beast didn't attack, only made pass after pass over the city, forcing people to their homes.

Worse, tarnished armor flashing in the sun caught my eye. Surrounding the city was an army that stretched, a blanket of iron and bone, all the way to the tree line. The city was under siege.

Behind us, the library door creaked open. I couldn't tear my eyes from the landscape below until a voice wrenched my attention away. "You won't get away with this."

We turned to find Amy standing behind us, looking very pissed indeed.

CHAPTER 35

In Which Boy Meets Ghoul

BRYCE

Judging by his expression, Amy did not care that we'd technically saved him. Clearly, he was just remembering the part where our sidekick poisoned him and considered us co-conspirators. His ratting us out to the king would put a big wrench in our efforts to save everyone, so I decided to do what I always did: run now and deal with it later.

"We're really sorry," I said, feeling for Courtney's hand behind my back, "and so glad you're not dead. We don't have time to explain now, but we'll talk later."

Courtney grabbed the potion book, then I pulled her down the nearest aisle, Amy's cries fading behind us.

Outside the library, the castle was in chaos. Ducking our faces, we pressed ourselves against the wall, hoping the shadows would conceal us while we came up with a plan.

"What are we going to do?" I asked, gasping for breath.

"I have an idea," came a tiny voice.

We looked down. There, leaning against the wall beside us like he was part of our crew, was Greg the mouse.

"Your ideas, historically, have sucked," Courtney snapped.

"This one is harmless," Greg insisted. "Amy is in there, is he not?" He pointed a tiny finger at the closed library door. "Simply ensure he stays in there."

I hesitated. "Lock him in?"

Greg nodded.

"Amy will be fine in there," Courtney said, like she sensed my hesitation. "We can blame a classic medieval door malfunction. Those have to be common enough. Once we handle the skeletons and the dragon, maybe he'll be more willing to believe we didn't mean to nearly murder him."

"How do we lock him in?" I asked. "There's no lock on the outside."

Greg sighed. For the first time ever, his endless adoration waned, and he almost sounded fed up with us. "The two of you forget you have magic with astonishing frequency."

On the other side of the door, footsteps tapped closer. Amy was coming. Panic rose in my throat—

Courtney pushed me against the wall and kissed me. Her lips glided over mine, and—she felt nice. So nice. So freaking nice.

Maybe too nice. Too easy. Too good.

All I wanted to do was drag Courtney back up to her room so we could be alone a little longer. But she'd suggested that potion, and a gnawing feeling of doubt made me worry that, despite vowing not to miscommunicate, there was something she wasn't telling me.

My mind started to spin like those cheap carnival rides everyone despises.

No. I refused to ride the damn ride—the overthinking ride that would end in nothing but feeling like garbage.

I wrapped my arms around her back, drawing her into me. Heat exploded in my veins. Her fingers closed over mine. As she guided my hand, I groaned against her mouth, imagining all the places she might lead it.

My imagination was pretty good, but I had to admit, I did

not expect her to guide my hand to a doorknob. Which was what she did.

"Wha . . . ?" I opened my eyes to find blue magic pouring off me. The visual evidence of how much Courtney cared settled my racing thoughts. I would not ruin this for myself.

The doorknob heated under my palm, and it finally registered why Courtney had kissed me. I focused, directing the magic down my arm, forcing even more of it out into the door. The metal burned. I held on until I couldn't, hand flying off the doorknob.

Courtney and I stepped back. The doorknob glowed red, smoke rising around the door. It jiggled, like Amy on the other side was trying to open it, but it held.

"You there," I said, stopping a servant who was passing by. "Watch this door. Find us if Amy comes out."

"Hurry, this way," Greg urged, and we ran after him. "I have something else to show you. To correct the mistake I made."

"Which one?" Courtney grumbled under her breath. "First you advise me to tame a dragon, then you nearly murder our mentor."

We went down several flights of stairs and many long halls, avoiding the frantic castle inhabitants, who ran in a great hurry to nowhere in particular. The walls turned to stone, and the air grew chillier the farther down we went. At last, Greg gestured for us to follow before squeezing under a door.

Squeezing under a door. Something about that prickled at my memory.

I tried to open the door to follow, but the wood was swollen and stuck to its frame. I gave it a good shove with my shoulder, and it popped free. Stumbling inside, I barely had time to look around before I was backpedaling, nearly bowling over Courtney.

There, standing in the middle of the gloomy room, was a figure in purple robes. Their hood was up, concealing their face.

"Amy?" Courtney asked. "How'd you get out?"

The figure flipped back its hood, revealing a pale skull and ghastly grin. A strangled curse tumbled from my mouth.

Courtney gasped. "Did we somehow accidentally melt Amy's face off?"

"Why does your mind always go to *melting*?" I asked. "You think we accidentally melted a guy instead of assuming it's one of the undead we accidentally raised because the dragon we accidentally freed made me accidentally—okay, I see how you got there."

The skeleton cocked its head.

Greg let out a long-suffering sigh. "She's one of the undead—their queen."

Courtney set her jaw. "You! You hit me with a battle-ax! I have a *bone* to pick with you."

That was Courtney, the joke at a funeral, and despite the situation, I snickered. "Nice."

Greg gave us a withering look. "We can use her as a stand-in for the old man. If you keep her hood up, nobody will know the difference. It will buy us time. If people notice his absence, they'll start asking questions."

A seed of doubt took root in my brain. For the first time, I began to wonder if the mouse was the undyingly loyal animal sidekick I first pegged him as. I took in the room. Shelves lined the perimeter, countless glass jars containing a sludgy green liquid packed across every surface. A large black cauldron steamed in a corner. And the skeleton standing in the middle, for some reason, was *not* murdering us all.

"Wait a minute." I took a step forward, then thought better of it and took two steps back. "You want Courtney and me to let one of the evil skeletons follow us around all day? One of the evil skeletons whose pals are outside right now *laying siege to the city*?"

"She's quite harmless," said Greg. "She longs for a new, less violent life, and so agreed to help."

"The queen of the skeletons happens to do whatever you say?" Courtney's eyes narrowed.

I caught on to what she was thinking, finally putting two and two together. The skeletons wouldn't even listen to Courtney, and she'd assumed she was the villain, their overlord. But they listened to a mouse?

"She's agreed to help on the condition you'll take her back through the portal with you," Greg said. "She wants to go to medical school."

The skeleton wanted to go to *med school*? When it came down to it, I didn't know what was a more absurd idea: signing a skeleton up for med school or having any hope of her paying off her student loans. Not to mention housing and—

"Why should we trust anything you say?" Courtney asked, bringing me back to the present before I could spiral into the logistics of becoming the primary guardian of a century-old undead skeleton. She turned to me. "Last time we saw Greg, he tried to kill Peepaw."

I squinted. "Did you just refer to our wizard mentor as *Peepaw*? Never mind—not important. Greg definitely poisoned Amy. He probably planned to do it from the moment he stole your peanut butter and was just waiting for an opportunity to make it look like an accident." My mind raced as pieces started clicking together. "Wait a second. Greg stole *all* of your groceries except for the pizza rolls, which he gave us to eat at the burial ground with instructions to make sure I cooked them well, probably *hoping* I'd drop them in the fire."

Courtney's eyes widened. "And then, when you didn't drop them, the dragon made sure you did—the dragon *Greg* told me about. He said it was part of the prophecy that the Chosen One can tame dragons. I bet that was never in the prophecy at all, and he made it up so we'd free it."

I gasped. "He probably only gave us back our condoms to keep us distracted so we wouldn't piece it all together."

Suddenly, a muffled yell sounded from somewhere deeper in the room. Courtney and I exchanged a glance, then dashed toward the sound. Greg yelled at us to wait, but we ignored him. We found another door behind a shelf, and Courtney threw it open.

Two people occupied the tiny space, which might have been a closet at one point but now resembled a prison cell. There was a tall woman wearing armor, leaning threateningly over a middle-aged man who was tied up in a chair.

"Is that General Thimblepop?" Courtney exclaimed. "She's working *for* you? Who's this other guy? Let me guess. The king's hand, Marty?"

"Yes, but listen," Greg began, and I whirled to face him.

"Does this mean General Thimblepop was never actually kidnapped?" I asked.

"Or maybe Greg kidnapped her and somehow turned her into his evil minion," said Courtney. "And now he's trying to do the same to Marty." She glared at Greg. "I bet you even ordered your skeleton to knock us out so we wouldn't be around to stop you from taking Marty. What about Winston? Did he escape before you could turn him to the dark side?"

As Greg watched our exchange, his entire countenance transformed. Where before he stood hunched, often with twitching whiskers and wringing hands, now he straightened. Crossed his arms. Hardened his face. Behind him, the skeleton mimicked his posture.

"You were the one who summoned us and created the portal," Courtney said, smiling radiantly. "I'm not the villain!" She lowered an accusatory finger of doom at the mouse. "We unknowingly worked as your minions the entire time. That means *you're*—"

"The Wicked One," I said grimly.

"Evil One," Courtney corrected under her breath.

"The Evil One," I said grimly.

Greg let out a long-suffering sigh. "No, you bozos. You have it completely backward."

"Seize him," I yelled but didn't move. There was, after all, a skeleton standing in our path.

Courtney and I exchanged a look.

She sighed. "Fine."

Courtney charged, diving for the mouse, but he sidestepped. She went crashing into a shelf, glass jars tumbling and shattering around her. She staggered to her feet, green slime coating her body. "He's getting away!"

Greg darted for a tiny hole in a wall. Fighting the fear clenching my stomach, I ran forward. A bony arm intercepted me, clotheslining me in a way that gave me flashbacks to Red Rover on the middle school playground. I hit the ground flat on my back, the air knocked from my lungs. My vision darkened as I struggled to draw in a breath. The shadowy form of the skeleton appeared over me. Her bony hands reached for my neck.

A blur to my right.

Courtney.

She swung the giant potion book like a baseball bat. *WHACK.* The skeleton went flying. Courtney bent, grabbed my arms, and hauled me up.

"Wait!" shouted General Thimblepop, but we ignored her.

We ran.

We were always running.

CHAPTER 36

IN WHICH WE TAKE PSYCHEDELICS AND GO ON A HERO'S JOURNEY

COURTNEY

We raced through the castle, running to Bryce's room like scared children. It seemed we spent a lot of time running from skeletons in closets, whether figuratively or literally.

Glancing out the window, I confirmed the undead army still hadn't attacked. In fact, they were completely motionless, staring sightlessly at the city. The dragon was nowhere to be seen either. Maybe they were waiting for commands from their minuscule overlord.

So many things made sense now: We sucked at being heroes because the Evil One, Greg, was orchestrating our every move. Greg was even the one who'd sneaked under the dungeon's key room door to steal the keys and kidnap Winston. Yet I still wasn't sure why a mouse wanted to take over the world. A severe case of little man syndrome? And I also wasn't sure why he'd kidnapped *Winston* of all people. Maybe because he thought Winston's predisposition toward chicken violence made him more likely to join his cause, but he ended up escaping instead? Or maybe he was just an easy target at the time, and it didn't really matter.

I looked at the potion book in my hand. It should have eased my mind to know I wasn't the real bad guy in this story. Yet it almost felt like another failure, like I wasn't even good enough to be bad. I was, as I always had been, a peasant—that nobody in the middle. At least Bryce was here with me. He clearly wasn't the Chosen One I thought he was either, considering we'd both been summoned by Greg to be pawns for his evil schemes.

Settling myself onto the bed beside Bryce, I laid the potion book between us. "We've been trying to save the world for days. If we took this potion, things could finally be easy." Bryce started to protest, but I cut him off. "Neither one of us is a hero, but we could be with the potion."

Bryce grasped my hands. "The mouse was steering us wrong before. We can defeat him now."

I raised my eyes to meet his gaze. "We can't know that. I know myself. I screw up everything I do. Maybe someone like me isn't good enough to save the day . . . and live happily ever after. I want to be better for you. I *need* to be better if there can be an *us* after this." I bit my lip. "That is, if you want there to be an us after this."

He shook his head, and for a moment, my heart dropped, but then he said, "Of course I want an *us*. There can be an *us* without the potion."

I pulled my hands away. Everything I ever wanted was within reach. One drink, and my life would stop feeling like an exhausting hamster wheel where I ran and ran and ran, achieving nothing, only to get spat out onto the dust.

"We have to be honest with ourselves," I said. "One day, things will get too hard, and I'll quit, or things will get too good, and you'll push me away." Ducking my head, I tried to catch his eye. "Bryce? No miscommunications, remember?"

"I'm thinking," he said, bloodshot, tortured eyes meeting mine.

I nodded grimly. "I will alert your grandmother as soon as we get home so she can document this occasion in your baby book along with all your other firsts."

A stunned moment passed before he broke into a smile. He tugged me onto his lap, and I wrapped my legs over his hips. "After we take this potion, and it turns you into a nice person, you're not going to have much left to say, are you?"

"Isn't that the point?" I settled my hands on his shoulders, serious now. "The potion will fix me. As the selfless epitome of human perfection, I won't ever leave you."

"Are you threatening me?"

Now it was my turn to smile. "And you, you'll be so brave you won't think about pushing me away because heroes don't worry about things like girls abandoning them, crushing their souls, and smashing their hearts."

"That's really comforting, Court," Bryce said brightly. "I'm touched. Like, by a taser in a hurtful way, but still touched."

"Look." I slathered a go-getter fun-loving tone into my voice that made me sound like a math teacher who unironically uses words like *hip*. "It'll also get us out of here. If we become good people, the citizens will like us, and our powers will grow stronger. We could even assemble a band of quirky misfits. The more unlikely heroes you assemble, the higher the chance of defeating Big Bads. That's Newton's fourth law of motion or something."

"Will the hero potion fix your compulsive lying—" Bryce began.

The bedroom door slammed open, revealing the servant we'd left to guard the library door. "There you are."

I sprang up. "What happened?"

"Amygronkphopoulozeetrop has left the library."

Bryce swept the book off the bed. "We need to make that potion and get the hell out of here. Now."

I nodded. Amy was probably fetching guards to throw us in prison for treason. It wouldn't take him long to realize we'd been working for the villain.

✧ ✧ ✧

I expected finding the ingredients the potion book listed would send us on the most intense scavenger hunt of our lives—a whole side quest that involved prowling through gloriously blooming castle gardens to snip blooms of wolfsbane or trudging through squelching swamps to pluck the eye of a newt—whatever a newt was.

Instead, Bryce and I found everything we needed in a kitchen cupboard, resting on a shelf that was neatly labeled: Potion Stuff.

Bryce ground herbs with a mortar and pestle while I cracked an egg into a bowl. Since the city was under siege, everyone was distracted, and there were no servants in the kitchen to ask why we were making the grossest-looking cookie dough ever. The recipe suggested mixing the concoction with your favorite ale to mask the flavor, but as we had no ale handy, we'd just have to shoot it down.

After five minutes of the least interesting potion-brewing scene of all time, all that was left was infusing the mixture with magic, which would add an extra kick of toxic positivity that would make us ooze likability and heroism.

I tried to conjure up some feelings to spark Bryce's magic, but I couldn't focus. I kept expecting Amy to barge in at any moment, or to hear the clank of bone or feel the heat of dragon fire as Greg came to destroy us.

I walked over to look at the chunky sludge inside the bowl. "God, that's disgusting."

"—said an angel, after god crafted your soul," Bryce finished without missing a beat.

It took me a second, but then I forced a smile. "Get it out while you still can."

We both went silent at that. Once we were heroes, we probably wouldn't mock each other anymore. Our whole dynamic would be different soon.

Bryce gathered my hands in his. He turned and dipped his head until we looked at each other, nose to nose. "Are you scared?" he whispered.

"Course not."

His face softened. "A wise . . . ass once told me that one day the sun will explode and consume the universe, and none of this will have mattered."

The feeling of loss only grew. It will have mattered. Mattered to me. The mattering was the whole issue. He mattered so much, I'd give up Nothing and everything for him all at once.

Winding his fists in my hair, Bryce brought his mouth down on mine. It wasn't like our other kisses, reckless and peppered with fits of uncontrollable laughter. It was heated and purposeful, overshadowed by unasked questions. *What happens after this?* It could have been an end or a beginning, and so we let it be neither. It just *was*, he and I, blocking out the world.

At last, I pulled away. I held my hand up, fading orange energy pooling in my palm. Wisps of blue light hovered over Bryce's skin as well. This man, this beautiful man who stuck by my side through everything, he should know how much I valued and admired him. He should know how much I cared. He should know that I was starting to wonder if, perhaps, I even . . .

I swallowed hard. "We should do it now, before the magic subsides."

Bryce nodded. Together, we cupped our hands around the container, willing our magic inside. As the last glow faded from our hands and began to shine up from the potion, I felt like I'd given something up I shouldn't have.

Bryce looked at me, and maybe, if we were different people, we would have said a few words, but we were us, so I said, "Bottoms up," and we each threw back a drink of the mixture.

The pulpy herbs, slick raw egg, and buttermilk hit the back of my throat, and I almost gagged, but I managed to muscle it down.

I didn't feel any different after the supersoldier serum. I didn't feel like I suddenly knew how to save the world, nor did I miraculously know how to properly wield a broadsword.

I looked at Bryce, who was grimacing and reaching for a cup

of water. I felt the same for him as before: craving his affection but scared what its cost would amount to.

Which was interesting. Because heroes shouldn't have insecurities, should they? Heroes shouldn't *still* be doubting someone who told her he liked her, even if she *did* hit snooze on her alarm seven times every morning, knowing his bedroom was on the other side of the wall, and even if she *was* bad with feelings.

"Do you . . ." I frowned. "Do you feel the same?"

"I feel like I might . . ." Bryce paused. Frowned. Tilted his head. "Be ill."

Ill was an unusually tactful word for Bryce. He had to be messing with me, pretending he'd been turned into some kind of heroic gentleman. I opened my mouth to tell him to stop faking, but what came out was "Oh dear. Can I help you in any way?"

Bryce opened his mouth. Closed it.

I wanted to know what he was trying to say, to ask if his brain was also stuck in a new, *polite* hellhole of a body. "Are you having a nice day?" was what came out of my mouth.

"Quite nice" popped out of his.

Small talk? We'd been reduced to pleasantries and *small talk*? I'd never been so sickened in my life. My mind spewed curse words. My mouth said, "What a lovely spring we're having, isn't it?"

"Quite. Nice." He clasped his hands together serenely.

How would *this* help us get home? We couldn't communicate now. My insides raged, but my body was infuriatingly calm as I walked over to the potion book and flipped through the pages. In addition to the hero potion, there were spells to make perfect peasants, blacksmiths, knights, bakers, and many more, but no antidotes for any of it.

"Is there no way to—" My jaw snapped shut, nearly biting my own tongue. I wrenched it back open. "We have to un—" *SNAP.*

I couldn't say what I wanted: *Can we undo it?* I supposed asking if there was a way to go back to being a bad person wasn't a heroic thing to do.

I read the hero potion description again: *Will turn the foulest person's actions pure.*

Actions. Not thoughts. Actions. I'd thought the potion would make me better all the way to the inside so changing would've felt like a good thing instead of a sacrifice. But my same old subpar spirit was trapped inside a prison of goodness.

I snatched the book off the counter to heft it over my head and hurl it against the nearest wall, but my muscles hardened in my arms, forcing my movements down. I gently closed the book and slid it to the side.

A scream ravaged through me but rose no higher than my chest. Angry, hot tears burned behind my eyes but weren't allowed free. I was trapped and frantic and *furious*, and all I could do was stand there, my face relaxed, save for a slight tension between my brows—the smallest, most delicate of frowns.

It felt like wearing a mask again. Like it was six months ago, and I was trapped, losing myself and wondering why people only cared when my outsides didn't match my insides.

"What now?" I asked, my voice happy and pleasant.

"We'll be heroes." Bryce's expression was unreadable.

"You're right," I said. "This is perfect." Evidently, as a hero, I could still lie, so long as my lies were agreeable. "We will take care of everything we messed up, and then we will find the mouse. We'll defeat evil and live . . ." My words petered out. I couldn't imagine how we could live *happily* like this for the rest of our lives.

CHAPTER 37

IN WHICH I GO ON A GIANT SIDE QUEST

BRYCE

We sneaked out of the castle and got to work. I knew Courtney's body was 100 percent controlled by the potion when she cracked her knuckles and asked, "What can I do to help?"

The potion made tasks that should've been relatively easy—like walking—many times more difficult. For instance, it forced us to walk with a skip to our step, which expelled way more energy than was necessary. It also made us stop every now and then to help people. In only a few blocks, I'd already loaded a supply wagon, paused to ruffle an orphan's hair, and approached a random villager to ask why they "held such sorrow in their eyes," after which I suggested they smile more.

The city was busy with soldiers setting up defenses and villagers gathering supplies, darting to and from buildings as the dragon swooped overhead. I quickened my pace as the dragon's shadow dropped across us yet again. Since Greg controlled both the dragon and the skeletons, I wasn't sure why he hadn't ordered an attack yet. Instead, the skeletons just stood there while the dragon ran surveillance overhead, keeping the inhabitants trapped inside the city.

It had been too dangerous to try to hunt down Greg in the castle when Amy could be hunting *us* down. So, for now, our goal was to assemble a team of misfits to aid us in defeating the zombies and the dragon.

In books, a band of overly capable warriors naturally gravitated toward heroes. There was usually at least one Greatest Warrior of All Time, and an elf, probably. Unfortunately, this wasn't a book, nor were we the good guys. We'd have to find them ourselves.

"Where will we find such . . . worthy companions?" Courtney's voice was robotic. Her mind, like mine, probably raged against the shell of her body.

"I can only assume they will be people we've met along the way. That's how these things usually work."

Courtney made a face like she was thinking. "Who have we met who has been capable of anything"—her face twisted, and her teeth clenched before she spewed out the rest of the sentence—"other than excellence?"

Her meaning came across loud and clear, even with the potion's interference. By this point, we should have encountered at least two to three of the best warriors in all the realm. Instead, we had Cuthbert and a family of innocent villagers we couldn't risk endangering, plus Amy, who was off the table for obvious reasons.

We'd have to settle for whoever we could find. "If we work together, I'm certain we will encounter noble persons who are strong of will, if not entirely strong of might," my mouth declared confidently.

Courtney's polished exterior made it hard to see anything past the surface, all traces of personality buffed away. I should've felt safer the nicer she was. Instead, my fear only heightened. Maybe the potion would make our relationship last forever, but I'd never know how she actually felt for me, her true emotions hidden behind a veneer of smiles and sympathy.

I'd never know if, one day, she stopped feeling for me. The exact way my mother did.

"Oy, you there," a gruff voice said, and I turned. It was the blacksmith from day one, the guy who'd tried to send me on a side quest for his daughter.

"Greetings, citizen," I said, even though my legs ached to run away.

"'Ello, sir. I heard you're looking for a crew."

Run, run, run, I begged my body, knowing exactly where this was going. "That's right." My mouth smiled brightly.

The blacksmith blinked. "If you don't have coin, mayhap we can arrange a trade. You look like a strong warrior. My daughter"—he wiped a dramatic hand across his brow—"she was taken by a band of giants not far from here, and—"

Was this guy for real? Even though we'd been in this land for—god, had it only been five days?—it still astounded me how everyone acted like people out of a video game or a fantasy movie.

"I have a proposition for you," the blacksmith said.

If I stood there much longer, I'd agree to assist him in exchange for his help—which didn't make sense; he was able-bodied, and I had the physique of a malnourished hermit. Why couldn't he help her himself?

But I physically couldn't run. Not only because of the aforementioned malnourished physique but because the potion wouldn't let me. Running away in the middle of a conversation was rude. I tried to find Courtney, but my eyes were only able to shift slightly before snapping back into place. Wandering attention during a conversation was also rude.

The blacksmith spilled his entire life's story to me, and even before he was done, my mouth was saying, "Of course I'll rescue your daughter from the band of giants."

CHAPTER 38

In Which I Assemble Subpar Sidekicks

COURTNEY

While Bryce was off negotiating with giants, I assembled a dream team—if that dream was one of those feverish ones where you had to give a presentation, and then you looked down to find you weren't wearing pants.

The problem with being nice was you couldn't tell people no, which was why my team consisted of the first four individuals who'd volunteered for the job. Even worse, I couldn't suggest they spend some time training because I couldn't hurt their feelings.

I'd gathered the group at a pub by the time Bryce returned from rescuing the blacksmith's daughter (it turned out she was just going through A Phase that involved hanging out with her giant friends). I'd recruited Cuthbert the swordmaster, and then I'd been approached by Winston, who was still bound and determined to use his life for good after narrowly escaping what we now knew to be Greg the mouse's evil clutches. He'd been desperate to help, and I quite literally could not tell him no. And I'd so wished to tell him no. Then, of course, there was also the blacksmith and his daughter, whose name was Chandelier Dew Bloodlava, but I'd taken to calling her Pants because she wore pants and would not shut up about how that made her different from other girls.

Bryce sat at the far end of the table. He looked at each person sitting around us, then at me. "What an excellent band of heroes you've gathered, Courtney." He smiled kindly. I didn't miss the elite level of sarcasm he sneaked under the hero potion.

I let my face remain in the neutral but pleasant expression that had become its natural state, completely replacing my previous resting bitch face. "Everyone, this is Bryce." I was going to leave it at that, but my mouth continued on without me. "Why don't we all go around the room and introduce ourselves?" I wanted to punch myself for suggesting the universally most hated group icebreaker activity.

"An inspired idea," Bryce said, that cheesy smile still plastered to his face.

I tried to drain my glass of ale, but my mouth only allowed small, responsible sips. I'd be enduring this hell sober.

"What kinds of skills do you all have?" Bryce asked, and though he smiled indulgently at each member of our crew like he was the father of the Brady Bunch, I imagined deep down he was on the cusp of a panic attack and wondering what was wrong with me that this was the team I'd assembled.

I tried to send him telepathic messages. *It's fine. Everything is fine.*

The smile slapped across his face didn't budge. All my usual methods of cheering him up wouldn't work anymore. There would be no more scaring the fear out of him, no more teasing him.

Winston fitted his hands together and shrugged modestly. "As far as skills, well, I don't want to brag none, but it was my rhubarb strudel that took first place in the village fall festival."

Bryce and I waited for him to say more. *Hoped* he'd say more.

Winston did not say more.

Cuthbert leaned forward. "He's being humble."

Bryce's smile widened, a silent *Thank god* screaming out of his eyeballs.

Cuthbert lowered his voice. "Blue ribbon winner *five years running*." Nodding, he sat back, brows raised with significance.

"You bake pies," Bryce stated with a bit too much cheer.

Winston puffed up. "Strudel, sire."

"*Strudel*," Bryce said exuberantly.

I turned to Cuthbert. "We know you can hold a sword. Any other skills we should know about? Maybe something niche and special that will come in handy later on?"

Cuthbert blushed. "I've been told I give excellent massages."

"Okay," I said, voice an octave higher than normal. "Cool, cool, cool. So, more handsy than handy. Amazing. Perfect. All skills have value. You're such an asset." I turned to the blacksmith's daughter. "What about you?"

"I wear trousers," she said, as though that one attribute qualified her to save the world.

I blinked. This poor misled girl. She'd someday learn that wearing any form of pants not preceded by the word *pajama* was literally the worst.

"So," Bryce said, "we have a baker, a masseuse, and a girl who wears pants." He turned to the blacksmith. With the blacksmith's big, burly frame and rough disposition, I was sure Bryce thought he was our group's saving grace. "What about you?"

The blacksmith looked surprised, running a hand through his beard. "Ah. I thought you knew. I did send you to fight for my daughter on my behalf."

"What are you talking about?" Bryce asked.

The blacksmith cracked his knuckles. "I'm a pacifist."

A long silence.

Winston leaned in eagerly. "What is our plan to obliterate the Evil One's army?" He smashed his fist on the table.

The blacksmith jumped. I did a double take when Bryce

didn't even flinch. But of course, heroes didn't do things like flinch. The thought of him enduring a silent flinch all by himself made my heart twinge. That was the problem with being perfect. No one could see you.

It took a second for me to realize everyone was waiting on me for an answer. In the corner of my eye, I noticed Pants on the other side of the table beginning to manspread (thanks to her pants), slowly taking over the bench as she glared.

"I . . ." I glanced at Bryce. He sat straight, the picture of supposed confidence, but didn't say anything. I had no idea how to go about saving the world either. "We will crush the undead scum like the vermin they are," I announced with gusto.

Amazingly, everyone nodded, grinning like that was a valid plan.

Great. Perfect.

"And how will we do that, my lady?" Cuthbert asked. His enthusiasm was insatiable.

"By using inspiration from mighty warriors in days gone by." *Fake it till you make it* had gotten me shockingly far in life, so why stop now? "You guys ever heard of Leeroy Jenkins?"

Attention glued to me, they all huddled in, except for Pants, who'd taken way more than her fair share of the bench by now. Cuthbert and Winston had to keep wiggling over to accommodate her, but their earnest expressions never wavered.

"I do believe I 'ave herd of ol' Leeroy," the blacksmith mused. "In that new ballad. 'Eard a bard sing it last week, I did."

"I sincerely doubt it," Bryce said, his unhinged smile still stapled to his face.

"No, I think he's right!" Winston said. "Weren't he the one who single-handedly fought off the trolls at—"

Pants manspread a little too far and Cuthbert toppled off the end of the bench. He amiably crossed his legs and sat on the floor as everyone else continued their conversation about Leeroy Jenkins.

"Okay, okay," I called over the increasingly impassioned discussion of a man whose one accomplishment had been shouting his own name while playing a video game and charging into a mass of enemies, resulting in the death of himself and his whole group of friends. Maybe not the best person to emulate. "The point is, if you call upon Leeroy Jenkins's name in your time of need, legend has it you will become unstoppable, and everyone will live in wonder of your great works for eons to come."

Everyone whispered Leeroy Jenkins's name in awed and hushed tones.

This plan couldn't possibly fail.

CHAPTER 39

IN WHICH WE STOP ZOMBIE-TING AROUND THE BUSH

BRYCE

Courtney's plan was very simple and very stupid: march up to the army and threaten them until they went away.

So simple, it might work. Or, at least, that's what my hero mouth told everyone. My Bryce brain told me we were going to die.

With Courtney on my right and four buffoons flanking us, we nobly stood together as the city gate creaked open—a side gate where no one could catch us, and the door only opened enough for us to squeeze through one by one. The blacksmith got stuck halfway, and it became A Whole Affair trying to get him out. The entire time, the skeleton army watched, which was really embarrassing.

At last, with Cuthbert pushing from the inside and the rest of us pulling tug-of-war-style on the other, he popped out like some kind of medieval Winnie the Pooh.

We reassembled our tough-guy formation and resumed our march, boots thudding into the soft grass as wildflowers swayed and bumblebees buzzed lazily through the pleasant spring air.

The stench of the undead was like roadkill on a hot summer day and only got worse as we approached. They stood motionless, wind flapping through the tattered remnants of their banners, their undead horses stamping flies off their rotting flesh. Some pesticide would've improved these guys' quality of life—er, death.

Courtney came to a stop before the army, and with some bumping and jostling, the misfits formed a line behind her. She squinted against the sun like John Wayne gearing up for a shootout. "Hi," she said. "I'm Courtney Westra of Lower-Middle-Class America, first of my name, rightful Chosen One, Protector of Nothing, Mother of . . . Pearl? Ruler of a Pretty-Okay Residential-Duplex, the Sunburnt, the Breaker of Toaster Ovens." Face set, Courtney looked up and down the line of zombies before addressing them again. "What you guys are doing here is not so chill."

"I don't think their being chilly has anything to do with their wanting to burn our city," Cuthbert piped up from the peanut gallery. "Though I do see how one might suppose so, fire being warm and them lacking skin and whatnot."

Courtney turned slowly, and I sensed her wanting to glare. "Thank you so much for your contribution." She'd apparently discovered, as I had, that if we made sarcasm sound sincere enough, we could sneak it through the potion filter.

"Right-ho," said Cuthbert. "Mayhap we could barter some blankets and coats in exchange for them leaving us alone. Things to keep them warm, like."

"Yes," she said excitedly, like she was genuinely encouraging him. "Maybe you could throw in a strudel as a peace offering."

Cuthbert rubbed the back of his neck and kicked the ground. "That be . . ." He pointed at Winston. "He makes the strudel, not I, though I'm flattered you mistook me for someone who could make such a fine thing as award-winning strudel."

I diverted my attention to a skeleton standing a little way ahead of the rest—an exceptionally ugly bastard with a caved-in skull, a missing arm, and a long skin tag dangling from his chin that I desperately wanted to cut off. "What do you guys want?"

The skeleton didn't blink. Partly because he had no eyes. But I also sensed he didn't blink figuratively either. Instead, he slowly pointed to the city behind us, tilting his head to the side.

"You can't take the city." Courtney stepped forward and poked a finger in the skeleton's face. "It's time for you to go."

His teeth chattered, which was disturbing and unhelpful.

"Don't give me that attitude," Courtney said.

He shrugged, rusty armor creaking, decaying skin tag wobbling off his bony jaw.

"We mean it," I said, the hero potion forcing me to stand my ground even though I wanted to grab Courtney's hand and run. "Get out of here."

The skeleton placed his hands on his hips and shook his head. A few surrounding skeletons caught on and began wagging fingers and wobbling their skulls in an obstinate way I didn't appreciate.

"The undead are making us look foolish, sir," Winston called helpfully.

"Yep, I got that," I said, my hero mouth adding, "Thank you. I love and appreciate you."

"Pack up and leave," Courtney said to the skeletons, "or we'll replant you so far down, you'll be able to make friends with what's left of the dinosaurs."

The skeleton recoiled, placing bony fingers over his wide grin in a mocking depiction of a gasp. Nearby skeletons chattered, slapping one another on their backs. Armor clanked. A few bones clattered to the ground.

Our friend with the bashed-in skull—or Bash, for short—started marching around, waving a hand like he was issuing orders. The most deeply unsettling mime, maybe ever. And mimes were already fucking upsetting.

In a truly impressive display of douchebaggery, more skeletons got in on the action, strutting around and wobbling their heads. A few pointed at me, then twisted fists comically over their eye sockets. The very skilled managed to squeeze out a few earthworms like tears.

"Hey!" Courtney said, more emotion in her voice than I'd heard maybe ever. She grabbed Bash by his breastplate and shook him so hard he rattled. "What will raiding the city get you? Why follow Greg's orders? Make your own choices. You think life is over for you because you're dead?"

"I think they do, my lady," Winston said. "I believe they do think it is over for them, seeing as they are dead."

"Marvelous observation," Courtney said, eyes bright. She dropped Bash, who barely managed to keep his footing. "Your life isn't over, okay? You've got a second chance. Maybe you got hurt—killed—once before," she went on, "but that doesn't mean you should get yourself killed again before you've had a chance to live." And though Courtney was talking to an ugly skeleton, it felt like she spoke to me.

My heart beat loudly in my ears. Courtney and I changed to be heroes, but in doing so, we erased the flaws that made us unique. Even if we were right and a relationship between us would've burned out, in changing ourselves, we doused the flames before they formed. The Courtney I'd fallen for was gone. She didn't like me this way any more than I liked her. We'd messed up bigtime.

My thoughts scattered as the skeleton leaned in, leering at Courtney, tilting his head this way and that, inches from her face. The rotten skin tag dangled in front of her nose.

"I hoped it wouldn't come to this," Courtney said in an overly cheerful way that made me suspect she didn't mind that it had come to this. She slapped the skeleton hard across his grubby skull. Palm hit bone with a hollow *thwack*.

The skin tag went flying.

We watched in slow-mo horrified fascination as it arced across the sky, descending toward Cuthbert's upturned face.

The skin tag landed wetly, flopping across Cuthbert's cheek.

Cuthbert let out a perfect Wilhelm scream.

Winston sympathy vomited.

Bash was greatly offended by it all and in silent hysterics, spread fingers quivering over his now-bare skull.

The blacksmith droned on about how he didn't condone violence in most circumstances, but he hadn't decided if his views pertained to people after they died—even if they were alive.

Pants picked lint off her pants, because that was all that mattered in her world.

Cuthbert screamed for someone to please remove the rotten chunk of Bash from his face.

"We will bring forth a champion," Courtney was yelling over the chaos, "to fight one of yours. We will settle this civilly—"

"Dear gods, not like this! Not like this!" Cuthbert howled at the sky, going cross-eyed as he stared in horror at the runaway piece of Bash's face, which had apparently decided Cuthbert's face was its new home.

"—and with integrity," Courtney went on. "I call forth"—she turned to the three-ring circus behind her and pointed at Winston, who tore himself away from his Important Work, which consisted of circling Cuthbert while waving frantic hands and accomplishing nothing of use—"I call forth . . . *you*."

Winston visibly gulped.

"I don't mean to be a bother," Cuthbert yelled, "but could someone . . ." He pointed at the piece of Bash. "We ought to return it to him, don't you think?"

That was when things went from bad to worse.

The dull pounding of hoofbeats thundered behind us. I turned. A group of horses galloped from the city gates. At their head was a figure on a dumpy donkey wearing flapping purple robes.

Amy.

Behind him rode an army of soldiers.

We needed to get out of here. Now.

I opened my mouth to scream *run*. Instead, I said, "Let's take a poll. I'd love to know where everyone's feelings are regarding the likelihood of our survival. Let's workshop some solutions. This is a safe space." It wasn't. "There are no bad ideas." There were. "We value your opinions." We didn't.

Pants said something about running and pants. The blacksmith said he felt uncomfortable overall, but he wasn't sure if that was because of the sickening displays of brutality or because he was breaking in new boots. Cuthbert gingerly peeled Bash off his face and announced he was okay with whatever the rest of the group wanted to do. Winston looked among Courtney, the skeletons, and the rest of us, and asked if he was still supposed to be dueling someone, or if that was off the table now. And Courtney . . . Courtney didn't say anything, which meant she wanted to say a lot.

The hero potion made me look each of them in the eye in turn and say, "We hear your concerns," like I was a politician who did not, in fact, hear anyone's concerns. "The team's morale and well-being are our primary focus."

Thud thud. Thud thud. Thud thud. Horses advanced from behind. Skeletons blocked us in the front.

With the whole team in obvious peril, the word finally ripped from my mouth. "Run!"

The group scrambled into action. Courtney and I hustled them onward, unable to move until everyone else was ahead of us. Cuthbert made a pit stop to gently tuck the piece of face into Bash's bony hand with an apologetic smile.

At last, Courtney and I brought up the rear. We barely avoided the reaching hands of the skeletons, breaking through their lines and running for the trees. For some reason, they didn't shoot arrows at us to stop our escape, which was weird, but I was too grateful to be alive to question why.

✦ ✦ ✦

We ran deep into the woods, climbing the foothills of the nearby mountain range. Winston swore he had a cousin who owned an inn at the next town over, and who would be happy to accommodate us. Everyone was greatly shaken, and we planned on taking the evening to regroup before coordinating another attack in the morning.

The next few hours were spent maneuvering around large boulders and towering pines, ascending the mountain. Mist hung like wet cobwebs across the valley below, veiling everything in shades of gray.

I looked over at Courtney. It was unnerving, seeing her like this. *Nice.* I wanted the girl who saw everything in a negative light and found it hilarious. Without her, everything felt hopeless.

A thumping sound drifted through the woods.

Courtney's head snapped up. "What was that?"

The thumping grew louder by the second. Our band of sidekicks was far ahead of us, nearly out of sight. But not so far away that we didn't hear their cries of fear.

My feet propelled me forward. The cowardly Bryce part of me wanted to hang back, but the hero potion forced my legs to pump faster. I spotted the crew a little way ahead, hunkered down behind boulders and bushes.

A shadow fell over us, and I looked up. Through the pine branches, I caught a glimpse of wings, bristly fur, and pinchers. The dragon. Staying low, I crouch-ran over to the huddle of sidekicks, Courtney on my heels. The beat of dragon wings throbbed against my eardrums as the beast passed overhead again. The blacksmith whimpered. Pants's pants rattled in fear.

"It knows we're here," Winston said shakily.

"We'll be all right," I said. My body forced me to continue speaking, the potion obviously having decided some kind of big speech was warranted. "Today we fight, not as friends . . ." I screwed my jaw shut before I could say we were family or some such nonsense. We had, after all, only known one another for a handful of hours.

Everyone exchanged looks.

"Not as friends," Courtney said, "but as . . . *more*."

I nodded. "That's right. More. If we die today, we will die as . . ." *Heroes* didn't feel right. "As people who really tried."

Winston slapped Cuthbert on the back, his eyes wet.

"So, until then, I say we fight," I spouted off.

"I'm a pacifist."

"Fight for those scared of spiders," I went on, ignoring the blacksmith, "and those who . . ." I'd talked myself into a corner. Speeches were hard. "For Sparta!" I finished.

Instead of cheering, everyone freaked out, hushing me and thanking me for the speech, saying they didn't want to interrupt, but really, I should keep it down, and had I forgotten about the dragon?

A wave of heat blasted across the back of my neck. Whirling, I looked up. The dragon's four dark wings splayed across the sky like spilled ink on paper. Its mouth gaped wide, flames churning in its throat.

An inferno of orange fire rolled down into the forest toward us. Cuthbert let out his signature warbling scream. Pants leaped agilely out of the way, thanks to her pants. The blacksmith and Winston flattened themselves against a boulder. I pulled Courtney with me and dove behind a tree as fire whooshed past us. The smell of burnt pine needles and singed hair stung my nostrils. Heat wafted over my face. I turned my head to the side.

With her hair billowing in the heat waves and fire reflecting off her dark irises, Courtney had never looked less like a sales associate. In that moment, I missed her. Missed her so badly it hurt. The things I would've done to see her back in that puke-green uniform vest, making me feel safe and comfortable as she shot idle threats of bodily harm my way.

The fire sizzled away, leaving behind scorched boulders and tree trunks. Everything seemed darker as my eyes adjusted back to the gloom of the woods.

A blur darted out in front of me. It took a second for me to realize it was Courtney. Running toward the dragon. I reached for my magic, but it slipped away, too faint to hold on to.

The dragon dropped into the forest in front of Courtney. The ground shook under my feet. The dragon's eight eyes snapped this way and that as it tried to focus on all of us at once.

Pants leaped from one boulder to the next, showing off the amount of dexterity wearing pants gets you. As she ran, she tugged a coil of rope free from a loop on her—you guessed it—pants. "We can use this to tie the beast's mouth shut," she yelled, which sounded like another terrible idea in a long line of terrible ideas, but I didn't have a better solution for subduing the creature.

"Watch out!" Winston yelled as flames licked around the dragon's maw.

Venom dripped off the ends of its talon-like pinchers, steaming and hissing from the heat of its fire.

The dragon roared.

Courtney jumped aside as flames exploded in the space she'd just occupied. I ran toward Courtney and the spider, intent on pulling her from harm.

"Catch!" Pants yelled, tossing me the rope.

I expected it to hit me upside the head and flop onto the ground, but my hand shot up and snagged it out of the air, my feet never breaking stride—which was probably thanks to the hero potion. Still, some part of me, underneath all that fear, felt pretty badass and hoped Courtney had seen my impressive moment.

I sprinted closer. The dragon snarled. Its legs bulged as it shifted its weight forward. Wind pounded against my eardrums as the dragon whipped its wings wide, sending Courtney staggering back. She sprawled to the ground, the dragon rising above her.

"Do it now, Bryce!" Winston screamed.

I ran forward, grabbing Courtney under the armpits and dragging her away. When she was out of danger, I sprinted back to face the beast. I looked up at it, its wings wide, muscles rippling, fire in its eyes.

The beast reminded me of Courtney—the way she was before the potion. Wild and furious and free. The dragon didn't want to be nice. The dragon wanted to be left alone to be itself. It ate livestock and spat fire because it was in its nature. It was not inherently evil just because the rest of the world couldn't condone its actions, afraid of something different and messy.

I finally fully understood what Courtney had been trying to tell me.

She wanted someone to like all of her, not just pick and choose her prettiest parts and look past the rest. Rejecting Courtney's faults would be like only accepting this dragon once it was muzzled and behind zoo bars.

I realized I'd been an idiot, always searching Courtney's actions for signs that she was more than what she appeared. But there was no mystery or secret joke behind Courtney and the KitKat, and that was the point. What you saw was what you got. She was a grouchy woman with blue hair who ate KitKats in a stupid way. I kept digging past her hard shell, excavating her softer attributes and showing them to her as if they were the treasures I valued most, when all along...

I didn't like Courtney's heart just because it had a soft center. I liked it for its hard shell too. She was tough and fierce and impossible. She had a heart as strong as iron, and that was why I liked it. Because if I ever managed to get in, she'd never let me out.

She never would have been the type to tell me she loved me one day and then leave the next. Why couldn't I have just said, *I like you, you asshole*, instead of making her feel like I needed more from her?

Instead, all my pestering to get her to reveal her softer side had probably contributed to her conviction she wasn't good enough, leading her to take that potion and change for me.

Or maybe she wasn't convinced she was unlovable. Deep down, maybe she'd only been afraid there wasn't *another* person alive who was good enough. Good enough to love her for her faults.

I'd failed her. I'd caged her into a pretty box the way I was about to tie down this dragon.

I tried to drop the rope, but I couldn't. My clammy fingers remained clenched around the scratchy fibers. The hero potion wouldn't tolerate beasts that hurled fireballs, only cheerful compliance.

Suspecting my death was very near, I tried to tell Courtney she never should've changed, that she was perfect how she was, but the words caught in my throat. Because saying she was perfect when she wasn't did not get the hero potion's seal of approval.

The dragon let out a hiss and shot forward, legs a blur as it charged me. It slid at the last second, turning broadside, flinging thick, sticky webs from its spinneret. The webs whipped around my body, clinging to my skin and pinning my arms to my side. The dragon reached for me with one spindly leg.

Courtney rammed into me, sending me rolling. I hit the ground hard, tumbling until I smacked into a tree. Pain shot through my body from the impact. Desperately, I fought to free myself from the spider's web, but the more I thrashed, the tighter it clung. Head swimming from lack of oxygen, I wrestled myself up enough so I could see Courtney facing off against the dragon.

She was running, not away from the dragon, but toward it. She bobbed and weaved, the dragon zipping jets of web at her like the world's deadliest silly string. "Grab Bryce!" she yelled, spurring the misfits into action.

Before I knew it, all four of them were trying to carry me at once, their hands matting the thick, sticky web more with every touch. With two of them at my head and two at my feet, they finally managed to hoist me off the ground, smacking me into every tree we passed and dropping me several times.

Meanwhile Courtney reached the dragon. It whipped around, stopping with its pinchers inches from her chest. The tiny arm-like appendages near its face stroked over its fangs as it huffed pillars of smoke like an industrial ozone-destroying factory.

Without hesitation, Courtney punched the spider squarely in its fleshy face. It recoiled, rearing up, hissing and screeching all at the same time, fangs clicking. Courtney somehow stared down the dragon towering above her. "Tell your boss he's not getting us back. That's why you're here, isn't it? If Greg wanted us dead, you would've burned us all up by now."

"Courtney," I rasped around a mouthful of web as the misfits smashed my head against a tree branch. I began to lose sight of her as I was jostled farther away. I needed to tell her—needed to tell her—

"Tell your boss we're coming for him," Courtney said, which wasn't wise, seeing as it ruined any chance we might've had for a surprise ambush. "We will find him, and we will kill him."

The misfits shuffled me farther away.

"Wait," I said, but everyone ignored me. "Courtney. I have to tell her . . ." The words wouldn't come out.

"There, there," the blacksmith said, aggressively patting my likely concussed head. "It'll all be all right."

"I need to tell her . . ." I needed to tell her about my revelation, that I finally understood her. "I realized how amazing she is." But we were too far away for her to hear anyway.

CHAPTER 40

In Which an Easily Avoidable Misunderstanding Leads to a Third-Act Breakup

COURTNEY

We sat together in the dining hall of Winston's cousin's inn. I straddled the bench, facing Bryce and picking cobwebs out of his hair. My ass was falling asleep from sitting with good posture for so long (apparently, heroes didn't slouch).

Bryce was telling me, "I was worried sick about you, darling," which I knew equaled *You idiot, what were you thinking?*

Our crew exchanged glances like worried children whose parents were fighting. Winston and Cuthbert sat so close they might as well have been the same person—actually, why did we need both of them? Pants had her legs on the table because she wore pants and could do so. The blacksmith picked at his nails with a knife, looking deceivingly threatening.

"I wasn't in danger," I said. "Think about it. The skeletons didn't kill us. The dragon didn't kill us. It flew off when it realized capturing us was futile. Greg doesn't want us dead."

It didn't make sense; most people wanted us dead.

"Perhaps the beast is simply in a foul mood because it's hungry," Winston said. "When I haven't had a strudel in a couple hours, blah blah blah."

◇ ◇ ◇

Later that evening, Bryce and I found ourselves alone in our room. We'd spent the majority of our time in this world alone, just the two of us. Now, the aloneness felt lonely where before it had felt anything but.

Bryce pulled his shirt off over his head and walked to the washbasin, where he went to work removing the last bits of spiderweb. He splashed water up his arms and face.

"I tried to use magic," I said, perching myself on the edge of the bed. "When the dragon tried to take you."

My unspoken meaning sat between us like an accusation.

Bryce scrubbed a towel over his face, wiping water from his eyes. "I tried to use magic too."

My stomach churned painfully. He searched for my affection and found the same thing I did when I searched for his. Nothing. After everything, I'd still abandoned him. Of course I still cared for him, but the easily accessible feelings that fueled magic . . . those were hard to find when I could hardly even find the real Bryce anymore.

Bryce tossed the towel over the basin, and I couldn't help but wonder if he was throwing in the towel in a metaphorical sense as well. When he looked at me, behind the unreadable mask of perfection there was . . . nothing.

Even if we were perfect, we couldn't be a perfect fairy-tale couple.

"We're going to be this way forever!" My mouth said it with celebratory cheer, the same way one might announce, *Happy birthday!*

I hugged my knees to my chest. Bryce closed the distance between us and climbed onto the bed, pulling me close, pressing his nose to my hair, and holding me tightly. I clung to him like, if I squeezed hard enough, I could pull out the real Bryce, *my* Bryce.

Maybe we could get through it. Maybe we'd learn to be content because it was the only way to be together. Maybe it would be enough to know that, under it all, we were still the same people.

"I want you," he whispered like he was saying, *I miss you.*

His thumb swept softly up and down my thigh with painful restraint, representing a million things he wanted to say but couldn't.

I turned in his arms. Sought his lips with mine.

A *tiny* bit of warmth flared inside me—the first touch of magic I'd felt since we'd taken the potion. Our lips met, and the warmth ignited into fire, giving me hope. "We don't need magic," I said. "Show me how you feel yourself." *Show me we're not so different now. Show me the mind I care for won't forever be trapped in the body of a stranger.*

Bryce deepened the kiss, lacing his fingers into my hair. I went to graze my teeth over his lip, but my jaw froze, leaving my mouth motionless for several awkward seconds. *No teeth. Got it.* Probably, inflicting any pain, even light pain in the name of pleasure, wasn't allowed.

Bryce pulled away and gave me a blank look. "Is something wrong?"

"No." I pulled him back. My tongue stiffened, forming unplanned words. "We should engage in sexual intercourse." I nearly melted from embarrassment. I'd wanted to suggest he bend me over the nearest surface and do some of those depraved things with his mouth he was so good at, but I guessed that kind of explicit language didn't represent heroism well.

"I'm going to—" He swallowed. "I'm going to make sweet, sweet love to you in the light of a full moon for hours. So gently."

I imagined the things he wanted to say were too filthy for his heroic mouth too. The potion had made him exactly like every other character in this world. He was a giant, freakishly happy cheeseball, and I half expected him to start trying to sell me a ShamWow or something.

With a feeling of impending doom, I recalled reading an

article about how Batman wouldn't go down on Catwoman because it wasn't "heroic."

I should have thought this through more.

We kissed again, all slow lips and long, dramatic sighs. I could practically hear the soaring dramatic music.

Bryce pulled back. "I have the sudden urge to light many candles."

What the hell? "Whatever do you mean?"

"Every moment with you is meaningful and should be treated as such," he said robotically.

He scrambled out the door and disappeared for a long while.

It took him several trips to gather enough candles to satisfy him. The act of lighting all of them took long enough that I propped myself up with pillows and was almost asleep by the time he was done.

"There, that's better." The mattress sagged as he crawled up beside me.

I cracked open an eye, and my heart sank. His mind might still be trapped inside his body, but I knew that Bryce was truly, *truly* not himself because he'd essentially created a fire hazard. Lit candles covered every available surface.

"Wow," I sighed dreamily, swooning with happiness I didn't possess. "I feel good about the number of open flames near my soon-to-be-sleeping body."

Bryce beamed. "I am glad you are glad."

He leaned over me, pulling the covers over his shoulders like we were in a PG-13 movie.

The mood was effectively dead.

We both looked at each other, smiled like it was the happiest day of our lives, and simultaneously claimed to have headaches.

✧ ✧ ✧

I left Bryce asleep and went outside for some fresh air. I leaned against the inn, cool night air raising the hairs on my arm. Focusing on breathing, I let my mind work out the complicated feelings churning in my head.

We'd taken the potion for the wrong reasons. Well, objectively, they were the right reasons, but subjectively, they were the wrong reasons for *us*, and now everything was ruined. I crammed myself back into a life that wasn't mine. I gave up Nothing, and it cost me everything. Maybe I was likable now, but I felt as unlovable as ever.

I'd once again started chasing perfection and a quintessential Happily Ever After, but I realized now that wasn't what I wanted. What I'd had with Bryce in Ohio before coming to this world felt more like a Happily Ever After than anything I could achieve now.

All I could do was hold on to the small scrap of hope that, somehow, Bryce liked the old me—the me I was before we even came here. Then at least a piece of our relationship could still be real.

"Are you all right, Lady Courtney?" The blacksmith leaned over the porch railing, looking down at me.

"Quite fine," I said. "A lovely night, isn't it?"

The blacksmith shook his head. "I know that look. That's the look of love lost." Pushing off the railing, he crossed to the steps, boards creaking under his girth. He lumbered off the porch and came around to me. "It's been a hard day, my lady. No matter what it might feel like, Sir Bryce loves you."

I would have snorted if I could have. Instead, I nodded and stared nobly into the blackness, looking at absolutely nothing. "Perhaps."

"He does care for you," the smith insisted. "He told me as much."

A little flutter went through my heart. "He did?" I breathed. "What did he say?"

"When you were fighting the dragon, he said he realized how amazing you are."

The fluttering inside me turned to ice. I'd hoped Bryce regretted the potion as much as I did. But after seeing me as a hero fighting a dragon, he'd come to his senses and realized he liked this new version of me more. Now he was yet another person who liked my outsides better than my insides.

I'd always suspected he'd like Chosen One Courtney far more than he'd ever cared for Normal Courtney. Normal Courtney was never enough. Normal Courtney was someone's brief infatuation until curiosity was satisfied, and they learned she was nothing more than exactly what she looked like. Normal Courtney was the selfish bitch, the lazy deadbeat, the washed-up loser.

Tears burned in the back of my throat. It was all too much. Pushing past the blacksmith, I ran. I didn't know where I was going, only that I needed space.

This world won its little game. I learned my lesson. I'd been put in my place and molded into something that the rest of the world could accept. I'd experienced "growth," and yet I'd never felt smaller.

I'd changed for the better. I'd worked hard, and people had faith in me. I was well on my way to defeating Big Bads and completing my hero's journey. I was perfect and lovable.

My old dream had come true.

Now, the dream was a nightmare.

CHAPTER 41

In Which I Go Through My Emo Phase

BRYCE

I woke up in the middle of the night with an aching dread in my chest telling me something was wrong. The space beside me in bed was empty. The panicked feelings of a nine-year-old boy consumed my body. It was irrational, I knew. Courtney could've just stepped out for a second.

Still, I sprang out of bed. At the last minute, I grabbed the pebble she'd given me off the nightstand, clinging to it like I was trying to hold on to hope. A knot formed in my throat. Images flickered in my mind. Scraped knees and slugs on rough concrete. Slammed doors, angry screams.

I ran outside. Turned in a circle. Saw only emptiness.

She'd left.

I fell to my knees.

It was all very dramatic.

Since the day I'd started to care, our relationship had been on a timer. Happiness was the beginning of the end. Always was. Always would be. Not even a potion could keep her from leaving me. Not even magic could keep her loving me.

I tried to slow the frantic spinning of my thoughts. I was jumping to conclusions. Courtney wouldn't have gone far.

Unless she went to save the world without me. That would mean only she could open the portal. That would mean she was planning to leave me here.

I'd already been left once by someone who I assumed would never leave. If I didn't know my own mother well enough to see the warning signs, I couldn't know Courtney well enough either.

"Are you all right, Sir Bryce?" a voice asked.

A strangled noise left my throat as I whirled around. The blacksmith stood there in the shadows like he'd been waiting for exactly this key moment to step in with critical information.

"I'm quite all right," I said, even though I wasn't.

"Nay. Your face speaks of love lost," the blacksmith said. "Your lady friend left you?"

"What makes you think that?"

"I saw her leave you."

I snapped to attention. "What do you mean? Did she say anything? Where did she go?"

"She were looking so sad, you see," the blacksmith began, and my gut sank. "So I told 'er what you told me earlier today. 'Bout how smitten you were with her while she was battling the dragon."

A wash of relief mixed with dread swept through me.

No wonder she'd left. She'd thought I couldn't love her without the potion, and I'd accidentally confirmed her fears. She thought I found her amazing *because* she was battling a dragon, not that I simply realized it *while* she was fighting a dragon.

We'd miscommunicated.

CHAPTER 42

IN WHICH I AM ~~HUNG~~ ~~HANGED~~ HUNGED?

COURTNEY

If my younger self had read this story featuring me, she would have thrown the book across the room.

When the first rays of dawn lit the sky, I stopped running and looked up to find myself outside the city, the army of skeletons separating me from the gates.

I settled onto a grassy knoll and watched the sunrise. The run dulled my panicked feelings so I could view the situation with more rationality.

Being in an adventure like the ones I used to read about brought things out of me I wouldn't have thought possible. Terrible things. Things that would make my younger self cringe mightily because suddenly, I'd become the annoying character who I used to shake my head at from the comfort of my couch and go, *What an idiot*.

I'd turned into the person who made rash and obviously incorrect life choices, the one often found running *up* stairs trying to get away from horror villains. I was the one who was too emotional, a cold bitch, and a wet noodle all at once. The one who felt the urge to blurt out an *I love you* after knowing someone for only a few days.

I needed to get my shit together and get us home, where there was no more magic and, hopefully, no more potion.

It wasn't the fear of failure that made me want to crawl back to my old life. It was the fear of my life being perfect. Because a perfect life didn't include bare feet in grass, Christmas lights in May, and ice cream without cookie dough. A perfect life didn't include the most ridiculously sexy accountant I'd ever seen.

Bryce liked me before I ever tried to be a hero. He even admitted he'd tried to push me away that morning with the Christmas lights because he was scared of the fact he was growing to care about me.

Drowning in insecurities made me latch on to the first sign of evidence my fears were real, but I knew Bryce, the real Bryce. I'd never needed the potion because I wouldn't have left him. He wouldn't have given me a reason to. The Bryce of two days ago took my carefully constructed ideas of the world and demolished them. He saw the real me, and he only wanted one thing.

No, not *that*.

He only wanted me to stay.

Making ourselves into heroes ruined everything and made us do ridiculous things like—

Miscommunicate.

Miscommunication was easy to do in this world, where no one was free to be themselves, tied down by the duties pertaining to their positions in the world—

Something clicked.

What was it I thought about Bryce? That the potion had made him just like everyone else in this world? Yet his mind was still there, and he could still sneak sarcasm under the potion . . . the way I could see that *something* in the flower stand girl's eyes when she said, *We can never not be peasants*. And Mama—she talked as though the less fortunate *couldn't* accept help. I'd thought it was some rule of etiquette preventing them from bettering their lives, but what if they *physically couldn't*? The way I physically couldn't be anything less than perfect.

In that potion book, there had been potions to make perfect heroes, perfect soldiers, and perfect peasants.

What if everyone in this whole world were trapped in their roles the way we were?

A shiver ran down my spine. On our first day here, Amy told us not to get close to the peasants. Then he'd passed Bryce and me a flask. "A toast," he'd said, "to the good we will accomplish together."

What if it was hero potion? We hadn't drunk it, but he must have thought we had. Must have thought we'd be his perfect pawns. Just like the entire world was.

Oh. My. God.

Amy's perfect peace was a lie, as much of a lie as my old life had been, everyone hiding behind masks, doing what was expected of them while they quietly died inside.

My first instinct was to run back to Bryce and tell him the truth, but I doubted the potion would allow me to plot against it. If it were so easy, Mama or any of the other peasants would have screamed the truth at us and begged for help. I was on my own. I'd have to find a loophole so I could get to Amy and demand he tell me how to undo the horrible effects of the potion.

It might be impossible. Because undoing the potion would undo the peace, and I was a hero, unable to cause chaos. But I had to try.

Setting my jaw, I channeled the perseverance of a lactose-intolerant person who consumes dairy anyway. Then I threw back my shoulders and headed toward the city.

I sneaked past the skeletons, even though I was beginning to suspect Greg the mouse and his minions weren't as evil as I once thought. Still, I wasn't sure what his role in all of this was, and it was best to play it safe.

Entering the city through the same conveniently unguarded side gate we used the day before, I plucked a long brown cloak off a clothesline and flipped the hood over my conspicuous hair, Jedi-style. The streets were mostly empty, thanks to the early hour and the looming threat of the dragon, but I still kept my head down.

When I reached the castle, I waited by a side door until a servant opened it. At the last moment, I shot from the shadows and jammed my foot in front of the closing door.

I slipped inside—

—and immediately ran into the real Evil One and douchebag extraordinaire Amy. The king stood at his side, flanked by half a dozen guards.

"One of the *imposters*." Spittle flew from Amy's lips as he pointed one gnarly finger.

I opened my mouth to scream at him. My muscles coiled, ready to tackle him to the ground, but I couldn't move. Couldn't speak. The potion kept me rooted to the spot, judging me guilty, forcing me to stand there waiting for my arrest.

A brief silence ensued, during which we all exchanged looks, waiting to see what the others would do.

The king waved an apologetic hand my way. "This is one of the traitors involved with the poisoning of our oldest and most respected historians." He nodded at Amy before turning to his guards. "So, well, I suppose, if it's no bother, you ought to seize her?"

Inside I was freaking out, but on the outside, I asked, like I was making small talk, "Historian? Amy, you're the castle *historian*? I thought you were something cool, like a wizard."

Amy shook with anger. "How dare you impugn my wisdom?"

"But how are you so old if you're not magical?" I asked.

"Superfoods," said Amy, like it was obvious.

"Seize her," the king said again. Evidently, he'd had a taste of power, and now he wanted more. What an untimely moment for him to grow a backbone. "She shall be hung for treason."

The soldiers stormed forward, barking orders, their boots stomping and armor jangling, flashing light into everyone's eyes as they jogged around, looking serious and generally accomplishing very little for several moments. Finally, they got their act together and formed a tight circle around me.

"Excuse me, sorry, one last thing." I held up a hand, and the guards paused. "I've been thinking about this a lot, and I'm like eighty-two percent sure it's *hanged*."

"No, no," the king said. "It's never *hanged*."

"I think this is the *only* case when it's *hanged*."

"Mmm, yes, she's right," Amy murmured thoughtfully.

"Oh," the king said, crestfallen. He perked right up a second later when he remembered he was in the middle of realizing he had massive amounts of power to abuse. "Seize her!"

✧ ✧ ✧

And that was how I found myself in prison.

The dungeon was dark and damp because of course it was. A fantasy world where anything was possible, but god forbid it have bright, cheerful prisons or disco prisons or, at the very least, not-moldy prisons. But no. The unoriginal medieval world had unoriginal, dank, dreary prisons with big burly guards and rusting iron bars.

Bending, I picked up a flake of loose cobblestone and turned it over in my fingers. It made me think of Bryce. He'd surely noticed my absence by now. I imagined him waking up and finding half of the bed empty. Guilt ravaged my insides.

No one would be coming to rescue me. Bryce would assume I didn't want to come back. Too late, I'd finally accepted the truth he'd been shouting at me this whole time; he never did have expectations for me.

I wouldn't have a chance to explain why I'd left, or apologize for it. He'd never suspect I'd been captured.

Wrapping one hand around a cold prison bar, I leaned as far as I could into the aisle and chucked the rock at the guard standing down the hall. The pebble fell short and skittered across the floor, stopping by his feet.

The guard looked up and, predictably, smirked, all mean and guard-like. "Much good that spunk will do you while you're standing on the gallows with a rope around your—"

"Come on, man. Lighten up."

The guard pondered that for a moment, then tried again. "Wonder how much of that spunk will be left in ya when you're danglin' off the end of a—"

I ran a hand down my face. "What has you so down that you have to be this way? All that's required of guards is for them to guard things. You're choosing to be grumpy all on your own. Life isn't so bad."

It was at that moment the guard was impaled from behind by a broadsword.

My lower extremities experienced an extremely negative visceral reaction in sympathy.

The guard slumped to the side. Standing in his place was a figure wearing long purple robes, their face shadowed by a hood.

"*Amy?*" I asked, withdrawing from the front of my cell.

The figure kicked aside the guard and strode forward. They stopped before me, head lifting slowly. Dim light washed over the ghoulish contours of a skull, each grinning tooth outlined in black shadow.

Chapter 43

In Which I Make a Grandly Stupid Gesture

BRYCE

It was hard to ride in on a white stallion to save the day when I didn't have a white stallion. Going on foot was also useless, as it was too slow.

I'd leveled my head enough to realize Courtney would not be so cruel as to leave me in this world for good, even if she had run away to get some space. Likely, her next step would be to start fixing her mistakes so she could get us both home as quickly as possible. Home, where she could stop spending so much time around me, her new least-favorite person.

As much as it terrified me, I knew what had to happen next.

I had to win her back before she did something stupid, like try to single-handedly face an army of monsters.

I slipped out of town and headed into the woods. My heart thudding in my ears drowned out the chatter of wildlife. Despite the cool shade of the trees, sweat coated every inch of my skin.

I hadn't climbed a tree since—I'd never climbed a tree. At most, I sat on a lower branch. Trees were wobbly and sharp and strangely rough and slippery all at the same time. Trees broke bones. I'd always thought the act of climbing trees served no purpose aside from recklessly endangering yourself, until now. Now it served an even stupider purpose.

I wasn't a hero, and no giant eagles were going to provide me with a *Lord of the Rings*–style Uber lift. But I did have a dragon hunting me that Courtney was convinced wanted us alive.

I selected a tree with branches spaced close enough together that I might stand a chance of hitting one on the way down, should I fall. As I wrapped my arms around the first branch and clumsily heaved myself onto it, I cursed my heart for getting myself into this mess. What I was doing proved what I'd always known: love was dangerous. The difference was now I'd decided it was worth the risk.

I scrambled onto the next limb, legs flailing. I began counting each limb, taking comfort in the orderly numbers. "It's worth the risk," I reminded myself a second time. "Worth the very risky risk." I grunted as I scrambled higher. "The very scary risky risk." I was close to the top now, the breeze swaying the trunk. I crawled up one more branch and gingerly got to my feet.

"The totally *stupid* idea," I said under my breath, looking over my shoulder as I scanned the sky. "Courtney, you'd better be right about something for once."

Courtney wasn't in on some secret joke, nor could she magically make me happy with my own life like I'd once thought. Deep down, I already knew how to be happy. I just had to let myself feel it. My whole life, I'd been emulating a slug. Feeling nothing, surviving. It was time to live.

So here I was, getting out of my own way, even though it scared the shit out of me.

A screech pierced my ears, followed by a distant *thud, thud, thud*.

I was in the dragon's web now.

If Courtney was right, and Greg the mouse wanted us alive, the dragon would deliver me back to the castle and Greg. Courtney was likely there, too, trying to recapture a dragon or defeat an army. I'd just have to escape Greg's clutches and find her. But first I needed to catch the dragon's attention.

Dread washed over my body, making my limbs tremble. My foot slipped a little, bits of bark dislodging under my boot and crumbling down through the leaves below.

I replanted my foot, but it was too late. My body bent one way, then the other. Hands flying desperately, I sought something to hold on to. I leaned for the trunk but misjudged how far away it was. My arms pinwheeled as I tried to regain my balance. My heart felt too light, like I was already falling.

And then I was falling. My stomach lurched into my chest as I plummeted off the branch.

Then suddenly, something snagged me around the middle, pulling me up, up, up, and sending my stomach right back down into my toes.

I pried my eyes open, then quickly shut them again when I caught an aerial glimpse of the forest below. My feet dangled over nothingness. The firm leg wrapped around my chest combined with the whistling wind made it hard to breathe. I risked another peek up, which awarded me an unpleasant sight of the dragon's bristly underbelly.

I didn't know why Greg wanted us alive, and I didn't care. If the dragon got me back to the castle before Courtney left, that was all that mattered.

◇ ◇ ◇

We made it back to the city in record time. The skeletons were closer to the castle now, but still out of range of the archers in the guard towers. The dragon swooped over them and into the city. Snatches of the cries from soldiers and villagers below caught my ears before the wind swept them away.

The dragon made two loops around the castle, and I forced myself to keep my eyes open even while my stomach churned.

The beast's head whipped to the side, gaze locking on to something below. I followed the direction of its stare and spotted a large courtyard. Many figures bustled about, but one, in a flowing purple robe, caught my eye. Amy.

For a second, I thought the dragon would incinerate him, but what happened was far worse. It folded its wings back, and we hurtled for the ground. Bitter bile tinged the back of my tongue as my stomach flipped yet again.

Cobblestones cracked from the impact of the dragon's landing. Villagers scattered every which way as the beast lumbered forward. The dragon kept me cradled close to its chest as its three other feet hobbled in a broken but quick gait. We swerved suddenly. When my brain straightened itself in my skull so I could see again, I craned my neck to find Amy flanked by a few soldiers standing directly in front of us, their mouths open.

My world spun for the millionth time as the dragon tilted me upright and planted me on the ground before them. With a strangely gentle nudge from its two claws, the beast pushed me forward.

Wind knocked me in the back as the dragon took off with one final screech, soaring away. I stumbled forward, nearly falling into a soldier's waiting arms. Thankfully for my dignity, I managed to keep my footing.

Unthankfully for my dignity, I still managed to find myself in the soldier's embrace a second later when he declared, "The imposter!" and seized me from behind, his blade zipping up under my chin.

Greg had his dragon hand me over to let Amy do his dirty work? It didn't make sense.

"What shall the imposter's punishment be, then?" the soldier yelled at maximum volume into my ear.

"Ah," said Amy, "a good question. Considering his crimes against the crown, our people, and the whole kingdom—"

Whatever words he had left—probably an abundance—they

were drowned out by the loud clanging of bells. Alarmed cries sang out from all the guard towers surrounding us.

"What's the matter?" my soldier shouted, deafening me.

"The skeletons, sir," another passing soldier yelled over his shoulder as he ran by. "They're on the move."

I squirmed, inching under my soldier's sword like I was playing a high-stakes game of limbo, poking it out of my way with one delicate finger. My valiant escape met an untimely end, however, both because the potion made me stop edging away, and because Amy saw me.

"Where do you think you're going?" Amy asked. "Did you think we'd forgotten about you?"

I gulped. "Yes, that's why I was leaving. Listen, I'm on your side. I'll help you guys do whatever, as long as it gets us home." I would too. Gone was my fear, and in its place sat determination. A sort of frantic, desperate determination because I didn't have any other options in the matter, but still determination.

"How can we trust you?" Amy scowled. "You betrayed the whole kingdom."

"If I were working for the Evil One, why would his dragon give me over to you to have me captured?"

Amy seemed to consider this, and my hopes lifted.

"The skeletons have breached the outer wall!" a guard yelled from a watchtower.

My heart quickened. "The mouse was manipulating us. I'll help you. I *need* to help you so I can get home. Please, I just want to find Courtney, then we'll be out of your hair."

"I'm afraid that isn't possible," said Amy. "Lady Courtney's crimes have been too many. We've already scheduled her hanging in the southern courtyard. Everyone's so excited, and if we cancel last minute, it will make for quite a faux pas. We were headed there to take part in the festivities ourselves when you *dropped* by." Amy chuckled to himself.

"What?" I said. My world closed in, and it was hard to

breathe. "What does that mean, you're hanging her? Like a picture of her?"

"Oh, bless," said the soldier, clapping me on the shoulder. "Hanged by the neck until dead."

I wanted to hurl. A tar-black abyss opened in my mind's eye when I tried to envision a future without Courtney. It killed me that she didn't know I'd been absolutely obsessed with her from the moment we met. She still thought I liked the perfect version of her, when really, I was smitten with the opposite. I pined over the Courtney who ate KitKats incorrectly. I had sex dreams about the Courtney who never took her trash to the curb. I'd fallen for the Courtney who revealed the worst parts of herself and stayed while I showed her mine.

"She's obviously corrupted, unlike you," Amy was saying. "We arrested her this morning. We can't save her. What would the people think?"

I jolted forward, my feet free now that Amy had decided I was one of the good guys.

Then I was running. For once, not away from frightening things, but toward them. My brain felt swollen and stuffy, my ears full of pressure, like I was underwater. My legs burned, but I pressed harder.

It was my fault we were here. If I hadn't let my trust issues take over my life, Courtney and I might've been home right now. Instead, I'd pushed people away. I'd pushed and pushed and pushed her straight to the gallows.

I ran around outbuildings and dodged squads of soldiers, ignoring the cries from the watchtower and the distant sounds of battle.

When I burst into the southern courtyard, it was like I'd stepped into a different world. It was the same garden where we'd had lunch our first day here. Purple and yellow flower beds surrounded marble statues. The spray from the Chosen One fountain misted over my skin. Royals were grouped together in tight clusters, fanning themselves and sharing gossip, and at the center, a scaffolding had been constructed. On that scaffolding stood two figures—one, a guard wearing a helmet with a full visor, and the other, a girl in a dress with a sack over her head, tendrils of blue hair poking out the bottom. That girl had a rope around her neck.

"*Courtney!*" I bellowed with the last remaining breath in my lungs, then sneezed because of the flowers.

Her head swiveled in my direction.

I tried to charge forward, but after one step, my muscles froze, and I couldn't move. I tried again. My foot remained stuck to the tiled path. Wrestling against the invisible force controlling my body, I strained, my muscles coiling, but still remained outwardly motionless.

The stupid hero potion. Amy had said Courtney was a traitor, and it wouldn't allow me to save her. "Courtney," I said again, but while my emotions raged on the inside, my voice was calm. A sob punched the inside of my throat, then sank deep into my gut. Every muscle in my body ached with emotion.

The guard shoved Courtney forward over a trapdoor. The crowd tittered with excitement.

I had to tell her before it was too late. Had to apologize for making her feel like she had to change. Had to say anything to stop the guard.

I love you, I thought, but the words lodged in my throat. Heroes couldn't love traitors. I was too late. Only now, when I quite literally could not express how much I loved her, was I ready to trust her enough to tell her how I felt.

"I hate you!" The words burst from my throat in a desperate, raw scream.

A few of the onlookers nodded approvingly. The guard and Courtney paused, both turning to face me. At the front of the crowd closest to the gallows sat the king. He waved a hand, indicating I should continue.

I lifted my chin even though, if I could have, I would've crumbled to the ground. My insides churned. I was going to be sick. I couldn't say what I wanted to, but maybe if I said what I *didn't* want to, she'd understand. We were forced to be enemies again, so when I told her all the ways I hated her, I hoped she'd know what my insults meant.

What they'd maybe always meant.

"Courtney," I called, "I hate how brave you are. I hate the way you prove me wrong. I hate how you barged into my life and ruined my plans. You have *not* made my entire existence brighter. Your morbid jokes have done *nothing* to keep me from losing my shit this week. And you kiss like most people play the saxophone—that is to say, not very well."

The guard shifted at that, so I hurried my words.

"You make about as much sense as any season of *Riverdale*, aside from season one." I paused. "The first season was admittedly pretty good." I had to try a few times to get the next sentence out because the potion kept cutting me off, but finally I was able to say, "You think you're not hero material because you're too flawed. Well, Bilbo Baggins was unambitious. Winnie the Pooh was a glutton. Luke Skywalker only started the adventure that led to him becoming a Jedi because he was attracted to his *sister*. Sure, maybe he didn't know Leia was his sister when he got her hologram asking for help, but he was still only compelled to rescue her because she was hot. Imagine only wanting to do good deeds—" *because you're hoping to get some ass*, I was going to say, but the potion cut me off. "Imagine only doing good deeds in hopes you might . . . fornicate with a grateful princess." I rubbed a hand through my hair, my eyes burning. I was afraid to blink, scared of what might happen. I drew in a ragged breath. "So yeah. I can't tell you you're a hero. I can't tell you it's okay because heroes aren't that great either. I certainly can't say that you don't have to try to be more because, to me, you're already more than enough."

A loud sniff caught my attention. It was Courtney's guard, apparently moved to tears by my speech. He was wiping at his eyes—or I assumed he was; his face was concealed by a hood. Another sniff, and he shifted, his elbow bumping an important-looking lever.

The trapdoor collapsed.

No. The word ripped through my brain, nearly strangling me as it got caught in my throat. I simultaneously wanted to look away and never look away.

The rope went taut, the sack flying off Courtney's head, revealing—

A pale, grinning skull with two blue ponytails roughly strapped to its head. My entire body convulsed in shock. The skeleton raised its hand, peeled off its glove, and waved with a little flutter of white phalanges.

On top of the scaffolding, the guard stepped forward and pushed back her hood, revealing a head of poorly cut hair. Courtney looked across the crowd at me with shiny eyes and smirked. "Hey, jerkwad."

The gentle insult caused every cell in my body to light up with joy. Somehow she was free of the potion.

CHAPTER 44

IN WHICH I RECEIVE A VILLAIN MONOLOGUE VIA TEXT MESSAGE

COURTNEY

How did I get to the position I was in? Well, it was simple.

Back in the prison, I breathed a sigh of relief when I saw the skeleton outside my cell door. Anyone was better than Amy. "Did Greg send you?"

The skeleton nodded, smile never wavering. For obvious reasons. (She had no face skin.)

I wasn't sure what Greg wanted from me, but I wasn't about to *hang* around and find out. I needed to get out of there. "Let me out."

When the skeleton began gesturing excitedly, I held up a hand. "No. I'm not doing charades again." I glanced around for something for her to write on, but my cell was, of course, bare (I was still upset about that). Thinking about my cell prompted me to think about my other cell, as in, my cell phone.

I whipped it out and powered it on before opening the Notes app. I scrolled past lists of preplanned insults for Bryce and opened a blank page. Stretching my arm through the bars, I experienced a surreal moment as I handed the skeleton my iPhone. "Here, Skelly. Just tap the letters."

Skelly, or Kelly, as I'd started to think of her, took the phone. Her finger bone tapped aggressively against the screen. As her tapping grew more irate, her head slowly tilted to the side. At last, she gave up and showed me the blank screen.

"Oh yeah. I didn't think about that. It only works with"—I grimaced—"uh, skin. And stuff."

Kelly promptly found herself a finger.

The broadsword was involved.

It was gross.

As Kelly tapped *not* her finger against my phone, I made a swift decision to burn the device as soon as possible. When she was done, she proudly presented the somewhat smudged screen. I read it from as far away as possible. She'd somehow turned caps lock on, which made reading easier.

GREGORY WANTS TO EXPLAIN HIMSELF. HE IS NOT EVIL, THOUGH HE IS THE ONE THEY CALL THE EVIL ONE. IT IS COMPLICATED.

"That makes no sense, Kelly."

She typed some more. The clicky button noises filled the echoey dungeon.

She shoved the phone in my face.

HE WAS TRYING TO CAPTURE YOU OR BRYCE SO THAT THE CASTLE FOLK WOULD ARRANGE A PUBLIC HANGING.

"See, you say he's not evil, and yet."

Kelly typed some more, then showed me the phone.

IF ALL IMPORTANT FIGUREHEADS CONGREGATE IN ONE LOCATION, IT WILL MAKE ADMINISTERING THE ANTIDOTE EASIER.

Antidote? Now she had my attention.

Tap, tap, tap, went the phone.

THE HISTORIAN HAS BEEN GIVING EVERYONE IN THE KINGDOM PATIOS.

"Well, that's . . . nice. A valuable use of tax dollars."

Tap, tap, tap.

APOLOGIES, THE TABLET SEEMS TO HAVE AUTOMATICALLY CHANGED MY SPELLING. HOW AMUSING. I MEANT POTIONS.

"I knew it!" I said.

After many texting and autocorrect mishaps, my theory was confirmed.

Amy had summoned the last Chosen One, Edna Johnson, to help him give everyone in the kingdom his potions by slipping them into her signature mulberry ale. He must have told her it was the only way to bring everlasting peace to the land and open the portal home.

Each person received a potion specific to their position in the kingdom. Ones for peasants, ones for soldiers, ones for bakers and blacksmiths and tailors. He'd been giving every new baby born into the kingdom potions ever since. Everyone who remembered a time before the potions was gone by now, so most didn't even know there was something wrong with them, aside from a few families who managed to tell their children the stories through sarcasm or speaking in opposites.

This was how Amy maintained peace for so long. It was also why everyone acted like stereotypes. *Because they were.* Peasants never strove for more. Blacksmiths did nothing but blacksmith. Even thieves and criminals like Winston stuck to their roles and committed petty crimes so neighboring kingdoms wouldn't catch on to what Amy was doing.

Except, Clementine the visiting princess *had* caught on. "Between you and me, something has always struck me as not quite right about this kingdom," she'd said the night of Winston's kidnapping.

The next time I spoke to her in the garden, she'd been unable to speak freely when she tried to accuse the king of suspicious activity or when she tried to hint that not everyone in the kingdom liked Edna Johnson. Amy must have heard what she'd said and slipped her a princess potion to make her docile and silence her.

"That's why Amy didn't want us talking to anyone!" I exclaimed. "He didn't want us to notice how unnatural everyone was acting for fear we'd catch on to what he was doing."

Kelly nodded and told me the rest.

The mouse was working on an antidote, but the potions would compel everyone to run from help, since, objectively speaking, curing them would make them "worse people" by freeing their minds.

He'd kidnapped Winston first because he was easy prey and, as a mouse, Greg needed all the help he could get. After secretly drugging Winston, Greg and a legion of mouse friends carried him off while he slept to a secluded wing of the castle and gave him the antidote. But when Winston woke up, he ran away before the mouse had a chance to speak with him and enlist his help. While Winston was free to renounce his life of crime, he didn't understand what it meant, nor had he known that his kidnapping had actually been a rescue attempt.

Since Greg and his friends lacked opposable thumbs, Greg realized he needed more help if his next attempt would be more successful.

First, Greg convinced me to free the dragon, then used it to catch General Thimblepop, who'd been helping him launch his campaign ever since. Next, he sent us to the field with oregano and made sure his dragon burned it, which raised the army. He used his army at the tournament to capture the king's hand, gathering another public figure to help lead the charge.

Now, the mouse was planning to use my fake hanging as a way to gather the rest of the kingdom's figureheads in one place, so he could successfully surround them with his army and free their minds. His primary target was the king, who could help by commanding his kingdom into compliance. Hopefully, the peasant potion would force the people to obey the king more than it urged them to run from a cure.

After finishing her story, Kelly put me in a headlock and forced the antidote down my throat, and then we were on our way.

After Bryce's declaration and after Kelly and I pulled off our switcheroo, I stood there on top of the gallows, my heart soaring in my chest. I was a raindrop, not a snowflake, and Bryce knew it. He made me feel like the only rain to drop in a thousand years, and he was dying of thirst.

I didn't have to give up my do-nothing lifestyle for Bryce. Rules had exceptions, but that didn't mean the rules ceased to exist. If my goal to have no goals were the *I* before *E* rule, Bryce was the word *weird*, a maddening anomaly that somehow fit right in.

He'd never pressure me down a path toward a future the world could accept. He'd help me build a hut at the crossroads of my life where I could go on existing as I had been, smelling the roses, looking at the stars, touching grass. A tiny space where we could just *be*.

I wasn't a hero or a peasant or a villain. I was me, and that was enough for me, and enough for him.

Thanks to Bryce's strange grand speech, I'd forgotten my actual reason for being up on the gallows until Kelly removed her skull, slipped off the end of the rope, then jammed her skull back on her spine as she landed nimbly on the ground. She looked up at me and waved her hand.

I remembered in a hurry that we were supposed to be ambushing the king to give him the antidote. Unfortunately, the king was now surrounded by a squad of guards and being led away by Amy toward the castle.

Holding the jars of antidote inside my coat close to my body to keep them safe, I jumped off the gallows. I landed hard, knees popping, more accustomed to sitting on a couch than performing feats of heroism. "Let's go!"

Which was when things really went to crap. The skeletons burst through the gate, pouring inside like a swarm of shoppers raiding a Best Buy on Black Friday. Soldiers charged for them, coming together from the perimeters of the courtyard to form a blockade, keeping the skeletons at bay.

Bryce stepped into our path, holding a discarded, rusted skeleton sword. The potion was compelling him to stop me.

I didn't have time for this. The king was getting away. I drew my sword—a handy bonus of taking the guard's uniform. "Look, Bryce. You know how we found that potion book? Amy's controlling everyone. Greg is the Evil One, but he's not that evil!"

Bryce took a step forward. "If he isn't evil, why didn't he tell us his plans from the beginning?"

He had a point. I didn't know, but I didn't have time to ponder it. I pressed forward. "Move."

"I can't let you." He said it hard, like a command, but he was also still under the influence of the potion. Even if he wanted to help Team Mouse, the potion would force him to try to talk me out of it. It would force him to fight against the antidote, against *me*.

Bryce lunged. I barely lifted my sword in time to block. Around us, the sounds of battle rang. Soldiers and skeletons fought in the corners of my eyes. Slowly, the skeletons were taking the upper hand, disarming and subduing the soldiers.

"Look around you," I grunted as I pushed away from Bryce and circled him. Maybe if I could convince the hero potion that Greg was being heroic, Bryce would be able to let me go. "The skeletons aren't hurting anyone."

"You're wrong," Bryce's mouth said, and he charged. Our swords clashed together again and again. Bryce spoke between jabs. "The mouse's dragon captured me and handed me over to be imprisoned. Why would it do that if they're on our side?" Obviously, the potion inside him was doing everything it could to convince me Greg was evil, but I refused to listen to him.

My arm trembled with fatigue. "Greg needed one of us captured so everyone would gather to watch our fake hanging. The dragon didn't know I'd already been captured when it took you."

"Lies!" Bryce spat.

Okay. Enough was enough. I tossed my sword aside and dove for his legs. My arms locked around his knees, and he fell back. We landed in the dirt and rolled, Bryce dropping his sword in the process.

Using the momentum, I hooked my legs around his hips and spun over on top of him. Before he got his bearings, I withdrew one of the vials from inside my guard uniform and popped the cork with my teeth. His body immediately resisted, thrashing under me, the potion compelling him to reject anything that would make him less than perfect.

I dumped the entire bottle over Bryce's face. The green potion splattered across his skin. He sputtered and sat up, nearly pushing me off him. As he wiped his eyes, I waited with breathless anticipation, hoping enough got past his lips.

Bryce's hands shot toward me. I tried to leap out of his lap, but not in time. When his fingers curled around the back of my neck, and I looked into his eyes, my heart stuttered.

"Bryce?" I whispered.

His gaze was intense. "I'm so sorry I told the blacksmith you were amazing."

I smiled as he grabbed a fistful of my hair and pulled our lips together. He let out a noise of relief in the back of his throat, and I clung to him as though I'd never let him go. Because I wouldn't. His tongue teased my lips, my teeth grazed his mouth, and I'd never been happier to be the type of assholes who would make out while their soldiers were busy fighting to save the world.

"All I want you to be is you," he whispered against my mouth, and tears wet my lashes.

All I want is for you to succeed. That was what Will had said, how I'd become convinced that true love didn't exist. Bryce made me wonder if maybe it did after all.

When we broke apart, we were both sniffling and wiping our eyes but trying to be sneaky about it, so we were basically just looking away from each other while carrying on a conversation.

"I'm sorry I left." My voice wobbled. "I should have talked to you, especially since you warned me about miscommunication."

"And I'm sorry if I ever made you feel like you weren't good enough," Bryce said shakily.

"You were right, though," I warbled. "I was being more of a jerk than I really am."

"It's okay. I like it when you're a little mean to me." He turned back to face me, tilting my chin so I'd look at him. "And yes, I'm crying. I'm on a battlefield, and I thought my girlfriend dumped me, which I seem to remember makes it okay."

"Correct," I said, biting my lip and trying not to look too pleased, even though him using the word *girlfriend* made my heart jump a little.

"Look, I don't expect you to promise you'll never leave." Bryce wiped grime and tears from my cheeks. "But here's the thing. Now you're free of the potion, I trust you'll at least provide a warning—preferably using colorful, unmistakably angry language—if you intend to walk out on me again. Don't ever pretend to like me, then blindside me. That's the one and only expectation I have for you."

I smiled. "You're allowed that one, Bryce."

Someone kicked me in the shin. I pulled away from Bryce to find Kelly standing over us. She shoved my phone screen in my face:

YOU HAD BUT ONE TASK. THE KING GOT AWAY.

Bryce's eyes went huge when he saw Kelly's . . . unique stylus. "Do I even want to know?"

"Probably not."

Bryce looked at me. "You do realize if we free everyone's minds, the kingdom will, objectively, be worse off."

"That must be why Greg didn't tell us his plan," I said. "If we knew what he was up to, we'd know the portal wouldn't open back up for us, and we might not have helped him."

In a flash, I considered helping Amy to restore peace so the portal would open, and we could go home. But then I remembered how it felt to be controlled, and a big part of me didn't totally disagree with what Greg was trying to do.

I'd been stifled twice in my life, once by society, the second time by magic. "People should be allowed to be less than perfect," I said.

"But the kingdom was at peace before. The people were safe and kind." Bryce groaned. "Why is this so complicated? I thought storybook villains were just supposed to go around doing evil things for the sake of doing evil things, not because they had a good reason for them. What's up with that?"

"We know what the right choice is," I said softly. "We were brought here for a reason." I stood and held out a hand, helping Bryce to his feet as well. "Let's be the bad guy's Chosen Ones."

If this world wanted to try to show me what a despicable person I was, fine. I'd prove it right and burn it down. The people should have been allowed to live outside of their prescribed capes. They should have been allowed to say what they meant, to question authority, to quit or fail or succeed in whatever ways they chose.

Kelly waved impatiently, so we took off, following her out of the courtyard and into the castle.

"All this running is going to be the death of me," Bryce said.

"Don't be insensitive, Bryce," I snapped. "Kelly was . . ." I dropped my voice. "Unalived."

We burst into the throne room, where we were immediately surrounded by many guards and told to drop our weapons.

"Now that I think about it," said Bryce, "we should've sneaked in here in the dead of night or something."

"Dead of night?" I whispered viciously. "Bryce, we talked about this. Kelly is *dead*. Her life is *over*. She was probably *murdered* on a battlefield or something. Why are you making her feel worse about it?"

"Well, well, well," said Amy, stepping forward. The king stood a little way behind him, surrounded by even more guards. "I can't say I'm surprised, Bryce. I should have never trusted you after you already betrayed us once." Amy shook his head mournfully. "Everything I've done has been for the good of the kingdom. We have never seen peace such as this, but you would rather have chaos."

The guards closed in.

"Bryce"—I drew out his name—"tell me you have a plan."

"Don't worry," he said confidently, "I have a plan." He reached into his pocket, drew out the pebble I'd given him days ago, and flung it across the room.

Everyone watched as it skittered over the marble floor. It wobbled for a few long moments before settling.

"Bryce," I whispered in the silence that followed. "What, and I cannot stress this enough, the fuck?"

"I thought, since I've been carrying around that pebble this whole time, it only made sense it would eventually come in handy to save the day. But, uh, instead of providing a satisfying payoff, it turns out it was useless deadweight."

"*Dead*weight?" I said around gritted teeth, nodding subtly in Kelly's direction.

"Sorry, Kelly," Bryce said.

"Seize them!" shouted the king, because that was apparently all he said anymore.

The guards closed in. I reached for Bryce's hand. Instead, Kelly wove her fingers with mine. I shuddered.

One of the guards grabbed me roughly by the arms, prying me away as another seized Bryce and a guard wrangled Kelly. We were dragged forward until we stood before the king. They forced us to our knees.

I looked over at Bryce, who gave me a wry little shrug. My throat tightened. I probably should've told him I loved him or whatever.

Amy stepped forward, sword drawn. "I bet you're wondering how I managed to get the last Chosen One to work for me." He chuckled, giving his sword a little shake. "She resisted for a while, but as soon as I slipped her a bit of hero potion, she realized the only noble choice was to help me. If only you possessed the same clarity of mind, maybe—"

"LEEROOOOOY JENKINS!" a voice roared. The throne room doors flung open, and our band of misfits barreled inside, led by the blacksmith.

The skeletons outside must've given them antidotes, because our little crew showed more skill in a few minutes than they had the entire time we'd known them. Cuthbert effortlessly disarmed half the guards as Winston silently knocked the rest out with a flick of his wrist and a puff of green magic. Pants carried Greg on her shoulder. The blacksmith gave everyone bear hugs as he administered vials of antidote.

Soon the misfits had everyone restrained.

Pants stepped forward then, and Greg dismounted her shoulder. "Well done." Greg strode over. "I admit, when I created a Chosen One portal, I only specified I wanted someone with questionable morals who happened to be holding oregano because I needed it to raise the dead. I had no idea Bryce would step through at the last moment and both of you would prove to be so cluelessly useful."

"Thanks?" Bryce said.

And I began to laugh. Because this whole time, there was no reason why Bryce and I had been drawn through a portal. It was all chance and bad luck. The whole time, I'd been convinced there was meaning behind it all as I battled with myself, trying to figure out if I was a hero or a villain, when all we'd only ever been were glorified pizza delivery people.

"What are you laughing about?" asked Bryce.

"We weren't sent on a quest to get over our flaws. We aren't the main characters. It's not that deep. You're, like, the cowardly bard, and I'm the self-centered comedic relief."

Bryce shook his head. "You were not the comedic relief."

"You're right, I should give myself more credit."

"That's not what I meant." He pulled me in for a kiss.

I hadn't been brought to this world to learn a lesson or change. It was okay to be messy and impulsive and wild. It was okay to fail. It was okay to never understand why there was a *t* in *mortgage*, or to be honest about the fact that no one enjoyed conversations about the weather, or to acknowledge that red dye #40 was delicious and drinking greens kind of sucked. I didn't have to be perfect to be worthy of love.

"I don't want to grow old with you, Bryce," I whispered against his lips. "I want to never grow up with you."

CHAPTER 45

IN WHICH THE END IS OUR BEGINNING

BRYCE

We spent all day turning people back into themselves. Courtney and I didn't get a chance to have the talk we both knew we needed. The *now what* talk where we had to face our feelings and the choices we made that got us stuck here.

By sunset, most of the city had been turned. Skeletons caught those forced to run from the cure. The dragon was off, netting stragglers. The mouse already had plans to march onward in the morning to liberate, and perhaps destroy as a result, the rest of the kingdom.

As I walked through the city, I took in the change we'd wrought.

Instead of villagers calling *good day* to each other, arguments broke out. Curse words zipped up and down alleys. Pent-up aggressions burst free at last. Lines were drawn and feuds formed. With the king gone, anarchy ruled.

Because the king *was* gone. With his mind clear, the king had a midlife crisis, realizing that his whole life, he had followed in the footsteps of his father without ever pursuing his dream of becoming a bard. He'd drawn up a business plan to use his fame from being king to springboard his music career.

Meanwhile, Amy was thrown in prison, and everyone was pleased to be able to complain, loudly and at length, about the number of council meetings it was going to take to decide what to do with him.

When I looked up, I found I'd reached the courtyard where Courtney and I first appeared.

"Hey." Courtney stood behind me. The fading sun lit her face in hues of gold and turned her short hair electric blue.

"Hi." I didn't know what else to say.

We stood there awkwardly.

With resolve in her eyes, she stepped forward, jabbing a finger my way. "You and I are never going to be one of those couples sung about in songs that bring out the best in each other. We don't make sense, not on paper and not off it."

"Talking about all the ways we suck as a couple is such a weird way for you to declare your feelings, Courtney."

"I'm not done." She avoided my eyes and gritted her teeth, like talking about her feelings made her experience physical pain. "Why can't we be a couple who brings out the worst in each other? Why do we have to look pretty on paper if we're so happy being miserable together?"

"We don't have to do a thing we don't want to," I said, experiencing the same sort of realization you have when you grow up and move out and discover you could eat ice cream three times a day if you want to. Courtney was my ice cream—probably bad for me, but worth the stomachache.

She stepped forward and ran her fingers along the hem of my shirt. "I don't wanna do the thing where we change. You know when people who are friends don't want to get together because they're scared of losing their friendship? You and I are like that, except I don't want to lose my enemy."

I nodded. What we had was fun and easy. It could stay that way.

"Love can't fix us, or anything else for that matter." Courtney raised our palms between us, interlocking our fingers. "Love is just glue that holds crap together."

"My broken fits with your broken." I brushed a soft kiss to her temple, and she sighed and shut her eyes.

"Yeah, but not like puzzle pieces, fitting together to make something whole. We don't complete each other or any of that bullshit. We're more like trash."

I raised my eyebrows. "Trash, huh?"

The way she smiled, you'd think she'd learned I'd died and was already plotting how many firecrackers to set off at my funeral. "Yeah, we're trash. Shattered glass and chewed bubble gum and crumpled newspapers. My mess and your mess, thrown together to create a priceless piece of art. Maybe a lot of people look at it and don't understand, but the people who matter—you and me—we get it."

Her smiling at me filled me with such intense joy that I could hardly stand it, so I pressed my lips to hers until she stopped, until words melted to soft sighs, and all that was left was her and me.

Kissing her didn't feel like something new and exciting. It felt like something old and precious and nostalgic. That one particular feeling that sometimes surfaces but you can't quite catch. Like when a certain smell hits you, but you can't place it, but you remember an old feeling of sunlight and safety and simplicity. Kissing her felt like those times.

We kissed, slow and lazy, until our sighs grew heavy, and our lips swelled. When I looked into Courtney's dark brown eyes, I knew she felt what I did. She buried her hands into the hair at the back of my neck, and I tightened my grip on her waist. We stumbled against the nearest building, losing ourselves in each other.

With nothing immediately threatening our lives, the peace was so *peaceful* it almost hurt.

I murmured something about how, if anyone tried to interrupt us, I'd show them how much of a villain I was. Courtney fondly told me to shut up, and I gently said she was the fucking worst.

Chapter 46

In Which We Refuse to Be in an Epilogue

COURTNEY

The wall of the building Bryce was pressing me against gave way, and I fell backward. I toppled through what felt like heavy fabric before landing against a cold, hard floor. It was dark, but overhead, stars glittered fuzzily. I blinked, clearing my vision, and the things I thought were stars sharpened into new shapes. Light fixtures.

Gasping, I scrambled upright and turned in circles, taking in my surroundings. We were back in the home improvement store. There was my coatrack, tipped over now, Bryce lying askew in the middle.

"Bryce?" I rushed to him.

With a groan, he rolled over. "What—" He stopped mid-question as he realized where we were. "We're back." He leaped to his feet and crushed me against his chest, swinging us in a circle. "We're back!"

"But how?" I asked when he put me down. "We ruined everything."

He gave me a teasing grin. "Maybe true love saved the day."

Feeling my face flush, I shook my head. "Maybe the good of

giving everyone their free will back trumped the chaos that it caused."

"Or true love saved the day."

My heart softened. Maybe the reason didn't matter. Maybe it was nicer just to believe. "Are you saying you love me?" I whispered, then quickly added, "Actually, wait. Don't tell me." I held out my hand. "Come here."

When he slipped his hand into mine, I dragged him through the store. The aisles were dim after closing, but I knew the path well enough that soon I broke into a run. We laughed, and it reminded me of that time in the library—him and me, away from everything else. Maybe every day with him would feel like this. Quiet, happy, while the rest of the universe kept on spinning. Not that the world revolved around us, but that we were a satellite, orbiting far from chaos in the peace of space.

I skidded to a stop. The glow of the freezer section cast blue light over Bryce's face. I slid open a door, the glass frigid against my fingers. I swiped a box of ice cream bars off the shelf, planning to pay for it later. Probably. "Come on." I tilted my head, and we walked, slower now, back to the coatrack.

With a heave, I pushed it upright. Sliding apart the coats, I ducked inside. When Bryce hesitated, I stuck my hand out and crooked my finger in a *follow me* gesture.

He crawled inside and settled across from me. "What if it sends us back again?" he asked, voice pillow-talk hushed. Shadows danced across his face from where the light from the fixtures glowed through the opening at the top of the coatrack.

"Be brave, Bryce." I smiled, popping the box of ice cream open with a thumb.

I unwrapped one of the chocolate-coated ice cream bars and handed it to him.

He didn't take it. "I don't like ice cream."

"Everyone likes ice cream."

Reluctantly, he took it.

"Now you're going to eat it, and when you're done eating it, nothing bad will happen."

His throat lurched. "How do you know?"

"I'll make sure of it."

I opened my own ice cream and dove in, raising a brow as though to say, *Your turn*. Giving me that look he was so good at—the look that said, *I can't believe you've talked me into this*—he took a stiff bite. As he chewed, his shoulders relaxed. He let out a little moan, his eyes rolling back.

"Told you," I said.

Eyes twinkling, he wiped a stray bit of chocolate off my lip.

But his face darkened as we finished the ice cream. One last bite, then he just sat there, the Popsicle stick clenched in his white-knuckled grip. Bracing for the blow part of him still expected.

"Bryce?" Leaning forward, I touched his arm.

He didn't look at me.

"I love you."

His eyes snapped up. Slowly, a smile spread across his face. "Yeah?"

"Yep. And every time you eat ice cream, I'll tell you that again."

Grabbing the back of my neck, he tugged me forward, pulling me into his lap and wrapping his arms around me in a desperate embrace. I wound my hands into his hair and held him close. I pretended not to feel the wetness of his tears against my neck or the tremble in his shoulders.

When he lifted his face from my shoulder, he was himself again, but *more*. A little less broken. A little more whole. He rested his forehead against mine, and I gazed into his eyes, smiling softly.

Someone tapped me on the shoulder.

With a yelp, I fell out of Bryce's lap, whirling awkwardly on the ground to find the bony silhouette of a skeleton peeling back the coats, peering in at us. Light bulbs glittered through Kelly's teeth as she lifted her hand in a little wave.

◇ ◇ ◇

My car had been towed, so we rode back to the duplex in the back of an Uber, disguising Kelly in a long floral dress, a cowboy hat, socks, Crocs, a scarf, sunglasses, and a puffy pink jacket.

We gazed numbly at the seat backs in front of us. Deep bags had taken up permanent residence under Bryce's eyes. Luckily—or perhaps unluckily—Kelly still had her disturbing stylus from the other world and was able to explain on my phone that she'd hitched a ride when she saw us vanish through the portal.

Now, Kelly sat to my left, happily tapping away at Candy Crush on my phone with *not* her finger.

"You shouldn't give her so much screen time," Bryce said from my right. "She'll get addicted to it."

"She's been good all day, so *excuse me* if I want *five minutes* of peace."

We exchanged a look.

"This is such a weird epilogue," I whispered.

"Epilogue?"

"You know, the culmination of everything that happened in our story that creates our Happily Ever After. They usually involve dream jobs, marriage, kids. Sometimes opening a small business and/or saving a town. Rarely adopting a member of the undead."

The Uber driver gave me a weird look in the rearview mirror.

"What does an epilogue look like to you?" Bryce asked, and I knew what he was asking. *Where do we go from here?*

"I don't want to epilogue," I said, like *epilogue* was a verb. "I don't want to do the picturesque Happily Ever After thing. I want to take it one day at a time."

"Whatever epilogue you want, as long as it's not like *The Lord of the Rings*, where we have to say goodbye six different ways," he said.

We rounded the corner onto our street and caught a glimpse of the duplex, which was still half-lit with furiously blinking Christmas lights.

"We're lucky the house didn't burn down." Bryce humphed as he opened his door. The blues and pinks flickered across his face, revealing the fact he was smiling.

The dome light spilled out onto the driveway, and the car dinged. Following Kelly, I clambered out and stretched. As the Uber drove away, Bryce joined me, holding my hand as we stared at the duplex. Bony fingers pressed around my shoulder as Kelly leaned between us, smiling her unnerving grin.

Bryce cleared his throat. "So."

"Yup," I said.

"Now what?" I asked.

"We'll figure it out," Bryce murmured as he dipped his head and brushed his lips to mine.

Being with him felt like messy private moments when no one's watching, and you're free to take off the mask, when you fill your house with off-pitch singing and dance around in your underwear. It felt like freedom. It felt natural and right and easy. Affection filled my heart, prompting magic to flare from Bryce's skin.

My eyes flew open. My own magic curled off my fingertips. Magic didn't exist here naturally, but we must have carried a bit home inside of us . . .

It was at that point that the last of the magic slipped from our bodies, conjoined, formed a portal—and the dragon burst through with a roar.

"It's fine," I squeaked. "The dragon isn't inherently evil, right?"

"It's also not inherently good," Bryce said.

And the furiously flashing Christmas lights were clearly pissing it off. Without the mouse around to communicate with it, the dragon defaulted to doing dragon shit—namely, burning our house down.

EPILOGUE

COURTNEY

"Maybe our epilogue was actually a prologue," I whisper.

Bryce's fingers lace with mine. "No. It's an epilogue. We're epilogue-ing, damn it."

Desperately, I look around, searching for a rope or anything I can use to try to capture the beast. Of course, there's nothing... aside from a new portal, which is still glowing in the yard.

Suddenly, I feel as though I've caught a glimpse of a new future where things could be different, the same way I did at Thanksgiving. But this time, there's an actual portal, lighting up a path I hadn't seen before, unexpected but full of things I long ago dismissed as impossible. Unicorns and trolls. Unconditional friendship. True love. The simpler way of life I've been craving. My Happily Ever After won't be perfect like I used to imagine, but I've grown fond of imperfect things.

I turn to Bryce. "I always wanted to be a hero so I could get my Happily Ever After. We're not heroes, but maybe we could have a Mediocre Ever After. We won't have a castle, but we could have a very quiet, safe hut. We wouldn't have to stock shelves or crunch numbers. We could have real friends." Like the village girls. "Sure, there won't be running water, but there also won't be Corporate America or motor vehicle accidents."

"Are you . . . are you actually suggesting we *go back* to the world we spent the whole time trying to leave?" Bryce asks.

I shrug. "Why not? We can always come back, right? Every time we need to stock up on Germ-X or tampons, we'll just do a few good deeds and open the portal again."

But he's already kissing me. Kissing me like he's never kissed me before. Bold. Daring. Brave. Irresistible. He breaks away. "Yes. No more being a slug. I want to be a person, to *live*."

I glance at the portal, which is beginning to fade. "We need to catch the dragon's attention so it will chase us when we go through."

Panicked that we're going to run out of time, I start jumping up and down, waving my arms and yelling, but the beast spares me no mind. It begins to rise higher in the sky, gaze searching for a new target.

"I've got this," Bryce says, reaching into his pocket and withdrawing a small pebble.

"You went back for it?" I breathed.

"Of course."

The portal darkens further. I don't feel any more power inside me, so creating another portal will be impossible, since there's no magic on Earth to replenish our supply. If we don't act quickly, our opportunity will be gone forever.

Bryce draws back his arm, hesitates only a second, then whips his arm forward, the rock slingshotting high into the sky.

It bounces right off the dragon's snout. With a smoky snort, the beast whirls on us, eyes narrowing. Fire blooms in its nostrils.

"Run," Bryce says, grasping my hand. He's told me to run a lot in the past few days, but this time his voice is not full of fear, but full of life, of hope, of love.

With the monster breathing down our necks, we plunge through the portal.

And when I blink, I find that all my dreams have come true.

EPILOGUE 2

BECAUSE EVERY FANTASY STORY NEEDS MULTIPLE ENDINGS

COURTNEY

It's Thanksgrieving here in the magical world, which is the holiday everyone celebrates to give thanks for the fact that they can now express their grievances freely.

We're all seated around a rough wooden table in the backyard of Mama's house. Bryce and I have a house next door—a tiny cottage that leaks water and barely has room for the two of us, but we don't mind. Nearly the whole street has been roped into the girls' game of Kill the Guy with the Ball, which means that our life is perpetually chaotic.

Everyone is here—our band of misfits, the mouse, Mama, Pop, all their children. With Greg the mouse here to tell it not to eat anyone, the dragon sleeps in a heap a little way away, the children using it as a jungle gym. Greg even helped us create a portal so we could run back to our world and pick up Kelly, who's thriving in her new career as a med school classroom skeleton—a solution that took care of her employment, housing, and education while avoiding the issue of her being alive. She's only accidentally moved in front of the entire class twice.

Mama spent all day bossing us around the kitchen, and the

food tastes three times better thanks to the work that went into it. Better yet, there isn't a turkey in sight. Meanwhile, the girls are sussing everyone out; their ball has been missing for hours, and nobody knows who has it. They've given me three pat-downs in the last hour alone, and I still don't even play the game.

As we near the end of the meal, everyone begins going around the table, joyfully sharing their complaints.

"I hate bath time," the toddler Poppy proclaims with adorably pouted lips and crossed arms.

Bryce's hand brushes mine beneath the table. I wind our fingers together, hiding a smile, my bare toes curling against the cool grass.

"It upsets me when people still come to my forge expecting weapons," says the blacksmith, who is now using his craft to make lawn ornaments.

Then, beside me, Bryce stands up. He clears his throat. "Before I share what I'm unthankful for, I have a few words."

My mind flashes back to the last Thanksgiving I attended, when Will stood up only to drop to his knee. Bryce wouldn't do that to me, would he? He knows I don't want an epilogue with marriage and children.

But Bryce reaches into his jacket pocket and withdraws—

"I've had your ball for hours, you absolute losers!" he exclaims with relish.

Love blossoms in my heart for this ridiculous, beautiful, imperfectly perfect man and our ridiculous, beautiful, imperfectly perfect life.

The newest member of the game, the blacksmith, rises, his shadow dropping across us.

"Oh, shit," Bryce says under his breath.

"Get him," the blacksmith growls, leading the charge.

Moments before everyone tackles Bryce, he passes the ball to me behind his back.

Without hesitation, I take it. It's not a ring, but it is a promise—a commitment to a lifetime of chaos, laughter, and love.

Bryce flashes me a wicked grin. "You're in it now."

And then the horde descends, plowing Bryce over. Whoops and laughter echo off the houses around us. Mama makes a valiant effort to save the pastries, flapping her apron at anyone who dares to get too close. Pop lights up a pipe. I smile, tucking the wooden ball into my pocket.

When I was little, I was 90 percent sure I was special. Thankfully, the 10 percent chance that I'm not won out, because now, Bryce and I get to be delightfully unspectacular together forever.

THE END

ACKNOWLEDGMENTS

First of all, thank you to everyone who saw this bonkers story and decided to give it a try. It's only because of readers like you that I get to do this, and I'm forever grateful and honored that I get to share my daydreams with you. A big shoutout to my agent, Lucienne Diver, who supported my underachievers, even when they were less than lovable. It's only thanks to your eye for finding the heart behind my chaos that Bryce and Courtney found their way into readers' hands, so thank you.

Of course, a huge thank-you also to Melanie Iglesias Perez and Elizabeth Hitti. Working with you both has been an absolute pleasure. From the moment we first spoke, I know you "got" what I was trying to do with this book. Your insightful notes made these characters come to life (if we don't count Tim, R.I.P.). I'm so honored and excited we get to create more stories together.

Thank you to the rest of my team at Atria, including Nicole Bond, Sara Bowne, Lacee Burr, Sofia Echeverry, Zakiya Jamal, Rebecca Justiniano, Alexis Leira, Paige Lytle, Maria Mann, Libby McGuire, Alexis Minieri, Davina Mock-Maniscalco, Emma Navarro, Katherine Nintzel, Meryll Preposi, Shelby Pumphrey, Kitt

Reckord, Dana Trocker, and Abby Velasco. I so appreciate all your hard work, more than words can express.

To my copyeditor, thank you for not burning my whole manuscript when you came across *Amygronkphopoulozeetrop*. You are extraordinary.

To Laywan Kwan for the absolute dream cover design and Mike Pape for the cover art (I'm still fangirling), thank you.

Of course, all the thank-yous to my critique partners, writing friends, and beta readers. This story had many, many rounds of edits, and I appreciate each of you for reading it in whatever disastrous state I thrust it upon you in. Your brilliant feedback turned it into what it is today.

A special shoutout to the SP crew. Our group chat is Charles Dickens's yard, where I, a less-talented Hans Christian Anderson, go to cry when my tender author feelings get hurt. (It happens like every day.) Thank you for your endless patience and support. Our friendship means more to me than you know.

Lastly, to my husband, Shawn, thank you for all the hard work you put in to help us both reach our dreams, and for your willingness to allow me to disappear into my office to scribble my little stories for hours on end. Also, thank you for helping me brainstorm the Evil One's diabolical plans that one night in the kitchen. Nothing brings couples closer together like plotting (fictional) world domination. I love you, and—since this book releases on your birthday—happy birthday!

ABOUT THE AUTHOR

Sloane Brooks loves writing stories filled with romance, humor, and magic. She lives in the Midwest with her husband, two cats, and too many houseplants. She is the author of *The Underachiever's Guide to Love and Saving the World* and, under the pen name Shannon Bright, her debut paranormal rom-com *Every Wish Way*. Visit sloanebrooksauthor.com and follow her on Instagram, Threads, and TikTok @sloanebrooksauthor for more.